The Key

FELICIA ROGERS

δ

Dingbat Publishing

Humble, Texas

First and foremost I would like to acknowledge my Lord and Savior, Jesus Christ, for the ability to write even one word. Next my cousin, Traci Conkle, for pushing me when I thought a published novel was a hopeless dream. And last, but definitely not least, the two ladies who read the original manuscript tirelessly and without complaint: Alicia Mountjoy and Kim Knoll.

PART I

CHANGES

1

The chain rattled and clanked against the aluminum bike rack. Pushing her hair from her face, Maddie released a breath. Customers passed her and entered the convenience store. The overhead bell rang in announcement each time.

Salt covered the icy roads and the sidewalk at the bike rack, but not the walkway to the door. Maddie cringed. How many times had she busted her behind? Since she'd moved to the southern town of Coal Creek, more than she cared to count. It would make her look like a dork... again. No matter how hard she tried to blend in, she always wound up making a dork of herself. No wonder she wasn't making any friends—who'd want to be friends with her?

The autumn weather was so strange, one day sunny, the next rainy, the next snowy. She'd never lived in the South before; was every year like this one, or was the world determined to mess with her?

Drawing in a deep breath for courage, she took a step and slipped. Legs spread wide, she reached out to steady herself against the paned glass window, but missed the mark.

"Whoa!" someone said. A masculine voice, nice and strong.

Heat flushed her face. The object she gripped wasn't the cool frame of the store window but a shirt covering the hard muscles of a well-developed chest.

Lifting her chin a fraction, she stared into the bluest eyes she'd ever seen. A smile tilted the corner of her rescuer's lips.

"Are you okay, miss?"

Miss! He called her miss! Not oaf or clumsy or… A thrill rattled up her spine, setting her brain askew.

Fighting a rising fog, she shook her head. "Yes." And cringed. She'd just dorked herself again.

His smile widened and he helped her straighten. "I was just going in the store. May I help you inside?"

She managed a nod without contradicting herself this time.

He gathered her small hand in his larger one and squeezed. He opened the door and waited. "You go first."

Don't act like an idiot, Maddie. He released her hand and a hollow place opened inside her, as if she'd lost her best friend. His lips tilted in a smirk as if this was a common occurrence between him and those of the female persuasion. She didn't doubt it.

Determined he not realize the full extent of how he'd affected her, she squared her shoulders and strutted inside. The warmth slapped her face and dispelled the fog. Removing her scarf, she turned to thank the stranger, but he'd disappeared. The store seemed filled with boys, but they were all the wrong boys.

She twisted her lips in disappointment and strode to the back wall housing the coolers. Milk and eggs gathered, she strolled past the candy bar aisle. Chocolate bars with nougat, chocolate bars with peanuts, chocolate bars with chocolate filled an entire row and her mouth watered in anticipation. Maddie closed her eyes, paused for a deep, settling breath, and reached forward. The plastic covering of a candy bar didn't fill her hand, but rather something warm. She opened her eyes, hoping her rescuer had reappeared.

"May I help you?" An elderly gentleman stared at her hand, closed around his coated forearm, and frowned.

She released him, heat searing her face. "I— I don't think I need a candy bar today." *Dorks don't deserve them.*

She ran to the cash register, checked out, raced to her bike without suffering a repeat of her earlier disaster, and stowed the groceries in the front basket. The lock fumbled in her hands and she dropped the key twice.

She almost sighed when she managed to open the lock. Unfortunately, the chain slid from her grasp and fell onto the ground. Angrily, she ripped it up, threw it in the basket on top of the milk, and took off down the road.

Just another day in her new and dorkish life.

Chase raced to the restroom. Hopefully the damsel he'd left could find her way around the store. The poor girl seemed lost.

When he returned, his family milled about. The damsel wasn't in sight. She hadn't been very tall; she might be hidden by the chip racks in the back. He peered around them. Not there.

"Look here, Mom! They have chewy caramel sticks. May I have one?" yelled Chris, who loved everything sweet and enjoyed at least two cavities per year.

Was that a flash of auburn hair, over by the back cooler? Chase frowned. No, just the lights reflecting off a display of sodas. The girl couldn't have left that quickly, could she?

His mother rolled her eyes and grabbed a handful of the caramel sticks from the shelf. "Now, don't ask for anything else. If we keep eating like this I'm going to be as big as a horse."

His father leaned over and planted a kiss on Mom's cheek. "Doesn't matter to me, Carissa, I'll still love you."

Mom smiled and slapped Dad playfully. Embarrassed, Chase moved away and squatted to study the store shelf. Jerky and healthy snacks as well as candy. Not bad for a small town, so maybe this wouldn't be the worst place on earth for his family to settle down.

The girl he'd rescued seemed to have disappeared, and he let the stab of disappointment trickle down deep. She'd been pretty in an unusual way. Waist-length auburn hair and jade green eyes had drawn him as soon as she had tilted her face toward him. But again, small town; he should be able to find her at school.

He groaned at the thought of settling in at yet another place. Sometimes being part of a military family had major drawbacks. Like traveling and moving multiple times a year. Hopefully this would be the last time for a while. His father had retired from the military and taken a job as a consultant at a weapons plant. Now they were moving to the sleepy town of Coal Creek, close to his father's employment.

"Chase!" Craig, his younger brother by two years, waved at

him.

Chase's legs cramped and he shook them as he stalked toward Craig.

"Hey, bro, what do you think of this? There's a comb in the honey!"

Chase rolled his eyes and patted his brother's back. "You need serious help."

"Boys, it's time to head out."

Colton and Cole, the twins, grabbed snack bags of chips, snagged candy bars, and plopped them on the counter. The pile grew as each of them laid down their snacks for the remainder of the trip. Dad paid, and they ran outside and filed into the SUV.

"Shouldn't be long now, guys. Your mom and I are really excited about this house. We know you're going to love it." They squeezed each other's hands and looked longingly into each other's eyes.

Cole groaned. "Mom! Dad! Do you have to do that in front of us? We're only ten! You might scar us for life."

Music poured through Chase's headphones, blocking the ensuing explanation. The twins received more lectures than a college student.

The vehicle sped along the highway. A cool breeze drifted through a cracked-open window and he shivered. November in the town of Coal Creek wouldn't be warm like sunny southern California. Surfing and sunning most of the year would be a thing of the past. He'd made some great friends in California. And what of the girls! Tanned, with that honey-colored hair that only comes from lying in the sun. He almost sighed aloud. Why did it seem like every time they moved somewhere good, they didn't get to stay long?

Chase bobbed his head to the music and stared out the window at a fast-flowing river. He blinked. A creature with glowing red eyes slithered into the water. Only a second's glimpse, that was all he got, then the car had passed it and trees blocked the view.

He rubbed his eyes and faceplanted against the pane. His heart raced. What was it he'd learned in school? Alligators lived in freshwater and their eyes reflected light, which made them look red. Could it be? Could that giant lizard-like creature have been a real alligator?

He fell back against the seat. It couldn't have been anything weird and bizarre, like something out of a strange novel—what was he thinking? Gators weren't weird and bizarre? Chase laughed at himself and settled deeper into the music.

Finally the SUV turned in at a driveway and shuddered to a halt. Everyone climbed out, but Chase hung back, watching. The two-story white house with a picket fence reminded him of an old sitcom set. Kids rode skateboards along the dead-end street. Older boys played ball in their driveways.

Coal Creek might not be such a bad place after all. Especially once he found that strange damsel again.

Next morning, Maddie fumbled into school, yawning and rubbing her tired eyes. The nightmares had begun again. The therapist said time healed all wounds. But what did he know?

She hitched her full backpack a little higher. She was still fairly new to Coal Creek High School. Because it was the middle of the year and there were no empty lockers, she had to carry her books everywhere she went, shouldering the heavy load. There'd been talk about finding her some space in the teachers' lounge. Wouldn't *that* be fun.

This school really needed a construction project, focusing on shiny new lockers. And the girls' restrooms, of course. Powder blue with wall-to-wall mirrors and soft lighting would be good. Yeah. Right.

Everything was different, so different from...

Stroking a stray hair behind her ear, she shook off the memories and wondered about the boy at the gas station. Was he just passing through? Did he live nearby? He'd had blond hair and kind blue eyes. He'd been nice to her, which was a rarity. These days she either received pitying or awkward stares. Nothing attuned to the friendships she'd enjoyed before she came to live in Coal Creek.

She entered English class and headed to the back corner. On her first day a couple months earlier, it had been the only available seat. Fortunately, it provided room for her to shove her books out of the way. It also gave her a place to hide from inquisitive eyes. Being the new girl was a pain.

But someone occupied her chair. The guy was dressed in black—black T-shirt, black jeans, black boots. Thick and wavy black hair lay across his forehead and caressed the top of his shoulders. He was handsome in a dark kind of way. And he was newer than she was. Excellent, she was off that particular hook.

What were the odds that she'd meet two handsome strangers in two days, in such a small town? Of course, neither would want anything to do with her, not with all the cheerleaders sashaying around. Not a dork like her.

But this handsome stranger lifted his eyes to her face and grinned. "Am I in your seat?"

His words dripped with both honey and venom in a strange sort of way. She gulped. Had he just spoken to her? The dork, the oaf, the friendless?

"Yeah, but umm…" *How do you tell someone like him to give your seat back?*

He folded his muscled arms over his broad chest. "Mr. Henley told me to sit in the back. How lucky am I?"

"Excuse me?"

"Looks like I was lucky enough to take the seat of a beautiful woman."

Maddie heard a gasp and glanced behind her. Stephanie— better known as Miss Popularity—gawked. She blinked rapidly and said to those around her, "What, what did he say? He can't be talking to *her*."

Maddie faced the new guy, her confidence renewed. If talking to the dark handsome stranger got Stephanie's goat, then she was all for it. "Yes, that's my seat."

Stephanie's voice rose an octave. "Did *she* just speak to *him*? Someone fan me!" Stephanie poured on the drama, and her sidekick Marley grabbed a book and waved it like a fan.

The boy in black stood and offered Maddie her seat. "Sorry about the mix-up." He held his hand out. "I'm Dougal Lachlan. It's nice to meet you."

Maddie glanced again over her shoulder. Stephanie was on the verge of stroking out, her face as red as a pomegranate as she gasped for breath. With a satisfied grin, Maddie accepted Dougal's hand. "It's nice to meet you, too. I'm Madelyn Clevenger. But you can call me Maddie for short."

They shook hands and a thud echoed behind them. Stephanie had slipped from her chair and toppled to the floor in a theatrical, deliberate move.

Maybe her lack of friends hadn't been entirely her own dorky fault.

Maddie fought a grin as she walked to her next class. Other students stared at her and she lowered her head, allowing her hair to drape across her face. Her Cheshire cat grin was for herself alone.

News of Dougal and their conversation had caught the school rumor mills and she'd become an instant sensation. She didn't like being stared at, but man, it beat the pity and indifference by a long country mile.

She entered her next class and strode to the back to take her seat. Again Dougal sat there, his legs crossed at the ankles and propped on the seat before him.

"Maddie, right?"

"Yeah."

"Looks like I've done it again."

"Looks like it." Heat flushed her cheeks and she stroked a strand of hair behind her ear. Wait, did she do that when she got nervous?

Dougal moved and swept out his arm. Maddie took her seat and shoved her books underneath. When she lifted her head, everyone stared at her. She cleared her throat and flipped her book open. Felt good.

Stephanie vigorously fanned herself with a folded piece of paper. "I don't get it. I just don't get it."

"Don't worry, girlfriend," Marley said. "I'm sure it's just an anomaly in the space-time continuum."

"What?" Stephanie glared and shook her head. "Marley, what are you babbling about?"

"I was trying to explain the new guy's odd behavior."

"How, by being odd yourself?"

Marley narrowed her eyes and fell back against her chair.

It was almost comical. If Maddie hadn't considered the entire situation weird, then she'd have been jumping in delight.

The teacher entered and Maddie shifted her gaze. A tingle raced along her spine. Dougal was kicked back and staring at her. He lifted his hand in a salute. Gnawing her lip, she lowered her gaze and studied her book.

It wouldn't do to gloat too much. Just enough.

"Chase, the principal will see you now," said the plump school secretary.

Chase nodded. He hated the first day at a new school, especially when the year was already started. Being the only one wandering around and getting lost, wondering between classes if he had enough time for his locker and the bathroom both, finding himself at the wrong end of a long hall with ten seconds before the bell...

At Coal Creek High, the principal met with all new students. Chase's parents thought of it as a great opportunity. He thought of it as a way to ruin a guy's reputation before it even started. And how many new students could a small, one-horse town possibly get?

He entered the office. The rotund, balding man behind the desk held a large pastrami on rye. He took a bite, laid it down, leaned forward, and offered his hand. "Chase Donovan? Welcome to Coal Creek. Hope you don't mind if I eat lunch."

Chase averted his gaze. A piece of lettuce was wedged between the principal's front teeth. "No, sir. I don't mind."

"Good." He waved Chase to a chair, then took another bite, chewed, and swallowed. "Young man, I believe you'll like it here. We're a small school with big opportunities. Do you play sports?"

"Only for recreation."

"What a pity. You've got the build." The principal chomped another bite. He picked up some papers on his desk and riffled through them. "I see here that your father was in the Air Force. I was a military man myself."

Chase critiqued the man's physique and refrained from comment about how long ago that must have been. "Yes, he's retired now."

"Ah, so he came here to retire. I don't blame him. This is a wonderful community. And now that the weapons plant is expanding... well, they're the big employer in the area. If they're expanding, it's really great for the town."

"That's good to know."

"Do you have any questions?"

"No, sir."

"Very well, then. See Mrs. Grady at the front desk and she'll help with your schedule. I'm sure you're going to love it here."

Chase left, rolling his eyes. Great meeting, really great. So worth the time and damage to his reputation.

Mrs. Grady arranged his schedule and he thanked her then joined the crowded hallway. The bell rang and he glanced at the papers she'd handed him. Third period. French. He swore under his breath as he studied his paper map. How was he supposed to use it to find his classes? The words were blurred, the floors unmarked. He lifted his chin. A sign, like you might see in the mall, dangled from the ceiling. Hitching his backpack higher on his shoulder, he set out in a jog following the arrows. Third period was in full swing before he slipped in and found a seat off to the side.

Stares, new guy, whatever. At least he knew he wouldn't be the only one, if the area's big employer was expanding. There would be at least several more newbies wandering around and the unwanted attention would be shared out. Hey, he had gotten something useful from the principal's little meeting—intel.

"Everyone turn to page fifty. You'll find your assignment on the board."

Groans mingled with the sound of shuffling papers. Chase bent and drew paper and a pencil from his backpack.

A pretty cheerleader type sitting in the middle of the room whispered, "I just don't get what he sees in her." She twisted a strand of honey-colored hair around her finger. She looked as if she might have come from a California beach. "Marley, you want to make a bet?"

"Sure, Stephanie. What's the bet?"

"I bet I can make tall, dark, handsome, and new forget all about Maddie before the week is up."

Yep, more newbies around. Excellent.

Marley scratched a pen lid against her forehead. "I don't know. He seems pretty into her."

A shadow fell across his desk. "Ladies, you should not be talking."

"Sorry," said Stephanie.

Chase started to say hello, but the teacher dropped a thick book on his desk. The flimsy metal legs vibrated beneath him.

The teacher walked away, saying, "If you need help, feel free to ask."

He nodded, but didn't get the impression the teacher really

meant what he said. At least one teacher just going through the motions. Not good. At least it was only French and not something important, like chemistry or pre-calc. He sank low in his chair and tried to blend.

"*Accueil. D'où êtes-vous?*" The teacher stared at him.

Keeping his face blank, Chase nodded. "California."

"Ah, California." The French teacher spoke rapidly and Chase lost the thread. Thankfully, he moved to another student. Chase breathed a sigh of relief. He could follow some of the chattering but couldn't bring himself to care.

The bell rang and he moseyed to the cafeteria. The line wound around the octagonal room and he found himself at the end. Tray finally filled, he looked for a place to sit. All the tables were full. A door to the outside stood open. Shoulders stooped, he found a seat underneath a small tree with drooping leaves on a brick planter. Thankfully the weather had warmed overnight. The seat was damp but not icy.

The pizza tasted like cardboard and the milk was warm. Could this school get any worse? He carried the full tray to the garbage can and let the contents slide off into it. Backpack hoisted on his shoulder, he dragged out his map.

Running his finger along the route as he walked, he mumbled, "If I take this hallway, and then—"

"Whoa!" came a feminine voice, but the warning was too late. Delicate hands fell against his chest.

Just like at the store yesterday. An electrical tingle raced over him and his pulse revved. "Sorry," he said, heat flushing his cheeks.

"No, it's okay. It was my fault." Before he could speak again, the girl moved past, not even looking up. The fresh ozone scent of a thunderstorm hung in the air.

He turned to apologize, but the words stuck in his throat. Auburn waist-length hair, clasped in a ponytail, swished behind her as the girl made a hasty retreat. She didn't glance back. It had been her, but his next class wouldn't wait. He'd have to find her again.

Shrugging, he left the atrium, entered the hallway, and studied the map again. As usual when starting a new school, it was going to be a long day.

A few minutes earlier

Dougal hid in the corner of the atrium, his leg propped behind him against the wall. A toothpick hung from his lips as he struck his casual pose. Teenagers—ugh! Always worried about appearances and what others thought. In five years none of it would even matter and after a hundred years of life, he should know.

He planted both feet on the ground and looked at his wide-soled black boots. He sighed. Why did teens have to dress in such hideous outfits? Fortunately the attire he'd chosen for himself after researching several teen magazines wasn't overly grotesque. At least he could stand the black. It also seemed to garner much attention. The adults eyed him warily and the kids expressed intrigue, wonderment. Perhaps he should have dressed more obscurely. Of course with his natural good looks, no clothes would have made him blend.

He rubbed a spot between his brows. Finding Maddie so quickly had been unexpected. Of course, that was just part of his assignment. Serena's continued haranguing that he 'get close to the key' was annoying. Why did she not do the work if she was dissatisfied with his performance?

A magical blue light glowed around the outer courtyard doors, getting closer fast. Dougal perked up. Maddie exited the building. Hair fell across her face and she bumped into a strange boy walking with his head bent. Dougal's stomach clenched as Maddie made contact. How dare the stranger touch her? Dougal made a move to intercept and tell him to keep his hands to himself, but the boy seemed slow-witted and allowed Maddie to walk away without offering an apology.

The new boy scooted past Dougal. The air between them sizzled with electric energy. It danced along Dougal's arms and lifted the hairs on the nape of his neck. Ozone tickled his nostrils. He frowned, feeling the heat in his eyes that meant they were glowing. He hadn't felt a surge like that since childhood. Who was this stranger? Had he come for the key as well? And if so, why?

2

The day was finally over. Maddie stowed her unneeded books in the teachers' lounge. A couple students had left, the principal told her after the last class, one dropping out and the other moving. But the two new guys had been in the front of the silly man's mind; it seemed he'd met with both earlier that day, when they'd registered. He hadn't remembered her, also new but not as new as them.

The two guys got the lockers. At least the staff had made room for her in the teachers' lounge. Goodie.

The remaining books weighed heavily on her back. She hauled the load to the bike rack, placed the backpack in her bike's front basket, put her helmet on, and set out.

She'd been living with her great-grandmother since her parents' unexpected death. The situation wasn't ideal, but at least she had a home.

Tall pines lined both sides of the highway. A wide strip of asphalt ran along both sides for bike riders and walkers. The community of Coal Creek loved their tourists and some employees walked to the weapons factory for their shifts.

Maddie pedaled and mentally reviewed her day. *Dougal Lachlan.* She lifted her hand from the handle and fanned herself. He was a hottie and a half. A smile twitched at her lips. Poor Stephanie. The girl had barely made it through the day without having to see the school nurse over Dougal's fawning toward Maddie.

Toward her.

The bike coasted downhill. The wind whipped at her hair and brought the scent of dying honeysuckle and pine sap; the unexpected snowfall yesterday had taken its toll. Soon the season would change and the temperature would turn even colder. The thought of riding her bike in extended winter weather caused her stomach to knot. Clumsy her, the bike, snow, *ice...* not a comforting combination.

Maybe she could convince Grandma Draoi to buy a car. With it she could take Grandma to the grocery store and they wouldn't need to depend on the kindness of strangers. The lady who volunteered to take her shopping seemed like a freeloader, always taking something with her when she left.

Maddie rounded the corner, their driveway just ahead. Gravel crunched beneath the bike's tires. She stood and pedaled faster. Maybe Grandma Draoi had supper ready. After the stomach-curdling pizza no one had eaten, she was starving.

Chase parked his truck in the circular drive, wishing again that he'd driven it across country rather than let the movers tow it behind the big van; that would have been such an experience, but Mom had vetoed the idea without giving it the consideration he felt it deserved. With a sigh, he entered the new house, which seemed to be exploding from his brothers' rowdy play. Ah, it was good to be home, no matter how new it was. A football flew through the air and he caught it with one hand. He was set to throw it back when his mother appeared from nowhere and grabbed it.

"Chase, don't encourage them. I told your brothers to go outside and play."

Cole and Colton grumbled in unison. Cole made a grab for the football. She raised it above her head with a frown.

"Where's Dad?" Chase asked.

"I think he's in the workshop, unpacking tools."

"And Chris and Craig?"

"They called to say they were staying at school to try out for junior varsity football." She handed over the football and shooed the twins outside, then lowered her gaze to the box at her feet. "This is such a disaster. I can't find anything. I don't know how I'm supposed to fix dinner. Can you believe it? The movers wrapped my dishes with the twin's underclothes! I've been working all day and I can't find a thing." She sent him a desperate look and asked, "Do you want to help me?"

"Uh, maybe we should just order pizza?" It would have to be better than the poisonous variety the school had served, if the company expected to stay in business.

"Men!" she complained, and opened the box.

Chase slipped out of the house. He found his dad in his workshop, in much the same state as his mother. "Oh, Chase, glad you're home. How was your first day of school?" He didn't wait for a reply but said, "Look at this. Your mother is going to have a fit."

"What is it?" Chase asked, leaning over the open box.

"Her fine silverware is mixed in with my drill bits. I guess I better go tell her." Dad stretched and walked past.

Chase straightened. "Dad?"

"Yeah?" He stopped at the door.

"I really need to talk to you."

"Right now?"

"Yes. Do you have time?"

Dad sat on a stool. "Sure I do. What do you need to talk about?"

"Well, school was..." He didn't finish, choosing instead to study his hands.

"Not so good, huh?"

"No."

A gentle hand settled on his shoulder. "Look, Chase, I know it's not easy going to a new school—again—especially during the middle of the year, but I promise this is the last time."

"Yeah, I know." Chase scuffed his toe against the concrete floor. "It's just that..." He couldn't finish the sentence. Of all the schools they could have finally settled into—uninterested teachers, bored students, lousy food, and a girl who made static electricity sizzle along his arms but wouldn't stop long enough to talk with him. Totally awesome.

"When I retired from the Air Force, I thought we would stay in one place, and here I am, moving you guys around again." Dad ran a hand over his still thick hair. "But I promise this is the last job transfer. If this place doesn't like my consulting, then I'll just stay home and pester your mom all day."

No, Dad already felt guilty. Chase couldn't complain. Maybe if things got really bad, he could talk his parents into home-schooling or letting him take online classes. That needed research into state and local laws, though. For now, he was stuck.

In turn, Chase patted his father's shoulder. "Don't sweat it. You're only doing what's best for us."

"I hope so."

"When do you start the new job?"

"Next week. They were kind enough to give us a week to unpack."

We'll need it. Chase started to speak, but Mom yelled from the back door. "Alexander!"

Dad sighed. "I guess I better tell Carissa I found her silverware."

Alone, Chase knelt beside the box and separated drill bits from forks. It seemed the right thing to do.

"Grandma, supper was excellent."

"Thank you, dear. I'm glad you liked it."

"Do you have any plans tonight?" asked Maddie. She leaned her elbows on the table and cupped her chin.

Grandma Draoi turned away from the sink and giggled. If she'd been much shorter, she'd have needed to stand on a box to even reach the sink. "I think I'll curl up with a good book. I received one in the mail today and it is positively scandalous."

No one knew precisely how old Grandma Draoi was, including Maddie, but age had softened everything about her. Only hints of fiery red remained in her greyed hair, and her kind green eyes seemed to have faded through the years with time and sorrow. Even her body had rounded and softened with age. Maddie thought her the perfectest grandmother of them all.

Maddie cocked her eyebrow as Grandma Draoi flashed a book showcasing a shirtless man. A really hot one. "I see."

"Don't you laugh at me, child."

"Me, laugh, at you?" Too late, Maddie covered her mouth. Grandma whacked her with a towel. Maddie raised her hands in defense and scooted away from the table. "I've got some homework to finish, so I'll leave you to your licentious read."

"Pshaw," Grandma Draoi said as Maddie hurried from the

room.

Upstairs, she stretched across her bed and dragged out her journal. She turned to the first empty page and cataloged the day's events. Dougal, tall, dark, hot, and actually willing to talk with her. But forgotten by the principal and relegated to the teachers' lounge. Blech. And not even a glimpse of the polite guy from yesterday's encounter at the store. And it looked as if Stephanie was deliberately isolating her from the other kids. So both a good day and a bad day at the same time.

In the margin she doodled a picture of Dougal. Using charcoal, she darkened in his hair and smeared it with her thumb, making sure it swooped over his dark brows and lay in a caress across his broad shoulders.

She rolled over onto her back and read what she'd written. Finished, she dropped the book onto her cedar chest and sighed. Too much to deal with. Why did Stephanie have to be such a selfish drama queen?

The phone rang. Sitting up, Maddie waited. Five rings in and her grandma still hadn't answered.

"Must be one good book," Maddie muttered as she leaned over and grabbed the receiver. "Hello?"

"Hello, Maddie?"

"Yes?" she asked hesitantly. Who could be calling *her*?

"It's Dougal."

Excitement exploded through her. She covered the mouthpiece, sprang off the bed, jumped up and down, and squealed. Drawing in a couple of deep breaths, she calmed herself and removed her hand. "What can I do for you?"

A snicker floated across the line and a wave of heat rushed up her neck and across her cheeks. She'd been busted.

He said, "I fear I missed the homework assignment in history."

"Oh." Disappointment welled inside her as she reached for her backpack. "Let me just pull out my notebook. I know I wrote it down."

"Thanks. I really appreciate it."

"Sure." The book free, she read off the assignment. She collapsed back on the bed, drawing her knees up and playing with a strand of her hair. "If you ever need help, just let me know."

Background noises filtered across the line. A feminine voice whined. "Dougal, get off the phone. I'm feeling neglected."

What? Maddie dropped her hair and sat straighter. She could not have heard that right. And that voice...

"Stephanie, I'll be done in just a minute." He paused, then added, "Thanks again, Maddie. I don't know what I would have done without you."

"Yeah," she said, her heart thumping madly against her ribs, her voice dull.

"I guess I better go. If I don't get started on my homework soon, I'll never finish."

"Sure."

"See you tomorrow?" he asked.

"Okay."

The phone clicked off. A tear slipped from the corner of her eye and down her cheek. She'd known the attention had been too good to be true.

Dougal glanced back. Stephanie stretched in the booth seat on the big room's far side. Decorated in a fifties style, the small town diner sported a long counter, swivel stools with vinyl tops, and booths. A malt machine hummed. Waiters and waitresses wore paper hats and red striped jackets. The checkered floor matched their Oxford shoes.

Dougal had excused himself on the pretense of selecting a song from the jukebox. He'd peered into the machine, covertly dragging out his cell phone and making his call. A thrill had tingled through him as he'd realized how excited the call made Maddie. Her muted squeals had radiated over the phone line. Presumably she would have kept that up had Stephanie's voice not intruded.

He looked over his shoulder again and sighed. A relationship with the popular girl was a necessary evil, mainly because Maddie was jealous of her. Who wouldn't be? Stephanie was a bombshell, long blond hair hanging down to her tush, tanned skin, pale blue eyes, and a voice that grated on the nerves like fingernails on a chalkboard. But she could be used to manipulate Maddie's emotions, to twist the key into the shape they needed. Tedious, but necessary.

He shoved the phone in his pocket, selected a ballad, and returned to his seat. Stephanie leaned over and ran a manicured nail across his exposed neck. He allowed his mouth to spread into a smile. All for the cause.

"Who were you talking to?" she whispered, licking her painted lips.

He waved a small strip of paper. "I called Maddie about a homework assignment."

Her lip protruded, her fingernail withdrew. "Why didn't you ask me?"

Because it's better to keep you guessing, too. "I didn't want to."

She narrowed her eyes and drew her hand into her lap. "So you called Maddie?"

"Yes."

"Well, I don't like it. If we're going to date, then you have to stay away from her. Being in the same room with that girl, and dating me, will totally ruin my rep and I won't have it."

The waitress brought their sodas while Stephanie went on, and on, and on, explaining how often they needed to be seen together. How he would take her home and pick her up, how she expected him to stay for cheerleading practice, how they would eat together at the "special" table in the cafeteria. Tedious. He only half listened. Students went in and out of the diner. He studied each of them; he had to find that strange boy again. He needed to know who he was; then he could pass the information on to Serena. She knew all the Ancient Ones. If one of them was still around, then she would know.

And that electrical surge in the school atrium had felt just like one of the Ancient Ones. A very, very strong one.

3

Chase drove into the school parking lot, picked a spot, and cut the engine. The antique truck backfired, and kids in the immediate area leveled heated stares and mouthed vulgar curses in his direction.

Sighing, he grabbed his backpack and walked inside. He went to his locker, kept the books he needed, and stored the rest. Homeroom was close by, and he entered and took the first available seat.

Students filed in. A group of girls huddled together and he recognized two of them from yesterday's math class.

"Marley, pay up." Stephanie held out her hand.

Chase didn't really want to listen. But her voice was too loud to be ignored.

"What for?"

"What for? Don't you remember our little bet? I told you I could get Dougal to forget all about Maddie and I've already done it."

Only a true drama queen would want the entire homeroom to know all about people they didn't know. Chase yawned and flicked through a textbook. It didn't matter which one, just that he show no interest in her performance.

"Impossible."

"Nope. Look there."

A guy dressed in all black plopped into an empty chair next

to Stephanie. He leaned over and flicked her hair. "Hey, baby. How you doing?"

Marley gawked, and Stephanie batted her lashes and twisted her face toward the newcomer. "I'm doing good. Are we still on for this afternoon?"

"I wouldn't miss it."

The Goth-dressed teen lifted Stephanie's hand and kissed it. She fanned herself and twittered like a bird until the teacher called roll. And Chase sighed.

Maddie hid behind her hair and forced herself not to watch Stephanie flirt with Dougal. Humiliating, how fast the witch had made him forget all about her. And betting with Marley—she needed a hole to hide in. For the rest of her life. Not that she blamed him, not when the choice was between the head cheerleader and the class dork.

Their affections were stymied briefly when the homeroom teacher entered and called the roll. But thirty minutes later the bell rang and Maddie threw her heavy backpack on her shoulder. It was time to escape.

The load lightened and she looked around. Dougal tugged at the top strap. "Let me carry that for you."

Maddie's thoughts hovered between disbelief and dull anger. She opened her mouth to protest but Stephanie pushed in beside them. Through clenched teeth, she said, "Dougal, sweetie, what are you doing?"

"I'm carrying Maddie's books." He said it as if it were the most natural, least questionable thing in the world—as if he hadn't been flirting with Stephanie throughout homeroom.

"Oh." Stephanie tugged her purse strap higher on her shoulder as if preparing to strangle someone with it.

Maddie grimaced. She didn't want to be that someone, at least not in the middle of homeroom.

"Stephanie, you go to class and I'll meet you there."

Stephanie froze. If looks could kill, Dougal would have fried, and Maddie right beside him. "I— I—"

Marley clutched her arm. "Come on."

They went, finally, but Stephanie made a point of showing what she thought of the arrangement. And instead of protesting, Maddie found herself tamely following Dougal to their next class. If it showed up Stephanie, whatever it was, she could be a fan.

He walked directly to her seat and dropped her bag in the corner. "The school should really provide you a locker. That pack is heavy."

She nodded and bit her lip.

"I guess I should take my seat."

She nodded again and followed him with her eyes as he found a spot in the middle row.

Stephanie plopped into the seat in front of him and crossed her arms over her chest. A pout covered her lips, and Dougal leaned forward and whispered in her ear. Maddie fought envy as she dragged out her textbook. For a few minutes there, it had seemed...

"Miss?"

She straightened in her chair and stared at the most gorgeous guy she'd ever seen. Blond hair hung two inches above the nape of his neck and feathered neatly across his forehead. His sapphire eyes twinkled like the sun glinting on the ocean. She gasped and stars swam before her vision. It was him! How had she sat down right beside him and never noticed?

He snapped his fingers, grinning, and she shook her head. "Sorry? What did you say?"

Chase studied the dazed girl. Brownish-red hair framed her face. A dusting of freckles peppered her cute button nose. She blinked and flashed eyes the deepest jade he'd ever seen. She shook her head and her hair swayed from side to side.

Wow. Just... wow. He'd never complain about small towns again.

He held out his hand. "I didn't have an opportunity to introduce myself the last time we met. I'm Chase Donovan."

She grasped his hand awkwardly. "Madelyn Clevenger, or Maddie, as most people call me."

"It's nice to meet you."

"Nice to meet you, too." He didn't say more, just stared at her, and finally she asked, "Did you need something?"

"Oh, yeah. Sorry." He paused and heat rushed across his cheeks. *Get a hold of yourself, Donovan. You've talked to pretty girls before. California girls, at that, the ones wearing bikinis.* He cleared his throat. "Today's my first day in this class and I thought maybe you could tell me about Mr. Holston."

"I guess so. What did you want to know?"

"Well, I guess I mainly need to know how to get a book. Yesterday a teacher just flopped one on my desk in front of me and then stalked off. So I didn't know whether I should make my presence known, or just wait for him to come to me."

"Hmm, I think I would just wait. Mr. Holston can be a tad eccentric."

"Okay."

"If you need a book before he gives you one, you can share mine. That is, if you want to."

Somewhere in Heaven, angels began to sing. He could feel the echo in his chest. "Thanks. I appreciate it."

The teacher entered and Chase straightened. The man was bald on top with hair wrapping around the sides of his overly large head. He wore a plaid polyester jacket with matching bell bottoms. Chase cocked his brow and Maddie whispered, "See."

He looked away as Mr. Holston opened a ratty copy of *Hamlet* and began to explain the deeper meaning of the play. It seemed to take forever, not just the entire first class. Finally the bell rang and Mr. Holston yelled out their nightly reading assignment. Chase hurried to gather his books.

"Thanks, Maddie."

"No problem. And just to be on the safe side, I would stop and tell Mr. Holston you're new. He might not have noticed you."

He nodded and found his way to the front desk.

Maddie watched Chase's retreating form. A person would have to be blind not to notice Chase Donovan. Biceps flexed with every shift of his backpack. His jeans clung to him like a second skin and like a California surfer, his tan contrasted with his white shirt, which stretched taut over his broad chest.

He turned and winked. Maddie blushed and quickly bent to finish the task of loading her backpack. For the first time, she was glad she didn't have a locker. The longer it took, the more peeks at Chase she could steal. But she could only drag the chore out for so long, and then she had to leave. Bummer.

In the hallway, throngs of people crowded around lockers

and talked in loud voices. Maddie ignored them—hey, they'd ignored her since she'd arrived, and fair was fair—and continued to her next class. She took her seat in the back and stowed her books. When she looked up, Dougal waved. She lowered her eyes to her desk. Wrong hottie, and he'd chosen Stephanie.

Others filed in and again she found herself staring at the back of Chase's head. He peered back at her and her mouth went dry.

"Hi," he said, a smile tugging at his lips.

"Hi," she replied.

"Fancy meeting you again so soon."

"Yeah," she said, fighting her own smile.

"This school is a lot different from my last two, in Texas and in California."

She gnawed on her lip. *He wanted her to ask questions, didn't he?*

When she didn't say anything, he continued, "My dad retired from the military and I've been to dozens of schools, but this one is—"

"Different. Yeah, you said that."

He opened his mouth, perhaps to explain what he meant, but the teacher interrupted. Mr. Sanders stood at the blackboard and worked mathematical equations, explaining each one in excruciating detail. When he finished, he listed their assignment.

Maddie worked the problems. A shiver raced along her spine. She shifted her gaze to the left. Dougal's dark eyes studied her. He lifted a brow and his lips twitched upward.

Ignore him, just ignore him, she thought as she focused on the calculus problem. The answer evaded her and she looked at the example on the board. She gulped.

Dougal still stared at her, his amber eyes glowing like a lit candle—the weirdest thing she'd ever seen in her life.

4

On the opposite side of the room, a boy dressed in black ogled Maddie. The stare was so intense it was palpable, and Chase's hackles rose. But he didn't own Maddie and he hadn't even asked if she had a boyfriend. He drew in a deep breath and focused on the calculator. Within a few minutes his heart rate calmed and the irritation passed.

The bell rang, and he packed up his things and headed to French. Without the Goth and Maddie, the class passed quickly. Maybe that meant he didn't handle distractions well.

He shouldered his pack and headed to the lunchroom. Most of the tables were full, save one. Maddie sat alone, her hair falling forward and draping her face.

He approached the table. "This seat taken?"

She lifted her eyes and shook her head. For a moment Chase hesitated. She didn't look overjoyed to see him. Maybe she wasn't attracted to him... and maybe he was creating problems. Maybe he should get to know her first. Maybe he should stop overthinking everything and eat before the lunch period was over.

Taking a deep breath, he set down his tray and took a seat. "Is the cafeteria always like this?"

"Most of the time. It's even worse on rainy days."

"I bet." He took a bite of the hamburger and moaned.

"Is it good?" she asked, a smile tugging the corner of her

lips.

He shrugged. "Let's just say it's not as bad as yesterday."

The conversation faltered and they ate in awkward silence. She fingered her burger wrapper. "Is Dougal staring at me?"

"Excuse me?"

"The guy dressed in black and sitting next to Stephanie, is he staring at me?"

Chase looked in the direction she gestured. That guy, yeah. "I think so."

Maddie groaned and pushed her tray aside, burying her head on her folded arms. He almost patted her, but stopped himself.

She glanced up. "I just don't get it. He hangs out with Stephanie but he still watches and flirts with me."

"Oh," he said, wadding his napkin.

"I just don't understand guys." She blew air from her mouth.

She had noticed that she was speaking with one, right? "Is there anything I can do to help?"

She pursed her lips. "I don't think so. Unless you can read minds."

"Afraid not."

The food on her tray grew cold. Determined to distract her from Dougal, Chase pulled out his schedule. "Do we have any other classes together?"

Maddie secured a strand of hair behind her ear and flashed him a timid smile as she ran her finger over the list. "Yeah, fourth period and sixth."

How had he not noticed her in class the day before? He must have been out of it to miss someone like her. He folded the sheet of paper and shoved it in his back pocket. "Great. You can guide me there after lunch."

They left the lunchroom and traveled the crowded halls. Several people did a double take, watching them walk together. He ignored their scrutiny. Hey, she'd been attending Coal Creek High for several months. If they'd wanted to walk with her, they could have done it at any time. Now that he was here, though...

"Here's chemistry," said Maddie.

They both stretched a hand forward, and his collided with hers atop the doorknob. An electric shock rocketed through his body. The hairs on his arm stood on end and he swallowed.

Maddie jerked away and rubbed her wrist.

"You okay?" he asked.

"Yeah, I'm fine. Must have built up some static."

That hadn't felt like static electricity. That felt like... he didn't even know. But nor did he know what to think, much less say. *Hey, that was weird. Let's do it again.* Yeah, right. So with a strange prickling feeling still in his thumb, he nodded and stood aside, allowing Maddie to enter first.

Maddie massaged her tingling wrist as she entered the classroom. What had just happened? She'd thought Dougal's bizarre glowing eyes had made her day weird. But that shock—that was worse, because it had been up close and personal. She needed time to think, but loud voices interrupted. Oh, great: Stephanie and her court.

"Have you seen the *other* new guy?" Marley asked.

"No. But I saw his truck. Yuck! And double yuck!" said Stephanie.

"What kind is it?"

A boy replied. "It's an old pickup, like from the eighties. Ancient, man."

Marley added, "Yeah, but wait until you see *him*. He's *so* dreamy, his body more than makes up for his vehicle."

Stephanie crossed her arms over her chest. "It doesn't matter! I wouldn't date a guy who drives an ugly truck."

Maddie's heart thumped. They were discussing Chase. One glance at his brows drawn together and she knew he realized it, too. But seconds later his face relaxed and Maddie hid a smile. Why should he worry about what Stephanie and her crew said? Chase had to know he was awesome. And besides, Stephanie had set her sights on Dougal, right? She hadn't even noticed Chase yesterday, because she'd been concentrating elsewhere.

In the middle of another nasty comment, Marley's jaw dropped.

"What's wrong with you?" asked Stephanie.

Marley lifted her shaky finger. "Th-that ain't natural."

Maddie gritted her teeth. It wasn't natural that someone would want to walk with her? Oh, one of these days Stephanie and her crew would go too far.

Stephanie stared at Chase and Maddie as they passed by.

"What's happening this week? Is it the coming of the apocalypse or something?"

"*That's him,*" whispered Marley, loud enough for everyone in the room to hear.

"Him, who?"

"The *other* new guy."

Stephanie groaned.

Maddie would've smiled if she hadn't been distracted, but Dougal sat in her seat again. She stiffened as she prepared to approach.

Maybe Chase sensed her discomfort, because he leaned down and whispered in her ear, his cool breath tickling her neck and sending shivers along her spine. "Is that your seat?"

She nodded.

"Do you want me to say something?"

Grateful, she shook her head.

Chase stopped at an empty stool and Maddie continued to her lab table. Dougal stood and held out his hand. "I hope you don't mind that I saved your seat."

She slid across the warmed wood. Dougal bent forward and blew against her neck. His bronze eyes grew dark as he straightened and walked away to sit next to Stephanie.

Chills raced along her body and she hugged her middle, hoping no one would notice. Finally the teacher entered. The lecture should have been a good distraction, but Maddie struggled to focus. Without wanting to, she kept glancing over to the other table, where Stephanie's eye twitched and her head jerked while she rubbed her hand along Dougal's thigh. He tweaked her nose and cooed. Her shoulders slumped, a lazy smile spreading over her mouth.

Maddie drummed her fingers on the lab table. When next she glanced up, Dougal was watching. He blew her an air kiss. Heat flushed her face and she lowered her eyes, vowing not to look back up.

The teacher listed instructions and her lab partner jotted them down. Chemicals mixed and the reaction complete, Maddie filled out their answer sheet and prayed the bell would ring soon. She couldn't make it much longer. Jealousy was eating her alive.

Dougal flirted with Stephanie then looked to see if Maddie watched. Her eyes darkened. Her pulse thumped against her neck. A smile tugged at the corner of his lips. She *did* watch. The thrill of his effect on her tickled him, and brought some relief, too. Serena would be pleased and perhaps ease up on her continued harping.

Stephanie squeezed his thigh, and he gritted his teeth. She reminded him of a girl from his childhood home. The Irish village had been filled with beautiful girls, but one had thought she was more perfect than the rest. And in truth, she had stood in stark contrast to the other girls, with her long blond hair and her skin unblemished by freckles. Her hands had been smooth and untouched by work, a lady's hands.

Every day she'd prowled the market, swayed her hips, and enticed the local men. Then one day she'd been found dead, face down in a pile of rotted fish. A scrawled note had been pinned to her back: *Now your outside matches your inside.*

The perpetrator had never been found. Dougal assumed it was like the death of Julius Caesar—there hadn't been one culprit, but many.

He covertly snuck a glance at Stephanie. An imaginary target hung from the girl's back. Students paid attention to her because of her popularity and head cheerleader status, but once that was gone, the adoration would leave with it and she would either self-destruct or someone would help her along.

"What are you thinking?" Stephanie asked, her breath smelling of mint.

"I was thinking about your future."

She knitted her brows together, but asked no more questions as the teacher began to lecture about covalents.

Chase couldn't believe it, but Dougal openly flirted with both Stephanie and Maddie. He gritted his teeth until his jaw ached and couldn't make himself stop. What was wrong with him? He couldn't be jealous. No, it wasn't jealousy; he just hated jerks.

The class bell rang and he ran to his next class. It was a complete bore and failed to occupy his mind. The teacher strutted about the room discussing supply side economics and Chase fought off yawns. He'd had economics before, both macro and micro. Why was he even in that class?

He lowered his chin and movement to one side caught his eye. In the back corner Stephanie filed her nails. Marley sat beside her, doodling in a notebook. Suddenly she glanced up and their gazes meshed. Marley's lips twitched and she waved. Embarrassed at being caught staring, Chase silently groaned and looked away. Hopefully she wouldn't think he was interested. The queen's lady-in-waiting wasn't his type.

Finally the boring class ended, and Chase grabbed his books and rushed to the gym. The locker room echoed with voices, and he picked an empty stall for changing clothes.

Voices drifted from the next row over. "Have you seen that Dougal guy?"

"No, man. I don't look at guys."

"No, stupid. I meant, have you seen him play football? He puts us all to shame."

"If you say so."

Maybe he should try out for the team, despite what he'd said to the principal, and take the guy down a few pegs. Someone needed to. Chase strode from the stall, shoved his belongings in a locker, and went to stand with the other students.

The gym class was co-ed. Girls grouped in the corner while the boys milled about. Some played basketball while others talked.

He grabbed a ball and took a shot. It bounced off the rim and tumbled in.

"Lucky shot." Dougal retrieved the ball. He lifted it above his head and sent it flying. It whistled through the air and swooshed in. "Nothing but net," he said, rubbing his knuckles across his chest and blowing on them.

Yep, he really hated jerks. Chase bent to pick up another ball when the gym doors slammed.

"Line up!" Coach Johnson yelled.

The students complied and Chase moved as far away from Dougal as humanly possible.

"Since the weather is nice, we're going to hit the track." The air filled with groans. Coach lifted his hands in defense. "If you don't want to run, then you can do push-ups. Your choice."

In a single file line, boys first, they moved outside and onto the track. Chase took off in a steady jog.

"So how do you like it here?" asked Maddie as she jogged

up beside him.

He couldn't stop the smile that spread across his face. But he needed to act like her interest hadn't affected him. He shrugged without breaking stride.

"Coach Johnson really isn't so bad. At least he didn't make us race each other." She smiled and he smiled back. "I wanted to thank you for your offer earlier," she said, a little out of breath.

"My offer?"

"Of help."

"Oh, that. No problem."

"Still, I wanted to thank you. Not many people will go to bat for me right now, so knowing I have a friend makes all the difference." Chase didn't respond and she hesitantly added, "I can call you my friend, right?"

"Absolutely."

She placed a strand of hair behind her ear and sped up. "See you at the finish line."

Ready to chase her, he was surprised by a rush of air blasting past. He blinked. Dougal had flown ahead of him and pulled alongside Maddie. Scowling, Chase slowed his pace and continued to the finish.

5

Dougal ran alongside her. Maddie grimaced. The guy was bad news. His behavior, flirting with her while dating Stephanie, testified to that. She needed to get away from him before he gave her emotional whiplash or worse. She pushed herself to speed up but quickly realized there was no point; she couldn't outrun him.

"Can I help you, Dougal?" she asked in a strained voice.

"Most definitely you can."

Great. Exactly what she needed.

They reached the finish line and moved off the track. She downed the contents of a water bottle, liquid dribbling off her chin, and bent over, placing her hands on her knees and sucking in air. He'd get the hint. He had to.

"Are you all right, love?"

Then again, maybe he wouldn't, not unless she made it more specific. Maddie straightened, leaned away, and placed one hand on her jutted hip. "What?"

"I asked if you were all right."

"I'm fine." She turned, intending to stalk away.

But he grabbed her arm. "Have I offended you?"

She glared at his hand, wrapped around her arm. "Offended me? Of course not. How could you have possibly offended me?"

That hint he got. He released her and she stomped into the

girls' locker room, showered, and dressed. Nestled between two rows of lockers, she pulled on her socks and shoes. Maybe she'd escape without further confrontation. But nearby a door squeaked and Maddie froze, heart thudding in her throat.

"I thought you said you won him over," whispered Marley.

"I did," said Stephanie, sounding steamed.

"Apparently Dougal didn't get the memo."

"Marley, I told you I'd convince him to stop staring at Maddie and I will."

"Whatever." There was a brief pause. Marley added, "Maybe you should work on someone else, like Chase."

"Don't drool, Marley, it is totally unbecoming."

"Do you think Chase would go out with me if I ask?"

"Nope. I don't think he would."

"Hurtful."

"I thought you would appreciate the truth."

Their voices faded as other girls swarmed into the locker room and hit the showers.

Heart still thudding, Maddie peeked around the corner. The coast clear, she left the locker room for the gym, settling into a quiet corner behind the stacked bleachers. Ear buds in and sketchpad in hand, she waited for the final bell.

Soft strokes covered the page as the portrait took shape. Feathered hair lay in a wave over his forehead and there was a playful tilt to his full lips. Gentleness shone from his shaded eyes. Capturing emotion in her drawings had always been easy for her, even when she couldn't get the details exactly right, such as the hard parts like hands and ears. Details were important, her art teacher used to say, but the soul was vital.

When the bell rang, she shoved the pad in her backpack. It slipped from her grasp and sprawled open, a sketch of the tower splayed across the visible page. Her heart hammered in her chest and she grabbed the pad and closed it with a snap. Why did the image from her dreams cause her to feel ill? It was only a dream, even if it was one she couldn't get rid of. Again she shoved the pad in her pack, and followed everybody else out of the gym.

Books stored in the teachers' lounge, she grabbed her bike helmet from a shelf and strode to the parking lot.

Covertly she searched the fleeing students. Chase climbed into a rickety old truck and drove from the lot. Dougal hoisted himself into his jacked-up SUV and peeled away. Neither of them sent her a second glance.

When the lot emptied, Maddie climbed astride her bicycle and headed home, exhausted.

Mom frowned at Chase across the table. "Is something wrong?"

"No." He pushed the pork chop around the plate again. Maybe she wouldn't notice.

"You've barely touched your food."

Nope, she'd noticed. Might as well exit gracefully. "Can I be excused?"

She nodded, and he pushed back from the table and rushed upstairs. At his desk, he stared at the blank computer screen. He checked his email and replied to a few of his friends from California. There were the general questions about his new home and school, and the rote words about missing him. He leaned back in his chair and threaded his hands behind his head. If he closed his eyes, he could visualize his old bedroom. Felt baseball pennants pinned to the dark brown walls, football trophies covering hung shelves, bookcases filled with novels. He opened his eyes to the white, sparsely decorated room. He'd decided not to paint or put anything up for at least three months, just to make sure they were really staying put.

Sighing, he hoisted his backpack onto his lap, drew out his books, and slapped them on the desk. Homework consumed the rest of the evening. Before bed Dad called him downstairs for a nighttime snack, but he declined and sacked out early.

But sleep eluded him. He drew back the corner of his curtain and studied the starry sky. If he closed his eyes he could mentally etch every one of Maddie's features. Her high cheekbones, her slightly upturned jade eyes.

He sighed, rolled onto his side, and punched his pillow. His infatuation with a girl he'd just met was driving him mad. Besides, she was clearly into the Dougal guy. Best to just forget her and move on. Yet why did it seem that was easier said than done?

Maddie finished her homework and decided to go to bed

early. Curled beneath the covers, she snuggled into her pillow and her eyes grew heavy...

The wind lifted her hair off her shoulders and the swaying grass tickled her legs. She glided in slow motion through an endless emptiness. A structure shimmered before her, a brooding tower gleaming white in the dark, and she reached out. Before its fullness materialized, before she could touch it, smoke engulfed her.

The field, the wind, the tower vanished. Instead she stood in her childhood home. Flames covered the floor and ascended the walls. She couldn't breathe. A hand grabbed her wrist...

The force of her own screams jerked Maddie awake. Cold sweat covered her brow and her heart raced. Covers knotted around her legs and she kicked until she achieved freedom, throwing them on the floor.

Her breath came in short rasping gasps as she paced the length of her bedroom. Fortunately Grandma Draoi removed her hearing aids at night. Concerned questions would only make it worse.

The dream had been the same, the strange empty place, the white sparkling tower, and then a return to the fire. It was always the same. It haunted her and refused to leave her alone.

She glanced at the clock. Four a.m. glowed red. Groaning, she thought about lying back down. But images of red hot flames flashed before her vision. They waited for her to close her eyes again. They always did.

Instead she grabbed her sketchpad and opened it to the tower. Grazing her fingers across the deep lines she'd drawn, she closed her eyes. She'd sketched it after one of her more extended dreams, when the terror of her past had felt vivid and alive. Would the images ever fade? Why did the dream repeat?

Sighing, she thumped the sketchpad onto her nightstand and cradled her chin in her palm. Sleep was over. Normally she left home by six, so what difference would an hour make?

She prepared for school, ate breakfast, and wrote her grandma a brief note. At the back screen door, though, she stopped and peered out. Dark gray clouds covered the sky. The first fat raindrops struck the roof and cascaded over the gutters. A bad storm, and it was just getting started. What lousy luck she had. She mumbled unhappy comments under her breath as she searched for a poncho in the hall closet. Two of them, one with a purple leopard design and the other with white kittens covering it. They must have been stowed away from when she'd visited as a young child. The kids at school would make fun of her, but what did she care? At least she'd be dry.

The kitty poncho, the smaller one, covered the backpack and she swathed herself in the purple leopard, tugging hard to cover her entire body. Finished, she strolled outside into the drizzle and climbed astride her bike.

The rain hampered her progress and she arrived in the school parking lot as Chase's truck shuddered to a complete stop. He looked out his side window, a frown covering his handsome face. Great, all she'd needed was for Chase to see her in full dork gear. She made a mental note to get a new poncho, one that wouldn't humiliate her quite so badly.

Quickly she donned her pack and headed for the protective cover of the school's awning. But she wasn't fast enough and a touch on her arm announced Chase's arrival. Oh, it was going to be a wonderful day. She looked at him and fought a cringe as a stray bead of water trickled under her collar and into the valley of her bra.

"Hey," he said.

"Hey." She reached for the school's glass door and restrained the wiggle she felt coming on.

"So you rode a bike to school in the rain."

"Yep." *Come on, just riff on the dork gear and get it over with.*

He sucked on his lower lip and her heart jumped in her chest. "If you ever need a ride..." His voice trailed off.

Wow, and not a word about the stupid purple leopardskin. He really was a nice guy. "Thanks." Water dripped from the poncho and pooled at her feet. When she tugged open the door, cool air struck her and she shivered. "I guess I better go to the restroom and dry off before class starts."

He nodded. Maddie didn't wait for further conversation. Instead she rushed to the bathroom. Ponchos folded and stored in a plastic bag, hair fingered through, she left the sanctuary and rushed to homeroom, unsurprised by rampant snickers. The weather had turned her naturally wavy hair into an unruly mass of frizz, and Chase hadn't been the only one to see the purple leopardskin. Everyone was laughing at her and her rain gear.

Ignoring them, she took her seat and glanced around the room. Her heart sank. Dougal was missing. Why she cared, she didn't know. But she couldn't deny that she did.

His claws had clutched the tree outside Maddie's window as he'd studied her through the night. The dream had wakened her and she'd jumped to her feet, racing around the room like a chicken without a head. Raindrops slipped through the leaves above him, fell onto his back, and slipped between strands of his thick fur. He shivered as the cool water touched his sensitive skin. The entire tree had shaken with the movement and he had peered through the window to make sure his presence remained hidden.

Maddie had moved downstairs, yet he had waited. When she left the house wrapped in mismatched ponchos, he had to bite his tongue to keep from snickering. The teenagers, some his *close personal friends*, would have a field day with Maddie's new attire.

He had waited until she and her bicycle started down the long drive before jumping from the limb and taking flight. He'd soared above her, spreading his wings as widely as he dared. He had hoped to block some of the rain from her person, but he couldn't risk her noticing a large bird-like shadow soaring overhead, even without direct sunlight. Serena would not be happy if he was caught.

Once Maddie had reached the parking lot, he'd changed course and returned home. He would be late to school, but that was alright with him. After all, absence makes the heart grow fonder, and the thought broadened his smile.

The lair was secured in the mountain ridges above Coal Creek. Few people knew of the location and fewer still could reach it. He landed in front of the cave's entrance. The smell of baking bread stretched from the dark arch and he lifted his snout to the air, sniffing.

"Don't procrastinate, Doran." Serena's voice echoed from inside.

He folded his wings to his sides, whispered a few words Serena had given him, and changed into his human form. The tunnels were dark, but he narrowed his eyes and his vision increased, allowing him to see. Before sitting at the table, he strode to his section of the cave and dressed. Black pants, black boots, and a clean black T-shirt. He thought about wearing a black beret, but it seemed like overkill. Did the modern crop of teenagers laugh at berets or think them cool? Frankly, they weren't worth the bother of finding out.

"How did it go?" Serena slithered across the floor and set a plate of hot bread on the table. Thick blond hair swathed her face. Serena looked like a beautiful mermaid, only instead of a fishtail, her lower half was that of a massive snake, like Echidna, mother of all monsters.

The steaming bread made his mouth water. He pulled the hunks apart and slathered them with butter. "It went well." He shoved a piece in his mouth and almost drooled.

She buried a butcher knife in the table close to his hand, but he didn't flinch.

"I tire of waiting. You've rescued her, you've inserted yourself into her dreams, you've flirted with her. How much longer will it be before she does your bidding?" She clicked her nails against the wooden tabletop.

"Serena, since you have no one else to do your work, perhaps you should stop nagging me about my progress."

She ran her finger along his arm. "I wouldn't say there is no one else."

He furrowed his brow. "What do you mean? I thought I was the only black gryphon left."

"Well, there might be one other."

That was news indeed. He'd wondered if any of the Ancient Ones lingered on, and now it seemed one did. But if he showed much reaction, he'd be handing her a weapon against him. Instead he took another bite and swallowed before saying, "Really. Who?"

"Ah, Ailin Colin." A dreamy look glazed over her slit eyes and he cocked a brow. She waved his curiosity away. "I think he goes by Gregory now or some such nonsense, but it doesn't matter. He and I, well, we have different goals." She sighed. "Did you know that I used to be a beautiful woman, admired by many? Now I'm a monster." She moved close and stroked his hair. "I have waited too long, Doran. I want to be normal again."

Of course he knew. She'd told him a hundred times. He kissed the back of her hand, a smile tugging at his lips. "Call me Dougal."

Chase headed to his locker. Mixed feelings assailed him. Maddie rode a bike to school? Even in the rain?

He flung his books inside and slammed the flimsy metal door.

Mrs. Grady, the school secretary, stared at him, her arms crossed over her chest and her foot tapping. When he didn't readily apologize for his behavior, she said, "I'm afraid I made a mistake on your schedule."

He cocked his brow.

"It seems you've already had economics so you'll be taking world history instead."

She handed him a slip of paper which he crammed in his pants pocket. The warning bell rang, and he grabbed his backpack and shuffled along the hallway.

Classes were pretty much the same and at lunch he sat with Maddie.

After chewing and swallowing, he asked, "If it's still raining this afternoon, how would you feel about me giving you a lift home?"

Maddie fiddled with a napkin. "I don't know. I live kind of far out."

"Not a problem. As long as I call my mom and dad and let them know what I'm doing, they won't mind."

She shrugged. "If you're sure."

He nodded, feeling a small measure of relief. She'd called him her friend and driving her home in the rain was something he could do to earn that. Besides, being with her wouldn't be any sort of punishment.

Lunch ended and they went to chemistry. Dougal sat beside Stephanie and whispered in her ear. She giggled and fanned herself.

Chase fought jealousy as Maddie stopped and studied the couple. He couldn't keep pretending that sharp, stabbing feeling was anything else. The jerk wanted to keep both girls guessing. Maybe if he broke things up, he'd surprise Dougal into showing his true colors, and once Maddie saw what a jerk he was, she'd quit watching him and his cheerleader. What could he do to break up their coziness? And did he really want to?

Yeah, he did.

Taking a risk, he approached Dougal, extended his hand, and said, "Hello, I'm Chase Donovan. It's nice to meet you."

Dougal ignored Chase's outstretched hand and looked past him. His eyes glowed amber, like something out of a weird, cheap movie. "Maddie," he whispered. The word echoed through the room like a caress. "I have awaited your breathtaking presence."

Maddie's eyes widened and she glanced at Chase. Shocked, he couldn't move. At first he thought it was surprise. Then he realized it was literal. *He couldn't move,* and fear pounded through him. Something bizarre was going on and he had to stop it.

Without glancing at him, Dougal swaggered past, lifted Maddie's hand, and kissed it. "You are like a ray of sunshine on this rainy day."

Maddie didn't respond, just sat there staring with wide eyes; however, Stephanie scooted out her stool, stood, and braced her hands on her hips. "Dougal, what are you doing?"

Dougal leaned over and whispered in Stephanie's ear. Her face morphed into an almost twisted expression, sensuous and ugly. Around Chase, the room blurred. It was like a videotape on rewind. Everyone but Stephanie froze. Sounds grew dull and distant as Stephanie resumed her seat and leaned her elbows on the lab table, propping up her chin. Then the usual noises resumed.

No one commented on the anomaly. Had anyone else even noticed it? Around him, everyone opened books, arranged glassware and Bunsen burners, shuffled papers and whispered. Wait, if only he had noticed it, had it really happened? Had the tree really fallen in the forest and made no sound?

Chase fisted his hands—easily, so maybe he'd imagined not being able to move—and struggled to regain his balance. What had just happened?

Chase couldn't concentrate. His plan to distract Maddie from Dougal had backfired. Dougal continued to peer over his shoulder and Maddie blushed like she enjoyed the attention.

The teacher seemed oblivious. Why didn't he call Dougal down and tell him to turn around?

Blue lines on his paper blurred before his eyes and Chase shook his head. A dull ache raced across his skull. He massaged his temples. Maybe he was coming down with something. That could account for the weirdness he'd witnessed before. Sure, a head cold, or the flu, or something like it, could be the reason the world had paused. It was logical. He hadn't witnessed it but imagined it.

Chemistry ended and Chase escorted Maddie to their next class. Dougal walked ahead of them. Odd sounds, like heavy footfalls, echoed in his ears, doubtless part of the cold he was catching. Chase cleared his throat and tried to ignore the noise. "Anything I need to know about this class?"

"I didn't know you had history."

"Yeah, they moved me."

"Didn't want to suffer through a year of economics, eh?" She smiled and butterflies danced in his stomach.

He laughed and rubbed a spot between his eyes until his stomach settled. "They decided to count the class from my previous school."

"Gotcha. Well, there's nothing special you need to know. If you're worried about not having a book, just ask the teacher when you walk in."

Chase followed Maddie's advice and stood in front of the teacher's desk for over ten minutes while the man riffled through drawers and shelves searching for an available textbook.

Book finally in hand, Chase was directed to a seat two spots from the back row. Maddie sat behind him, still hidden in a corner, and Dougal sat two chairs to his left.

Chase had to give the jerk credit. He didn't miss a beat. During world history, Dougal stared, waved, winked, whistled, and passed notes to Maddie, anything to get her attention. Stephanie wore a sour expression. Chase didn't envy the tongue lashing Dougal would receive. It wouldn't be of the pleasant variety.

Class ended and Chase thought about approaching Dougal and telling him to get lost, but confusion over his feelings for Maddie and what she really wanted held him back. Maddie hadn't expressed an interest in him other than friendship and she seemed to enjoy the extra attention from Dougal, while at the same time being creeped out. At least that was the vibe she was giving off.

Backpack slung over one shoulder, he stood and scooted out his chair. He'd never really liked a girl who'd had another interest. Not that he was vain, but generally he was enough. Of course he hadn't really told Maddie he was interested, either.

Hot breath struck his neck. He turned. Maddie waited for him. "Want to walk to gym together?"

He swallowed, his heart skipping a beat at her nearness.

6

Again, gym started with the classic line up—guys on one side, girls on the other. A volleyball net stretched across the gymnasium. Coach Johnson separated the kids into teams by alternately pulling one guy and one girl from each line.

Maddie mentally counted, hoping to be on Chase's team. In the few days he'd been a student at Coal Creek High, they had developed a friendship. Being in his presence made her feel comfortable, and it didn't hurt that he was drop dead gorgeous.

The die was cast and Maddie found herself on the team opposite Chase. It figured. Before she could reconcile herself to it, moist hot breath struck her naked shoulder.

"Loving the tank top," said Dougal as he jogged to his position on her team.

Heat flushed her cheeks and she tried to ignore her heart, which had just kicked into overdrive. The situation was absurd. How could she be absorbed with Chase one minute and then with Dougal the next? That had to be what happened when a girl used to zero attention suddenly was inundated with it. Maddie had no idea how to react. But she wouldn't blame herself for being fickle; instead, she was going to enjoy every minute of it while it lasted. No doubt the sun and planetary alignment would change soon and she would return to being just Maddie the Dork, with no catcalls, whistles, or hot breath against her neck.

Maddie shook, jumped up and down on her toes, bent over, and stretched her elbows down to her knees. She was ready to play.

A sudden, jerky movement caught her eye through the net's webbing. On the opposite team and huddled next to Marley, Stephanie frowned, a vein throbbing in her forehead.

A slow smile spread across Maddie's lips. She tried to control the internal gloating, but why should she? Didn't she deserve, if just that once, to be on top of the world? She certainly thought so.

The first serve, and it headed right for her. Sudden pounding in her chest. She could handle it—of course she could. But her overly long shoelaces caught under her feet. She reached for the ball, tripped, and landed face down on the shiny wooden gym floor.

Two shadows cast over her. Two hands jutted in front of her face. Instead of choosing between Chase and Dougal, she pushed up herself. Red rashy burns covered her thighs, but it was nothing to the heat scorching her face. She'd just dorked herself again, in front of the entire class, including both guys.

"You should sit down, Maddie. I'll get you a towel," said Dougal.

Chase wrapped his arm around hers and tried to escort her, but Coach Johnson stepped in their way. "Where are you two going?"

"She was hurt, sir. I thought I would help her to the bleachers," replied Chase.

"Miss Clevenger, are you hurt?"

Maddie bit her lip and shook her head.

"That's what I thought. Now get out there and play."

Maddie limped back onto the court.

Chase caught up and whispered, "Why didn't you tell him you were hurt?"

"Because if I did, then he would make me write a five-page report on volleyball or something stupid like that. I would rather stumble through the game than be tied up in my room all afternoon, slaving over a paper."

Chase sighed and assisted her to her spot before slipping back to his own side. Dougal had already resumed his spot behind her; a dark brooding frown tightening his forehead.

For the rest of the game Chase purposefully struck the ball

away from her. Chase's teammates weren't as generous, but her other guardian angel picked up the slack. When it headed toward her, Dougal jumped in front of her and returned the ball.

Coach narrowed his eyes and settled his hands on his hips, but he didn't comment. Gym over, Maddie shuffled to the showers, ignoring his posturing.

Maddie vanished into the girls' locker room. Chase watched her go, but didn't head for the showers right away. It was time for that confrontation he'd intended in chemistry class. Dougal tried to pass him, and Chase called, "Hey?"

Dougal ignored him and kept sauntering.

Jerk. Chase raised his voice. "Dougal, I'm talking to you."

Dougal turned and Chase closed the distance. When he was near enough to see the jerk's eyelid twitching, he asked, "Why don't you leave the girl alone?"

Dougal narrowed his eyes. Their amber color morphed to black and Chase's heart rate doubled. He hadn't just seen that. No, he really hadn't; it was the coming confrontation that got his blood up.

A smile twitched at the corner of Dougal's lips, but didn't quite reach his eyes. Casually leaning against the end of the bleachers, he crossed his legs at the ankles. "I fail to see how this is any of your concern."

"So you *do* talk."

Dougal straightened in a graceful rush. They stood toe to toe, eye to eye, nose to nose. Chase wasn't backing down. He'd faced intimidation tactics before. The only way to beat a bully was to stand up to him.

He narrowed his eyes. "It's my concern because I've made it my concern."

Dougal reared his head back and roared with laughter. "You have no idea who you're dealing with."

Fury roared through Chase and he clenched his fists. "What do you want with her?"

And suddenly Dougal no longer looked like a teenager. His face stayed the same, his hair, his stupid black T-shirt and the way he stood—only his eyes changed. But the effect sent a startled shiver racing down Chase's spine. No high school kid, not even the toughest gang member, had such flat, dead, ancient eyes.

Something was wrong. Very wrong.

With a bored sigh, Dougal waved him away. "You wouldn't understand. Now run along and find yourself another lass. Maddie is mine."

Aghast, Chase stared after Dougal's retreating form. The guy was a total egomaniac. But the wrongness extended deeper than that. Chase didn't know what that wrongness was, but he intended to find out.

He hurried to the locker room, showered, and changed. He waited outside the girls' room, Dougal's flat black stare etched in the air before him, until Maddie exited. Then he straightened. "Are you ready?"

Startled, she jumped and placed a hand over her chest.

"Sorry, I didn't mean to scare you."

"I'm okay."

"So, are you ready to go?"

"Sure. Just let me get my backpack." They walked to the bleachers, and she grabbed her pack and hoisted it onto her shoulder.

"Can I carry that for you?"

"I'm okay." They entered the emptying hallways. "I'll have to grab my bike. You don't mind if I put it in the back of your truck, do you?'

"That's fine."

They reached the bike rack and he insisted on rolling the bike to his waiting truck and lifting it into the bed. They settled in the cab amongst creased vinyl. Foam stuck through the sun-cracked dash. For the first time in ages, Chase critically examined his truck. Stephanie's insistence that she wouldn't date a guy with an ugly truck came back to him. What did Maddie think about such things? Did she think his truck was ugly? He hadn't thought about it for a long time.

The vehicle had belonged to an elderly gentleman who'd lived on their street in California. The man had treated the truck like it was a baby, his prized possession. But he grew too old to drive and finally needed to get rid of it. Chase's father had purchased the truck for a steal. Although the body wasn't in great shape, with only 50,000 miles on the odometer it would last Chase for a long time.

The engine at least sounded good and Chase drove from the parking lot. He needed to find a subject to discuss. Something other than the worries—Dougal, his truck, Dougal, did she like him, Dougal, the weird stuff going on, Dougal—racing through his mind.

As casually as if she hadn't had a worry in her life, Maddie asked, "How are you adjusting?"

He breathed a sigh of relief. "Okay, I guess."

"Is it really different from what you're used to?"

"Not as much as I thought it would be. I guess being an Air Force brat and moving around a lot helped prepare me for the change in routine."

"I used to live somewhere else, too." She studied her hands.

"Oh. I didn't know that. So what do you think of Coal Creek High?"

She shrugged. "Pretty much like my old school. The popular kids rule and the nerds get picked on."

"And what are you?"

She laughed under her breath. "I can't believe you have to ask."

"I thought it would be rude to assume." She playfully slapped his arm and he smiled. Good, she was relaxing and so was he.

"My driveway starts right up here."

He took the next right and hit a rut. She grabbed the dash and grimaced.

"Sorry about the road."

"Don't worry about it. That's why I love my truck; you can't hurt it."

The sun glinted off a two-story wooden house. Patches of dried grass dotted the landscape. Untrimmed hedges created an imaginary fence along a cracked sidewalk.

The truck shuddered to a halt and he got an even closer look. White paint chips littered the ground, creating gray splotchy areas. Alternating planks, running the length of the porch, sported large gaping holes.

He drummed his fingers on the steering wheel and scratched the bridge of his nose. Maddie lived here? The house reminded him of something from a horror movie. Before he lost the courage, he blurted, "I was wondering, would you like to study for the chemistry test together? I could really use the help. Joining a school after the year's already started makes me feel so far behind."

She looked up from her lap and the corner of her lip twitched. "I'd like that."

An elderly woman stepped onto the porch and yelled, "Is that you, Madelyn?"

Maddie opened the door and climbed from the truck. "Yes, Grandma Draoi, it's me."

"Who brought you home, deary? Tell him to come meet me." The old woman turned and waddled inside.

She turned back to the truck. "Come on and I'll introduce you."

Chase stepped down and tugged on his shirt. He dusted his hands on his pants and smoothed his hair. Hey, that old woman looked tough.

The porch steps sagged under his weight and he tiptoed across the unstable planks. Inside the foyer, Chase blinked.

Through an open door on the right, he could see the living room walls were lined with rich mahogany paneling. The vestibule was painted a soft blue. In the corner, a spiral staircase led upstairs. In both rooms, floor-to-ceiling windows covered in thick drapes blocked prying eyes. Decorative tapestries dotted the stairwell. A giant chandelier, with swagging crystals, hung from the foyer ceiling.

Chase looked left and right. Maddie lived here? Relative to the outside, the inside appeared huge, and much better cared for. He did a double-take before following Maddie to the kitchen.

The old woman shuffled her feet and prepared glasses of iced tea. Without prelude, she asked, "Okay sonny, who are you? Where do you come from? And what are your intentions toward my great-granddaughter?"

"Grandma!" said Maddie as fiery red color mingled with her freckles.

Chase held his hand out and grasped the old woman's firmly. "I'm Alexander Chase Donavon, or Chase to my friends. I'm a military brat, so I come from a little bit of everywhere. And Maddie and I are friends." *At least for now.*

"If you say so," said her grandma, cocking a brow.

Maddie breathed a sigh of relief and Chase smiled. She wasn't so tough.

"Grandma, Chase asked if I might be allowed to go home with him tomorrow and study some for a test."

Her grandma glared again. "Will you two be alone?"

He laughed. "Hardly. I have four younger brothers. Plus my mother is always home."

"Okay, Maddie can go. But I expect her to be returned in the same condition you found her."

"Grandma!"

The old woman cackled. "I'm just playing with you, sonny. My name is Draoi Casey-Brennan. I'm Maddie's great-grandmother, on her mother's side."

"Do I detect an Irish accent?"

"Aye, laddie, ye do indeed." She thickened her accent and Chase smiled. With a wave, she said, "You better be gettin' home. Your parents might be worried."

Chase thought about explaining that they knew his where-abouts, but she seemed eager for him to leave. Maddie escorted him to the porch and he asked, "Would it be okay if I pick you up tomorrow morning?"

"I'd like that." She twisted her hands. "And Chase?"

"Yes?"

"Thanks."

"It was my pleasure."

He skipped down the steps, stopped at the truck bed and hauled out her bike. He rolled it to the porch and propped it on the kickstand before climbing into the cab and rolling down the window to yell, "Bye, Maddie."

"Bye, Chase."

"He seems nice."

"He is," replied Maddie.

"Do you not want to talk about him?"

"Oh, Grandma, I'm sorry. It's not that. I'm just very dis-tracted."

"Did something happen at school?"

"I guess you could say that," said Maddie, gnawing her lip and twirling a strand of hair around her finger.

"Tell me about it."

Maddie hesitated, but Grandma Draoi had a way of drag-ging information out of her and she found herself saying,

"There's this guy."

"Another one?" Grandma Draoi asked in a shocked tone.

Heat flushed her cheeks and Maddie wished she could hide her head in a hole like an ostrich. "No, not like Chase. He's new to school, too, and we have similar classes and he, well, he stares at me and flirts with me, like all day. He follows me to class. He offers to carry my books. Just normal stuff, I guess."

"Hmm." Grandma stalked around the kitchen stacking clean dishes. Over her shoulder, she asked, "What's his name?"

"Dougal Lachlan."

A plate fell and splintered on the shiny tile floor. Maddie drew her bare feet up in the chair and covered her head with her hands. When the shards settled, she stood on the chair, took a big step, and reached her flip-flops. Feet protected, she joined her grandma. Silently they cleared up the broken pieces. A strange look settled on Grandma's face.

Maddie gnawed her lip before whispering, "Grandma?"

Her expression changed and her lips lifted, but the smile didn't quite reach her eyes. "Yes, dear?"

Maddie's heart hammered against her ribs. Something didn't feel right. "Do you know him?"

Maddie thought she wasn't going to answer, but she said, "I once knew a man named Dougal. But he lived a long time ago."

"Then it couldn't possibly be the same guy."

"Of course not." Grandma's tone held a hint of skepticism. She stood and carried the full dustpan to a cardboard box.

Maddie sat back on her haunches, confused.

"That was a good supper. Wasn't that a good supper? I think I need to go check on the garden. Don't wait on me." Grandma vanished out back, holding up one hand in passing to keep the glass door from slamming behind her.

Maddie rose to her feet and dusted off her pants. She scrunched her face at the door. Beyond it, Grandma paced the squash patch and mumbled under her breath. Occasionally she would lift her hands to the sky and close her eyes, then she would lower them and start pacing again. It was a good thing no one was watching; they might have thought her grandma had lost her mind. Maddie kind of thought that was the case herself, but she let it go. Old people did weird things, right?

Turning her back on the odd scene, Maddie climbed the stairs to her bedroom. Sitting at her desk, she finished her homework, then stared at the bed. She hated going to sleep. The shrink had said the dreams would fade with time, but after six months they were no less vivid. The sparkling tower, the smell of smoke, her parents' death... nothing had changed.

She sighed. She was blessed to have a home with Grandma, but sometimes it was so boring. There was no cable, no computer, and no car! A friend took Grandma shopping once a week. Other than that, Grandma Draoi never left the house. The place was not the ideal environment for a teenage girl, even if she did think so herself.

Sketchpad spread out on the table, she held her pencil aloft. Visions of Chase and Dougal danced before her eyes. The first stroke of the pencil felt awkward. She dropped it and palmed her chin. She just wasn't in the mood to draw.

Maddie grabbed a book and sprawled across the bed. She would just read a little. Her eyelids grew heavy and she shook her head. Words blurred before her...

Dougal swooped onto a nearby tree. Branches filled with evergreen needles hid him from view. Wings tucked to his sides, he shuffled back and forth like a bird. The branch wiggled beneath him and he tightened his grip.

Chase had left in his ancient truck and Draoi and Maddie had settled down to dinner. Potent aromas had drifted through the open window. He had salivated; the acid drool dripped onto his talon and he'd grunted.

Moving closer to the tree trunk, he kept watching. Maddie spoke, but he couldn't make out her words. What he had noticed was a brief expression of fear that passed across Draoi's face. Moments had passed and then Draoi excused herself.

She paced in the meager garden. The once beautiful druid had aged considerably. Her bright fiery red hair had changed to a stunning silver, and her formerly lithe body carried extended girth about the middle. However, one thing hadn't changed... her power.

Grace and poise oozed from her ambling form. Words of incantation were almost visible as they left her wrinkled lips. The invisible blue veil, more a suggestion of color than something he actually saw, thickened its coating around the house, yet he could still see through it. Serena's own spell kept him from being locked out.

Why would Draoi be strengthening her protection spell? What could Maddie have said to worry her grandmother? Had she mentioned him? Even if she'd said his name, how could Draoi possibly remember him? Their one chance meeting had occurred years ago when her own daughter had been born.

He'd hidden then, too, behind the doubly thick glass windows, and sought a glimpse of the newborn Casey. She'd been beautiful, with dark hair and bright green eyes. A blue aura of protection had glowed around her. He'd touched the glass and it had practically hummed.

His heart had hammered in his chest when the door to the nursery had opened and a shadowy figure had entered. In the dark, an unrecognizable creature had hovered above the child, a dagger in hand glinting in the nightlight's glow. Dougal had screamed and banged against the window until the creature became scared and fled.

After that he had covertly watched the young Casey. He'd waited in anticipation of her maturity. For a time when he might be able to convince her that her role as the key was beneficial to all, but that time had never come. Before he'd been able to succeed in his mission, she'd given birth to a girl of her own and transferred her powers.

A whistling sound reached Dougal's hearing and he peered through Maddie's window. The curtains fluttered and he caught a glimpse of her sitting at her desk. He would love to fly over to her window, hang from the frame, and get a closer look, but with Draoi in such close proximity and so worked up, the idea seemed riddled with flaws. Perhaps another time.

When Draoi turned her back, Dougal jumped from his position and flew into the sky.

She turned around and around in the dark wood. Sounds—a growl, the flap of wings, the hiss of hot air. Her heart pounded. A creature landed before her. Wings flared on either side. Venom dripped from pointed fangs. She gulped and ran.

Branches smacked her face, cutting her skin. Her long flowing white dress billowed behind her. Tree limbs snagged her as she raced to escape.

The hot putrid breath of her pursuer closed in. She looked over her shoulder and screamed...

"Maddie, wake up!"

She struggled to open her eyes, clawing the air around her. A cool hand caressed her forehead and it slowly drew her back. She fluttered her lids open. Grandma Draoi stared down with a face full of concern. Behind her, the window still showed the night.

Maddie gulped and rubbed sleep from her eyes. "I'm okay. It was only a dream." *Of all the nights for Grandma to keep her hearing aids in place...*

"Yes, only a dream." Grandma paused. "Why don't you go wipe your face and then lie back down?"

Maddie managed a nod. She felt Grandma's stare on her back all the way to the bathroom, and she couldn't quite bring herself to close the door between them. But the mirror—it reflected a harrowed young girl. Auburn hair lay in a mass of tangles above her shoulders. Rounded jade eyes stared back at her. Maddie shook her head, and her hair moved. It showed... She touched her face and gasped.

A thin moist line marked her pale cheek. She was bleeding.

Chase awoke in a cold sweat with his father shaking him.

"Chase, are you okay?"

Breathing heavily, he stared at the ceiling and tried to calm his racing heart. For a moment longer the white-clad form fled into the forest...

"Chase, talk to me."

He shook his head, shook it off. "It was only a nightmare," he croaked.

"It wasn't just a nightmare. You were screaming."

"I was?"

"Yes. What were you dreaming?"

"I'm not sure." A figure in white, a forest... he held onto the dream's last vestiges but kept them to himself. Dad had enough on his mind already. Chase rubbed his eyes and struggled up, sitting on the side of the bed.

Mom stood in the doorway, her face white as a sheet. "Alex?"

"Carissa, he's fine. Go back to bed." She left and Dad asked, "Do you remember anything?"

He shook his head again.

Dad pulled up a chair and handed him a glass of water.

Chase took it gratefully. The cool liquid soothed his dry throat. "Thanks."

"Do you feel better?"

"Yeah."

Dad patted Chase's shoulder. "Okay. Why don't you lie down and see if you can go back to sleep? I'll see you in the morning."

Chase nodded and handed over the empty cup. The door clicked shut, and Chase pulled the covers to his neck. He closed his eyes and willed the nightmare to stay at bay.

"Do stop jumping," crooned Serena from a pallet on the opposite side of the cave.

Dougal sat up and wiped sweat from his brow. The dream of Maddie had been so vivid, he wasn't sure it hadn't been real. He'd landed before her in his transformed state and she had run. She had fled like a scared rabbit being chased by a hay baler. He'd pursued. He'd wanted to stop her, to explain, to tell her he wouldn't hurt her, he couldn't hurt her. He needed her. But she'd awakened before he could.

He ran a hand through his hair and dropped his elbows on his knees. He wasn't a saint, but he wasn't a monster, either. Well, maybe he was. He'd done some terrible things, very terrible things. If only he'd...

There was no need to rehash old memories. What was done was done. The dream was just a small indication of how much harder he would have to work to make her comfortable before they could claim her help. Somehow he would convince her that, by helping them, she was doing the right thing. She would see. They all would.

7

The next morning, the truck's engine rumbled outside early. Before he had time to exit his truck, Maddie placed a peck on Grandma's cheek, grabbed her backpack from the kitchen floor, and skipped down the steps. She dropped her pack in the truck's floorboard and buckled up.

His initial smile morphed to a frown. "What happened to your cheek?"

"Oh, nothing," Maddie said, allowing her hair to fall forward and cover the neutral-colored bandage. At least Grandma's first aid kit had been well supplied and she hadn't had to wear neon pink or cartoon characters or anything seriously dorky.

"Why does it need a bandage if it's nothing?"

"Okay, so it's something."

"Well...?"

"It's silly, really. I scratched myself in my sleep. No biggie."

"Humph. That was some sleep." Chase drove the truck out of the driveway. "Were you dreaming?"

"Um, yes."

Chase grew quiet and flashed a glance much like the one Grandma Draoi had given her.

The rest of the trip passed in silence. They arrived at school, and Chase was testy and moody. He gathered Maddie and her stuffed backpack and marched her straight to his locker. Handing her a small slip of paper, he said, "Here's the combination. I don't know how I got a locker and you didn't, but until you get one, we can share."

"They probably just forgot me. That happens a lot. But Chase, are you sure?"

"Yep, I'm sure."

She kept the books she needed and shoved the rest inside before making her way to homeroom. The students seemed subdued, like something bad had happened and they were all afraid to speak. She swallowed. As if her dream had spread its wings across the entire town of Coal Creek.

Studying the roomful of students, she frowned. Dougal was missing again.

Chase followed Maddie to homeroom and took his seat. He reviewed the dwindling memories of his nightmare. He'd stood on the sidelines and watched as a girl swathed in a gauzy white dress was chased through the woods by a horrifying creature, kind of like a gryphon from legends, with the lower half of a lion and the upper half of a massive eagle. He'd tried to yell when he first spotted the beast, but his screams had been silent. He'd tried to help her when she ran, but it felt as if roots held him to the ground. There was nothing he could do but watch, and he hadn't even been able to get a good look at her. And then the vision had blurred and faded. The girl disappeared. The gryphon stood in a clearing and looked around in bewilderment. And then Chase had awakened with Dad calling his name.

The bell rang and he went through the motions. During the classes he shared with Maddie, he kept staring at her. Something wasn't right. The scratch on her cheek oddly matched the place the girl in the dream had been struck by a branch.

By lunchtime Chase had settled it in his mind; Maddie was definitely the girl from his dream. He needed to talk with her about what he'd seen, what he'd experienced, the strangeness that seemed to surround them. But not here. Maybe at his place, after they'd studied for the test? It should be quiet there, with his brothers outside playing.

That felt like a good idea and he breathed a sigh of relief. The remaining three classes passed in a blur as his mind totally focused on Maddie and their afternoon plans.

It was kind of odd when she thought about it, but Maddie found herself actually missing Dougal as the rest of the uneventful day passed. His presence had brought excitement into her normally boring school life.

After school, Chase drove them to his house. He grimaced when he turned the knob and the front door didn't automatically open. The key rattled in his hand as he used it.

They stepped into the foyer of the Colonial-style home. A broad staircase led upstairs. A hall ran along either side. Black and white shiny tile covered the floor.

A middle-aged woman with warm eyes, whom Maddie presumed was Chase's mother, ran toward them, covered head to toe in bubbles, and slid to a halt, leaving wet skid marks on the tile. "Oh, Chase, I'm so glad you're home! I was bathing Max and he jumped out of the tub. Can you help me catch him?"

"Sure."

The woman thrust a soap-covered hand toward her. "Carissa Donovan. It's nice to meet you."

"Maddie Clevenger. It's nice to meet you, too." Even if her hand did need wiping afterward.

A large dog brushed past Maddie's legs and she couldn't help it; she squealed. Chase smiled, dropped his books on a hall table, and charged after the mutt. Maddie regained her balance and followed Chase as he raced through the living area, into a dining room, and through a set of sliding glass doors that led to the backyard. Maddie took a position on the porch as Chase wrapped his arms around the dog's middle, but Max slid right through. She covered her mouth and giggled.

Chase looked at her and his lips twitched. "So you think this is funny?"

"No," she replied, her body shaking with unrestrained laughter.

Chase stalked over, scooped her into his arms, and crushed her to his soapy chest. Surprised and a little shocked, she squirmed and kicked, but he squeezed tighter. And lifted.

"Chase! What are you doing?"

His smile broadened and an almost devilish look covered his face as he headed further into the yard. Wait—over his shoulder she could see... She squirmed harder, trying to break his hold. "Chase! I don't have any dry clothes!"

"You can wear mine."

Whoa. The thought sent a tingle through her body and she stopped struggling. Maybe she could distract him from his goal. She leaned into him and brushed her lips against his. A current shot between them. *Double whoa!*

Chase's eyes widened and instead of kissing her back, he dropped her... into the dog's bath water. Large gobs of soap suds clouded her vision and the water engulfed her. At least the water and the day were warm. She got her hands on the tub's bottom, rose above the bubbles, and gasped for air.

Two small identical-looking boys hooted, hollered, and pointed.

Maddie sent Chase an accusatory glare. "You dropped me!"

His smile was totally self-satisfied. "In my defense, you shocked me."

Fortunately, soap bubbles covered her blush, not to mention the rest of her, too. Maddie had learned her lesson. She wouldn't try that tactic again, even if she wanted to.

Wait, what?

Chase offered his hand, but she refused. "No, I can get out myself."

He backed away. Maddie grabbed the metal tub's side and pushed upward, but her hands slipped on the wet surface and she splashed back into the suds. More whoops from the twins when she resurfaced. She needed to rethink her strategy, but nothing came to mind. Giving in, she asked, "Chase? Can you help me?"

He nodded and slid his arms under hers, lifting her effortlessly and looking surprised himself. Finally Maddie stood dripping in front of him, water pooling at her feet. She'd never felt more like a dunked cat. A wet tendril of hair clung to her face and Chase gently stroked it behind her ear.

The world seemed to freeze. All sound, all movement stopped as he leaned forward. Excitement flared within her. She closed her eyes, anticipating another electrifying kiss.

Instead of feeling his lips on her own, however, she got a bump to her back. She stumbled forward. Chase's legs tangled with hers and they flipped, splashing into the tub together. Chase rose sputtering and yelling. "Craig! I'm going to get you for that." He sprang from the tub and raced away.

It was impossible to sort out exactly how she felt while kneeling in a tub of sudsy water—for the second time. Strange, but she didn't feel embarrassed, not by their amazing kiss, not even by her wet sweater. She gnawed on her lip. How was she going to get out this time? But before she could abandon all hope, a hand appeared before her. "May I help a damsel in distress?"

Maddie looked up. The bright sun was blocked by a rather tall man, the light blazing around him like a halo. Even an adult's presence didn't embarrass her, not after... whatever had happened. She grasped his hand and he pulled her free. This time she ran a good distance from the tub, to make sure she wouldn't be pushed in again.

When she stopped, she found her rescuer had followed, and he was staring at her with a wrinkle between his eyes. "Who are you?" he asked.

Still not embarrassed, and that was *weird*. She smiled and offered her hand. "Madelyn Clevenger, but you can call me Maddie. You must be Mr. Donovan. I can see the family resemblance."

"Yes, I am. But please, call me Alex. I don't feel like a Mr. Donovan."

Chase joined them, wet from head to toe and laughing. The twin boys ran behind him, pulled along by the huge dog, now on a leash.

"Hey, Dad, I see you've met Maddie."

"Yes, in quite unusual circumstances. I think you'd better find your mother so she can get Maddie some dry clothes." Alex paused. "I need to go to my workshop. No disruptions, son."

Was something wrong? Maddie examined Alex more closely. She'd taken an instant liking to him, but perhaps something had irritated him. Or actually, he seemed more worried, which didn't make sense at all.

Chase drew his brows together, but said, "Sure, Dad." He placed his hand on the small of Maddie's back and guided her inside.

She glanced back as they walked, but his father headed in the opposite direction, walking fast. Yes, definitely worried; his shoulders hunched stiffly.

"I'm sorry about that. My dad doesn't normally act so strange."

"That's okay."

Water dribbled down her legs and pooled at her feet. She arched her back and discreetly tugged at the front of her sweater. Finally they found Carissa. She scolded Chase for allowing Maddie to get soaked and found some clothes for her to wear.

In the bathroom, she toweled dry. The sweat pants and oversized sweatshirt were warm and smelled like flowers. Maddie hugged them and inhaled deeply. It was like the perfume Mom used to wear, back before... Tears pooled in her eyes and she wiped them away, sniffing. But it took a while before she could stop crying.

The Donovan household felt so... so comforting, welcoming. Almost as if she belonged there. She loved Grandma, of course, but her house seemed silent and even cold in comparison. There was something here that she'd been missing and hadn't even realized. And how long had it been since she'd had so much fun?

Tucking that stray strand of hair behind her ear, she studied her reflection in the oval mirror. She hadn't stopped crying in time. Red rimmed her eyes. Hopefully Chase wouldn't notice. Clearing her throat, she grabbed the waistband of the slightly oversized pants, and entered the hallway.

Chase waited. He'd changed, too, and leaned casually against the hall wall. "Mom is washing your things. Are you ready to study?"

"Sure."

They trudged upstairs to Chase's bedroom. He pulled out the desk chair for himself and motioned for Maddie to sit on the edge of the bed. The mattress sank beneath her, also comforting. They laid their books across the bedspread and pored over them. While they quizzed each other, little heads poked around the corner of the open bedroom door and snickered.

"You must not have girls over very often. They seem to find me being here very amusing."

"Yeah." Chase dipped his head but not before she saw the red color flooding his face.

Is it possible he'd never *had a girl over?* Her heart pounded at the thought. She'd been joking. With his good looks and charm, it seemed unlikely that his girlfriends hadn't visited. And visited a lot.

Her heart beat harder.

8

Mom announced she'd put out snacks downstairs, yet they didn't move. Light filtered through the parted curtains and struck the bandage secured to her cheek. He should ask her about the dream and just get it over with. But as she faced him, her jade eyes twinkling, his mind froze.

"You have a wonderful family," said Maddie, staring at the pages of notes scattered across the bedspread.

Not where he wanted the conversation to go. Licking his lips, he drew in a deep breath. "Yeah, sure. Loud, nosey, obnoxious, and a whole host of other words I shouldn't repeat in polite company."

Maddie snickered, and without thinking Chase grabbed her hand and intertwined their fingers. Volts of tingling energy shot up his arm and she had to feel it as well. Didn't she? It was so weird, but so cool. Outside the sky darkened to night and as his room dimmed, her eyes shone a deeper jade. The air around her seemed tinged blue. His heart hammered in his chest in sudden panic and he deftly withdrew his hand, grimaced, and rubbed it on his pants like he was wiping away sweat.

She didn't comment on the electric shock or his hasty release. Had he imagined the electricity, the blue aura? Was he losing his mind? For lack of anything better to say, he asked, "Do you wear contacts?"

"What? Uh, no. I have perfect vision. Why?"

"Your eyes. They're the most unusual color I've ever seen."

"Yeah, I get that a lot." She lowered her chin, her hair falling in front of her face.

He sucked on his lip. Nothing was coming out like he'd hoped. The dream, the shocky feelings, the blue air, all of that made his brain feel fried. Running his hand through his hair, he struggled to find a safe subject. "I'm sorry about earlier."

She lifted her chin and quirked a brow.

"I mean, I'm sorry about dropping you in the water when, well..." He scratched his head, being evasive. "...when you kissed me."

Maddie avoided his gaze; a red hue covered her cheeks.

He continued, "I mean, I *was* going to drop you in the water. That was my plan. But your kiss shocked me and I just let go." He paused before adding, "So I'm sorry."

"Don't be."

Did that mean she liked it? Not being dropped in the water, but being kissed.

She pushed off the bed and made her way to the open window. A cool breeze drifted in, lifting the sheer curtains and Maddie's waist-length auburn hair. He gulped. She was so pretty. Bright yellow sunlight glowed around her, casting a halo above her hair and highlighting the freckles peppered across her cute button nose.

He stood and eased toward her, unsure of his own intentions but knowing he wanted to be closer to her. That feeling of electricity that seemed to pass through him when they touched drove him to close the gap between them. If he could just experience it one more time, then maybe, just maybe, he would know if it was real or imaginary.

"Supper!" his mother called from the bottom of the stairs.

Great timing, Mom.

Maddie turned and he stopped. "We should eat," she said.

"Yeah, we should." Mesmerized by her jade eyes, he didn't budge.

She stroked the strand of drying hair behind her ear and tilted her head. When he didn't move, she cleared her throat, poked her tongue against her cheek, and walked around him.

"Do you like horses?" he blurted as he turned to follow.

Maddie glanced over her shoulder, her brow arched. "Sure. What girl doesn't love horses? They're so romantic; all that riding-off-into-the-sunset-with-the-hero kind of stuff. Why do you ask?"

"Oh, I just noticed a horse next to your grandma's house. Is it hers?"

"Oh, no. That's Gray Beauty. She belongs to our neighbor, Mr. Temple."

The change in subject seemed to put Maddie at ease, or at least she seemed to relax again as Chase led them to the dining room.

Settling in her seat, Mom asked, "Chase, will you call your father?"

He nodded and pulled out Maddie's chair before excusing himself. Happily, he sauntered to Dad's shop.

The day had been productive. He'd studied for the dreaded chemistry exam until confident he could make at least a passing grade, and he'd had time to visit with Maddie. There were still many unanswered questions, but somehow just being in her presence helped. All in all, he would count the day a success.

Chase stood before the workshop door. Weird noises seeped through the cracks. He drew his brows together, slipped outside to the uncovered window, and peeked in.

His father writhed on his cot, gripping his stomach as if pain shot through his body. He stood, removed his shirt, and leaned on his hands flat against the wall. His back muscles rippled. His skin moved in ways human skin shouldn't move. Then claw-like appendages poked through his back.

It was bizarre. Terrified, Chase reeled back around to the door, his heart pounding against his ribs. He couldn't have seen what he thought he'd seen. It just wasn't possible. There had to be an explanation. Shaking the door knob, Chase stuttered, "D-dad?"

"Yes?" came a muffled reply.

Chase swallowed and said, "Supper is ready."

"Tell your mother I'll be in in a minute."

"Sure." Chase hesitated, then added, "Are you okay?"

"Yes." The terse reply sounded as if his father clenched his teeth.

Hesitantly, Chase returned to the house, unable to believe what he'd witnessed. He gave his mother the message and took his seat beside Maddie.

Mom frowned. "Your father knows we have a guest. What can he be doing that he can't finish later?"

"I don't know," said Chase, forcing himself to stare at the table and not think about his father or his father's back.

"Maddie, I'm sorry for the delay."

"It's fine. I really don't mind."

Colton and Cole beat their silverware against the table like a drum. Craig and Chris tossed a football across the table.

His mother said, "Chase—"

Chase knew exactly what she wanted. He drew in a ragged breath and scooted his chair back. "I'll check on him again."

"No need, I'm here." All eyes turned to the head of the table as Dad settled into place. He seemed pale, but otherwise perfectly normal. "Looks like a fine meal, Carissa."

"Thank you, dear."

"Let's say grace."

Dad blessed the meal, then heads rose around the table and the scramble for food began.

"Mom, pass the potatoes."

"Dad, pass the rolls."

"Do we have more peas?"

"Can I get more to drink?"

On and on it went. It felt kind of embarrassing, but beneath the homey camouflage it provided, Chase covertly studied his father. He appeared more and more normal, gaining color, jumping in and filling his plate with the others. No claws extended from his fingers. Nothing weird seemed to poke from his back.

Chase exhaled a breath of relief. As he'd thought, he must have been mistaken. Attempting to redirect his focus, he studied Maddie and tried to gauge her reaction to his family. She smiled, but her plate remained empty. Leaning over, he said, "Jump in and grab something or there may be nothing left."

"I will as soon as it looks safe."

As plates and mouths were filled, Dad said, "Maddie, you said your last name is Clevenger. Could you tell me the names of your parents?"

Maddie tensed. "Tom and Abigail."

"Do you have any Caseys in your family?"

Maddie answered, "Yes, my maternal great-grandmother is a Casey who married a Brennan."

"Where are your parents?"

"Dad!" Chase was appalled.

"It's okay, I don't mind answering." She focused on his father. "They're dead."

The rest of the meal passed in awkward silence. Even the younger boys didn't seem to want to talk. Maddie regretted her blunt words.

She forced down each bite of food, unwilling to hurt Carissa's feelings regardless of her diminished appetite. Finally dinner ended and she scooted away from the table, said her goodbyes, and headed to the bathroom, once there changing into her own clothes.

Jeans on, she paused and studied her reflection in the mirror. Her normally wavy hair frizzed around her face. Splotches of pink covered her freckled cheeks.

"Get a hold of yourself, girl. You didn't do anything wrong."

When she left the bathroom, Chase waited outside, her books on the floor beside him. He carried her backpack as he led her to his truck. They pulled out of the driveway and Maddie chewed on her lip. Should she explain her bluntness?

The air in the truck grew thick with tension as Maddie concentrated on the passing scenery. She couldn't think of anything to say, so the trip stayed silent. Finally, just before she thought she'd die if it continued, the truck shuddered to a halt outside Grandma's house. She jumped out before Chase could even open his door. She waved, ran up the porch steps, and didn't stop until she was safely inside.

In the living room, she peeked back out through the window. His truck idled in the driveway. Wearing a forlorn expression, he stared at the house.

She leaned against the wall. Tears pooled in her eyes. Why hadn't she said something, anything, to him? He was her friend. He deserved better.

The truck roared as Chase drove from the driveway. Maddie raced upstairs, past Grandma's room, to her own. In the window seat, she grabbed a pillow and hugged it to her body. Chase's taillights retreated along the rutted road.

The tears slipped down her cheeks as the memory of her parents' death played fresh in her mind. There would be no sleep tonight.

Chase slammed his hand against the steering wheel. What had possessed his father to ask Maddie, practically a stranger, such a personal question? Not that he'd done much better. During that awful drive, he'd wanted to speak numerous times. First, he would apologize for Dad's nosiness. Second, he would offer to listen if Maddie ever wanted to talk. Third, he'd find a way to broach the subject of all the weird things happening around them, especially that dream. Fourth...

...he needed to talk to his father.

He waited for the light to turn green. But suddenly a sharp pain shot through his middle and he grabbed his stomach. The agony was like nothing he'd ever felt before and it threatened to rip him in two.

All thoughts of questioning Dad fled. The pain eased and Chase waited, clutching the steering wheel, terror pounding through him. Another jolt of agony stabbed him between his shoulder blades, then a weird sensation crawled up his back, on either side of his spine, as if the muscles beneath his skin fought to escape... or as if some alien something inside him tried to burst out through his skin.

The light changed and Chase slammed down the accelerator, not letting up until he reached home. The truck skidded to a halt; he threw it into park and killed the engine. Thankfully his parents knelt before a flowerbed out front. He fell from the cab and cried, "Help me."

In slow motion, his parents rushed to his side. He knew they sprinted across the yard; he could tell by the way they moved, the horror twisting their faces. But it seemed to take forever before Mom skidded to a crouch beside him.

"Chase, what's wrong?"

Dad grabbed her shoulders. "Carissa, listen to me. He'll be fine. But I need to take him to the workshop. Don't let anyone come in. Do you understand?"

"Alex, you're scaring me."

His face tightening, he pulled her close. "Carissa, you have to trust me."

"Okay," she said, a tremor in her voice.

Hey, Dad, Chase thought, *what about me? She's not the on-*

ly one who's scared.

Before he could voice the thought, his father heaved him upright, shouldered his weight, and practically dragged him to the workshop. Inside he laid him down on the old camping cot, the one where Dad had contorted and writhed earlier that evening. At the memory, Chase's heart pounded harder.

Lying down didn't ease the pain again rippling up and down his back. Chase rolled to his side and pulled his knees into his chest. "Dad, what's happening to me?"

Dad didn't reply as he dabbed a damp cloth to Chase's forehead. The pain intensified again and Chase clenched his teeth. Even in agony, he couldn't miss the fear on Dad's face, which was even scarier. His dad had deployed during the First Gulf War; he'd faced enemy missiles. He didn't scare easily.

Noticing his attention, Dad dropped the rag and turned away. He ran his hand through his hair and paced the workshop. "I can't believe this. It's unbelievable."

"What?"

It was as if Dad couldn't stay away. He prowled back across the workshop and hovered over Chase. "There are things about our family that I haven't told you." He blurted the words out in the same tone Maddie had used when telling of her parents' deaths.

The shivering increased. Chase's flesh felt like it was on fire, like millions of tiny pokers stuck him. Inside his shoes, his feet felt as if they'd grown several inches. He kicked them off, ripped off his socks, and stretched his toes.

They'd grown claws.

"Yes, son, go ahead and strip down. That will make it easier."

Chase screamed.

PART II
D A N C E S

9

The next morning Maddie waited for Chase as long as she dared. When he didn't show, she grabbed her bicycle from the shed and shoved her pack in the basket. Icy air struck her cheeks as she pedaled down the driveway. The world had chilled overnight. The sky appeared less blue, almost as if ice crystals lingered in the air, ready to fall. She wouldn't be surprised if it snowed. Coal Creek was notorious for its unusual weather, as she had good cause to know.

The five-mile ride to school gave her time to think. Chase was probably angry. She guessed she deserved it. He'd gone out of his way and accepted her into his home, and she hadn't even thanked him. Instead she'd sat like a mute while he'd driven her home and allowed him to believe she was upset by his father's questions. She owed him an apology. Big time.

Despite the cold, perspiration gathered on her forehead as she pedaled into the school parking lot and locked her bike to the rack. She looked for Chase's truck. No sign of it in the student lot. The bell rang and she held back tears as she ran for the door.

Lockers slammed as students hurried to homeroom. Maddie scurried inside, holding her books tightly to her chest.

Stephanie and Marley smirked. Stephanie said, "I told you it wouldn't last. Even with his poor choice in vehicles, Chase is still too good for her."

Maddie raced to her seat and bent her head, causing her hair to drape across her reddening cheeks. Maybe Stephanie was right. Maybe Chase *was* too good to be her friend. Who wanted to be friends with the school dork?

The metal desk chair creaked beneath her weight. A shadow danced across the floor and she lifted her chin. Dougal leaned across in his seat with a look of smug satisfaction.

"Where's your friend?"

Maddie wanted to say "Out sick" to keep from admitting she had driven Chase away, but she couldn't lie. So she said, "I don't know."

He straightened and patted her hand. "Don't worry. I'll protect you."

Maddie looked out the window. Maybe Chase was just running late.

But even though she watched the doors during all their classes together, he never came bounding through any of them, nor did he join her for lunch. Maddie went through her day much as she had before meeting Chase. Only now Dougal followed her from class to class. True to his word, he kept a close eye on her and few others attempted to approach, not even Stephanie. His behavior confused Maddie, twisting her thoughts and feelings around inside her, but she couldn't help feeling grateful, all the same.

The final bell rang and she slipped outside. Snow dappled the sidewalk and gathered atop the bare branches of trees. *Great.* What more could go wrong that day? Her teachers had loaded her up with homework, the library had been closed for fumigation, she'd let the teachers have her shelf space back in their lounge, it didn't feel right to use Chase's locker until she'd apologized, and so she had no choice but to bring most of her books home. Her bike tilted as she worked to yank it from the rack.

Light flurries coated her hair and wet her collar. She shivered beneath her sweatshirt, wishing she'd brought a coat. Such unpredictable weather, one day sunny, the next snowing. Now, if she could just make it home without sliding on ice...

Her hair stood on end as if lightning struck close by. A shiver of electric static tickled her hands. Aboard her bike, one foot on the ground to hold her upright, she twirled and searched the lot. Did someone watch her?

There, in the student lot. Not exactly watching her, but close enough. Dougal lounged, wedged between his SUV and Stephanie. He smiled as he slipped his hands around her waist, and she wrapped her arms around his neck and kissed him with disgusting smacking noises, audible even through the noises of the last students slamming car doors and calling goodbyes to friends. For all his flirting with Maddie, he seemed to really enjoy Stephanie's affections.

Repulsed by their display, Maddie turned away and headed for home.

Dougal glanced over Stephanie's shoulder even as his lips stroked hers. The cool feel of her flesh did little to excite him. The kiss ended, and she laid her cheek against his chest and sighed. He smoothed her bangs away from her forehead like an automaton, feeling nothing.

Maddie had shot a disgruntled expression in their direction before pedaling out of the parking lot as fast as her legs would take her. He should have pushed Stephanie away, and he knew he'd regret not doing it. Maddie would not be won through jealousy, as he'd first thought, but rather by constant, positive attention. Her shy, embarrassed facial expressions as he flirted with her told him as much. Yet having Stephanie on his side provided a way for him to stay connected with the school's pulse, and it was hard to be in tune with the students when you were eighty years their senior.

A pinch on his abdomen drew his attention.

"Hey, I'm down here."

Dougal lifted Stephanie's chin. If he pressed up just a little harder, he could snap her neck. It would only take a second and for a moment he let the temptation soak through him. No, that was self-defeating. He squelched the idea and covered his hardened face with a smile. "Indeed."

She failed to notice his anger and made swirling motions across his chest. "I was thinking... why don't we go out? We could go see a movie, or we could find a place to park and just be alone..."

The unspoken words trailed off and he thought about throwing her onto the ground like a used rag. The woman offered her charms too freely. They barely knew one another. In the old country she would have been shunned and branded. No decent man would have sought her affection. But this wasn't the old country and he wasn't a decent man. No, he was something entirely different.

He combed a strand of hair behind her ear and contemplated his answer. "Perhaps a movie would be nice. I will meet you at the theater at 6:30." He released his grasp, moved her back a step, and climbed inside his SUV.

As he drove away, he glanced in the rearview mirror. Stephanie gawked after him, yearning in her stare.

Chase's father helped him stand. Worry etched lines in his face around his eyes and lips. "How do you feel?"

Dad had asked the question off and on for the entire night and the following day, between bouts of pain and rare moments of lucidity. The torment would wane and Chase would sleep, only to wake in the same state. His alarm had blared and he'd slapped his phone, breaking it into a million pieces. When next he'd awakened it was afternoon, and Dad still hovered over him.

Chase licked his rough lips. The room spun around him, wobbled, then settled into its proper place. "I don't know. Weird?"

"It'll become more familiar."

Oh, that sounded great—*not*. Standing at the cot's side, he faced a mirror Dad had bolted to the wall, between a bookcase filled with the old family journals and a rack holding drill bits and screwdrivers. In the dim workshop light, his new features seemed bizarre and monstrous. How could *this* become more familiar? He whispered, "What am I?"

Dad collapsed onto a stool and clasped his hands. "You're a gryphon."

"A what?" Breath lodged in his throat and his heart hammered in his chest. He'd stared at his own body all night while it had changed, and he couldn't stop shaking.

"A gryphon. Half eagle, half lion."

"B-but I still have human features." Shouldn't a gryphon have a snout or a beak or something? His nose and mouth were only slightly larger. Chase touched the planes of his face. In the mirror, the grotesque caricature of himself did the same. *This isn't happening. It isn't possible.*

"True."

Dad didn't say more and Chase grew frustrated. How could he be so calm? Overnight his son had gone from normal teenage boy to freak of nature, and Dad had sat there and watched every moment of the transformation.

"Why is this happening?" Chase asked. A lengthy explanation would be nice, something that included radioactive vats of chemicals or an alien invasion.

His father studied his hands. His chin lifted. "The girl."

"You mean Maddie?" Chase drew his brows together.

Dad sighed. "Yes. Since…" His voice trailed off.

Chase coaxed. "Since…?"

"Since it happened to me, I've been reading up on our family history." He waved one hand at the journals in the bookcase.

Under Chase's breath, he said, "I knew it!"

"What?"

Explaining what he'd seen the day Maddie visited—*had it only been yesterday? it felt like forever ago*—probably wasn't the best idea. What good would it do, since he was looking in the mirror at a clearer version? He wanted answers, not a reasoned discussion. "Nothing. Tell me what you've learned."

"First we should get some things clear." Dad paused. "I know you saw me."

Oops. Chase lowered his eyes. His feet had grown enormously large and sprouted pale fur. Not anything he wanted to look at. He turned away, but his first step pacing clicked a claw onto the concrete floor. He froze. Not anything he wanted to hear, either, and instead Chase hunched his shoulders and waited.

Dad nodded, as if none of Chase's reactions surprised him. "In the gryphon state, as I found out yesterday for the first time, our hearing is better. A lot better."

"So last night, why didn't you just tell me what happened to you?" *Especially when you knew it might happen to me?*

"I didn't want to alarm anyone."

Oh, yeah, right. Good one, Dad. "Is that why you asked Maddie all those questions at the supper table?"

"Yes."

"Will you tell me now?"

Dad paced and tapped a finger to his forehead. "In the

yard, Maddie touched me. I felt a distinct tingle, and then pain. Not much later I changed, and then changed back." He paused. "That never happened to me before, so it had to have been caused by her touch."

"She's touched me lots of times. So how come I'm only changing now? And how come it took so much longer for me to complete my change?"

"I'm not sure." But then Dad blinked. "And what do you mean, she's touched you lots of times?"

The heat of embarrassment flushed his face. "Well, I mean, umm, touching in passing and stuff."

"Chase?"

"Dad, it's not like that. I've only known her a few days."

"But you still have feelings for her?"

"Yes." Why did the thought make him uncomfortable? He'd liked other girls.

"I'm sensing there's more to your feelings than her just being another pretty girl."

"Yeah." Chase ran his overly large hands through the fur atop his head. He pulled them down, stared at them, and frowned. Pointed nails protruded from his fingertips. Thick pale fur covered both sides. Sighing, he said, "I can't explain it. It's like, the first time I met her I wanted to get to know her. She thinks we're just friends, but..." He let the words drift away.

His father didn't respond and Chase continued. "Dad, you asked about her parents and her last name. Has that got anything to do with this?"

Sagging as if defeated, Dad settled back onto his seat, hunching with his elbows on his thighs. "When I was young, my father told me wild stories about flying creatures. At the end of each story, he would tell me to beware of any female with Casey blood. I just assumed it was a scare tactic. Some kind of family rivalry, like the Hatfields and McCoys." He paused and rubbed the spot between his brows. "I didn't mean to upset Maddie by asking about her parents."

Chase sighed. His dad would never hurt or embarrass anyone on purpose. But before he could say something to break the tension, his wings brushed his legs and he groaned. "What am I going to do with these things? I don't think they'll be too accepting at school." The wings would make driving difficult, not to mention sitting in the school desks, playing volleyball or running in gym, fitting through doorways... and thinking that way was stupid. He had bigger concerns, like finding some way to change back. Dad had managed it, so theoretically it was possible, as the chemistry teacher might say.

But Dad laughed. "We'll work on it. After a few moments I was able to transition back to normal, so I would think you'll be able to do the same."

"What do we have to do? Mutter some kind of special words? An incantation? Perform a special dance?"

"Don't be flippant."

"I've got to inject a little humor."

If possible, Dad's tone became more serious. "I think if you're away from Maddie long enough, the effects of her presence will wear off and you'll naturally transform. Or maybe you can will it. I don't really know."

Sarcastically, Chase said, "Great." So it was up to him. He relaxed, meditated, chanted silly words, counted backward from a hundred, anything and everything he could think of while Dad pored over the family journals, volume by volume, starting at the oldest and working his way forward through history. Pages turned in the background of Chase's thoughts. Finally he exhaled loudly and slumped, closing his eyes.

"I know you're tired, but we can't quit. Don't worry, we'll find a way to get you back to normal." Another turning page. "Might miss another day of school, though."

"So there's nothing in those books that mentions this?" It seemed a strange thing to leave out. *Of all the things for someone to forget...*

"If there is, I haven't found it yet. Honestly, I'm having trouble sorting out what is relevant to our experience and what is just some oldtimer trying to share a personal experience."

Chase moaned and tried to get comfortable. But the wings made sitting awkward. They were heavy, the feathers too thick to bend easily, and they splayed on either side of him across the cot's rumpled blankets. Leave it to his family to have a zillion journals about their history. Granted, it seemed to have been a really weird and fascinating history, if changing into a gryphon was part of it.

The workshop kept him cramped and he would have given anything to be outside where he could stretch his legs. And his wings... the thought tingled, like a shiver across his skin.

Wings were made for flying, right? Having wings meant...

That would be entirely too cool.

Unable to lie still, he leaned his head back against the wall, straightened his legs before him, and closed his eyes. His wings stiffened, then sagged with him, pushing into the blankets. But before he could totally relax, a strange image flashed into his mind and he sat bolt upright.

"What's wrong?" Dad leaned over the workbench, another journal open beneath one hand.

"I *see* something."

"You mean, like a vision?" Dad tensed.

Chase squeezed his eyelids tighter. "Yes. There's someone riding a bike on a country road and there's a—a car behind her. It's coming fast. Too fast. I don't think it can stop. Oh, no! It hit her! She's lying in the snow and not moving. The car didn't stop!" He squinted. "She doesn't appear to be breathing."

"Can you tell who it is?"

"It's Maddie." Chase opened his eyes. Around him, the workshop swam back into sharp focus, as if the adrenaline brought out every detail. "What does it mean?"

Worry lines tightened across Dad's jaw. He shook his head. "It could mean Maddie just got hit by a car."

"What?" Chase pushed to the edge of the cot and squeezed the table's end. Suddenly the wood moved beneath his enlarged fingers. When he glanced down, a dent had appeared.

He could damage a thick slab of solid wood. That was pretty awesome, too.

But Dad grabbed his upper arm. "Or it could be a future event. Whatever the case, she mustn't be allowed to die."

"How do you know?" No, wait, what did it matter? "I'll go to her."

"But how?"

Chase stood and fanned his wings behind him, bumping shelves and knocking tools onto the concrete floor. A whole rack of carpentry tools fell with a crash and clatter. He cringed. "This is how."

"But you're not ready!"

"I don't have a choice. I have to help her."

Dad hauled out his cell phone and dialed 911. But Chase pushed past him, opened the outer door, and stepped into the backyard. Hopefully he hadn't attracted Mom's attention with the racket. Unsure how to begin, he muttered, "Up, up and away. Abracadabra. Olé, olé, oxen freeze. Up. Go. Move."

Nothing worked. Now what? How was it possible to have these really cool wings and not make them work?

Closing his eyes, he focused on his goal. A deep breath, another, then he opened his eyes and ran. Tall trees loomed before him at the yard's far end. He spread his wings and air rushed beneath them. His feet left the ground a fraction of an inch, like a small biplane attempting to take flight. Trees and bushes closed in. Fear sent his heart into overdrive. He was going to crash. And if he did, Maddie might die.

Dipping his chin to his chest, he prayed. But on their own, his wings angled against the cold air rushing past him. The crash never happened and he opened his eyes. Objects on the ground grew smaller, and he flapped his wings and ascended. He didn't even need to think about it; his wings knew what to do and all he had to do was let them.

He let out a whoop of joy as he soared above the countryside. The wind blasted past him and wet flakes of snow splashed against his face like cold raindrops. It felt so natural, so easy, as if his body had developed flying muscles and instincts when it had changed. The fear had vanished. He didn't even mind the cold; his fur kept him comfortable.

He needed to turn—and with the thought, his wings tilted, banking him above the river and its line of trees. In the distance he could see the high school, tiny figures moving around the outdoor track in some after-school activity. Only a few cars still waited in the student lot.

The highway lead away from the school, into the trees, and the road to Maddie's house broke off from that. A few flaps of his marvelous wings brought him over the line of pavement and there she was, biking home from school, her backpack bulging in the front basket. She struggled to pedal up a small hill as snow lightly fell on her tiny frame. She seemed so small, so defenseless, from his eagle's-eye view, head down as her legs pumped.

He heard the car before he saw it. Brakes squealed. Fractions of seconds, that was all the reaction time he had.

Without thought, his wings folded. He swooped down, surely in full view of the careless driver, wrapped his arms around Maddie's middle, and lifted her from the bike. His wings fought for altitude. Chase cringed as the bike crumpled beneath the car's tires.

He tightened his hold and flew until they reached a clearing. Landing—should he pretend he was a plane? But again his wings knew what to do. They backpedaled, then folded, setting them down lightly beside a stand of trees. He released her and waited for her to scream, but she remained strangely silent. She slumped to a sitting position on the whitening ground and stared at him, her eyes huge and glassy.

Awkwardly, he bent over her. "Are you hurt?" His voice had somehow become gruff and it didn't sound like him at all.

She shook her head. White puffs of air escaped her parted lips. Sirens wailed in the distance. He wanted to hold her, warm her, but feared imminent discovery. Bad enough that the driver must have seen him.

Squatting before her, he said, "People are coming to help you. Stay here until they arrive. Okay?"

She nodded and looked down.

The sirens were getting closer fast. Chase turned, spread his wings, ran a few steps, and lifted into flight. Tempting to soar overhead and watch the rescue, but instead he flew low over the trees toward home. When he arrived he knocked on the workshop door and his father answered.

Dad pulled him inside. "Well?"

"I got there before the car hit her." He fell against an empty wall, his chest rising and falling from exertion. Flying had felt natural, like breathing, but it left him panting as if he'd run for miles.

"What did she say when she saw you?" Dad asked.

"Nothing."

"Nothing? She didn't scream?"

"No. It was like she was in a trance. I don't think she realized I was real." Chase stretched his wings—they felt cramped, maybe overworked—but managed to keep from tumbling more tools from the racks.

Dad whistled quietly through his teeth. "Astonishing."

"Maybe I can transform back now?"

"Maybe." Dad stepped back, tapping his forefinger to his chin.

He'd done what he'd set out to do. Chase relaxed. Knowing Maddie was safe caused his heart rate to slow and the adrenaline seeped away, letting his breathing ease. Nerve endings awoke and it felt like a thousand tiny needles pricked him at the same time. He gritted his teeth to keep from crying out. The transformation to his human form took only a minute. Then he shivered on the cot and Dad threw a blanket over his bare shoulders.

Gnawing his lip, Chase asked, "Will I change again?"

"It is a distinct possibility," Dad shrugged, "although I haven't transformed again. But then, I'm not touching the girl constantly."

Not something he wanted to discuss with his father. Chase ignored the accusation. "So you think it might happen again if Maddie touches me?"

"I don't know."

"Don't those books say anything?" Chase pointed to a new stack littering the workbench.

"If they do, I haven't found it."

Chase crossed his legs and pulled the blanket tighter. Being fully human again felt strange. "Exactly what have you discovered?"

"Just a bunch of random facts about the Donovan family, like that we have sons, not daughters."

"Has it always been like that?"

"For as far back as the family kept records."

Yep, he was in a weird family. "You've learned nothing else?"

"I'm afraid the things I've learned are more confusing than helpful."

Chase didn't care if all he ever had was a son. Considering his pack of brothers, that felt *normal*. Right now he had more immediate concerns. "Let me get this straight. You're saying I could go to school, and if Maddie touches me, I could transform right there? In front of everybody!"

"That's a possibility."

Chase threw his hands into the air. "This is impossible. Senior year, Dad! Senior year! I can't avoid the whole year just because I'm afraid of changing into a freak. I'll just have to find a way to control it."

"One way might be to stay away from Maddie."

"Dad!"

"I'm not telling you what to do, just that it might work."

"But I can't. It would break her heart. We're friends. She's already lost so much; if I abandon her..." He shook his head, unable to finish the thought. Not only would staying away hurt Maddie, but him as well.

Dad opened his mouth as if to speak but was interrupted by a timid knock on the door. "Alex?" said Mom's voice.

"Yes, Carissa?" Dad straightened.

"Maddie's grandma just called. She's frantic. She said Maddie never made it home from school today. Do you know if Chase has heard from her?"

Chase whispered, "But what about the fire trucks and police? When I left, flashing lights and sirens were headed her way. I told her to wait and they would find her. Why didn't they find her?"

Too late, he felt the now-familiar tingle and pain in his gut. Eyes closed, he visualized Maddie sitting where he had left her. Chase's voice took on a gruffer tone as he asked, "What is she doing?"

Dad hissed. "Chase! Your mother is right outside."

"I know." But he couldn't help what happened next. One moment he was curled on the bed and the next he was standing, his wings flared at his sides. "I'll go out the back."

"But Chase—"

Before his father could say more, Chase left.

10

How long have I been here?

Maddie slowly awoke from her daze. Her breath came in short rasping gasps and stars swam before her vision. She grabbed her purse, which somehow hung at her side, and searched the contents for her inhaler, coming up empty-handed. When she was younger, she'd been prone to asthma attacks and had never gone anywhere without her inhaler. Recently, however, the attacks had been much further apart and she no longer carried the life-saving device. That might have been a mistake. She opened her purse and breathed into it like a bag until the stars disappeared. As soon as she reached the house, she would stick the inhaler back in her purse.

She wanted to stretch out her legs and lean back on her hands, but she shivered so violently that she knew exposing more of herself to the icy air would be a mistake. Hugging her knees to her chest, she tried to remember how she'd gotten there, in a field away from the road and without her bike or backpack.

She'd been biking home from school; that she knew. Vaguely she recalled skidding tires and stopping her bike to glance back. Sliding on the icy road, the car had been so close that the cold hard reality of death had seemed imminent. It had been too late to move. Eyes closed, she had waited for the car to strike. Then the wind had been knocked from her as she was snatched away. The ground had grown smaller beneath her. *Something* had lifted her and carried her to where she presently sat.

She closed her eyes and imagined her rescuer.

The— the *creature* in her memory had been at least seven feet tall, with legs and feet like the hindquarters of a dog. Its arms, however, had been human, with regular hands and long fingers that ended in sharp, pointy claws. Massive wings had spanned wider than he was tall. Fine gray fur had covered both its human and animal features. And it had talked!

She laid her hand against her forehead. She didn't feel feverish. If she thought she'd seen that, then she should be.

Maybe the car had hit her and she was in a coma. Perhaps the creature had been a hallucination. She checked herself for injuries but found no signs of trauma or bleeding. Of course, if she was in a coma, she might not be seeing herself as she really was.

Maddie struggled to stand on her wobbly legs. Sirens still wailed in the distance and she waited, but no help arrived. She thought she'd seen the road when she'd first sat up, but now it was gone, hidden by the deepening dusk and lowering clouds. Not even flashing emergency lights showed through the night's fall. That morning she'd expected heavier snow. Looked like it had arrived.

Her sweatshirt and jeans were wet and cold, and she shivered harder than ever. She'd been in danger from the car, but now the cold was a bigger danger. She needed to move before she froze. She stumbled forward. Several trails branched off from the clearing. One should lead to the road, another out toward home, and another back into town. But she didn't know which went where. She chose one and forced herself to walk.

Within a few yards, the trees thickened on either side of the trail she'd chosen. Pine needles rustled. Fear squeezed her heart. "Get a grip, Maddie. It's just the wind."

It blew again, moaning through the trees like a lost soul. She shivered harder and kept up the monologue. "What have you gotten yourself into? You should have walked toward the road. But you can't find the road. This is crazy, stumbling around in the woods while it's snowing." Her teeth started chattering, interrupting her flow, and she clenched her jaws together.

She wrapped her arms around her middle. Her fingernails were turning blue. The sweatshirt stuck to her and a deeper shudder wracked her body. The fear inside her was colder than the surrounding air. Wandering around through the woods like this, she'd never find her way home. She'd die of exposure and maybe they'd find her in the spring after the thaw...

But before she could complete the thought, massive wings pumped overhead, sounding like a blacksmith's bellows. She looked up and stopped, leaning against a rough pine's trunk for support.

The gryphon-like creature stared at her, blocking her path ahead. Her heart thumped loudly in her ears. She took a step back and swallowed.

Its eyes narrowed as it closed the distance between them.

Hands behind her, she backed up until another pine blocked her retreat. Closing her eyes, she chanted in her head, *It's not real, it's not real.*

A wisp of warmth struck her cheek. She opened her eyes. The back of the creature's knuckle lightly stroked her cheek and she sucked in a breath. Quickly, she said, "I did what you said."

It didn't answer. Its expression was blank.

She gnawed on the inside of her mouth. Would the creature slide his nail across her exposed throat? Throw her to the ground or attack her? With the tree to her back she couldn't get away, couldn't outrun his wings—but instead he lifted his snout and turned his head from side to side, like a cat does when hunting.

Intent on figuring out the creature's intentions, she said, "Um, thank you for saving me from the car. I thought I was a goner." *Thought I was a goner? Couldn't I have come up with something more original?* Wait, why should she bother impressing a creature? Was she going to take him home as a pet? Since he refused to vanish the way a figment of her imagination would.

It's not real, it's not real... okay, maybe it is.

If she wasn't mistaken, the beast raised an eyebrow. Encouraged by still being alive, she added, "Do you find something amusing?"

He coughed behind his hand. *He*—yes, the beast had to be male. He looked rugged and tough. No clothing, but the thick, pale fur protected his body better than the sopping sweatshirt did her.

She shivered again, harder. She'd forgotten the cold in her fear, but now anger filled her. "Don't you have *anything* to say? You told me to wait. And I waited. What was I supposed to wait for?"

"The authorities." His gruff voice made her heart skip a beat. It was so deep, it seemed to come from his nonexistent boots.

Sudden weariness overcame her. She slumped, slid underneath his arm, and continued along the trail. Over her shoulder, she yelled, "Well, they didn't find me, so I'm going home." If she could find home, of course. Maybe if she stayed mad enough, her boiling blood would keep her warm, along with the exercise.

Two steps and the creature scooped her into his arms.

Instinctively she struggled, but his hold tightened and he pulled her tight against his warm chest. The beast ran, spread his wings, and flapped, one incredible downdraft, lifting them skyward.

The ground disappeared in the still-lowering clouds. Maddie buried her head in the creature's chest, clenched his forearms, and held on for dear life. At first she hid her face because she didn't want to look. But once his warmth melted the ice within her cheeks, she snuggled and relaxed. Somehow, she knew he wouldn't hurt her.

They landed at the wooded perimeter surrounding her grandma's land. He didn't immediately let go and she absorbed his heat. She almost felt warm and the shivering had mostly stopped.

"You have to go the rest of the way alone," he whispered in her ear as he finally settled her on her feet.

Cold seeped in again. She wrapped her arms around her middle and stepped back reluctantly. He didn't move.

"What are you?"

He didn't answer.

"Am I dead?" she asked.

Still he said nothing.

She bit her lip and stared into his amber-colored eyes. They were beautiful, glowing in the gloom like golden coals. "Thank you."

He nodded.

She turned on her heel and ran. Within a hundred feet, she broke free of the trees and raced onto the gravel road leading to her grandma's house. Two police officers turned, staring, and started toward her. Through the pine needles and bare branches behind her, she felt the creature's heated gaze.

Grandma Draoi stumbled beside one officer. "Maddie!"

Maddie fell into her arms and accepted her fierce embrace. It felt so good, so much like home.

"Child, where have you been? I've been worried sick."

Grandma Draoi looked much older than she had the night before, and Maddie fought pangs of guilt.

"A car almost hit me, but I—I avoided it. It destroyed my bike, though. I ended up in a clearing and my mind was foggy. It took me awhile to find the road."

"You poor dear," said Grandma Draoi, hugging her even tighter.

Maddie hoped the beast had supersonic hearing so he would know she hadn't turned him in. Besides, everyone would think she was crazy if she told them what had really happened. *She* thought she was crazy, when she thought about it.

After she'd explained further to the police, they left. Finally warm, Maddie rushed through her dinner of hot soup and retired to her room. Throughout the evening she had shot glances out the window in hopes of catching the gryphon still watching over her, but she had been disappointed. Sketchpad in hand, she drew every feature she could remember. The gryphon took life on the page, his height and breadth filling it. Carefully she sketched in the glorious feathers of his wings and the amber heat of his eyes.

Pad sitting like an easel on her nightstand, she fell into bed and stared at the image. Lids fluttering closed, she dreamed of a gray furry beast flying amongst the clouds.

Chase waited until Maddie entered the house and the police left before taking flight and returning home. He entered the sanctuary of the workshop and waited while his body relaxed and transformed back to normal. Folded clothes rested on the edge of the cot and he smiled at Dad's foresight.

He joined the family for dinner, but barely made it through

the event. His eyelids drooped from the previous night's lack of sleep. Finally, exhausted more than sated, he made a hasty excuse and retired to his room.

Laptop flipped open, he checked his email and thought about corresponding with friends in California, but as he set his hands on the keyboard to type all he could see were the hands of his gryphon form. He leaned back and sighed. He would never again be the young, carefree boy he'd been just a couple of days before. Now he was something entirely different. Some sort of superhuman or monster, he wasn't sure which.

Maybe he should find a mask and create himself a secret identity. Then he would need a really cool name. He could be Gryphon Man or Furry Flying Fellow or...

He was so lame. He lay down, hoping to forget the day and what the future might hold.

11

Not until the next morning did Maddie realize she had a huge problem—no way to reach school, no backpack, no books, and no completed pile of homework. The teachers were going to kill her when she told them she'd lost everything... that is, if they believed her story at all. She paced the living room and gnawed on her lip. She should have asked the police for a report before they left; that would have been proof positive. She plopped onto the sofa and laid her elbow on the arm. Maybe she should call Chase. She hadn't seen or heard from him since Wednesday afternoon. Maybe he'd changed his mind about being her friend?

She didn't like that question at all. When she thought about Chase not being her friend any longer, it felt as if she'd swallowed a brick... whole. *Yeah, that's the kind of thing a dork would do.*

Since her grandma had yet to come downstairs, Maddie wrote a note saying she'd left early for school. She didn't explain it was because she was walking. Some things Grandma didn't need to know.

Bundled up, Maddie left, locking the door behind her. The cold morning wrapped frigid arms around her and she shivered before she reached the road. The wind whistled past her ears as she strode on the roadside, facing traffic. She raised her collar to block the chill. Snow flurries fell, but didn't stick. Boy, did she miss her bike and the warmth of summer.

A blaring horn from a jet black SUV startled her and her heart thumped wildly in her chest. It pulled up on the opposite road shoulder. The driver's window rolled down. Dougal leaned from the window and opened his mouth, only to be interrupted by Stephanie's high-pitched wail. "Why are you stopping?"

Dougal pulled back inside the SUV. "Because she needs a ride."

"I don't care." Stephanie pouted.

"I do." Dougal's tone sounded stern. Again he leaned out the open window, and his voice sweetened when he spoke again. "Would you like a ride to school?"

Maddie would have loved to say no, but her lips were chapped, her hands numb, and she wasn't even halfway there. "Y-yes, thank you."

Dougal jumped out and opened the rear door. But three kids were crammed into the back and there was nowhere left to sit.

"Hmm, seems I've been a tad too generous today." He shut the door and reopened his own. Maddie was afraid he'd changed his mind and was about to tell her she'd have to keep walking but instead he said, "Stephanie, scoot over."

Stephanie mumbled in a disgruntled tone as she complied.

Dougal's Irish brogue thickened as he stood aside and with a gentlemanly sweep of his arm, he said, "Your chariot awaits."

His eyes glowed bronze. A chill climbed her spine, but this one had nothing to do with the temperature. Maddie averted her gaze and hugged her purse to her chest. "Thank you." His eyes had glowed that way before, a few days ago in school, hadn't they?

Sarcasm poured from Stephanie's mouth. "Of course you'll accept a ride. I'm crammed against the door with the handle jabbing me in the ribs and you're enjoying it."

Dougal climbed in and Maddie was caught between them, sitting atop the center console without a seatbelt. Even though she sat above him, her thigh pressed down against his. She attempted to wiggle away, but there was nowhere for her to go and all she accomplished was igniting a spark of friction. The smile he flashed in her direction exuded an animal magnetism, wicked and handsome, that had heat flushing her face. How could she avoid his attention in such close quarters?

Stephanie shifted and grunted. Classical music filled the interior and Maddie forced herself to relax. Propped up on the console as she was, her legs spread for balance and her hands gripping both bucket seat backs, it wasn't a comfortable ride. "What an interesting choice of music."

"More like boring." Stephanie studied her painted nails.

Dougal flexed his thigh against hers again. "I prefer instrumental music to the music of today. What do you listen to?"

If only her left thigh had one more inch of room. But she had to admit, tweaking Stephanie had its good points. "A little bit of everything."

"Easy listening?"

"Sometimes."

"Pop?"

"Occasionally."

"What about heavy metal?"

"Not really."

Tension oozed from Stephanie and Maddie fought a rising sense of satisfaction. Okay, so she didn't fight it all that hard.

They eased into a parking spot, and Stephanie jumped out before the vehicle stopped. Maddie waited until Dougal slid from the behind the wheel and climbed out his side with his gentlemanly assistance.

"Thanks."

"No problem. If you'll wait until I can grab my bag out of the back, I'll walk you to your locker."

She gnawed on her lip. She would love to be escorted by Dougal, but that would mean she couldn't search for Chase. "Umm, don't worry about it. I need to make a stop first, so I'll see you inside." She didn't wait for him to protest but threw her purse over her shoulder and crossed the pavement, searching for Chase's vehicle for the second day in a row.

Breath whooshed from her mouth. The heaviness in her heart increased. She allowed her hair to drape across her face as she passed his truck and entered the school. Perhaps if she'd apologized for her behavior, Chase wouldn't have felt the need to leave her stranded two days in a row. *Or maybe he's just tired of the dork.*

She made a beeline for the office and explained her lack of books. The principal chastised her for not taking better care of school property, but wrote a note of explanation for her teachers to see.

Chase had driven to school, but hadn't stopped to pick her up. That meant something was definitely wrong. She would avoid his locker until he told her everything was again copacetic, not that she needed a locker since her books had been lost when her bicycle was crushed. Hopefully he'd rush up to her in one of their classes together and she could explain and apologize. The alternative would be to carry all her books home, once the teachers replaced them... or use the space in the teachers' lounge again. Lovely.

A fake smile plastered on her face, she entered homeroom.

Chase leaned against a desk on the room's far side. Football players and cheerleaders surrounded him, all laughing and chatting together. Maddie couldn't reach him without pushing through them, so she took another route to her seat, sliding between desks and trying not to notice all the sideways stares. He laughed and cut up with the group, acting like a completely different person.

She tried a little wave to capture his attention, but he ignored her. Her hopes sank. Yep, he'd tired of the dork.

Class was a blur. Maddie couldn't focus. She tapped the pencil's eraser on the desk. Chase had been her friend. There were so many things she had wanted to share with him, so many things she yearned to tell him.

Tears welled in her eyes and she swiped them away as she doodled a broken heart on her composition book. If this was how she felt because he didn't want to be friends, what would it have felt like if she'd loved him? The pain would have been unbearable.

Second period was the same, with Chase hanging out with his new buds. Maddie tried to convince herself that lunch break would be different. He would sit across from her and stare at her with his big blue eyes. They would talk about classes and their upcoming tests, and the past places he'd lived, and everything would return to normal.

Tray in hand, she carried it to her usual table. Chase entered and sat at another table with his new best friends, clearing avoiding her.

Dougal sat with Stephanie and her pals. He sent her pitying looks and Maddie stared at her tray, trying not to meet his gaze.

Her throat burned and her chest ached. In a rush, Maddie picked up her tray of untouched food, walked to the garbage can, and dumped it. She shouldered past teachers and students and headed toward the bathroom. She could hide there for the rest of the day. But halfway there she changed her mind and went to the principal's office.

"Mrs. Grady?" Maddie said.

"Yes, dear?"

"I need to go home."

"Are you sick?"

"Yes." *In my heart.*

"Do you have a way?"

"Yes," she lied.

"Okay. You can leave. I hope you feel well enough to return tomorrow."

"Thank you." Maddie left the office and crossed the parking lot. She should've known having a friend was too good to be true. Who'd want to be friends with her?

She trudged along the deserted highway and cried. If her life had to suck that badly, why did people keep saving her? Why didn't they just let her die?

Tears blurred her vision, but she recognized the path veering off the road into the forest. On impulse, she followed it. In a small clearing hidden from the road, huge rocks dotted the turf and she scrambled onto a boulder. Her shoulders shook. Tears finally spent, she laid back across the granite and studied the sky. If she was lucky, maybe the careless driver would pay her another visit.

Maddie disappeared from the lunchroom and Chase allowed himself to relax. The close proximity had had him feeling her tension and sadness, and it had been almost more than he could bear. Besides, fighting off her sinking emotions was giving him a headache. Making her miserable... he hadn't signed on for that.

Around him at the table, his new best friends chattered on. They hadn't stopped yet, making him wonder if they ever would.

"I can't wait for the game this weekend."

"Yeah, we're just now getting good."

"I bet if we could get Chase here to join the team, we'd be even better."

Chase listened, but didn't reply.

An elbow dug into his ribs. "Come on, buddy. The coach is always looking for new players. I bet with your secrets from other schools, we'd be able to take the entire division down."

He managed a shrug. It seemed to satisfy them. They huddled together, absorbed in their discussion.

Football; not anything he cared to discuss. Chase pushed the unappetizing food around on his plate. It could have been a gourmet burger and it wouldn't have interested him. Silently he stood, dumped his tray, and exited into the atrium. He found a bench surrounded by bushes, took a seat, and cradled his head in his hands.

His skull pounded. He closed his eyes and tried to force Maddie out of his head. Instead, fuzzy images flashed behind his closed lids. She lounged on a jagged rock, facing the sky. Tears rolled down her cheeks; her body racked with sobs.

He gulped and grabbed the bench. The wood had been polished smooth by generations of student fingers, but he still managed to nail a splinter.

After much persuasion and stern warnings, Dad had convinced him to steer clear of Maddie. Chase had argued every point he could think of, but his father had refused to relent, arguing that the safety of their family, especially his younger brothers, had to be his first priority. If Chase morphed during school, they would all be in danger, and they didn't even understand the powers they faced. Against his better judgment, Chase had finally agreed.

"Dad, she doesn't have a way to school!"

"But you're not supposed to know that."

"But I do know! Even if I didn't know about her accident, which I do because I was there to save her—but even if I didn't know, there are ways I'd figure it out. You just don't understand. How could you? I see her. And I know what she is feeling based on what I see. She's hurt because she thinks I abandoned her."

"I'm sorry. It can't be helped."

"Yes, it can! I'll just tell her the truth."

His father grabbed his arm. "No! I don't know enough for you to tell her the truth." He paused, clutched Chase's shoulders, and stared intensely into his eyes. "You must promise you'll tell her nothing, at least until we know more of what's going on."

That morning his resolve had almost broken. Seeing her so forlorn, so alone... He didn't believe Maddie was a threat—how could she be?—but Dad had acted so terrified, so uncertain. Chase had reluctantly agreed not to tell Maddie about changing into a gray beast until Dad deemed it appropriate.

The pressure of his fingers on the bench increased, driving the splinter deeper. Maddie had hunched over against the morning cold, against his betrayal. Dad didn't understand the visions or the depression he felt at being separated from Maddie, nor what the separation did to her. If he did, he'd agree with Chase that the risk was worth it.

What would his father say if he knew Chase had waited in the parking lot until Maddie had arrived? He'd wanted just one glimpse of her, just one, before starting his day.

But when she'd exited Dougal's vehicle and looked over at Chase's truck, he could tell by her deepening slump that she'd hit rock bottom. The bush had hidden him, and he'd almost jumped out and apologized as she'd passed, but his promise to his father had held him back.

Barely.

He'd scurried past the janitor and entered a side door to beat her inside.

She'd entered homeroom and found him surrounded by people who would never accept her. He'd known in advance what effect it would have. That was why he'd sat with them. She had to hate him or he would never be able to stay away from her.

He yanked the splinter from his finger and watched a drop of blood well out. Her dejection, her silent tears... his choice was tearing her apart.

If only Chase could control the beast within. Then he could be with her.

He *needed* to be with her.

Chase closed his eyes, letting a fresh wave of anguish assault him. Maddie draped backward over a boulder in the woods. Regret. She regretted that she was alive. He dropped his head into his hands. She had had no one and he had given her hope, only to snatch it away.

Footsteps alerted him and he straightened. Chase tensed as Stephanie stalked outside and looked around, but she barely glanced at him. "Have you seen Dougal?"

"No."

"Is he with her?"

"Who are you talking about?" Chase asked.

"You know exactly who I'm talking about. That Jilly-come-lately. If she thinks she can just waltz into my school with her unusual eyes and make all the guys swoon over her, then she has another think coming." Stephanie flipped her hair and stalked away, muttering, "It just isn't done. People like her aren't supposed to have two guys fawning over them."

Well, at least Maddie had *that* going for her. But Chase's worry increased. It wasn't encouraging that Stephanie didn't know Dougal's whereabouts. The two of them had been like peas in a pod since he'd arrived at Coal Creek High. Other than the brief moments Dougal spent pretending to be interested in Maddie, of course. Although maybe he wasn't pretending. Stephanie was pretty, in her cheerleader sort of way, but Maddie was stunning.

One good thing about having a monster inside him was all the enhanced abilities. Taking advantage of his new skill set, Chase peered through the atrium's bushes and through the glass door, narrowing his eyes to increase his visional acumen, and swept the student lot. Dougal's SUV was parked out front.

Chase shoved off the bench, jogged to his truck, climbed inside, revved the engine, backed out of the lot, and drove out. He had to find Maddie.

Maddie left the lunchroom. Dougal excused himself, raced across the atrium, and leaned back against the brick building. She didn't notice him as she crossed the parking lot and trudged toward her home.

The bell rang, ending the lunch break. The clamor of students banging their trays against plastic garbage cans echoed behind him as Maddie disappeared around a bend. Dougal didn't know whether to follow or let her go. Clearly the young blond boy had hurt her. She moped like a teenager who had lost her first love. It was the perfect time to swoop in and soothe her broken heart.

He kicked at the student lot's gravel.

"You should go to her," the wind murmured.

Moving his lips but making no sound, Dougal asked, "Where is she?"

"She sits alone in the wood, bemoaning her ill-fated life."

"Show her to me," he whispered.

Maddie was in a clearing. Tears rolled down her cheeks as her frail human body racked with sobs. A part of him longed to comfort her. Her sorrow aroused ancient feelings of sympathy within him. He staunched those urges by reminding himself of his goal. Maddie was the means to an end, nothing more. Even though her sweet, silky voice cut straight through his heart, he wouldn't give in. She served a purpose; he couldn't allow himself to become physically or emotionally attached.

Even though she was at least a mile away, he could hear the thump of blood pumping through her heart. He jogged across the parking lot, picking up speed. When the curve hid him from the school, he changed into his natural form and streaked through the sky to his waiting damsel in distress.

Maddie fussed at herself.

"Why do I have to run everyone off? It's all my fault! It would be better to never make friends. What could I have done differently? Maybe I was too blunt about my parents. Maybe that was it. I should have just told them the details. Or maybe if I hadn't been so secretive and just told Chase the truth in the beginning, then his father would have known and there would have been no need to tell them at the table and scare the family away."

Maddie ranted and threw granite pebbles fallen from her boulder at a solid oak tree. Each one smacked into the bark, making a plucking sound. She threw another, but it vanished into the surrounding brush without a sound. Shocked, she gulped and jumped down. A dark shape separated from the tree's trunk, tossed a rock into the air and caught it, and she backed away. Someone had caught it?

"Don't be afraid," said a musical voice.

"Dougal?" she asked, blinking rapidly.

He walked from behind the shadows, again tossing and catching the pebble. "Yes."

Her heart skipped a beat. "What are you doing here?"

"I saw you leave school and you seemed upset." He ambled

closer. "Is there anything I can do?"

Maddie shook her head. Something about Dougal seemed strange, different. Dangerous? But that was silly. Wasn't it? "No, that's okay." Her heart raced as his gaze intensified. The black part of his eye grew and fear tightened its grip on her. Realizing how vulnerable she was, she said, "You should go back to school before you get in trouble."

"Are you worried about me?" He took another step closer. His grin sent cold chills along her spine.

She gulped and a thought struck her. "How did you get here?"

His eyes glowed bronze, shining through the forest gloom like a cat's eyes in the night. He flashed a set of white, pointed teeth. "I flew."

No, it couldn't be! Stars appeared before her eyes and she crumpled to the ground.

12

Light-headed, Chase pulled the truck to the side of the road and cradled his head. No clue where that had come from. Guys who got invited to try out for the football team didn't usually get dizzy spells. Maybe some side effect from the beast within, or from his relationship with Maddie?

Slowly his equilibrium returned and he drew in a shuddering breath. But when he reached for the gear shift, he couldn't force himself to drive on. A vision flashed through his mind, a second there and the next gone, and Chase gasped. Not far away from where the dizziness had hit him, Maddie sprawled on the ground beside the boulder where he'd seen her earlier. A black form shaped like a bear hovered over her.

Chase threw the door open and stumbled from the truck. A path led away from the road. He raced through the brush and erupted into a small clearing. "Get away from her!"

The creature lifted its head. Chase tried to stop and fell backward onto the bank. Fangs bared; the creature snarled. Horror rocketed through him. It wasn't a bear. It resembled his other form, only much darker, and this one was angry.

Pain stabbed in his stomach and lanced up his back. Beneath his skin on either side of his spine, nerves rippled and shifted. Under his breath, he muttered, "Not now, not now."

The sharp point of an extending tooth poked into his lip. Chase fought against the transformation. If this similar creature saw him, everything Dad feared could come true... whatever that was.

The black beast leaned over Maddie again. Drool dripped from its lips. Its claws extended. One bony black finger flicked out and stroked her cheek. Maddie's unconscious form shuddered.

Chase closed his eyes and willed himself to stay human. Maddie smiling. Maddie shoving books into his locker. Maddie playing with her hair while they enjoyed lunch, such as it was... she'd made school lunches a good thing. His breathing slowed. The wind shifted. Was that her perfume? It smelled so good.

He opened his eyes. Maddie lay in the clearing alone, one hand reaching toward the granite boulder as if seeking support. The beast was gone.

Whirling in a circle, he searched the vicinity, narrowing his eyes and using his enhanced senses to ensure they were truly alone. Then he stumbled over downed branches and fell to his knees at Maddie's side. Her pulse beat strong and steady against his fingertip.

The creature had touched her cheek. The wound from her dream had reopened and a small streak of blood spread across her pale skin.

The sight of Maddie's injury caused Chase's body to tingle again. Her eyelids fluttered open and he struggled to regain control. Deep calming breaths weren't working. The pain began in agonizing waves. If she saw him change...

"Chase?"

He closed his eyes and focused on the sound of her voice. No, that wasn't working. He had to touch her. The need outweighed the risk and he pulled her onto his lap, nestling her head beneath his chin. It felt right. The emotional roller coaster of the last few days ended. His heart rate returned to normal and the pain faded away.

He'd won.

Her words were muffled. "I'm sorry."

Tears wet his shirt. His sin against her stung. "What do you need to be sorry for?"

Maddie leaned away from his chest and swiped at her tears. "I'm sorry for how I behaved when I met your family. Please don't leave me."

He held her tighter and fought the guilt that tightened his

throat. "You did nothing wrong. I'm the one who should be sorry. Will you forgive me?"

"Yes," she whispered.

Chase cradled her. Nothing had ever felt more right. His hands on either side of her face, he dipped his head and brushed his lips across hers. Electrical pulses shocked his lips and coursed through his body.

She trembled, and that set his pulse pounding again.

The energy faded and he cleared his throat. "I'm so sorry, Maddie. I won't ever leave you again. That is, unless you ask me to."

She didn't speak, and he swallowed. That day might actually come. Shakily he stood, lifted her into his arms, and carried her back to the road, to his truck. Deposited inside, she flashed him a small smile.

He lifted his finger for her to wait, then jogged back to the clearing and retrieved her purse. A cursory glance around the area, but he couldn't see any proof of the black beast's existence. There were no obvious signs that anyone had ever been there, much less a monster he still barely believed in, and he huffed a sigh of relief.

Chase returned to the truck and slid behind the wheel. "What now? Do you want to go home?"

She nodded. He started the truck, checked the rearview for traffic, and pulled out.

While he drove, Maddie stared out at the passing scenery, her face turned away. He gnawed on his lip. Had she seen the black beast? Did she think it was him? What was she thinking? The silence was deafening. Picking what he thought was a safe subject, he asked, "Where's your bike?"

She frowned. "You mean you don't know?"

"Know what?" He bit the inside of his cheek to mask the lie.

Maddie pushed her hair from her face. "Someone ran me off the road yesterday."

It wasn't hard to create appropriate fear and concern. "Really? Were you hurt?" Stupid question. After all, she'd gone to school, at least for the morning classes.

If she thought the question stupid, no sign of it showed in her voice. "No. I was rescued."

"How?" *Here it comes. She's going to blurt it out.*

She grimaced. "I'm not exactly sure. When I figure it out, I promise you'll be the first to know."

Surprised by her answer, Chase asked, "You're sure you're okay, then?"

"Yeah, I feel one hundred percent better now."

She felt better because she was with him, or because she'd left school and wouldn't have to suffer through chemistry and gym, or... the possibilities were endless and agonizing. But before he could figure any of it out, Maddie twisted on the bench seat to face him, twirling a strand of hair around her index finger.

"Why have you avoided me for the last two days?"

Too late, Chase realized he should have expected the question and had an answer ready. No way could he say, *Hey, I'm a mutant beast and I was afraid you would set off my powers.* Although maybe he should, just to see what she said... no, not a good idea. Instead he shifted and fidgeted. "Well..."

Maddie studied her hands and sighed. "Listen, I'm sorry about the dinner table conversation. My parents' death is still fresh on my mind and I was way too blunt."

"Maddie—"

"It's okay. I understand. I come with a lot of baggage."

No time to figure out something to comfort her; they'd arrived at her grandma's house. Chase guided the truck into the rutted driveway. Without thinking, he blurted out, "Maddie, do you have plans for tomorrow evening?"

"No."

"Would you like to go with me to the school dance?" Coal Creek High sponsored one each month in the gym; the flyers had been posted in each classroom.

Her eyes and smile widened. "I would love to."

"Great! I'll pick you up around six."

"Okay."

He parked outside the house. "And on Saturday morning we could go hiking and have a picnic, if you like."

She climbed from the truck and leaned in through the open window. "I would like that. And thanks for the ride home."

"You're welcome. See you tomorrow morning, then?"

"Yeah, see you tomorrow morning."

Chase watched as she walked away from the truck and went inside. His body relaxed as he felt her tension ease. Perhaps tomorrow they would have a long talk. They really needed one.

13

Maddie bounded into the living room, bent over, and kissed her grandma.

"You're home early." Grandma Draoi tilted her face, accepting the kiss, and patted Maddie's head.

"Yeah, I wasn't feeling well."

Grandma Draoi raised an eyebrow. "You look fine to me."

"I feel better *now*."

"I saw your note this morning. Did you walk home?"

Maddie shook her head. "No, Chase drove me."

"Oh, was he not feeling well, too?"

"No. He's fine. Why would you think he felt bad?"

"Because he left school early. Lean down here and let me check your head. Something ain't right about all these questions you keep asking."

Maddie grinned and bent down for inspection. "No, Grandma, he's fine. I'm fine. In fact, we talked about hiking on Saturday and going to the dance tomorrow night."

Grandma removed her hand. "Maddie, do you think that's a good idea?"

"Yeah. Why wouldn't it be?"

"Well, I just mean you haven't known this boy very long and you seem to be getting very attached to him."

"And?"

"Well, I don't want to see you hurt is all." But Grandma

Draoi's eyes glared so intently that Maddie's pulse jumped.

"I'll be fine." Maddie grimaced at the lie. For the last couple of days, she had suffered Chase's indifference and that had definitely hurt. If he ever decided he no longer wanted to be her friend, then she would never be fine—but her grandma didn't need to know that.

Before Grandma Draoi could ask more difficult questions, the phone rang. "I'll get it." Maddie skipped from the room and grabbed the phone. "Hello?"

"Maddie?"

"Chase?"

"Yep."

"Are you home already?" Maddie leaned against the door facing and twirled her hair. A veritable geyser of happiness sprouted within her.

"Not yet. I just wanted to hear your voice."

Heat rose to her cheeks. "You did?"

"Yes, I did."

"Who is it, dear?" Grandma, from the other room.

Maddie covered the mouthpiece. "It's Chase."

"Oh." The single word said it all.

Time for privacy. Maddie carried the cordless phone upstairs to her bedroom and dove across her bed. She felt like a Valley girl (did they still have Valley girls?), lying on her stomach with her legs kicking behind her and talking to a boy on the phone. All she needed now was a wad of gum. "Sorry, my grandma was curious."

"No problem. I guess it's not every day that a guy calls you. I mean, I hope it's not. That is, for my sake."

She laughed at his worried tone. "Hardly! I think you're the first boy to ever call me!"

"Now, I find that hard to believe."

"Well, don't, because it's true." Except for Dougal, who'd called her for homework. But that didn't really count and she saw no reason to mention it.

"What about at your other school?"

Maddie wanted to clam up. Would the pain of her past never cease? Swallowing the feeling, she said, "Not even at my other school."

"I don't believe it. It's too hard for me to fathom that someone as beautiful as you has never had a serious boyfriend."

Maddie rose and studied herself in the dresser mirror, glad he couldn't see her blushing. "And what about you? You're the hottest thing on two legs. How many broken hearts have you left behind?"

He snickered. "Hottest thing on two legs, huh?"

The mirror reflected her increased redness, but she continued. "Chase, please, you have to know how attractive you are. This can't be news."

"Actually, it is news. I don't have a clue how attractive I am. Why don't you explain it to me?"

Maddie groaned. Now what had she gotten herself into? She stuttered and stammered, unable to form a coherent thought, much less a sentence. She'd never told a guy what she liked about him before; what was she supposed to say? Finally she blurted, "Well, you know what I mean."

"Nope, afraid not."

She blew out a rush of air. "Do you want me to spell it out for you?"

"*Please*," came his drawn-out reply.

And the light dawned. "You're really enjoying this, aren't you?"

"Immensely," he answered in a deep voice.

A chill shivered up her spine. They were just friends. Right? What had she been thinking, telling him he was attractive? She would probably scare him off and he would never speak to her again.

But hadn't the kiss changed things? Couldn't she be his friend and still find him attractive?

As if she wasn't herself, she lowered her voice until it took on a smooth, velvety sound. "You have the body of Adonis. When you look at me with your baby blues, I grow weak in the knees. I can't be with you for more than a few minutes without hoping you'll take me in your arms and kiss me." *Oops, did I really just say that aloud?*

No. Couldn't have.

The sound of squealing tires carried over the line. "Chase? Chase? Are you okay?"

"Yeah," he said, a little breathlessly.

"What happened?" she asked.

"I— I had to pull over."

"Why?"

"You're a real piece of work, Madelyn Clevenger."

"I'm sorry. I didn't realize what I was saying." She laughed. "Are you mad?"

"Nope, but no one has ever talked to me like that. Do you realize I want to turn around, whisk you from your room, and kiss you senseless?"

Maddie gulped. How could she be around him tomorrow after all this? She changed the subject. "Are you going home?" Her heart beat faster and faster as she waited for his reply.

"I'm not sure. What do you think I should do?"

Why did he ask her? She wanted him to come back and do all the things he'd threatened. Starting with the whisking away and finishing with kissing her senseless. No one had ever paid so much attention to her, and she didn't know how to react. But from the way her heart hammered... she swallowed and spoke her honest feelings.

"I want to tell you to come back, but you should go home. I feel vulnerable and maybe this isn't the best time."

A long pause. "You're right."

The line fell silent and Maddie bit the inside of her cheek. "I think you avoided a question that I asked."

"What was that?"

"Girlfriends? How many have you had? How many broken hearts have you left behind?"

She hoped he'd say none, but realistically if he said none, would she believe him? A guy like Chase didn't walk around without a girlfriend.

"I've dated, but I've never had a serious relationship."

"Oh." What was she thinking? She'd only known him for a week! What right did she have to feel possessive? But she couldn't help it. The thought of him dating other girls made her want to unsheathe her claws.

Chase interrupted her thoughts. "I'm home. I guess I better let you go. I see Mom peeking from behind the curtain. No doubt she wonders what I'm doing home so early."

"Yeah, you should definitely explain. I'll see you tomorrow."

"Yes. Yes, you will."

After Chase hung up the phone, he sat in his truck a little longer. Hey, Mom could wait. But Maddie's admission of attraction had set his blood to boiling and it felt like steam rolled from his ears. It hadn't been her words, or her tone, but her emotions. His pounding heartbeat matched hers as if a single heart beat in both their chests. Not something he wanted Mom to see.

Something about the beast within him was tuned to Maddie. Every ardent thought, every passionate feeling that raced through her mind, he shared it. He could feel her emotions, sense her racing pulse, taste her yearning. Adding that to his own emotions had forced him to pull over and catch his breath. Either that or wreck the truck.

Uh, oh. Mom no longer peeked through the closed curtains, but rather had pulled them completely aside. She stood in front of the window with her hands on her hips, waiting. She would want to know why he'd left school early. He preferred to be honest, but how could he? His father had expressly forbidden him from seeing Maddie and he had clearly broken that rule. Dad seemed either unable or unwilling to understand.

How could Chase make his father realize he could control the change, but only if Maddie was safe and happy? When Maddie was in danger or distressed was when he lost control. And in the meantime, what could he say to Mom?

Shifting in the seat, Chase unbuckled the seatbelt and reached for the release handle, only to be stopped by a soft tapping. His father stood at the truck's open window.

"What are *you* doing home?" Chase asked.

"I could ask the same of you. Did you have a problem at school?"

"No. Did you have a problem at work?"

Dad's brows knitted together in surprise. "You're being a little rude, aren't you?"

"Sorry."

"Apology accepted. But still, I want to know why you're home."

"I wasn't feeling well."

"You couldn't do it, could you?"

Chase dropped his chin to his chest. "Dad, I'm sorry. But you just don't understand." He shoved open the door and slid from the truck. "I did try, honest, I did. But I can't stay away from her. I wish I could explain it to you. This girl, she's... I don't know, different. I can feel her emotions. I can't read her mind or anything like that, but when she's sad, I know it. When she's happy, I know that, too. When she's troubled... and today she was so depressed. I couldn't handle her pain."

The tension drained from Dad's face and he squeezed Chase's shoulder. "She's special, besides just the obvious stuff, right?"

"Yeah, she's special. I can't let her go. She's a part of me. I know you said she's probably related to me changing, but it isn't her touch that does it."

"Let's go into the workshop."

Chase grabbed his backpack and followed his father. Mom waved from the window and he waved back. She seemed satisfied Dad had the situation under control, and vanished from view.

Inside the workshop, Dad asked, "How do you know it's not her touch that sets it off?"

Chase ran his hand through his hair and heat rushed to his cheeks.

"That's the way of it, then."

"Dad, I—"

"No need to explain."

"Really? You're not upset?"

"Well, I'd hoped you'd be able to stay away, but clearly it's beyond your control." Dad slumped on the stool by the workbench and pushed the journal he'd been reading aside. "I think the best we can hope for is that you can keep from revealing your other form until I can find out exactly why it's happening."

"What are you two doing out there?" Mom yelled from behind the closed workshop door.

"I think we better let your mother know you're all right. That is, before she comes in here and finds out things she isn't ready to know."

"Yeah." Chase paused. "Dad?"

"Yes?"

"Thanks."

His father nodded and opened the door.

14

Maddie hung up the phone. One thing she hadn't discussed with Chase was meeting Dougal in the woods. He'd said he'd flown to reach her. The shock had caused her to pass out. When she woke, he was gone and Chase crouched in his place.

Just thinking about it made her head ache and she massaged her temples.

Maybe Dougal had meant he'd gone really fast? Or had he literally meant that he'd flown through the air? Was he the gray-winged creature that had saved her from the swerving car? Anything seemed possible.

Pacing her room, she tried to think it through. There had to be a rational explanation. Maybe she had fallen asleep on the rock and dreamt the entire thing. She hadn't imagined the gray gryphon, but perhaps Dougal had been a dream.

The psychiatrist had said the mind could conjure many things, including a person to offer comfort.

Maddie drew in a deep breath. She was so tired. Separation from Chase had caused sleepless nights. Now that they were still friends, and maybe more, she would rest like a baby.

Grandma called and she hurried downstairs for supper.

"You must ssstop being ssso ssstupid!" Serena hissed.

"Don't nag me." Dougal lay back on the chaise and ran a hand through his hair. When she was upset, she always drew out her words like a snake. What would she do if she realized her primordial actions? Maybe throw a rock at his head. The thought made him smile.

"When will you learn? Your time trick in the classroom only hindered your power! The *eochair* will never appreciate someone who gives up their energy so freely."

"Shut up! You know nothing of her."

"Oh, and you do?" Serena paused, paced to one side of the room, whipped around, and exhaled loudly. "You like her, don't you?"

Dougal hid his reaction. Serena was too nosey for her own good. She would never understand his feelings for the *eochair*. "As I told you before, I don't like her. She is a fragile creature. A breakable being. She is nothing to me."

"I do not believe you."

He jumped up, grasped her by the throat, lifted her off the ground, and shoved her head against the wall. "I don't care what you believe."

"Touché. But it matters not to me if you have feelings for her. Her fate was decided long ago. As was ours."

He dropped her to the cave floor and turned away. "You're right. My feelings for her are none of your concern."

"Ah, so I was right."

Dougal grabbed a chair and hurled it across the cavern. It crashed into the wall above her head. "Of course you're right. She is supple and full, like a big red juicy apple. I want to take a bite of her sweetness and allow the juices to dribble down my chin."

She laughed, a deep guttural sound that filled the cave. "Serena knows. I always know."

"Her smell is intoxicating. I can't get enough of her. Why must we wait?"

"The timing must be perfect. Besides, she must be willing to fulfill her task. We cannot force her."

"Who made up these stupid rules?"

"Modern language," she said with a sigh. "The Ancient Ones, of course. The door may only open with a willing key and no other."

"How am I going to make her willing?"

"It is simple. Let Chase woo her."

Maddie awoke with a start, a nightmare fresh in her mind. Not anything she wanted to remember. She tried to run from it, gathering her clothes and rushing to the shower. Hot water cascaded over her shoulders and down her back. But she couldn't forget the dream.

The black flying creature had leaned over her and with its claw had reopened the wound on her face. Blood had dribbled along her cheek in a steady flow, seeping into the hard-packed earth. From the blood a tower had grown. Ivory doors with intricate carvings had appeared, bigger than her grandma's house. They had shone amidst the fog. They hummed and vibrated and she wanted to touch them, if only for a moment. She'd reached forward, but before she made contact the ground opened up and swallowed her. That was when she woke.

The human mind was such a mystery. How did it string such fanciful images together?

Thinking about the dream, she took too long in the shower and had to dress fast. The gray gryphon was clearly why she'd created the black one in her nightmare. The tower was obvious since it dominated most of her dreams. But what about the ivory doors? What about the ground swallowing her? Maybe she had read about it in a book, or saw it in a movie?

A glance at the clock—oh, great. Chase would be there any minute. She rushed downstairs to find Grandma Draoi preparing breakfast.

"Hello, dear. How are you?"

"So so."

"Did you sleep well?"

Maddie grabbed a piece of toast, a couple slices of bacon, and scooped eggs onto her plate. "Not sure. I had some weird dreams."

Grandma Draoi frowned. "Do you want to talk about them?"

"Nah." Not enough time to describe her dream and eat, too. She spooned scrambled eggs into her mouth. Cheese in them. Yum.

She rushed back upstairs, brushed her teeth, and grabbed her purse and an empty backpack. Hopefully the teachers would replace her books today; she'd been so miserable the day before, she'd forgotten to ask even in the classes she hadn't cut. The truck's horn honked as she reentered the kitchen. She planted a kiss on Grandma Draoi's wrinkled cheek and raced out the back door.

Chase stood beside the truck, holding the door like a true gentleman. She grinned, climbed inside the cab, and stowed her empty backpack at her feet. He climbed behind the wheel, started the engine, and drove off.

For a while, it felt as if nothing had changed between them, as if their friendship had never been tested. Chase said, "I've been thinking of places to hike and I thought it would be cool to try out the park with the waterfalls. What do you think?"

"Sounds nice."

"Have you been there before?"

She shook her head.

And so on. When they arrived, the school was abuzz with chatter about that afternoon's dance. For a few moments, Maddie felt a warm glow. She had a date and they were gonna dance.

But then Stephanie passed them in the hall, speaking to Marley in an overly-loud voice. "I have the perfect dress planned. I'm going to knock Dougal's socks off."

The warm glow vanished and Maddie gnawed her lip. She hadn't even thought about what to wear. Maybe she should back out of the date, rather than embarrass Chase by wearing jeans or worse.

After that, the day dragged. At lunch Maddie picked at her food while Chase scarfed his down. Clearly if there was a problem, he didn't see it and she'd get no help from him. The bell rang and they went to his locker. Maddie threw her new books inside and stuffed the ones she'd need for homework in the backpack.

He leaned against the locker door. "What's up?"

It was time to be honest with him. "Maybe this dance isn't such a good idea."

He looked outraged, not understanding. "Why not? I thought you wanted to go."

Nope, no understanding there. "I do, but..."

He waved his hands in circular motions, egging her on. "But..."

He waited and finally she shrugged. "Nothing. Just take me home so I can get ready."

He bowed and swept a hand in front of him. "This way, madam."

Chase left her in her driveway. Slumped, she shuffled into the house as the truck's engine noise receded into the distance. The door banged closed behind her.

"Is that you, Maddie?"

"Yes, Grandma."

Grandma Draoi stepped around the kitchen door and wiped her hands on a dish towel. "How was school?"

"The usual."

"That bad?" she asked with a smile.

Maddie returned the smile, even though she didn't much feel like it, and shrugged her shoulders. "It wasn't bad. It's just that I'm having regrets."

"About what?"

She sighed. "I agreed to go to the school dance with Chase tonight."

"And this is a bad thing?"

"No, it's not a bad thing. I really want to go. It's just, well, I have nothing to wear."

Grandma laughed. "A woman's age-old problem." She tossed the towel onto a nearby hall table. "Come with me."

Up the stairs to the very top. Grandma led her to the attic. The door creaked open and light filtered through dusty curtains. With a broom handle, Grandma knocked spider webs from the corners. "Can't keep this place free of the critters."

Cobwebs aside, the attic was surprisingly neat. A row of trunks ran the length of one wall, as if they'd been pushed into place moments ago. Grandma Draoi opened the middle trunk and crouched on one knee. "Let's see what we can find." Solids, calicos, plaids, and other colorful fabrics dropped beside the trunk as Grandma lifted each and tossed it aside without looking at it twice. At last she lifted one and held it up. "This is it."

An old person's dress. It had to be, and Maddie couldn't turn her head to look. But the dress reflected in the full-length mirror on the other wall. Knee-length, pale blue, with spaghetti straps—it was perfect and she couldn't stop a gasp.

Maddie grabbed it and held it to her, then twirled in front of the mirror. The silky soft material settled about her knees.

"Grandma, this is gorgeous. Where did you get it?"

"It belonged to your mother, dear."

The material slid along her body toward the floor, but Maddie grabbed it and held it tight to her chest. *Her mother's...*

"Do you want to wear it?"

She swallowed the flood of emotion. "Yes. Yes, I do."

"Then we'd best get downstairs and wash it up."

"I don't think I've ever seen you so nervous."

"That's because I've never been this nervous," replied Chase.

Dad laughed. "You better get control of yourself. If this girl knows you're afraid, then you'll really be in trouble."

His mother straightened his collar. "Alex, leave the boy alone. There is nothing wrong with being a little nervous when you're dating someone you like."

Chase refused to snort. *Or even when dating someone you don't like.*

Dad shook his head. He yelled over his shoulder as he walked toward the living room. "Have a good time with Maddie and remember to be home at a decent hour. You can't take her hiking tomorrow if you don't get some sleep."

Mom fingered his hair and slapped lint from his jacket. "Ignore your father and just have a good time."

He kissed her cheek. "Thanks, Mom."

She smiled and nodded.

Chase grabbed his keys, ran out the front door, and climbed into the truck. One glance at the digital clock on the dash sent his heart racing. He was barely going to make it on time, at least if nothing went wrong. With his luck...

He shifted gears and backed the truck out. Thoughts of what to say raced through his mind as he shifted to drive and accelerated. The things they had in common were limited. They were both seniors and out-of-towners. They had similar classes. Obviously she didn't detest the outdoors or she wouldn't have agreed to the hike. After that... after that, he didn't know of anything they had in common.

The one main thing was off-limits. He guessed the night's conversation would have to flow as it happened, and hopefully naturally.

The truck shuddered to a halt and he opened the door, expecting to climb out, but his attention was arrested as Maddie descended the porch steps. A pale blue gown hugged her curves. Strappy blue sandals highlighted her shapely calves. He held his breath as she approached the driver's side. All he could do was stare at her.

She blinked back, confusion tightening her forehead. "Are we still going?"

He shook his head to clear the Maddie-induced fog. "Yes, of course." If he could find his brain from wherever he'd parked it. He jumped out, placed his hand to the small of her back, and guided her to the passenger door.

"Thank you," she said once she'd settled in the truck, a red hue covering her freckled cheeks.

He ran to the other side and slid behind the wheel. Overwhelmed by her beauty, he found that the simplest tasks became hard to accomplish. The keys slid into his lap and he nearly shoved the house key into the ignition.

She smoothed the skirt. Against the pickup's worn fabric, it looked like a princess' gown. "Do I look okay?"

He leaned on the wheel and faced her. "You're more beautiful than I can describe."

Her lips twitched upward and her face morphed into a darker red. He looked away, put the truck in gear, and drove to school.

When they arrived the dance was in full swing. They had to park across the student lot, then walked inside and a chaperone directed them to a photo booth. They took a picture, both smiling broadly, before joining the other kids. The music thumped loudly, and they found an empty table and sat down.

"Can I get you something to drink?" asked Chase.

"Yes, please."

Maddie tapped her foot to the pop music as Chase went in search of refreshments. She couldn't wait to wet her parched throat.

On the trip to school, Chase had sent covert glances in her direction until she'd thought about having him take her home so she could change. The unusual attention had caused her to sweat. The restroom! That's where she should go. Somewhere to hide. *Dorks don't do dances. Not very well, at least.*

But before she could leave, a shadow fell over the table.

"May I have this dance?" Dougal asked. In a black suit, he looked even hotter. But not as hot as Chase in his white button-up shirt and khaki pants. The white against his surfer tan made her want to fan herself.

Maddie gulped. "I don't think so."

"Oh, come on. I'm sure Chase won't mind. Look, he's at the punch bowl with Marley."

She glanced where he pointed. Marley filled Chase's cup and handed it over. Her hand lingered on his, then she stroked her hair behind her ear and tilted her head, listening to something he said. Then she laughed and fluttered her hand to his shoulder.

"You want to dance now, right?"

Dougal didn't wait for an answer, but grabbed her hand and hauled her to her feet. Dragged to the dance floor and forced into his arms, she didn't readily move. The beat changed to something slower, and before she knew it she was following his lead.

Even though she didn't really want to. Did she? Did she really believe Chase was flirting with Marley?

Eyes closed, Dougal sniffed. "Your hair smells of flowers baked in the sunshine. The scent reminds me of..."

Maddie waited, but he didn't finish the sentence. "Of?"

He shrugged. For the first time since she'd met him, he seemed off balance somehow. "Of an Irish lass from my past."

"Oh." She paused, but the opening was too good to resist. "Do you want to talk about her?"

He snickered under his breath. "Women are often attracted by my good looks, charm, and mysterious nature, but I fear they don't truly know me."

Oh, yeah. Right. But Maddie's heart rate accelerated. What had she gotten herself into?

He should have resisted the urge to dance with her. The only thought on his mind had been goading Chase and creating a rift between the burgeoning couple. Serena's idea, that the more Maddie felt for Chase the more leverage they had, didn't thrill him. He had other plans. Like causing her to love him, not that cretin, so she would willingly do as he wished. It was a much better idea than anything Serena had suggested.

Too late to run. Dancing with Maddie had opened old wounds. *Merissa*. Ah, if he closed his eyes he could still smell the fresh scent of her hair and feel her silky smooth skin.

Merissa had been Cian and Arin's daughter and the most beautiful girl in the entire village. Even though her father was part gryphon, she held no hint of being anything other than human. And she had loved Dougal, really loved him. He hadn't discouraged her love, nor had he encouraged it. She was too young to know the ways of the world. Too young to know her part in it all.

He'd spoken to Cian of marrying Merissa only once. He'd frowned and agreed to consider the matter. Days after Cian had accepted his offer of marriage, Dougal had done something stupid. When the boys in the village had goaded him, made him angry, his black nature had reared its ugly head and the village had never been the same.

After that he had been ashamed to show his face. He'd hid in the mountains and stayed away from his people. And there he'd met Serena, mother of monsters.

Merissa had married, had several daughters of her own, and eventually passed away, leaving Dougal at the same age he'd been when they'd met, and alone. It was always the same. Everyone he loved died before him.

Trance-like, he smoothed a stray hair across Maddie's temple. Her cheeks grew rosy red and he wanted to plant a kiss on her forehead. What would she do if he did? Just one tiny kiss? A gentle, respectful kiss? Would the butterflies he heard in her stomach increase? Would her heart race even more?

The heavy thud of footfalls approached behind him. Sometimes increased abilities ruined all the fun. No doubt Chase would be cutting in at any moment.

15

"Thanks, Marley."

She batted her lashes. "Anytime."

Chase ignored her obvious flirting, sipped the strong punch, and watched the dance floor. The music slowed and the lights dimmed, but even so, he knew something was wrong. He narrowed his eyes and peered around swaying bodies until he found his table. Maddie was gone.

In the low light everyone looked similar. He tried sniffing, but the extra odors blocked Maddie's scent. At least she didn't seem to be in danger; he hadn't started shifting.

On the dance floor, couples floated aside. Chase bit his tongue until a metallic taste filled his mouth. In the crowded center, now visible, Dougal clutched Maddie's waist, dragging her ever closer. Their bodies seemed to meld into one. Maddie appeared relaxed, comfortable, as if she enjoyed Dougal's nearness. Chase squeezed his fingers into a fist and punch splashed on the floor.

"Ch-Chase, would you like a napkin?" Marley said.

He threw the paper cup in the trash bin, grabbed the napkin, dried his hand, threw it ditto, and stalked onto the dance floor.

"May I cut in?"

He expected Dougal to resist, but he didn't even seem surprised by the interruption. Instead, Dougal stepped aside with a sweeping flourish. A gloating smile graced his lips and Chase forced himself not to punch it away. It wasn't easy.

Chase guided Maddie into the middle of the crowded dance floor. His initial grip was tight and she tensed beneath his hands. Relax; he had to relax, and he concentrated on slowing his breathing. Within a minute, their hearts again beat as one.

Next to her ear, he whispered, "Are you okay?"

"I'm fine."

"He didn't hurt you, did he?"

She shook her head, and then laid it on his shoulder.

He smoothed her hair. He wanted to ask if she'd been forced to dance with Dougal, but if she said no, that she'd gone willingly, the answer would hurt. So he kept silent.

The music finished and a new one began, its tempo faster. Strobe lights flashed, covering the ceiling and walls in a plethora of colors. Bodies gyrated across the wood floor. Maddie joined them and swung her hips in time to the music. Surprised, Chase could barely keep up.

They'd called her a dork? What idiot had started that? Watching her dance, Chase marveled at her grace, the fluid way she moved with the music. A smile spread her lips and she let her hair fly. It was the happiest he'd ever seen her and her mood was infectious.

The deejay announced, "Now for a blast from the past. What's a dance without a little yearly shout out? We'll start with the Roaring Twenties and dance our way to today. So guys, grab your gals and let's boogie."

With a whoop, Maddie intertwined their hands and kicked her legs out to one side. The first kick nearly pulled him over.

"What are you doing?" he whispered, sending wayward glances at their watching peers.

"The Charleston!"

Giving in, he followed her lead as best he could. Maddie's laughter and enthusiasm grew with the music. As they covered the dance floor, students moved aside and cheered them on, clapping in time to their rhythmic steps.

"Now that was a sight to behold. Let's give our dancers a big round of applause as we start 'Puttin' on the Ritz'!"

Maddie pulled him to a chair, her chest heaving. Sweat glistened on her face, but it only made her more stunning.

"Don't you know this dance?" He plopped into a chair and

swiped his brow. She wasn't the only one working out.

"Of course!" Her smile broadened. "But I have to save my energy for the 50s and 60s. Those are my favorites."

"How do you know this stuff?"

"I took dance back in my hometown. And, well, I guess I should confess that my parents were dancers, at least on the weekends. People paid them to teach dance lessons at parties."

"Really?" He couldn't keep the surprise from his voice.

"Yes, really. Surely it isn't that hard to believe."

Chase studied his hands. When he lifted his chin and looked into her face, he became serious. "Since I've come to Coal Creek, nothing is hard to believe."

Her smile faded, but the frown replacing it was short-lived. Elvis Presley belted out "Jailhouse Rock" and her face lit up like the Fourth of July.

"We have to dance this! Come on!"

She dragged him back to the dance floor and he tried to shake his hips with her. Heated gazes bore into him, but the elation on Maddie's face was enough to keep him going. He ignored the leering and let himself go until the song ended.

"Where did you learn to do that?" Maddie asked as they strolled back to their seats.

Chase shrugged. "I may have watched a couple movies with my mom." She snickered under her breath and he poked her in the ribs. "That was quality time, girl. Don't be laughing about that."

They shared a smile and Chase drew out her chair. As he held it for her, he noticed Dougal across the room, leaning against the stowed bleachers and furrowing his brow. Unable to resist, Chase saluted. Dougal threw his cup in the garbage can, grabbed Stephanie's arm, and hauled her onto the dance floor.

Excellent. The troublemaker could stay with the other troublemaker and her friends. Chase kept his eyes fixed on Maddie, the beautiful girl sitting beside him.

They danced for hours, resting every few numbers and talking about everything and nothing. It was a great evening, and Chase reluctantly drove Maddie home. "Did you have a good time?"

"Most definitely." Sure seemed that way; she hadn't quit grinning yet. "I can't wait until the next one."

Mind racing, he tapped his fingers on the steering wheel.

Should he spoil it by asking about that first dance with Dougal?

Before he could, she shifted in her seat. "Look, I'm sorry about the dance with Dougal. He just kind of appeared and led me onto the floor before I even knew what was happening."

Fortune had shone on him. Relieved, he cleared his throat. "Dougal has that affect on people."

"What?"

"Nothing." But he'd never forget the image of the world going fuzzy, as if Dougal had rewound time.

"Are we still on for the hike tomorrow?" she asked.

"Sure." If his legs didn't fall off overnight. She'd worked him out but good.

At breakfast, Grandma Draoi smacked her empty coffee mug on the table and looked Maddie up and down. "You look like you're going somewhere."

"I am. Remember, I told you Chase asked me to go hiking."

"Oh, yeah, I remember."

Her grandma lowered her gaze. Guilt plagued Maddie. Why hadn't she considered that Grandma might be lonely?

Maddie laid down her fork and wiped her hands on a napkin. "Hey, Grandma, how about when I get home we watch a movie together?"

A quick breath as Grandma Draoi's aged eyes brightened. "Are you sure you don't have homework or something else you need to do?"

"Nope. I'm all done. So, what do you think? Can you fit me into your busy schedule?"

Grandma giggled like a schoolgirl. "Aye, I believe I can."

Maddie yawned. Oops; she hadn't intended to do that.

"Are the dreams really bad?"

And she hadn't intended to do that because she hadn't wanted to discuss it. Maddie clasped her hands under the table. "I'd hoped you couldn't hear me."

"Do you want to talk about it?" Maddie didn't reply and Grandma continued. "When I was a little girl, I had this one recurring dream. I was in a field of heather in Ireland, and in the distance there was a tall, white, shimmering tower. In my dream I would walk and walk, but I would never get close enough to touch it. The dream wasn't scary but I was always afraid to talk about it. I didn't want anyone to think I was weird."

Maddie gasped and quickly covered her mouth. How had she known? "Grandma?"

"Yes, dear?"

"I'm really freaked out right now."

"How come?" But she didn't seem all that surprised.

"Because I think I might have had the same dream." Maddie shared the details—the purple flowers, the field of tall grass, and the tower that shimmered just out of reach. She didn't bother explaining about the dreams' shift to her parents' gruesome death, since it wasn't part of the mystery. "What does it mean?"

"Do you ever touch the tower?"

"No."

Without looking up, Grandma drummed the table with her fingers.

"How could we both have the same dream?" Still no answer, and not even a glance. "Grandma, if you know something..."

Finally she raised her head. "Do you dream about other stuff?"

Maddie shifted uncomfortably in her chair. Should she tell her about the dream from last night? But before she could decide, Chase knocked on the back kitchen door. Shading his eyes, he peeked through the door's parted curtain; a goofy grin covered his face.

Out of time. But Maddie wasn't quite ready to give up. "Grandma, I—"

"You go. Have a good time. We'll talk about this when you get home."

Something prickled at the back of her soul and Maddie hesitated. Grandma Draoi opened her arms and Maddie hugged her before opening the back door.

"Would you like to come inside?"

"Sure." Chase entered and took an offered seat.

Grandma Draoi said, "May I get you something to eat?"

"No, thank you." He patted his flat stomach. "My mother forced me to eat before I left home."

"A growing boy can always use more." She plopped a plate with a biscuit down in front of him.

He smiled, slathered it in honey and butter, and shoved it into his mouth.

Maddie sipped at a glass of milk until he finished.

"I guess you two kids better get a move on."

Chase stood and scooted his chair underneath the table. Grandma Draoi shook her gnarled finger. "Be careful. The woods can hide many secrets."

Strangely enough, she didn't seem to be teasing.

Outside, Chase opened the truck door and Maddie climbed in. As he started the engine, he didn't speak, and Maddie worried he had bad thoughts about her grandma.

"Sorry about Grandma. She can be a little—cryptic."

With a surprised glance, he shook his head. "Not a problem. Parents and grandparents are always concerned for our safety." He shifted gears and drove off.

Maddie studied her hands then the passing scenery. No, that hadn't sounded like normal concern. Something had disturbed Grandma, but she wouldn't learn about it until that night.

In the silent truck, the drive seemed to take hours, even though it was less than one. When they arrived at the park, Chase found a spot in the nearly deserted lot. "Ready to go?"

"Yup, lead the way."

He grabbed two filled water bottles and several granola bars from behind the bench seat and stuck them in a backpack. Then he pulled out two wooden walking sticks. Both were twisted, gleaming wood and they shone in the afternoon sunlight.

"These are beautiful. Where did you get them?"

"I made them."

"You did?"

"Yeah. I didn't make the wood, of course." Chase grinned, a lopsided grin that lifted only one side of his mouth. "It was really simple. Nothing more than cutting down a small tree, shaving off the bark, sanding it down until it was smooth, then adding a little bit of stain and polyurethane."

"Well, I think it's amazing." She took off for the park entrance.

He walked behind her and leaned forward, whispering, "It's yours."

Maddie stopped and he bumped into her. "It's mine?"

"Yeah, I made them a while back. I was just waiting for the right person to give one to."

She turned to face him. They were so close their breath mingled as one. Her pulse beat a rapid tattoo in her chest as his head lowered toward her mouth. She drew in a swift breath and prepared for the shock of his touch. When their lips met the electricity pulsed through her whole body. Every nerve ending burned as if it were on fire.

As he kissed her, their bodies melded. Right when she felt she would be consumed and that reality was slipping from her grasp, Chase stumbled as a passing hiker bumped him, and they separated. It was like a splash of cold water, more painful than losing a limb. They struggled to steady their breathing, their eyes seeking one another.

Maddie spoke first. "We should walk."

"Yeah, we should." Chase glared at the apologizing hiker, who scurried away.

The crisp, cool autumn air kept the park from being crowded, and at times no other hikers were in view. Alone, they hiked the trail around the wilderness area, stopping to admire the waterfall that cascaded over the mountainside. Chase wrapped his arms around her waist and pulled her against his chest. When he nuzzled her neck, chill bumps raced along her spine.

"You have an amazing effect on me," she said.

"I do? How so?"

"I don't think I should tell you. You don't need any more evidence that testifies against my sanity."

He laughed deep in his chest, and it reverberated through her. The breath of hot air he blew on her ear tickled and he pleaded, "Tell me."

"Hmm... you're not fighting fair."

"Have you ever thought that perhaps you have an extraordinary effect on me, as well?"

The thought had never occurred to her. Floored, she didn't know what to say.

"Well?"

She leaned back in his arms. "Let's say I believe I have an effect on you."

"Good."

"Uh, are you going to tell me what it is?"

"Tell you what?"

"Chase!" Really, the man exasperated her.

He laughed. "Do you really want to know?"

"Of course!" She paused. "Wait, maybe I don't want to know. I mean, if you are going to say something like you're disgusted by me, then you can keep it to yourself."

"Okay, and if I'm going to say something else...?"

"Do you enjoy baiting me?" she asked.

"Yes," he said with a smile.

She punched him playfully.

He pretended to rock from the blow. "Do you know when you're happy, your eyes take on a deeper shade of green? It's very pretty."

"Oh." Heat flushed her cheeks and she tried to hide behind a veil of hair.

But he brushed it back. "I know we haven't known each other long, and that we haven't talked of being anything more than friends, but I have to tell you that when I touch you, I feel a spark, an electric sensation." His gentle hand lifted her chin. "And I never want it to stop."

"Chase," she whispered and tried to look away, but he held her in place.

"Let me finish. There's something about you I can't get enough of."

Hot tears slipped down her cheeks.

He pulled her close and hugged her. "Don't cry."

Crying on his shoulder; what a dorky thing to do. Maddie sniffed, pulled away, and swiped angrily at her wet cheeks.

"Maybe we should finish the hike." He clasped her hand, his fingers sliding between hers.

Thankful for the distraction, Maddie agreed and allowed Chase to lead the way. They finished the trail loop and returned to the truck around two o'clock. Instead of eating lunch on a park bench, they opted to eat inside the cab. The motor hummed and warm air whooshed into her face.

"Are you ready to go home?"

No, she thought but said, "Yes. I hope you don't mind. My grandma seemed kind of lonely this morning and I promised to watch a movie with her."

He nodded, put the vehicle in gear, and pulled onto the road.

Chase concentrated on the road and sang along. The radio crooned a smooth tune as they drove the miles back to Maddie's house. She hummed under her breath. But the words flowed from his mouth and she stared at him with wide eyes.

"You can dance, and I sing." He shrugged. No big deal.

"Anything else you want to share with me?" She crossed her arms over her chest like she was upset, but ruined the whole effect with a charming smile.

And he loved that smile. "Hmm, let's see. I play guitar, secretly love old church hymns, and really like to play football, but hate being forced into it because I look the part."

"I see. Very revealing, Mr. Donovan."

"And what about you? Anything you'd like to share?"

She gnawed on her lip and studied her fingers. Dirt spots covered her fingertips and she rubbed them against her jeans. "I like to draw," she said, so low he had to lean in to hear her.

"Really? My mom loves art. Maybe you guys could talk about it sometime. She tries to corner us, but we're not interested and we just make her frustrated."

Maddie looked at him, and again tears shone in her jade eyes. "I would like that."

He loved how little things meant so much to her. Chase squeezed her hand before turning in to her driveway. He put it in park and let the truck idle in front of the house. Parting was such sweet sorrow. Shakespeare had been spot on with that one.

"I guess you better go inside and visit with your grandma."

Maddie stared at the house through his dirt-streaked windshield. "Yeah, I guess so." She took a deep breath and swung around. "What are you doing tomorrow?"

"I think we're trying out the church next to our house."

"That's where my grandma and I go."

"Oh." Okay, he was supposed to do something, say something. But nothing came to mind.

"How about we go together?" she said.

Relieved, he said, "Sure. I'll tell my parents I'm coming to pick you two lovely ladies up in the morning. I'm sure they won't mind."

"Great! I'll tell Grandma that her friend doesn't have to

come get us." Maddie jumped from the truck and closed the door. She waved and he waved back.

Chase waited until she vanished inside. He hadn't wanted to take her home so early. Every time they parted it was like separating from himself.

He couldn't explain it, but he felt closer to her with each passing moment. It was as if they were two ropes intertwined. With each touch shared, the binding twisted tighter, causing them to be stronger.

He drove away, consumed by an ominous feeling. A change was coming; something was in the air that he couldn't explain.

PART III

E N D I N G S

16

Maddie hated leaving Chase, but she needed to visit with Grandma. She eased the front door open. Soft snores echoed from the living room. Grandma Draoi stretched upon the couch with her arm thrown over her eyes. So much for that plan. Maddie grinned, tiptoed into the room, retrieved a cover from the back of the couch, and spread it over her. Static covered the television and Maddie turned it off.

She skirted the coffee table, walked to the window, and lifted a curtain. Chase and the old truck were gone. Not even a dust cloud still hung over the driveway. Outside, the late afternoon sparkled, sunlight, and some magical feeling stealing her thoughts away...

"Mom, when are we going?" she asked impatiently, tapping her foot.

"Soon, dear."

"But I want to see Grandma Draoi," she whined.

"I know, I know. But we have to wait on your father."

"Okay." She hopped on one foot and looked out the window. When finally she spotted the sedan pulling in the driveway, she let out a cry. "He's home, he's home!"

Her mother patted her on her head. "Of course he is, dear."

Her father entered the foyer. He placed a kiss upon her mother's cheek then bent down, picked her up, and threw her into the air, catching her before she crashed to the floor. She gig-

gled, knowing no fear in his arms.

"Oh, do stop doing that. You're scaring her."

"You always say that. But look at her. She isn't scared, she's laughing."

Her father tickled her chin and she tried to lower it to her chest. He put her down and she held onto his legs, looking up at him. "Can we go, Daddy?"

"Go where?" He winked.

She fisted her hands on her hips. "Did you forget?"

He patted her head and laughed under his breath. "No, my little peanut, I did not forget. Just let me remove my coat and tie and we'll be on our way."

She skipped around the room chanting, "I'm going to Grandma Draoi's, I'm going to Grandma Draoi's."

The car pulled from the concrete drive and Maddie could barely contain her excitement. She was Grandma Draoi's pet. Whenever they visited, she always received some kind of gift and lots of special attention.

When they arrived at the farm, Grandma Draoi was in the flower garden. She beckoned Maddie to her for a big hug. Then she popped her on the bottom and told her to go find their favorite plant.

Maddie scampered through the surrounding trees looking for their special flower. She bent to pluck it, but a shiver raced up her spine, like someone watched her...

"What is she doing?" Dougal scratched his chin as he watched Maddie skip through the woods and bend before a patch of grass.

"She's in a trance. Her memories are driving her." Serena never looked away, weaving her hands around in strange circular patterns.

"She's smiling at me."

"She thinks you're her father and she is a little girl on a mission."

Ruddy witch. "Serena, couldn't you have made me someone else?" Her father was exactly what Dougal didn't want to be.

"Retrieving memories isn't as easy as you think, *dear*."

Maddie spread her arms as if flying. She giggled, pretended to pick up her imaginary skirt, and ran past them.

In his human form, Dougal offered his hand. Maddie hummed a tune as they danced to music only she could hear. He hated Serena's plan, and taking part in it made him hate it even more. Chase would be their ultimate leverage, but in case that didn't work Serena wanted to insert memories into Maddie's mind. They needed to convince her that she was supposed to help. But pretending to be her father was more than Dougal could take. As their daisy chain dance passed by her a second time, he whispered to Serena, "I can't take this."

Serena huffed. "Fine, do you want me to wake her?"

"Yes."

"Then step back and hide yourself."

Dougal shifted into his gryphon form and hid in the tree line. Serena waved her arms around and whispered a few words. The humming ceased. Maddie stopped and shook her head as if trying to clear away a mental fog.

"What? What am I doing here?" Maddie blinked and looked around the clearing.

Dougal stepped from the shadows. Evening sunlight warmed his eyes in the way that made them glow. Her eyebrows rose and her pulse throbbed in her neck.

"What— what are you doing here?"

"It's quite simple. I've come for you." His gryphon form always deepened his voice; he thought it sounded commanding. "I believe we need to get to know one another better."

"I— I don't know what you are." She wrapped her arms around her middle, her eyes shifting nervously.

The poor girl. She probably thought he was the gray that had rescued her, meaning she just didn't get it. He would have to help her understand, and he flexed his claws at the thought.

Maddie backed into a maple tree. He took another step toward her.

"I— I don't know how I got here, or what you are, but I really think I should leave."

He shook his head. "I don't think so. I like where you are."

She licked her lips and his heart raced. In his fantasy, he stroked his knuckles across her cheek. He'd longed for the moment when he could reveal himself. Maddie was the *eochair*, and the legends spoke of the *eochair* falling in love with a gryphon. Of course it wouldn't be him, he was the wrong color, but still the idea sent a thrill through his body.

And maybe, just maybe, the legends were wrong about the color.

"You seem different from before." Her breathing turned ragged, as if she imagined racing away from him. "You're kind of scaring me. Could you move back?"

He reared his head back and laughed. When he faced her, drool dripped from his fanged teeth. "Trust me, dear, I am different."

Her eyes widened, her jaw dropped, and she screamed, a sustained sound ripped from the bottom of her lungs.

Ouch. That hurt his sensitive gryphon hearing, and he waved a finger at her. "None of that."

Another step, almost close enough to touch her, and she bolted. Tree limbs shook as she crashed through them in her haste.

A purr rumbled through him. "Oh, my dear, you've made my day. I love a good game of cat and mouse."

The door slipped from Chase's hand and closed too loudly. It echoed through the house, and the eerie silence hit him. His brothers... something had happened. He ran, but in the den, Mom rose from a chair. Worry lined her once youthful face.

"Your father is waiting for you in your room."

He still couldn't hear his younger brothers, and that wasn't a good thing. "Is something wrong?"

She collapsed in the chair and shook her head. Tears coursed along her cheeks.

Not good at all, and horror filled him. "Mom, please. Is it the boys? Is it Dad? Did something happen?"

"No, everyone is fine." She sniffed. "Except you."

Oh, so Dad told her. His fear twisted, a strange dose of guilt joining it and weighing down his stomach. Chase sighed. Maybe there'd been no way to spare her from the truth. She'd have realized something was wrong when either Dad or he entered the house wearing wings. And if he morphed while wearing his clothes again, ripping them to shreds from the inside out, she would surely start to ask questions.

She babbled. "Alex always told me his family was different. He even told me we would never have girls. I tried four separate times to prove him wrong. But he never told me what might happen to you!"

The tears overwhelmed her and she wailed louder. Awkwardly Chase patted her shoulder. "Mom, I'm fine."

"But... but you're a monster!"

He knelt before her. "I don't look at it that way. I believe I've morphed for a reason."

She sniffed and her fingers entwined with his. "Your father thinks he may have discovered that reason."

"He does?" His heart hammered against his ribs and he fought the urge to run upstairs. About time they learned something helpful. "Did he tell you what it is?"

"No."

He couldn't stand it any longer. "Mom, please don't worry. Everything will be okay."

"How do you know?" She squeezed his hands.

"I can't tell you how I know. I just do."

His father's voice floated down the stairway. "Chase? Is that you?"

He rose. "Yeah, it's me."

"Come upstairs, son."

"Okay." Chase patted his mother's shoulder again and she released him.

Ascending the staircase was like walking in front of a firing squad. Dad waited for him at his bedroom door. His clenched jaw seemed grim. "Come in and sit down."

The hope died within him. "This doesn't sound good."

Dad drew in a ragged breath. "I don't know if it's bad or good, but it may shed some light on our situation."

Chase sat at his desk and leaned forward with his elbows on his knees. "I'm ready."

For a moment Dad paused, staring out the window. Beyond the glass, the first pink of sunset touched the clouds. "There's a legend that surrounds our family. One I assumed wasn't true, but I'm realizing I was wrong. The legend claims there a clan who settled in a sleepy little town in Ireland. Most of the people were commoners and farmers, a peaceful people. Then one day they were attacked by giant flying creatures."

Chase's muscles tensed.

"Their villages were burned, their crops ruined, and their women stolen. But one girl, Arin, wasn't taken because she was different. She was blind." His father paused again, staring out the window at the brightening sunset. "During the raid, Arin became disoriented and stumbled through the woods, searching for her sister, only to confront a stranger. The stranger introduced himself as Cian Conn, an ancient war chief. Because Arin couldn't see, she befriended him and enlisted his help. He would help, but for a price. Arin agreed to grant any favor he asked if he would help her find her sister and save them from the same fate her village had suffered. They found her sister, but it was too late. She was dead."

Chase bit his lip and imagined the pain of losing your village and your sister.

"Their search complete, Cian made his requests. First, he asked for her to marry him. Second, he demanded that she and her descendants accept a special job." Chase opened his mouth but Dad stopped him with an upraised hand. "Don't get ahead of me. You need to understand a few things. From what I read, the person who helped Arin was not a person at all. He was one of the *gryphons.*"

"Gryphons? You mean those half-lion half-eagle creatures from mythology that you think we're morphing into?"

"Yeah, that's what I mean. I've been doing some research and it seems no one really knows what the gryphons are or where they came from. Most people believed they had the body of a lion and the head of an eagle. Some believed they roamed mountains guarding precious treasure. Whatever the case, Cian's original gryphon clan were defenders. For some reason he left them and joined a different gang, so to speak. He was actually one of the gryphons that destroyed Arin's village."

Chase drew his brows together. "Wait, what? I don't understand. You just said Cian helped Arin."

"Cian had been a participant of a sort, although halfheartedly. He didn't truly want to harm anyone, but he'd been forced to by his new gryphon gang. It was like a rite of passage. If he wanted to belong, then he had to do what they asked. As the fighting continued in the defenseless village, he snuck away. He didn't want to engage in destroying innocents. He hid in the woods, far from his new brothers' watchful eyes. When he'd seen Arin wandering about he'd taken pity on her because of her blindness. The journal insinuates that Cian felt they had something in common. She was different, as was he. Like her, he had an infirmity that made him less desirable."

Dad paused as if waiting for Chase to speak but when he didn't say anything, Dad asked, "Don't you want to know his infirmity?"

"Sure." What was he supposed to say? None of it made sense.

"His fur was gray."

Um... Chase cocked his brow.

"I know it sounds odd, but it's true. He wasn't like the others in his new group, because they were all black. This made him an outcast among his new gryphon clan. But after he helped Arin, he was in even more danger. Cian and Arin made a pact to imprison the black gryphons, the dangerous ones. Cian built a tall white tower and with some help, he tricked them and led them inside. Once they were in, he snuck out and Arin locked the door."

"And?"

"That's it."

"That's it. But that doesn't make sense. Why did he leave his first gryphon clan? Why did he trap his new one? What happened when he married Arin? What was the special job he gave her and her descendants?"

Dad shrugged and waved at the family journal open on the desk beside Chase's computer keyboard. "I don't have all the answers yet—still reading—but what I think is that Maddie is a direct descendant of Cian and Arin."

"And us? Where do we come from?"

"I can only speculate that after the pact made with the gray gryphons, more of them morphed into humans and married." He ran a hand through his hair and sighed. "I'd know more if some of the journal's pages weren't missing."

"Figures," said Chase with disgust.

He rose and paced. What did all of it mean? The legend only raised more questions. No doubt he was related to the gray creatures, but how? When he transformed, gray hair sprouted all over him, and presumably Dad was the same. And how did this all transmit back to Maddie? Questions floated through his mind. But before he found any answers, he doubled over. Pain warped through him and his back muscles shivered.

"What's wrong?" Dad gripped his forearm.

"I don't know, but I think I'm changing again."

17

Maddie's breath came in loud gasps as she ran, tripping over roots and fallen dead branches. She peered back over her shoulder. No one followed. Maybe she'd lost the gryphon. Maybe he hadn't even followed her. She stopped and spun in a wide arc. Night had fallen in the woods and shadows surrounded her. If the black creature stood before her, would she even see him?

A shape moved from the foliage, closer than she thought possible. All she could see was the motion, then the full moon came from behind the clouds and pale light gleamed off dripping fangs. Tall, blacker than the night, bronze eyes reflecting the moonlight, and her heart accelerated again. The beast slipped toward her. He'd caught her already. There was nowhere to hide and no one to call for help. Grandma Draoi was too far away, even if she'd awakened and missed her.

The beast narrowed its slit eyes. A rumble echoed in its chest. She stopped and spread her legs apart, terrified and defensive. "What do you want?"

He came closer, stepping into a beam of moonlight slicing through the leaves. He growled again and bared long white teeth. A putrid odor wafted from his mouth. Maddie stared at the hideous form. It stood on two legs that looked like the back legs of a lion. Her throat constricted. The creature did indeed resemble the one that had saved her, but this one was darker.

Was it possible it was the same being? And if so, why was it acting so hostile now?

Maddie jutted out her chin. "Are you the one who rescued me?"

"Yes," came the gravelly answer. "I saved you."

But she couldn't quite believe it. "From the crash?"

"What crash?"

Maddie heard the words as if from a distance. No, this one hadn't saved her, and that meant there were two such strange beasts flying around. Her stomach rolled, sweat beaded her brow, and she felt weird. Why did these things keep saving her? Gathering all her strength, she rushed the creature and beat his black-furred chest with her balled fists. "Why? Why did you save me? You should have let me die!"

He clutched both her hands in one of his and lifted her off the ground. She hung there, kicking her legs. Maddie's shoulders burned with the strain, feeling as if they were going to pop from their sockets. She stopped moving, dropped her head, and whimpered.

"Are you done?"

Maddie sent him a pointed stare and spit in his face. He wiped the slime with his free hand, and she leaned backward, then flung her head forward and head-butted him. He released his grasp—startled, she thought, probably not hurt badly—and she fell to the ground and curled into a defensive ball. But he didn't pounce on her. He cradled his head and moaned. Her arms ached as if stabbed with pins and needles, and she pushed to her feet. The world swayed.

Again the gravelly voice. "You shouldn't have done that." A darkness there, inside as well as out, and fear tingled through her. She'd made him angry.

She didn't let herself shrink away. Haughtily, she shot back, "And what are you going to do about it? Are you going to kill me?"

His head leaned back and again he roared with hoarse laughter. "Hardly, my dear. I have waited for you for a hundred years."

Her heartbeat pounded in her ears. "What do you want from me?"

"Not yet, my dear. As they say in books, in time, all will be revealed."

"I'm not doing anything for you," she spit out.

"Oh, but you will. And you'll do so willingly. It's quite a shame your parents died in the fire. They would have been the perfect leverage."

How dare he speak of my parents that way! Fury overwhelmed her fear. Maddie ran at him again, her foot placed for a well-aimed kick. She hoped his anatomy was enough like a man's for it to count.

He twisted and her toe bounced off his thigh. His arm snaked out, grabbed her by the hair, and yanked her off the ground once more.

She screamed, this time in agony. Every hair in her head felt like it was ripping out at the roots. Maddie screamed for her grandma, she screamed for her mom and dad, she even screamed for Dougal, then as suddenly as the pain began, it stopped. The forest whirled past her, then she slammed into the ground.

A thundering noise echoed through the clearing, louder even than her pulse in her ears. She rolled over and sat up, crawling away backward. Not one creature, but two. Fists flew as the gray gryphon turned the black gryphon into a punching bag. Claws flashed in the moonlight. They spun together, then fell apart.

The black gryphon held his chest and backed away. "Who are you?"

A snarl filled the pause. "I'm Alasdair, protector of mankind. Who are you?"

"I am Doran, your worst nightmare."

They circled each other like fighting predators. "What do you want with her?" Alasdair, the gray gryphon, bared both fangs and claws.

"That is none of your concern."

"I fear that it is."

Darkness fell harder, as if clouds hid the moon or a dragon ate it, and Maddie saw only shadowy movements. Fists connected and it sounded as if thunder rocked the sky. They slammed each other on the ground and the earth shook. She wobbled and struggled to maintain her balance. A panicky voice in her head told her to run, but her feet were rooted to the spot.

The pounding ended. More terrified than ever, Maddie strained her eyes, but saw nothing. A distinct whooshing sound, like bird wings fluttering, echoed around her. Moonlight suddenly flooded the clearing. A dark figure flew straight toward her and loomed ever closer. She shrieked and wrapped her arms around her head, then shrieked again when strong arms grasped her around the waist and hauled her into the night sky. Massive wings beat the air like a heavy drum. She struggled against her captor, then in the moonlight she saw his gray fur. Alasdair, the one who had rescued her from the car crash. She wrapped her arms around him and held on.

His arms tightened in return. His deep voice sounded strained. "Hold on."

Maddie had no intention of doing otherwise. Her head wanted to droop, and with one hand he cradled her neck in place.

Deep within the woods surrounding Grandma's property, Alasdair landed. For only a moment he stood and panted, deep breaths heaving his chest. Then he grabbed her hand and dragged her between the trees at a trot. An eerie fog hovered over the lake's surface. Crickets and cicadas rasped loudly as Alasdair found and drew her along a well-formed trail.

Roots and rocks poked from the ground and Maddie stumbled over them. The terror wouldn't leave. It seemed to have poured itself into her bones like rivers of ice, and she couldn't stop shivering. Her breathing grew sporadic and labored. *Not an asthma attack. Not now.* Gasping for air, she tugged on Alasdair's furry hand, but he just kept moving. How was she to get his attention? "Alasdair?" she squeaked.

He glanced back. "Madelyn, we must keep moving. He's coming."

In between ragged breaths, she managed to say, "I can't breathe."

If a creature with the face of an animal could express worry, then Alasdair did, his brows drawing together. "What must I do?"

"I need my inhaler or a bag. I think I'm having an asthma attack." Each word needed its own breath, and the need for air screamed through her, as if she fought under water.

Alasdair glanced around at the trees, as if unsure what to do. "Where is this inhaler?"

"Back... at... my... house." She didn't know its location— she didn't know where they were—but from his furrowed brow she assumed home was too far away.

He became agitated, stalking around her and growling. His claws pawed the hard earth; his hands waved wildly. Maddie picked up her shirttail and attempted to form a sack to breathe into but it didn't work.

They were going to die; it was as simple as that. They were supposed to be hiding from the dark one, but with all the noise Alasdair was making, not to mention her own attempts to breathe, they wouldn't remain hidden for long. Then breathing would be the least of her worries.

A howl rose then faded in the distance. Maddie cringed at the fierce sound. It was him—Doran. He was coming for her. She would die one way or the other, either because she couldn't breathe or because the dark one would rip her apart. Because she'd never help him, never.

Chase pawed the ground while Maddie wheezed. How had everything gone so wrong?

He had been in his room with his dad, discussing their family's absurd history, when the change began. Instinctively, he'd sensed Maddie's danger. Dad had attempted to dissuade him from leaving, assuring him the feeling would pass, but he was wrong. The intensity of the blood pounding in his head, the fear that coursed through his new form, was not his own. Chase had opened the window and flown out into the night sky, leaving Dad stammering behind him.

When he'd come across the black figure chasing Maddie, instinct had taken over and Chase had attacked. The dark one hadn't given up and Chase had known he was losing. Maddie's feelings of fear had interfered with his ability to protect her.

To keep her safe, Chase had abandoned the battle and carried her deep into the woods. And now when they were almost free, she was having an asthma attack!

Think, Chase! Think! This new form must know something you don't.

Somewhere in the forest, an angry, wounded beast howled. It caught him off guard. His body jerked as Maddie's heart rate accelerated, inside her chest and echoing in his. Her panic pounded through him like a runaway locomotive. He had to gain control soon or Doran would find them. It would help if he could calm Maddie. But how?

Kneeling before her, he pulled her face toward him with a gentle claw. She leaned back and tried to turn away. "Madelyn, look at me."

She did, her lip trembling.

"You must concentrate. You're not having an asthma attack; you're having a panic attack." At least he hoped she was, because a panic attack would be easier to resolve. "I will not allow you to be harmed, but you must trust me."

Her eyes focused. The first raw edge of their shared terror eased. Maddie coughed and her labored breathing began to steady.

Branches snapped. Chase whipped his head around. Off in the distance but approaching fast, limbs sailed through the air like a giant slapped them.

"Madelyn, we have to hide. I'm going to carry you. Do you understand?"

Her color started to return to normal—strange, how he could see her face so well in the night—and his worry calmed. She made no verbal reply but he sensed her acceptance, although she was still scared.

Chase scooped her into his arms and took flight with a single powerful pump of his wings. It was harder to maneuver in the dense forest, but it provided the cover they needed. He flew around trees and through hanging branches, his arms folded around her like a shield. His eyes narrowed like the eyes of a cat. There, against the hillside and above the tree line, a jagged dark triangle between two rock walls. He circled through the air, swooped low, landed, and carried her inside the cave. Past the entrance it opened enough to stretch out his wings. Gently he laid her on a rock shelf, walked back to the entrance, and strained his ears. No noise, no movement in the treetops. Nothing. Turning, he bumped into Maddie.

She tiptoed and peered over his shoulder. "Did we lose him?"

"Madelyn, you must not take such risks."

"What risk? You're standing in front of me."

"You have too much faith in me." He settled a hand in the small of her back and ushered her deeper into the cave.

Faint footfalls echoed as she followed his guidance. She whispered, "You didn't answer me. Do you think we lost him?"

Chase ignored her question and explored the depths of the cave. The full moon shone brilliantly through a chimney above them, where the two slabs of stone separated. It provided light and air, but not an exit; flying, he'd never fit through there, especially not carrying Maddie.

Using his increased visual abilities, as well as his increased hearing, he searched their sanctuary. He combed the back wall, searching for another exit, and sighed heavily. No other way out. If Doran found them, they'd be sitting ducks.

Maddie grabbed his arm. A shock flashed up into his chest as if a live wire held him. Tiny hairs stood on end and he shivered. The electrical feeling was more pronounced as a gryphon than as a human.

She jerked her hand back, staring at him with wide eyes. Hesitantly, she reached forward again and ran her fingertips across his bicep, stroking his soft fur. The electrical charge reverberated through them both. The more it happened, the more normal it felt.

"What causes that?" she asked, looking at him with genuine interest.

"I don't know." Her touch was driving him to distraction. He slid away from her hand and returned to the entrance, straining to hear through all the night sounds, a hooting owl, rasping crickets, and praying she wouldn't remember having a similar feeling with a boy named Chase. He'd called himself Alasdair; for some reason the name had just popped into his head. But with that shock, she had all the evidence she needed to figure out his real identity.

Besides, they weren't yet safe. How obvious was the cave entrance? Would Doran look on the ground level or would he stick to the sky? Could he sniff them out through the chimney's vent? Did the black gryphon have the same sensory abilities?

Doran seemed older, more experienced, and comfortable in his skin. If that was the case, he probably knew his abilities and limitations better than Chase.

He lifted his hand to run it through his long hair before he realized it wasn't there. He hoped his hair-combing habit didn't give him away further. He wasn't prepared to tell Maddie who he really was and accept his freak status. Not yet.

In the pool of moonlight on the cave floor, Maddie swayed and tittered. Chase rushed to her side as her legs crumpled. He caught her in midair and swung her into his arms. Her slight frame seemed to weigh nothing. Against the cave's back wall, he sank to the damp rock floor. He found a comfortable position, wrapped his arms around her, and laid her head against his chest.

Her hair smelled like honeysuckle and he stroked the soft locks, careful not to poke her with his claws. Soft snores reached his hearing. Maddie's slow steady heartbeat echoed in his head and ribcage.

If her touch had been distracting before, with such nearness it was overwhelming and exhilarating. It was like their first kiss. He wanted to envelope her whole body and never release her. *Whoa, boy.* Slow deep breaths helped, and he tried to calm his raging pulse.

Was this the same way Cian Conn had felt for Arin? Dad claimed Cian had risked his life to help Arin find her sister. And although it had never been specifically said, Chase knew Cian had done it all for love. Otherwise, why would he? Cian had to have fallen for the helpless, beautiful girl at first glance.

As he stared at Maddie, stroking strands of hair from her face, he could understand Cian's feelings. There was nothing he would not do for Maddie, and he'd known her for, what, a week?

She stirred in her sleep. He patted her head and smoothed her hair. "Shh... little one, you are protected," he said, holding her tighter as he drifted off to sleep himself.

"Leave them be," Serena hissed.

Dougal yearned to pound his fists against the cave, or better yet, against that meddling boy. He'd run back to Serena in her bolt hole, more than a mile from where he'd lost Maddie and Alasdair, and now he wondered why he had. "No! She is mine!" The words twisted in his heart. *She should be.*

"It would appear as if history repeats itself," she crooned.

"Serena, I'll warn you only once. Shut up."

She slithered toward him, rubbing her body against his. "We are the lassst. Why will you not give in to me? Together we could..."

Disgusted, he flung her aside. "Together we can do nothing! You do not want me. You only want what I can give you. Do you think I am foolish? I know why you have waited with me these last hundred years."

Scowling, Serena pushed herself up. She might resemble the mother of all monsters, but she was hardly the mothering type, and the murderous ice in her eyes made him pause. "Why do you not enlighten me as to my designs, then, since you know them so well."

"You wish to gain revenge on Cian."

She hissed and flashed her claws. "You know nothing!"

"Oh, but I do. You fell in love with Cian, but he cast you aside because of your black heart, choosing Arin instead. So to make him regret his decision, you pledged yourself, your loyalty, your body, your very soul to Cahal. The only way for your beauty to return is for the tower to be reopened and Cahal to be freed, and for him to love you in return." Dougal smiled. "I would like to meet the druid who cursed you."

She bared her fangs and hissed. But Dougal ignored her tantrum. He had bigger questions. "Were you able to insert memories into Maddie's mind? Does she believe she is to help us?"

"You made me stop the process too soon." She didn't sound disappointed.

He rammed his fist into the cave's rock wall. A shard flew between them and rattled off into silence. "And now you want me to let *them* grow closer."

Serena rose upon her tail and slithered to his side. She ran a claw along the side of his face. "I do, because asss I said before, once she cares about him, she will do *anything* to sssave him."

18

A painful crick ached in Maddie's neck. She tried to readjust her position, but something held her in place. Soft fur tickled her nose. Briefly she snuggled closer, but the pain in her neck and shoulders intensified. She wiggled free, stood, stretched her arms above her head, and worked her sore muscles.

Darkness still blanketed most of the cave. The last rays of moonlight filtered through the vent overhead. Eyes adjusted, she could just make out Alasdair. Even as big and powerful as he was, he looked harmless and peaceful sitting upright against the wall, his arms still positioned in a circle as if they held her.

A strange energy surrounded him, calling to her. She squatted. Heat flushed her face. They had spent the night together and she hadn't been terrified. She'd slept in his arms unafraid.

Light in their hiding place brightened as dawn approached. Grandma would be frantic with worry. Maddie groaned aloud as she remembered her plans with Chase. She needed to get home. What would she say if she was late? *Sorry, but I spent the night in a cave with a furry gray gryphon?*

Maddie bent over, grabbed Alasdair by the shoulders, and shook. "Wake up!"

His eyes popped open. Before she could blink, he jumped, whirled through the air, and threw her to the hard earth. She sucked in a swift breath as the wind was knocked from her.

"Why did you do that?" she gasped.

His lion-shaped face grimaced. "It was a thoughtless action." His deep voice sounded gruff, as if he was angry with himself. He crouched beside her. "Are you all right?"

"I'm not sure. You may have broken a rib." She felt her ribs, but nothing hurt worse than bruises. She started to rise.

But he pushed her down with a gentle touch. "You mustn't move."

She ducked beneath his arm and stood anyway. "Alasdair, I have to go home."

"What? B-but you may be injured. We mustn't move too quickly. Perhaps we should—"

She interrupted. "Look, I have... well, I have a date and I don't want to miss it."

"A date?" He sounded displeased.

So she tried to explain. "Yes. A boy from school is taking me to church and he'll be coming by to pick me up any minute now. Plus my grandma is sure to be worried sick."

"Who is taking you to church?"

Did she detect jealousy in his tone? Could a flying beast be jealous? She hedged. "I don't think you know him."

"Tell me," he said, grabbing her chin and forcing her to look at him.

Maddie stared into his eyes. His nostrils flared and his eyes narrowed. *Yup, he was jealous.* "His name is Chase."

"*Chase,*" he repeated, drawing out the name.

"Yeah, Chase. We go to school together. He's expecting me to be home this morning, not buried in a cave with a— well, whatever you are. He's going to think I'm crazy when I tell him what happened to me last night."

Alasdair clenched her shoulders. "You mustn't tell him."

"B-but—"

"You must not tell him. Promise me."

"But why?"

"Promise me!" he said through clenched teeth.

She shook his hands off. "All right, all right, I promise. He wouldn't believe me anyway. Now will you take me home?"

He nodded and swooped her into his arms.

"You don't have to carry me yet."

"Maybe I want to," came his gruff reply.

Alasdair stepped from the cave, his wings flared and flapped down, and they took flight. Maddie held tight, burying her face against the fur at the nape of his neck. The air rushed past her like a small storm. Strange, how safe she felt in his arms.

They arrived at the edge of the woods and he backstroked down. He'd done the same the time he saved her from the swerving car. He seemed to always be protecting her.

They landed like a feather. Alasdair placed her upon the solid ground, but she didn't move away. They stood a hair's breadth apart. It felt colder than it had in the cave. The morning air wafted around their bodies and their breaths came in white wisps. She waited for him to speak, but he remained quiet. Finally she said, "Thank you."

He nodded.

"Will I see you again?"

He lowered his gaze.

Something unhappy stabbed at her heart. She twisted a strand of hair around her finger. "No pressure, of course. It's just that— well, quite frankly I don't have that many friends and I could use all I can get."

Again he didn't respond.

"Okay." She drew a deep, shuddering breath. "I guess I'll go."

Maddie wanted him to say something, anything. Would he be there if Doran returned? Would he continue to watch over her? But he stood like a statue, unmoving and not speaking. She gave up, turned, and walked away, and her footsteps squeaking in the wet grass sounded like the shards of her heart pattering down around her.

A tear dislodged from his eye as Maddie turned her back. He hated disappointing her that way. But extreme agony wracked his body. He had stayed in his gryphon form for too long. The threat to Maddie had come and gone and the urge to turn human nearly overwhelmed him. And he just couldn't face her learning the truth, not yet. Not after Mom's reaction.

Flying toward home, he rehashed the morning's events. Something drew them together. For no matter what form he took, the desire to protect Maddie seemed ingrained in his soul.

It was as natural as breathing and he was powerless to stop.

Chase reached his bedroom window, flipped his wings along his back, and slid inside. Immediately he transformed. The relief left him shaking. Weak, he fell onto the floor and gasped in shock as a blanket fluttered through the air and covered him. Before he could thank his father—

"Where were you all night? What happened? Are you okay?"

"Dad, please. I'm very tired. Give me a moment and I'll tell you everything." *Well, not everything, but at least what you need to know.*

Resting took a while, plus some biscuit sandwiches stuffed with bacon. After Chase regained his strength, he relayed the events. Dad listened with rapt attention. When he'd finished, Dad pointed to the pile of books littering Chase's bed.

"What is it? More information on the legend?"

"Kinda, yeah." Dad grimaced, as if his thoughts tasted sour.

"Well, what do they say?"

"I haven't read them all. But look at this."

He handed Chase the top journal, open halfway. Beneath the sketch of a gryphon, someone had scrawled a single word. His pulse thumped madly in his ears as he spoke the word aloud. *"Doran."*

Maddie had waited on the front porch, her heart thumping strangely, until Alasdair flew off into the morning sky. For a moment he had hovered, a beast with agility and grace. The first morning sunlight flashed off his damp feathers, then he pumped his wings down, gained altitude, and vanished over the treetops. She'd wanted to stand there and stare, remembering that reflection from his feathers, like sunlight on window glass. But too much time had passed since she'd left home.

She eased the front door open and slid into the hallway. The house was silent, eerie and strange, as if it were empty, abandoned. No pots or pans slammed on counters in the kitchen. No water ran and jarred the ancient copper pipes.

Two steps took her into the living room. Her lips tilted in a smile. Grandma Draoi lay on the couch bundled in a cover, just as she'd left her. Maddie bent and kissed her forehead.

Grandma Draoi stirred and blinked. "Good morning, dear."

She stretched and grimaced. "Did I sleep on the couch all night?" Maddie hesitated—*what to say?*—and Grandma continued. "I guess it doesn't matter. Help me up from here and we'll get ready for church. Unless I've got the wrong day..."

Maddie shook her head, pulled her gently upright, and Grandma shuffled toward her room. She released a pent-up breath and ran to her own. Dresses flew from her closet and onto the bed as she sought the right one. They'd found so many great outfits in the attic chests... then she'd had no choices, now she had too many. Smooth, silky fabric stroked her hand and she tugged a green dress from the rack. She held it before her and surveyed the effect in the mirror. The dress had no straps and wasn't weather appropriate, but it made her jade eyes sparkle. Maybe if she threw on a sweater? Yeah, that would work.

"What do you want for breakfast?" Grandma Draoi's voice drifted up the stairs.

Maddie leaned over the top railing and yelled, "Toast is fine." She headed back to her room, but stopped. "Oh, and Grandma?"

"Yes?"

"Can you call your friend and tell her we won't need a ride this morning? Chase is picking us up."

No reply, just an unneeded pot banging back on the shelf. Maybe Grandma didn't care for the idea. The clock chimed nine, and she rushed to her room and gathered her morning supplies and her clothes. She would ask about the trip to church after a shower. She couldn't detect any smell on her skin from sleeping with a furry creature, but if someone at church was allergic, it could be awkward.

Dressed and downstairs, Maddie asked, "Are you okay with Chase taking us?"

Grandma plopped into the opposite chair and brought a piece of toast coated in strawberry jam to her lips. She chewed, causing Maddie's stomach to knot. Just when she thought she would burst, Grandma nodded. "I don't mind riding with your beau, but that truck of his is awful small, and high. I'm not sure I can get in the cab. Maybe you should just go on without me."

"No, I didn't—"

"Nay, it's no problem. I'm a little tired today anyway. I think

I stayed up too late watching movies. I keep telling myself I won't do it on Saturday night, then I turn around and forget how old I am and I do it anyway."

"You're not old."

"Ah, don't play that game with me, sweetie. I know I'm old and I don't consider that a problem. I've learned a lot in my lifetime and one of the things I've learned is that when you've got to rest, you've got to rest. I'll catch the service on the radio."

Maddie didn't argue, sure that Grandma would ask her to stay if she really wanted her to. Besides, she couldn't say she minded sitting alone with Chase in his truck again, and she chewed toast to hide her grin.

Chase dressed for the morning church service while his father argued against it. "You can't go."

"But I have to go," said Chase.

"Why?"

"Because she's expecting me! She doesn't know I was with her all night and if I don't show up this morning, it's going to look suspicious."

"But Chase, you need to rest. There are black circles under your eyes."

"It doesn't matter."

Dad's voice rose an octave. "How can you say it doesn't matter? This is your life!"

"That's right. It is. And my life is to protect Maddie and to love her."

"You can't know that already," Dad said, his voice breathless.

"Yeah, I can. I understand Cian Conn's feeling for Arin. She was in his blood. Life meant nothing without her. He was born to protect her, to love her."

"But..."

He gazed into his father's eyes. "No, Dad, listen. I know you're worried about me, but I know what I'm doing. I'm not giving up my life; I'm gaining a happier, fuller one."

"But you're just a child!"

"It's true I have a lot to learn. But one thing I know is that I love Maddie Clevenger and there's nothing I won't sacrifice for her."

Finally Dad relented, but made Chase promise they would discuss more family history after church. Headed down the highway, the old truck rattling around him, he found it hard to believe he'd just left Maddie two short hours before. Okay, Alasdair left her. But he was Alasdair, only she didn't know that.

This could get complicated real fast.

Chase pulled in front of the house and honked his horn. When Maddie didn't run out, he parked then jogged to the front door and knocked, peering through the parted curtains. She grabbed her sweater and raced out to greet him, tugging it on.

"Is your grandma coming?" She looked pretty in her green sundress and taupe sweater, her auburn hair loose atop it and her eyes sparkling like emeralds. He reminded himself to breathe.

"She doesn't feel up to it."

He paused, remembering the active old woman who'd stuffed a biscuit down his throat. "Are you sure you should leave?"

Maddie gnawed on her lip and looked back at the house. "I'm sure she would have asked me to stay if she wanted me to."

Surely she knew her grandma best. He shrugged and they climbed into the truck's cab. The trip to the church was quick. He parked and assisted Maddie. His parents waited for them at the door, but he could barely see them through the crowd of strangers around the ragged lawn.

"Who are all these people?" he whispered in Maddie's ear.

"All the townsfolk of Coal Creek."

"Everyone?"

"Pretty much."

"But—"

"I'll tell you what my grandma told me, but don't go sharing it. The fact is, Coal Creek Community Church is the only church in town and anyone who is anyone attends. Whether you have a faith or not, you come to church. Some come to worship, but there are those who come to socialize and be seen."

Stephanie and Dougal passed them. He winked in their direction and Chase stepped in front of Maddie so she wouldn't see. Yeah, that made her point.

The service was interesting even if he was distracted by all the people and their oblivion to the proceedings. Didn't they know they were there to worship and not make noise?

He laid his arm behind Maddie, along the top of the pew, and forced himself to relax and pay attention.

The service riveted Maddie to the edge of the pew. The pastor explained a Biblical passage in Revelation that described a throne made of jasper and sardine stone, which he said was also called carnelian, with a rainbow top like an emerald. She couldn't visualize what he said, but just the thought kept her enthralled.

Service ended and the Donovans invited her over for lunch, but Maddie declined. She'd already been away from Grandma for too long. For some reason worry had started to gnaw at her. Going home would settle her mind.

Chase held her hand as they drove home. "What would you think if I called you later?"

"That would be nice."

He nodded.

She studied their intertwined fingers. It had only been a week since they'd met and somehow it felt like years. She still found Dougal attractive, and his flirting made her heart race ten times faster than normal, but Chase was the one. He was attractive, sweet, and considerate. He also didn't like anyone but her, which was the biggest plus of all. If Dougal hadn't taken up with Stephanie... no, Chase was it.

He parked in front of the house, cut the engine, and faced her. "I had a good weekend."

She leaned forward, her hair covering her face. "Me, too."

He lifted her chin and rubbed the pad of his finger over her bottom lip. "Call if you need anything."

She gulped. He released her, jumped out, and strolled to her door. It was open before her heart went back to a normal rhythm.

He leaned against the truck, his arms crossed over his muscular chest, ankles crossed, until she entered and waved at him through the curtains. She stayed put, her nose pressed to the glass like a loyal puppy until his tail lights disappeared.

Her back to the door, she slid to the floor and sighed. Her

legs felt like jelly. *Wonder when you get used to attention.* She hoped it never happened.

She pushed herself up and strolled into the living room. The lights were out. She flicked on the switch. Grandma Draoi again lay on the couch. But something wasn't right. Her breathing was shallow, her skin pale.

Pulse quickening, Maddie yelled, "Grandma Draoi! Grandma Draoi!"

But she didn't respond.

Maddie grew frantic. "Answer me, please!" She dropped to her knees. "Oh, no. She's not waking up. No. No. This can't be happening. No!"

She stood, tripped, and stumbled into the hallway, grabbing the phone and dialing 911.

"911 operator, how may I help you?"

"I need help."

"Slow down, miss. Tell me what happened."

Maddie tried to be calm and rational, to give clear directions, but it was impossible. The operator gave up and agreed to send the paramedics.

The phone died in her hands and she hung it on the old dial phone's hook. Frantic and shaking, she paced. *Wasn't the operator supposed to talk me through CPR or something?*

The lady probably thought she was too crazy to administer it. She was probably right.

Oh, why had she left? Tears slipped from her eyes and ran along her cheeks. Grandma Draoi couldn't die; she just couldn't. Maddie had no one else.

Back and forth she paced the length of the room. Each pass she stopped and made sure her grandma still breathed.

Sirens wailed as the ambulance shuddered to a halt before the house.

After another quick glance at Grandma, Maddie ran to the front door and jerked it open. She pointed the paramedics in the right direction. Outside, the emergency lights mesmerized her...

Fire trucks with flashing lights lit up her driveway. Neighbors filed along the sidewalk and gawked. Gurneys rolled onto the pavement. Paramedics shook their heads...

Maddie jumped when a paramedic touched her arm.

"She has a pulse but it is very faint. We're taking her to the county hospital. You can follow us."

"No, I can't. I don't have a car."

The paramedics settled her in the cab's passenger seat. The driver talked nonstop, asking questions and trying to get a response, but she didn't feel like speaking.

It was all her fault. She brought death to everyone around her.

Church had ended, and Dougal was settled next to Stephanie and her entourage at the diner. Stephanie twittered on and on about what people had worn to the service and he looked away.

He'd lost Alasdair and Maddie in the woods. Sure, he could have kept chasing them, but by then he'd been bored with the entire event. There were other ways to get to Maddie. He'd flown back to the lair and fought with Serena, then made his way to Maddie's grandma's house. While he'd waited and watched, he'd wondered about that Alasdair. Serena had hinted that another gryphon, an Ancient One, still survived, but the grey he'd fought felt like a pup, strong but green. Where'd he come from?

Then Serena had materialized. She rarely left the lair, so why had she now? Questions, nothing but questions.

She had slunk inside the house, looking both ways as if searching for him. He made sure she was inside, then he'd lowered himself to the window and peered in. Serena had leaned over Draoi and spoke, but Dougal couldn't hear what was said. Sometime later, Serena had left, a chilling smile on her face.

Dougal had stuck around until Maddie arrived home. He'd wanted to grab her before she went inside the house, but decided to wait. It wasn't long before Chase had showed. He'd followed discreetly until he determined they were headed to church. He'd rushed to call Stephanie and invite himself. Of course she'd been more than accepting and he'd shown up at her door fifteen minutes later, ready to escort her.

And of course after the service Stephanie had clung possessively to his arm. He'd found himself carted off to the diner, trying to devise an excuse to leave.

An ambulance sped past, lights blazing and sirens wailing. Heads turned.

"Wonder who that is?" said Stephanie, sipping her drink.

160

Dougal sensed Maddie. She was in that ambulance. He shoved Stephanie's side and she slid from the booth with a frown. "Why are you pushing me?"

"I need to get out."

"But what about our food?"

"You can eat it. I have something I have to do."

He wanted to transform and fly, but he couldn't leave his vehicle at the diner and nor could he afford that kind of attention, not yet. He climbed into his SUV and followed the ambulance at a safe distance, arriving at the hospital not long after Maddie. Now he needed to find her and make sure she was okay. The *eochair* could not come to harm.

19

Maddie entered the hospital and the paramedics spoke behind their hands, doubtless informing the doctor about her odd behavior. Orderlies wheeled her grandma away. A nurse directed her to a nearby room and ordered her to wait.

Settled in a navy blue plastic seat, Maddie palmed her chin and stared out the window. Guilt hammered through her. But before she could sink into its ocean, a woman in professional garb settled in the chair beside her. She crossed her long slim legs, swinging her high-heeled pumps through the air. "Miss, may I speak with you?"

"Yes."

"The lady they brought in, she's your grandmother?"

"Great-grandmother, yes."

"We have some paperwork we need to fill out. Do you think you could help with that?"

"Yes."

"Very well, let's begin. Her name?"

"Draoi Casey-Brennan."

A smile touched the woman's face. If her makeup was any more perfect, her face would crack. "Ah, Mrs. Casey-Brennan. I believe she may have visited us in the past. I'll just pull her chart for the information. Before I go, though, maybe you can shed some light on what happened this evening."

"Well." Maddie shifted uncomfortably. The guilt rose higher.

"Last night I was out with a friend and I came home and Grandma Draoi was lying on the couch, but she got up and ate breakfast and acted fine, but she said she was too tired to go to church. So I left and when I came back, she was back on the couch and unresponsive."

"I see." The lady flashed her a disapproving glare.

Ignoring the look, Maddie asked, "What do you think is wrong with her?"

"We won't know until we run some tests."

Her heart broke into so many pieces, they could probably hear them falling all over the massive building. "Please don't let anything happen to her. She's all I have left."

The lady patted her hand and offered reassuring words before leaving Maddie alone.

After the family dinner, Chase raced to his room and pulled out his cell phone. He dialed Maddie's number, but there was no answer. He frowned, puzzled. They had made plans to talk on the phone, so why wasn't she answering?

His chest tightened and his throat constricted. Something wasn't right. But he didn't feel like he was changing. No, the feeling was different.

Downstairs, he grabbed his truck keys and raced outside. He would call his parents after he got there.

He pulled up in front of Maddie's house and honked his horn, expecting to see her bubbly self bound down the steps any minute, but he saw nothing. Long seconds passed. She didn't appear.

Chase left the warmth of the truck, walked to the front door, and knocked. Minutes ticked by and he pressed the doorbell. When there was still no answer, he strolled around the house and peered in the windows. If Mrs. Casey-Brennan had any close neighbors, he might have been confused with a peeping Tom. But even with all his nosiness, he found nothing. The house remained deathly quiet.

Back in the truck, he dug out his cell phone and called home. His pulse echoed in his ears and his breaths were shallow. Dad answered on the first ring.

"Chase, are you okay?"

"Yeah, I'm fine. Has Maddie called?"

"No. And where are you? We went up to your room and you were gone."

"I called her and she didn't answer. Now no one is home and I'm afraid something is wrong."

"Why don't you come back here and we'll try to find her."

The will to fight drained out of him. Help; that was exactly what he needed. He murmured, "Okay."

The undercarriage of the truck bounced along the rutted driveway. On the highway, he attempted to focus on Maddie's feelings, but he got nothing.

Chase entered his house to find Dad on the phone. He lifted his finger and Chase waited.

"Okay. Yeah. Thanks for returning my call." He talked a moment more then hung up, his brows drawn together.

"What is it?" Chase asked, fear knotting his gut.

"Now, don't get upset, but Maddie's at the hospital."

Instant nominee for the most useless advice in history. Chase fell back into a chair. "At the hospital? But how? Why? What happened?"

"I don't know. All I know is that 911 received an emergency call for an ambulance at the home of Draoi Casey-Brennan."

"That's it?"

"That's all the police department knows. The only way to know more is to go to the hospital. Let me get ready, and we'll go together."

"You're going with me?"

"Yes." And Dad ran up the stairs without looking back.

They traveled in the family car. Sick to his stomach, Chase was in no condition to drive. He clenched his fists in his lap while random thoughts about what might have happened rushed through his mind. Who had called the ambulance, Maddie or Draoi? Was the reason he couldn't sense Maddie because she was injured? The unanswered questions were driving him crazy.

By the time they arrived at the hospital, Chase was ready to crawl out of his skin. They strode into the emergency room and he grabbed the first person he saw.

"Where is she?"

The startled nurse jumped. "Excuse me?"

Dad placed a restraining hand on his forearm. "Forgive us. We're looking for Madelyn Clevenger."

"One moment, please." The nurse clicked a mouse beside the terminal. "Sorry, we've no one by that name."

Chase slammed his palms on the counter. The nurse jumped again. "We know she's here! She arrived in an ambulance. Now, where is she?"

"Excuse me, sir, but as I said, there is no patient listed by that name."

Dad glared at him and Chase fisted his hands to his sides. "Try Draoi Casey-Brennan."

The nurse tapped more keys. "Yes, there is a Mrs. Casey-Brennan in ICU."

"Where is that?"

She gave directions. Chase practically ran to reach the elevator, then stood in front of the closed doors and tapped his foot. "What is taking this thing so long? I could have run up the stairs quicker than this!"

Dad stopped beside him. "You need to calm down."

"How can I? She must be terrified. Her grandma is all she has. There *is* no one else."

"Did she tell you this?" A vertical crease wrinkled between Dad's eyebrows.

Chase paused, thinking back. "Not really. She doesn't say that much about her family. I know what she said at dinner, that her parents died and that she lives with her grandma. And she never mentions anyone else."

Dad shook his head. "But how do you know for sure?"

"I just do." There was no other answer. Chase knew in the core of his being, but where the information came from—*well, it could be osmosis.*

"You're linked to her," Dad whispered, his shoulders drooping.

Chase blinked. "What?"

"Are you feeling her feelings, sharing her dreams?"

He couldn't deny the way their hearts had beaten in sync. "Yes," he admitted.

"The journal explained a similar link between Cian and Arin."

"How can something like that even be possible?" He threw out his hands. "Wasn't Cian a beast all the time? That's kind of gross."

Dad shoved his hands in his pockets. "While you were gallivanting around with Maddie last night—" Chase cocked a brow, daring him to continue the thought "—I found an interesting passage in the family journals. It seems that when a gryphon of either color, black or gray, finds his one true love and that love is reciprocated, then he's able to take either form at will."

It felt like a light bulb lit up inside him. "Are you saying that if a gryphon loves and is loved by a human, then he can change to a human or gryphon and back again?"

"Exactly."

"Kind of like that old saying, 'love conquers all.'"

"You could say that in this case, love makes it possible for the couple to be together."

"So you're saying I was right?" asked Chase.

"Yes, and I'm beginning to see why you feel the way you do. Without her, you can never be permanently human again."

20

There were two hundred floor tiles, fifteen wall cracks, twenty-five chairs, three small tables, two soda machines, and no people in the ICU waiting room of Coal Creek Community Hospital. Maddie knew; she'd counted them all.

No doctors or nurses visited with an update and she grew afraid to leave, even to go to the restroom. She just knew the messenger would come in her absence. Hours passed and she felt like she was going stir crazy.

Hard, cracked plastic formed her body to itself and she shifted, again and again, looking for comfort. Tears filled her eyes and she swiped the drops away.

Looking up, she gasped. There he stood, staring at her. Gone was his usual attire. Gone was his attitude of superiority. Dougal sauntered to her side, lifted her hand to his lips, and kissed her palm. "I came as soon as I heard. How are you holding up?"

Maddie didn't want to answer. She wanted to shun him. How could he waltz in and ask her questions when there was so much unexplained between them? For example, how he pretended to like her but dated Stephanie? Or their unexpected after-school meeting in the woods, his odd words and subsequent disappearance?

But in her loneliness, her defenses melted. She needed someone. She didn't want to depend on him, but he was a familiar face, and he was there. The dam burst and she sobbed uncontrollably. He pulled her into his arms, stroked her back, and murmured soothing words. She relaxed against him. He placed his fingers under her chin and she held her breath as his head began a slow descent.

The elevator doors shrieked open. Chase dropped his jaw and wondered if he'd ever be able to pick it up again.

Maddie and Dougal stood in the middle of the waiting room. His arms were wrapped around her trembling frame and their lips were on the verge of touching. She jerked her head around and her fixed stare meshed with his. Her red-rimmed eyes widened and glowed a brighter shade of jade. Tears dripped off her chin and splashed on the cold tiled floor.

She leapt from Dougal's arms and rushed to Chase, throwing herself into his protection. She buried her face against his neck and Chase glared over her shoulder, sending a heated stare at Dougal.

Hands fisted at his sides, Dougal glared back. His eyes burned a darker bronze, glowed like flares in the ugly fluorescent lighting, and he twisted his lips into a snarl.

Side by side with the fury, a blaze of victory burned in Chase's soul. Dougal had tried to kiss Maddie, but the attempt had been futile. Even if he had succeeded in placing his lips to hers, it would have meant nothing. When push came to shove, she had run to him. He'd won.

Ignoring Dougal, Chase smoothed Maddie's long auburn hair. "Are you okay?"

Choked with emotion, she managed a nod.

"Take your time." He led her to a set of chairs, found one that looked like a couch, and sat with her, pinning her body to his side. Her warmth soaked into him, soothing the fretting beast within.

Dougal remained where she'd left him. He looked different. Instead of his usual black, he wore jeans and a navy blue T-shirt. His coal black hair seemed to have grown longer overnight and now the ends graced the top of his shoulders. But his glare hadn't changed, and if looks could pin a person to the wall, Chase would have been skewered.

In his arms, Maddie seemed exhausted and overwhelmed.

Again and again he stroked her hair, and her breathing slowed to match.

"Ch-Chase." She laid her head against his shoulder. "Th-thank you for coming."

He grabbed her hands and squeezed. "Where else would I be?" She didn't reply. When he realized she wouldn't, he continued. "I would have been here sooner, but I didn't know you were here. What happened?"

Maddie told him about finding Grandma Draoi unresponsive and how she had called the ambulance.

"How is she now?"

Her hands rose in frustration. "I don't know! No one will tell me."

Dad piped in. "Perhaps I can find out."

"Would you mind?" Maddie asked.

"No, I wouldn't. I'll be right back."

He left the three of them and an awkward silence filled his absence.

"How come you're here?" Chase asked Dougal when he could stand it no longer. Would Dougal make up a lie and say Maddie invited him? Unless she said it herself, Chase would never believe it. The embrace they had shared must have been forced; he was sure of it.

Dougal shook himself, a little ripple like shaking off some distant thought. "I happened to be in the hospital and heard someone mention Maddie's name. I was afraid she was hurt so I came to check."

A distant thought. Right. One about a kiss, without a doubt. "Well, now that you know she's fine, you can leave."

"She doesn't look fine to me." Dougal crossed his arms over his chest.

He hadn't had much to begin with, but with Dougal's stubbornness, Chase's patience was wearing thin. Maddie trembled beside him. He wanted to take her into his lap and comfort her as he had done hours before, back at the cave, but Dougal's presence restrained him. How could he love her the way he ought with that black glare prickling his skin?

Without warning, Maddie burst out in an agonized wail. Dougal strode over, knelt before her, and placed his hand upon her knee. It would feel so good to break the bones in those fingers. He would start with the ring finger first, making sure to break one tiny bone at a time, then...

"Maddie," Dougal said, his voice as smooth as silk, "can I get you anything?"

"Water," she choked out.

Instinct begged Chase to do her bidding. *He* should be the one to retrieve the water, if that would make her comfortable. But worry gnawed at his gut. If he left, then it wouldn't take two seconds for Dougal to slide in and assume his place. Let Dougal get the water. He would stay glued to Maddie's hip and protect her from predators, that one in particular.

Dougal nodded. "I'll be right back." And he left.

Chase didn't waste a moment. He tugged Maddie onto his lap and kept stroking her hair. He whispered, "Why didn't you call me?"

She used the back of her hand to swipe at her tears. "I was so upset I couldn't think straight. I even confused the 911 operator. Will you forgive me?"

"You don't have to ask. There's nothing to forgive. I just wondered." Chase struggled to feel her emotions. But for some reason, he couldn't. The only one he could decipher was guilt, because it was written all over her face.

One hand played with the buttons on his shirt. "This is entirely my fault. I should have insisted she come to church with us. Or I should have stayed home with her. She didn't act like herself."

He lifted her chin and looked into her eyes, choosing his words carefully. "Maddie, none of this is your fault. Your grandma wouldn't want you to blame yourself."

Her lashes trembled. "I know, but I should've been there. She might die because I wasn't there for her." She slid from his lap and strode to the window, wrapping her arms around her body in a hug.

Well, somehow he'd blown that. And he still couldn't feel her emotions. Chase sat with his elbows on his knees and waited with her.

Finally Dad arrived. Tension lines tightened the corners of his eyes, and Chase sensed the news wasn't good.

Maddie turned from the window, but didn't speak. Her eyes begged for answers.

Dad paused beside one of the hard plastic chairs. "Maddie, sit down with me, will you?"

She obeyed and folded her hands primly in her lap. The pose should have expressed serenity, but her trembling lips proved it was an act.

"Maddie, your grandmother is in stable condition, but she's fallen into a coma."

"What?"

"They don't know what happened yet. They're still performing tests." Dad slid an arm across her shoulder and hugged her sideways.

She nodded, stood from beneath his arm, and returned to the window.

"What excuse did you give them?"

The voice startled him. Dougal whirled and glared at Serena as she slithered from the deepest shadows in the concession room.

Annoyed, he turned away and dug change from his pocket. "I'm getting Maddie water. Don't raise your eyebrow at me. This is all your doing. What did you do to Draoi?"

Serena shrugged, her movements sinuous. "Just a harmlessss herb, my love. Blocking her abilities proved difficult. She was also more resssilient to my persuading than I expected."

"Well, all that is just great, isn't it? Now you've landed the old lady in the hospital and given Chase more opportunities to keep Maddie away from me."

Her eyes hooded, like a cobra's. "What of the kissss?"

He snarked and yanked the bottle of water from the machine. "You know there was no kiss! You know he interrupted my plans. Why must you continue to make me voice my failures?"

Her shoulders rippled in a shrug. But her eyes gleamed.

Dougal fought the urge to strangle her. The feelings he had for Maddie continued to grow, despite his best efforts, and he found it hard to think straight. "Sometimes, Serena, I wonder whose side you're on. You know I must convince the girl to help us. She must be a willing participant." *And I prefer to have her help us because she loves me.*

"Aye, I know. And she will be. As I have told you before, Chase will be a great motivator. She doesn't have to love *you* for it to work."

But I want her to. "Are you sure? If we allow them to fall in love, and threatening him doesn't work, then it'll be too late."

"I know. But trust me, I'm right. I'm always right."

Dougal headed back to the waiting room. Serena had better be correct. He'd waited on his family for too long.

21

Unsurprised by Mr. Donovan's news, Maddie struggled silently with her fear of loneliness. She found a seat in the corner of the room and cried softly. The hospital minister offered words of comfort. When he left, Mr. Donovan mentioned the ICU's visiting hours, yet his presence barely registered.

She bit her lip. Would they stick her in foster care? If she went home, how would she get back to the hospital? What could she do about school? How long would it take for Grandma to recover? Where was Dougal with her water?

The last thought floated through her mind and as if by magic Dougal appeared at her side. "Sorry it took so long."

He offered no excuses and she asked for none, instead taking the bottle and guzzling the cool liquid. "Thank you."

Dougal nodded. Clearing his throat, he asked, "Is there anything else you need? A ride home to pick up clothes? Someone to retrieve your schoolwork?"

As if she'd go to school the next morning directly from the hospital. "Thank you, Dougal, but I'm fine for now."

"You'll let me know, right?" Strange, but he seemed sincere when he asked. Maybe he didn't prefer Stephanie after all.

Then again, maybe he did. Maddie swallowed more water. "Sure."

"Then I guess I'll leave. I'll call later to check on you and see how your grandma fares."

"Thanks."

Mr. Donovan had left to call home. Chase sat in the corner, rubbed his hands together, and knitted his brow.

Maybe she should explain. Chase had walked in on what must have looked like a kiss-in-the-making. Still uncertain, she rose on wobbly legs and took the seat next to Chase, laying her hands over his. "I need to say something."

He looked at her. His uncertainty matched hers, and the pain beneath his nearly drowned her.

She lowered her eyes. "Dougal's not all bad." Granted, some days he seemed it. "The other day he drove me to school and today he's been so considerate. Saying thank you was the least I could do."

A muscle twitched in Chase's jaw. "Do you like him?"

Maddie flashed a smile and shook her head. "I don't like him like that. But do you know who I do like like that?"

"No," he whispered.

"*You*," she murmured, a tad breathless. Her eyes never wavered as she leaned forward. Their lips met and a tingle, both electrical and emotional, raced through her entire body.

A door slammed and she yanked back, startled and guilty. A doctor wearing a white coat crossed his arms and tapped his foot against the tile floor. He didn't look like he was joking, either.

Heat flooded her cheeks.

The doctor dropped his arms. "You may see your grandmother, but only briefly."

Brief or long, she was ready. "Yes, of course."

"After your visit, I recommend you go home and rest. You may see her again tomorrow."

"Will someone call me if she wakes up?" asked Maddie.

"Yes. Just make sure to leave your number at the nurses' station."

She excused herself and followed the doctor along the hallway to a set of double doors. He hit a sequence of buttons on a keypad and the doors swung inward. The smell of antiseptic assaulted her nose. Fluorescent bulbs reflected off the glossy floor tiles, threatening to blind her. Machines whirred, creating their own musical patterns.

The doctor led her down the hallway, stopped at an open door, stepped aside, and directed her onward with his outstretched arm. "You have thirty minutes."

She nodded. *Thirty minutes?* That hardly seemed enough time to pour out her soul and confess her sins.

Grandma Draoi lay on the hospital bed. Her long hair lay unfettered across her pillow. An oxygen mask covered her face and taut blue lips. She looked much older than Maddie remembered, and horribly ill.

Unbidden memories of visiting Grandma came to mind. Always they had a good time, playing in the garden, riding Gray Beauty, and canoeing on the river, then everything had changed.

The fire. Her parents had perished and Grandma Draoi had offered to take her in. Fear of hurt made her distance herself from Grandma Draoi and their closeness had dissipated. Foolishly she had believed if she didn't get too close and Grandma died, then it wouldn't hurt as bad. What a stupid lie!

She held Grandma's unresponsive hand and talked. Everything that had happened over the past week poured forth. Fresh tears flowed. Before she finished, a nurse stood at the open door and casually announced the end of her visit.

Maddie leaned over and whispered in Grandma's ear. "I don't want you to worry. I have Chase and his family to help me. And believe it or not, I think I may have made another friend. His name is Dougal."

She kissed Grandma goodbye and left the room.

From his perch on the window ledge, Dougal watched as Maddie took her grandmother's hand and began talking. Hanging branches covered him and his clawed toes gripped the concrete. His hawk-like ears listened to Maddie's speech. His pulse raced from her presence. The evil, black part of him wished to grab her by the throat and strangle her until dead. Of course then he would be forced to listen to Serena's harping. But there was the other part, the part that Cian had noticed in him, the good part, that longed to hold her, possess her. What was it about this daughter of a Casey that made his blood run hot and his soul yearn for her love? Was it because she reminded him of Merissa or was it because she could help him free his family?

She told Draoi of her adventures, beginning with his unusual arrival at school and ending with her night away. Most of the juicy details were left incomplete. He kept waiting for her description of the fight, or her take on her harrowing escape, but she kept silent about those events. Maybe she didn't want to risk frightening Draoi, even subconsciously.

Never once did she mention that she'd been hanging out with gryphons. He was a tad insulted. Then it happened—she told Draoi not to worry, she had friends. She gave his name.

A friend. She considered him a friend.

Shock gripped him. His claws went lax, releasing their hold on the ledge, and he fell backward, smashing his head into a tree limb on the way down and landing on another. Dazed, Dougal lay awkwardly along the limb, listening to its strained creaking. No one had ever called him friend. Even in his own village, he'd been despised and feared.

He remained in beast form. When his shock faded, he took to the sky and landed silently on the hospital roof. There, by the emergency stairwell; standing there, he could see the entire parking lot. He held no desire to return to the lair where Serena was sure to ask too many intrusive questions. He would need to steady himself against her probing. His current thoughts he'd keep private. They were none of the witch's business.

Chase paced the waiting room. Although she'd absent-mindedly excused herself, Maddie had followed the doctor without even saying goodbye, and with her gone he didn't know what to do. Didn't help that he'd spent the first five minutes of her absence rubbing his tingling lips. He'd never get used to the surge of electricity when they touched. No matter what else happened, he had to find some way of keeping Maddie in his life.

The waiting room door opened and Chase lifted his head. His parents entered, already deep in conversation.

"Where's she going to go?"

"Home, I assume," said Dad.

"But Alex, she doesn't need to be stranded out there alone."

Chase interrupted. "What if I stay with her?"

They glared at him as if he had sprouted three heads. Raising his hands defensively, he added, "Their house is huge. I'm sure there's a spare bedroom I could use. And it's not like we could offer space in our house. I mean, where would she sleep? We're packed in like sardines as it is. And like Mom said, Maddie shouldn't be alone."

Dad nodded, but Mom glanced back and forth between them and straightened to her full height. "Alex, are you really considering this? That's too big a temptation. They'll be out there by themselves!"

With a shrug, Dad clasped her hands. "They'll get up, go to school, and then come to the hospital and spend time with Maddie's grandmother. They can eat dinner with us. When they get home, they'll have homework and by then it'll be time to go to bed. I think it'll be okay."

"It's that last part I'm worried about. And, well, what about his, you know, *condition*?"

Chase couldn't wait to hear Dad's argument on that point.

Dad scratched his head and massaged his chin. "You'll just have to trust me."

Oh, yeah, *that* was convincing. Chase grimaced and went back to pacing while Dad pulled her aside. The whispers grew louder, almost heated, then fell silent. When Chase glanced back up, she relented with a reluctant nod.

Chase arrived back in the waiting room before Maddie. His books, clothes, and essentials he'd stashed behind the truck's bench seat; a basket full of food would separate them on the drive to her grandma's house. Despite the serious situation, he couldn't help feeling excited, almost giddy, and more than a little nervous. After serving as big brother to all the Donovan youngsters, responsibility didn't often faze him. But despite the nerves in his stomach, serving as Maddie's support seemed so natural, he couldn't regret his decision.

Granted, they'd arranged her life without consulting her. Hopefully she wouldn't be angry at that.

She arrived a few minutes later. Her eyes were puffy and her shoulders slumped. She reminded him of a lost puppy trying to find her way home.

Instead of talking, he wrapped her in his arms. She melted against him but didn't cry.

"How is she?" he asked against her hair.

She shrugged.

"Would you like to go home?"

She pulled back and looked at him. The misery in her eyes tugged at his heart and settled his nerves. "How?"

"If it's okay with you, my parents agreed to let me stay at your house until your grandma is well enough to return home."

"Really?" She sniffed and brushed a strand of hair from her face.

He combed it back with his fingers. "Yeah. That way I can drive you to school, the hospital, and home. That is, if you're comfortable with it?"

She lifted one shoulder. Red dotted her cheeks. "I guess so."

"I don't want to rush you, but we can go anytime you're ready."

She glanced around the empty waiting room, her nose wrinkling as if she'd seen all of the places she could stand. "I'm ready. Let's get out of here."

22

Chase pulled into the driveway and killed the engine. He drummed his fingers on the steering wheel in time with the pounding of his pulse in his ears. It sounded like a rock band on triple espressos. *What in the world was I thinking?* "Well, we're here."

"Yes, we're here."

Just act cool. You'll get through this. "Should we go inside?"

"Probably."

Might help if she'd use more than three syllables per answer. "Maddie, are you worried about me being here? Because if you want to do something different—"

She spoke over him. "No, it's not that. I like being with you. I just wish…" She paused and ran a trembling hand through her hair. "I blame myself for this whole thing."

He frowned. So much for his worries. "But you shouldn't."

Maddie didn't argue. He couldn't possibly understand, because he didn't know everything she'd done. She'd left Grandma for more than just church. Heat rushed to her cheeks as she thought about the night spent with Alasdair. To cover her embarrassment, she climbed from the truck. He did the same and grabbed his bags while Maddie carried the basket of food

179

inside.

The fire had gone out. Devoid of its earlier warmth, the entrance was cold and uninviting. Fighting an ugly sense of foreboding, she directed him upstairs to a spare bedroom and then carried the food to the kitchen.

Yummy aromas wafted to her nose and her belly growled. She unpacked the basket, found a chicken breast, pinched off a piece of the juicy meat, and popped it into her mouth. She smacked her lips as flavor struck her tongue. Pure heaven with a crispy crust. Next she ate half a flaky biscuit. She removed the gravy lid and raised the other half of the biscuit aloft.

"So this is what you've been up to." Chase leaned casually against the door facing, his arms crossed over his defined chest.

She smiled and covered her puffed jaws with both hands, one still holding the biscuit's second, doomed half. But she didn't stop chewing. Strange how the promise of a good meal made the situation lighter and calmed her guilty nerves.

"I thought you were following me and when I turned around you weren't there. I called but you never answered. Now I know why." He pointed an accusing finger at the food-laden table.

She swallowed. "I was hungry."

He laughed. "Then by all means, eat."

She offered him a biscuit. "Do you want some?"

"Yes, I believe I do. Do we need plates?"

"Sure." She put the biscuit on a paper towel and opened a nearby cabinet. The plates were on the top shelf and she tiptoed to reach them.

Chase came up behind her. His chest grazed her back as he reached over her head and grabbed the plates. She turned and was engulfed in his arms, the plates somewhere behind her head. He laid them on the counter.

Shyness overwhelmed her. "I don't know why the plates are so high up. There's no way Grandma Draoi could reach them. She's shorter than I am." *Am I babbling? I am. I have to be. Dork dork dork.*

His blue eyes lingered on her face, looking longingly at her lips. A kiss... would be as good as the biscuit. But they played a dangerous game. Alone in the house and physically attracted to one another could get them in big trouble. And suddenly Maddie knew without a shadow of a doubt that she wasn't ready to go there.

Without warning, he swooped down and stroked his lips on top of hers, taking her breath away. Whatever she'd been thinking vanished. She snaked her arms around his neck and pulled him close. Like a buoy in a storm, like a lifeboat, a lifeline, he became the only sane thing in her world.

Finally they pulled apart, breathing heavily. His hands splayed along her waistline. She played with the hair that caressed his collar, thankful that he wasn't insistent or demanding. *A dork could get used to this.*

"I've wanted to do that all day," he said.

"Hmm... it was nice."

He laughed loudly. "Nice? I was hoping for amazing, spectacular, earth-shattering..."

She pursed her lips. "Did I say nice? I meant exhilarating, titillating, passionate..."

"Hmm, I like your adjectives much better than mine."

"You do?"

"I believe I do."

He moved as if to kiss her again, but when their lips hovered mere inches apart, her stomach rumbled. Without releasing her, he pulled back. "Have you eaten anything today?"

"A little piece of chicken and half a biscuit."

"Maddie! You need to take better care of yourself."

"Um, Chase, I haven't exactly had time."

"Yeah. I guess I just don't want anything to happen to you." He ran a shaky hand through his hair.

She studied the buttons on his shirt to hide her curiosity. "Does it ever seem odd that you feel so strongly about someone you just met?"

"Sometimes."

"Me, too. I've never met anyone like you." Suddenly she felt so close to him, closer than any two near-strangers had any right to be. Words she hadn't intended to say tumbled from her. "Besides my parents, you're the only one who's ever expressed any feeling for me."

He straightened, blinking twice, three times. "Surely that's not—"

"True? Yes, it is."

"What about your grandma?"

"Yes, she loves me. But that's not what I meant." She

should be blushing from the unintended revelation. But she wasn't. Speaking with Chase, being with him, made everything all right.

"What did you mean?"

"I don't know." And suddenly the day just seemed like too much. The kitchen spun around her. She closed her eyes and her legs weakened.

Chase guided her to the table. "Come, sit, and I'll fix you a plate."

She settled in a chair and palmed her chin, letting him fuss with the food. "When I was younger, I loved to visit my grandma. She would tell me the most fascinating stories about our family and she made me feel so safe and happy. But as I grew older, she would sit and stare at me with a distant, absent look. I talked to my mom about it. I thought maybe I was dying or something and they didn't want me to know, but my mom said she thought Grandma was just sad because she was growing older."

He placed a loaded plate before her and she shot him a grateful look, picked up a chicken breast, and enjoyed a succulent bite. She smacked her lips and he laughed at her enthusiasm.

"Good, is it?"

"Yep, reminds me of my mom's." Huh. She'd never before mentioned her mother without feeling sad.

Maybe the thought showed on her face, for he froze as if afraid to respond. But Maddie found she didn't need to stop and recover any composure. Instead she took another bite, and another, and by then he'd finished fixing his own plate and sat across from her, the open containers between them and the entire kitchen smelling like a cold-chicken picnic.

"My mom was a fabulous cook and my dad never failed to tell her so. I remember this one time when she made a pineapple chicken dish. Dad ate it but he was kind of picking and choosing, and she said, 'It's not that good, is it?' And he laughed and said, 'No.' He told me later it was terrible but he was determined to eat it just to keep from hurting her feelings. Turns out after he ate the entire thing, she admitted she didn't like it much, either. He and I laughed about that for weeks."

Chase fixed a chunk of chicken between two biscuit halves and dipped it in gravy. "That reminds me of the time my mom made biscuits and Dad picked one up and it was as hard as a rock. He tried to eat it but couldn't get his teeth to bite through it. He put it on his plate, and when Mom saw it, she asked him why it was still there. He told her straight up that the biscuits were hard. She stood up, cleaned off the table, and dumped the food in the garbage. He was afraid she would never cook again."

"Obviously she did and her biscuits got better." She reached for another one.

He licked his lips, catching a trail of gravy obeying the law of gravity. "Yep, they sure did."

They shared more laughter and finished eating. Everything cleaned and put away, they retired to the living room and took a seat on the couch.

"TV or talk?" Chase asked.

She didn't hesitate. "Talk. That is, if you want to."

"Of course I want to. I'd like to hear more about your family."

Maddie studied the couch cushions. Grandma had been lying there just a few hours ago, her head resting on that very pillow. Sighing, she said, "There's not much to tell. I'm an only child. My mom was a housewife. My dad worked at a local plant and we lived close to his job in a small town about two hours away from here. Until they died."

"Do you want to talk about it?"

She'd spent hours with a therapist talking about it and nothing had changed. Why should she resurrect the incident? But then again, didn't she want to share everything with Chase? The good and the bad? And maybe he'd do more for her than any therapist.

She swallowed. "We had just come home from visiting Grandma Draoi and it was late. We said our goodnights at the top of the stairs and I went to my room. I was so exhausted from the day I didn't even change my clothes. I think I fell asleep before my head hit the pillow.

"The next thing I remember, the smoke alarms were going off. My room was all smoky and hot and I dropped to the floor and crawled to my door. I nearly grabbed the metal door knob but I remembered a fire safety class from school that said to touch the door with the back of your hand first. I did and it was blazing hot. I hadn't shut it completely the night before so I pulled it open a crack."

She twisted her hands in her lap and her throat burned from holding back tears. Telling the story always seemed too much like reliving it, like letting the horror take her over, and part of her wished she hadn't started. "The hallway was engulfed in flames. The walls looked like they were rippling. The heat was so intense I could feel my arm hairs singeing."

A tear slipped onto her cheek and she swiped it away. "My parents' door was directly in front of me. Flames licked at it from floor to ceiling but I thought I could save them."

A sad laugh refused to stay inside her. "I never made it to their door because someone grabbed me around the waist and hauled me back. Still not certain exactly what happened. One moment I was running across the hall. Next thing I knew, I was sitting on the pavement outside. Firefighters, police, paramedics were everywhere. They fought the fire for hours, but it was no use. The house was so hot they weren't able to go in until it was little more than a pile of ashes."

Maddie twisted the hem of her shirt. "Of course they investigated for over a month, but they never discovered what caused the fire. A faulty electric wire was the biggest suspect but one investigator said the fire was too hot. They couldn't find any traces of gasoline or kerosene, though, nothing like that. So I guess I'll never know for sure."

Finally she glanced up, and the compassion in his eyes was too much to bear. They'd been having a fun evening and she'd spoiled everything. *Dork.* She pushed off the couch and crossed to the window. "On second thought, I don't think I want to talk about it." She hadn't meant to be sarcastic but her tone came out that way. *Dork dork dork.*

Nothing would change what had happened. Her parents were gone and she remained.

A guilty glance over her shoulder showed Chase studying his hands as if he was at a loss for words. His expression hadn't changed, and she knew she'd ruined the evening. She shouldn't have dumped all that on him. It had been such a trying day; she had just blurted everything out without thinking.

He leaned forward and placed his elbows on his knees. "We should probably get ready for bed. It'll be time for school before we know it."

"Yeah. I'm going to call and check on my grandma first."

He went upstairs. With a hollow feeling in her stomach despite the wonderful supper, she called the hospital. No news. She hung up the phone and dragged herself up the stairs.

He met her on the landing. "Any change?"

She shook her head. "They said I can visit tomorrow after school."

"Okay."

He leaned against the door jamb. His sleeveless T-shirt highlighted his bulging biceps. She pointed toward her bedroom door. "I really should go to bed."

"Yeah." But he didn't move and his eyes followed her.

She felt their touch as she passed him. Then she closed the door and his spell was broken. Maddie laid her head back and drew in a deep breath. She wished she hadn't said anything about her parents, but at least now he knew. He knew what happened to people who got close to her.

And she wouldn't let him make that mistake. She hoped.

He hadn't commented or given advice, for which she was grateful. Curling into a ball under the covers, she tried to free her mind. How would she sleep knowing Chase lay across the hall? Probably not very well.

23

Hands clasped behind his head, Chase stared at the ceiling. Sympathy flooded him until he thought he'd drown. He'd known about Maddie's parents dying, but hearing the full tragedy and seeing the emotions flit across her features as she described her failure to rescue them broke his heart.

It was one more problem he couldn't fix. He couldn't bring her parents back or protect her from the sorrow of loss. *Growing up stinks.*

Chase rolled onto his side and punched the lumpy pillow. Tomorrow he'd make sure to grab his from home.

He stared at the paisley wallpaper. Typical old lady's house. Even though he mocked it, the house had stood the test of time. No doubt many generations had lain in this very bed, stared at these very walls, and contemplated their future. A couple years ago, he'd figured out what he wanted to do and at eighteen, he looked forward to a career in aeronautical engineering and design. He hoped to build the fastest plane known to man.

What would it be like to sit on the sidelines of an air show and witness his plane streaking across the sky? To have millions of people cheer and clap at his invention? To know that he had created something?

As he envisioned different scenarios, he remembered sitting with Maddie at the table and sharing a simple meal. It had seemed so right, so natural, to be by her side. The rush of success would mean nothing without her.

They would hole up in his design room, which in his thoughts looked an awful lot like Dad's workshop, and she would lean over his shoulder and study his blueprints, making knowledgeable suggestions. They would sit down for a meal and she would listen with rapt attention, and in turn he'd listen to her innermost thoughts. They would hold each other through the night, discussing their various ideas.

Heat stole over his cheeks as he thought of the other things they'd do, once they were married. Lying together…

He jerked awake as a blood-curdling scream rent the air. He leapt from the bed, fighting rising panic and kicking the blankets to the floor.

Without asking, he flung Maddie's door open and— stopped. His first instinct was to run inside and battle whatever disturbed her. But she sat bolt upright, barely breathing. Her hair stuck out in all directions. Her eyes were wide as she gazed into space and tears coursed along her cheeks. She didn't seem to notice him, and he got the strange impression she was sound asleep where she sat.

Afraid to startle her, he crept into the room and perched on the edge of the bed. Slowly she turned toward him with a strange, distant expression. She still didn't seem to see him, even though she stared right through him.

Hand shaking, Chase touched her forearm, then stroked his fingers up to her shoulder. She relaxed, her chest rising and falling in a deeper, more regular pattern. Carefully he guided her back down onto her pillow and smoothed her damp hair away from her forehead. A zing raced along his arm like he'd plugged into her mind, harder than their usual electrical zap. His heart thumped loudly in his ears.

Darkness enclosed them, at first so dark he could barely see her beside him. Seemingly oblivious to his presence, she strolled through a field of tall grass toward nothingness, but as she moved a shape materialized in the distance. A tall, beautiful white tower shimmered into existence, sparkling and glimmering in the growing starlight. It held a magnetism that pulled her forward, literally floating her off the ground. He ran to keep up. She reached out, her fingers outstretched in anticipation. But even though she continued to fight the grass and gravity, she never quite reached her destination.

Frustration covered her face. Then the scene changed and they were in a cave. She snuggled close to Alasdair's beastly form and a sense of comfort pervaded her.

Chase drew in a quick breath. With the shudder, his hand flinched from Maddie's forehead and the connection was lost. He rocked on the edge of the bed. The vivid images still lingered in his mind. If he closed his eyes he could still see Maddie and Alasdair in the cave huddled together, the little smile on her face.

Agitated, he massaged the bridge of his nose, stood, and retreated to the window. He'd joined her in her dreams. He'd seen them, even though she hadn't seen him. Beyond the lacy curtains and windowpanes, stars lit the clear night sky. A gentle wind blew, scattering leaves across the yard. Chase laid his head against the cool pane. *Control.* He needed to regain control. No matter how impossible the night's events.

Soft snoring behind him. Maddie relaxed and stretched deeper into the bed. Sensing her contentment and his invasion into her space, he retreated back to his borrowed room. It seemed cold and empty. Shivering, he straightened the tossed blankets and lay down, wishing she were with him. His alter ego had all the luck.

The alarm blared and Maddie slapped it off, then rolled back onto her pillow. So incredibly comfortable... but her eyes didn't want to close again, and she realized how refreshed she felt, not drowsy or loggy at all. Had her normal nightmare visited her? She couldn't remember it, but she knew she'd dreamed of overprotective guardians and massive, sheltering wings.

No, there'd been one nightmare. She vaguely remembered running from... from Doran, the black gryphon. Dark woods had engulfed her. Her breath had come in short rasping gasps as she'd stumbled between trees. Cracking and splintering branches had echoed behind her and she had been too afraid to find a hiding place. Up ahead a two-story house with a white picket fence had beckoned her. Brilliant multicolored flowers had offered welcome. She had increased her pace.

A dark winged creature had appeared and hovered overhead. Flames had shot from his eyes and a fireball lit the sky and struck the house, causing it to explode. As the flowers had melted, she'd screamed. Then the scenery had changed.

Maddie flipped onto her back and twisted a strand of hair around her finger. A smile teased the corners of her lips. *Alasdair.* He had played a major role in her dreams. Heat flushed her cheeks as she remembered. He'd swooped in from the sky like a super hero, wrapped his arms around her trembling frame, and carted her off to the cave. Ah, his gentle touch. Settled in his arms, she had feared nothing. He had pushed stray hairs from her face, stroked her forehead, and whispered words she didn't fully understand.

She rolled onto her belly and grabbed her sketchpad from the nightstand. With sure strokes she outlined Alasdair's features. Darkening in certain areas, she considered his eyes. Something about them seemed so familiar. Colored pencils in hand, she shaded them blue. She knitted her brow and tapped the pencil to her temple. It seemed right, but...

Again remembering her dream, she snorted. The flowers had *melted*. Right, had they been plastic stuck in the ground?

Pleasant smells wafted to her nose. Her belly rumbled, as if she hadn't eaten nearly enough last night. Sighing, she placed the pad and pencils on the nightstand and checked the clock. There never seemed to be enough time.

Clad in her robe and slippers, she padded downstairs and sauntered to the kitchen. In her head she calculated the time needed to prepare for school. Time to shower and dress... time to fix her hair... time to— the thought failed as she pushed through the kitchen's swinging doors.

Chase stood in front of the stove. He wore a pair of jeans, a shirt partially buttoned, and tapped his bare foot in rhythm to his whistling. Light shone on the droplets of water that clung to his blondish hair. Defined shoulder muscles rippled as he moved.

He spun on his heel and came to a dead stop, holding a spatula. How could he look so domesticated?

"Omelet?"

Maddie's gaze lowered and she gulped. Washboard abs led to a tapered waist. Heat flushed her face and she looked back up, her face burning hotter.

He grinned and repeated, "Omelet?"

Oh, yeah. She nodded.

He lifted the skillet and poured the prepared omelet onto an empty plate. She grabbed it and hurried to the table in the corner of the room, where they'd sat the night before. She bowed her head and said grace. When she finished, he sat across from her with another omelet and a mischievous glint in his eye.

Surely he knew how attractive he was and what he was doing to her. She took a bite of the omelet and choked. He pushed back his chair and rushed to her side, patting her on the back. If he did the Heimlich maneuver, she'd faint.

"Are you okay?" he asked.

His cologne took her breath away and she struggled to nod.

He seemed unsatisfied and squatted beside her. "Are you sure you're okay?"

And suddenly she was furious. She wanted to yell that she'd never be okay. Her parents were dead, her grandma was in a coma, and she was cooped up with him! A handsome, attractive, caring male! She wanted to throw caution to the wind and beg him to love her. But she didn't want to just love him now; she wanted to love him always. Yelling wouldn't accomplish that. Again she nodded.

He returned to his seat. The heat from his gaze, stolen in between bites, made her squirm.

Finished eating, he leaned back in the chair and she snuck another good look at his physique.

"What time should we leave for school?"

Maddie averted her gaze because she couldn't speak and look at him at the same time. "In about an hour, I guess."

"Okay. I'll stay and clean the kitchen while you get ready."

"Okay." Slowly she chewed the omelet, making each bite last. Drat school. Once the plate was empty, though, she couldn't readily move. It would be so much nicer to stay home instead. They could go to the hospital... Her smile died.

Chase grabbed her hand and squeezed. "Are you sure you're okay?"

"Yeah, I'm sure." One more fast change of directions from her emotions, and she wouldn't be.

Their intertwined fingers lay in the table's center, between their empty milk glasses. It seemed symbolic, but of what, she wasn't certain. She tried to relax, but though her mind commanded it, her appendages refused to obey. Maddie lifted her eyes and their gazes locked.

"*Maddie*," he said in a ragged whisper.

Longing raced through her veins. She couldn't take it and ripped her hand from his grasp, pushed back her chair, and fled upstairs. Too much. It was all just too much.

Maddie gathered her clothes and escaped to the bathroom. The hot water fell from the shower tap and she stepped into the spray. It cascaded over her head and down her frame, washing away her thoughts and worries. When she stepped from the shower, she felt like a new person. As she dried off and dressed, she whispered the mantra, "*I can do this. I can do this.*"

Right. And if she chanted for much longer, she'd make them late for school. She tossed the towel over the rack and exited the bathroom.

Chase stood in the hallway. He had buttoned his shirt and put on his shoes. His blond hair had dried and neatly curled atop his collar. Their gazes caught and held. How long they stood mesmerized by each other, Maddie didn't know. She wanted to throw herself in his arms and crush her lips to his, she wanted to...

"Are you okay?"

No, she didn't want to. She fisted her hands and said, as rudely as she could manage, "Chase, please quit asking me that."

A crestfallen expression settled on his face. She had hurt his feelings. Great, now she had another reason to feel guilty. She hadn't wanted to be harsh but her erratic, uncontrollable emotions were making her crazy. Opening her mouth to apologize, she closed it just as quickly. If he was mad at her, then it would be easier to keep her distance.

And boy, oh, boy, did she need to keep her distance for right now. Maybe for all day. Maybe for...

She fled to her room, grabbed her books, and returned to an empty hallway. Glancing through the foyer windows downstairs, she cringed. Dark clouds covered the sky. She sighed and grabbed an umbrella from the big vase by the door. The knob rattled in her hand as she stepped onto the porch. A loose board cracked beneath her boots, and she moved to the left and made a mental note not to step there again. She'd better tell Chase, too. Chase...

He sat behind the wheel, staring into space and looking forlorn. Maddie squared her shoulders and made her way to the truck. The first drop of rain splatted on her nose.

It was going to be a long ride.

24

The drive to school was a silent affair. Chase gripped the steering wheel, his knuckles bared white, and concentrated on seeing the road through the heavy thunderstorm. Wipers swished back and forth as rain descended in solid sheets. The wind howled and pushed against the truck. Thunder rumbled and lightning struck a tree nearby. Maddie jumped. He would have asked if she was okay, but she'd pretty much cured him of that and he kept his mouth shut. The darkening sky fit his mood perfectly. At least they didn't have to worry about forest fires from the lightning strikes, not with that downpour.

He pulled under the school's drive-through shelter. She unzipped her backpack and removed an umbrella. Placing it on the seat between them, she sent him a pleading look.

"Thanks," he said as she opened the door and slid out.

Maddie shifted the heavy pack higher on her shoulder as she vanished into the building. He parked and grabbed the umbrella. Even shaded by its breadth, he was drenched by the time he made it inside.

She waited at the front door, wearing a grimace and holding paper towels. "Let me take the umbrella and you can dry off."

He took the offering and dried. Entering students, half sheltered passengers and half drowned drivers, flowed around them, and without conferring they stepped sideways into the corner while he finished.

"Chase?"

"Yes?"

"I'm sorry. I didn't mean— well, it's just..." She stopped and shrugged.

He placed his finger over her lips. "It's okay. I should have realized you get asked that a lot."

Her eyes flashed gratitude. "We better get to homeroom or we'll be late." She grabbed her backpack and led the way.

The day dragged. Rain beat against the roof in a steady pattern. As the math teacher droned on and on about cosines and how to work their scientific calculators, Chase's mind wandered and his gaze drifted. He latched onto the brightest spot in the room—Maddie.

Her hair fell forward on one side of her face as she concentrated on her calculator. She worried her bottom lip, sending chills through his body. Since she'd shut herself down and snapped at him, their emotional connection had faded even more and now he couldn't sense her emotions. He ached for that closeness, wanted to touch her and see if it would return. Not knowing how she felt was driving him mad.

The thunder boomed and he glanced toward the window. Dougal sat there and stared at him. Good. As long as the jerk stared at him, then he wasn't staring at Maddie.

And he could handle that game. Chase returned the glare, but something about it nagged at him. *That look... Where had he seen it before?*

He glanced again at Maddie. She sent him a shy smile, sending his pulse into overdrive.

"Mr. Donovan, would you mind repeating the instructions I just shared with the class?"

Heat flooded Chase's face. "Well, I..."

"That's what I thought. May I request you refrain from staring long enough to listen to me?"

The classroom snickered and Chase replied, "Sorry." *You know, if you weren't quite so boring...* Not that he'd ever say that aloud.

The teacher cleared his throat and continued. With great effort, Chase managed to pay a modicum of attention.

Finally the torture was over. They left math class and Maddie asked, "What were you doing? If you get in trouble, your parents won't let you stay with me."

He ran his hand through his hair. "Yeah, I know."

"Then what gives?"

He kept it light. "I don't know. There's just something about you."

"What?" she asked, blinking and playing with a strand of her hair.

He pulled her next to the row of lockers. "I can't help myself. It's like I'm drawn to you and I can't stop."

"Chase—"

"Don't interrupt. I need to get this out. Somehow you're a part of me." The words of the old 80s song "Simply Irresistible" by Robert Palmer ran through his mind. She was that and so much more.

Maddie squirmed, but it was a delicious sort of squirm. "Chase, you don't really know me."

"I know enough."

She sighed and tugged hard on his hand.

"Where are we going?" he asked, hoping it was away from the crowds and some place private.

"To class. We can't be late."

Figured.

Would the day never end? The rain pounded nonstop, Dougal and Chase both stared at her, and she felt awkward, more of a dork than ever. What was Chase's problem? He claimed he was drawn to her, and she could understand that as she was irresistibly drawn to him as well, but couldn't he resist the urge to stare?

She worked hard to ignore them and concentrate on her classes.

At lunch Maddie sat with her tray, waiting for Chase to join her. But behind him, Dougal hesitated. For a moment she had the horrible impression he intended to join them. When he grimaced and headed for his regular spot next to Stephanie, she relaxed and released a sigh.

"Maddie?" A tray settled beside hers.

If he asked the question, she'd explode. "Chase, I'm fine. I had a fear Dougal might sit with us and I didn't think I could handle it right now, so I sighed. No big deal. So how do you like your chicken sandwich?"

The change in subject didn't distract him. "Why would he do that?"

Maddie regretted her decision to share her worries. "Who knows? Why does he do anything he does? Why did he show up at the hospital? Why does he continue to follow me? Why does he stare at me?"

"All good questions." A frown tugged at his lips as he glanced in Dougal's direction.

"Let's not worry about it. We should eat."

"Good plan."

It took her a moment to realize the silence wasn't just Chase gingerly examining the so-called chicken sandwich. The rain had stopped.

The day refused to end. Maddie thought she'd scream and run crazy first, but finally it did and they strolled to the truck. When Chase's fingers brushed hers, she slid hers between his and squeezed. He helped her in, gave her a kiss on the cheek, and clicked her seatbelt.

"What was that for?" she asked, fighting the flutter of butterflies in her stomach.

"Just something I wanted to do."

"Oh."

"Should we head to the hospital?"

"Yes."

Mondays should be outlawed.

Chase was happy the day was over and he could finally take Maddie away from there. Their physical closeness intensified their relationship and sharing her presence with others, especially Dougal's staring, was becoming painful. He closed Maddie's door and turned to circle the truck. But Dougal stepped in front of him, blocking his path.

Through clenched teeth, Dougal said, "What do you think you're doing?"

"I'm taking Maddie to the hospital."

"No, you're not. She's mine."

Oh, yeah? Chase cocked a brow. All day his temper had seethed beneath the surface and finally he had an outlet. Excellent. His parents would kill him if he got into a fight on school property. But a guy had to do what a guy had to do. They'd understand once he explained. "Yes, I am."

Dougal threw the first punch. Chase leaned right and Dougal's fist slammed into the passenger side window. The glass vibrated and Maddie squealed, jumped, and scooted across the bench seat.

Ignoring Maddie's reaction, Chase twisted and delivered an uppercut to Dougal's chin. It landed with a purely satisfying shock that ran up his arm through his wrist and elbow to his shoulder. Dougal's head snapped back. He staggered across the parking lot and landed on his backside. For a moment he sat stunned, then he shook his hair from his black eyes and Chase flinched as they took on an eerie bronze glow. They looked like cat's eyes, gleaming across a darkened room, and he remembered he'd seen Dougal's eyes do that before. In the excitement of Maddie, he'd forgotten.

A crowd gathered. Stephanie rushed to Dougal's side and helped him up, her lip curling in disgust when she glanced at Chase. The guys from the football team, the ones he'd hung out with when trying to forget Maddie, pushed each other and pointed. Maddie climbed from the truck and gawked. Dougal dusted off his pants, pushed past simpering Stephanie, climbed into his SUV, and peeled out of the parking lot, leaving her standing.

Why had he given up so easily? Dougal liked to start things then leave at the first provocation, like when Chase had interrupted his dance with Maddie. But this had been physical, and Dougal hadn't seemed the sort to leave a fight unfinished.

Concern tingeing her voice, Maddie said, "What a punch! You sent him halfway across the parking lot. How did you do that?"

Good question. Chase wasn't prepared to answer, not even for Maddie. "Just get in the truck."

People stared as he helped her in again and closed the door. He walked to the driver's side and slid behind the wheel, flexing his hand.

Furious, Dougal bit the inside of his cheek, keeping the metallic taste sweetening his mouth. It seeped not only from his cheek but from where he'd bitten his tongue when the stupid interfering human boy had hit him. Pain radiated along his arm from his smash with the truck's window, his knuckles were bruised and bleeding, and he'd skidded across the concrete parking lot, ending with his bruised posterior in a cold puddle. But worst of all, confusion and shock pounded at him.

Impossible. What had happened was impossible. It could *not* have happened.

In the rearview mirror, Stephanie balled her fists and ran across the lot in his wake, screaming for him to stop. He ignored her tirade and drove on, exiting the parking lot with a satisfying squeal of tires. At the first intersection, he turned the wrong way, deliberately heading out into the forest where none of the students who knew him lived.

Several miles down the road, he parked on the side of the road beneath the shelter of overhanging pines and climbed out. The SUV could stay there without risk. He entered the dense forest and listened for passing cars. When none were forthcoming, he transformed into his gryphon shape and flew to Serena's lair.

The tunnel inside was narrow and dark and it took someone with special vision to *see* the way. Deliberately he flew too fast, risking his wings and shoulders at twisty corners and pushing himself all the way. The danger felt good, like the squeal of protesting, accelerating tires as he'd left the humans behind. Especially her.

He entered the living area and hovered. Serena sprawled across her velvet chaise with her tail hanging off the edge. One arm lay across her eyes. Was she in a trance? Was she asleep? Did he care?

Yes. Yes, he cared. Because he needed answers and in her trance, if she hadn't spent her energy looking elsewhere, she might have seen the impossibility he'd experienced.

He returned to his human form and stomped across the cave floor. Being a beast in the little open area cramped his wings. Without the fulfillment of danger and risk from flying too fast, he much preferred walking around on human legs. Plopping down next to Serena, he asked, "Did you see that?"

She opened one eyelid a fraction and nodded. Her eyes remained unfocused; she'd been distance-watching and it would take awhile for her normal sight to return. If he'd ever wanted to kill her...

Not before he got answers. "What happened?" He leaned his elbows on his knees and gently massaged his jaw.

"I don't know," she replied softly.

"Well, something happened. How did he avoid my punch? How was he fast enough to hit me? And how did he hit me so hard?" None of it was possible.

"I don't know."

Rage boiled inside him. "I grow weary of your non-answers, woman."

Her eyes closed again. "Do not worry. Even if Chase is strong, you are stronger."

Frustrated, Dougal stomped back into the tunnel, ignoring his swelling jaw and various aches. He should follow Serena's plan and let Chase be the lynchpin that brought Maddie to her knees. Yet there was something about her quiet, gentle spirit that made him wish she *wanted* to help him find his family. He wished...

He refused to punch the cave wall. His knuckles already hurt too much.

Maddie didn't know why Dougal and Chase had fought and Chase seemed so furious she didn't want to ask. He drove in silence, eyes on the road, the muscle in his jaw twitching. But one thing was certain. Dougal could hit hard. The whole truck had shuddered when he'd hit the glass.

When Maddie could stand the silent treatment no longer, she asked, "What did Dougal want?"

He screwed up his face, but didn't answer.

"Please. What did he want?"

Chase opened his mouth, snapped it shut, and then opened it again. "Do you really want to know what he wanted?"

"Of course."

Chase parked the truck in the hospital lot. He leaned on the steering wheel and shot her a brief glance. She thought he wasn't going to answer and she opened her mouth.

"You. He wanted you."

Stunned, Maddie couldn't move. She stared out the windshield. The most logical answer, and it had never occurred to her. *That's because nobody fights over dorks.*

The imposing brick hospital sat atop a small knoll. Flowerbeds surrounded the facility and the last faded blooms looked like twigs after the early snowfalls. What did it say about her that the building didn't frighten her? Grandma Draoi was inside, so it had to be a good place, right?

Chase reached over and grabbed her hand, giving it a faint squeeze. "Let's not think about that right now. It'll be okay. Let's just go in and visit your grandma."

Inside, the ICU waiting room was empty; even the attendant was missing. Maddie paused at the double doors. "Come back with me? That is, if you don't mind."

"I don't mind. I did promise not to leave you."

Her lip twitched at the corner and she intertwined their fingers. Hand in hand, she leaned over, pushed a red button, and spoke into an intercom. The doors swung open and they quietly entered another world.

With Chase beside her everything looked different than the day before, somehow safer. A brightly lit hallway stretched in front of them. Beeps and mechanical whirring noises floated through the air. A nurse looked up, smiled, and offered a wave of acknowledgement. Maddie waved back as she pulled Chase into the darkened room at the hall's end.

Chase leaned against the farthest wall as Maddie approached the pale figure lying on the bed. She'd told him what to expect, but the knowing hadn't prepared him. Draoi Casey-Brennan appeared completely lifeless, and it disturbed him on a deep level he didn't understand.

Maddie stroked her grandma's hand. Only the machines' beeping and whirring broke the silence. Chase wished he'd stayed in the waiting room. No, he had promised. He'd be there for her, no matter how his stomach twisted.

The door pushed open and a doctor entered, the nurse with the electronic recording machine behind him. He reached out his hand. "You must be Madelyn Clevenger."

"I am."

"I'm Dr. Gomez. I've been treating Mrs. Casey-Brennan." He spotted Chase. "And who might this young man be?"

"He's a close personal friend."

"All right," he hesitated, "would you mind coming with me? I would like to discuss some things with you."

Chase swallowed. Things like, would her grandmother ever recover, and how Maddie would have to be brave. He felt sick.

Maddie must have been expecting something like that, though, because she didn't blink. "Of course. Chase, do you mind sitting here and talking to her? I know she'll remember your voice."

"Sure." Surprising, how normal he sounded.

The door creaked closed behind them. Hesitating wouldn't help. Chase swallowed, settled into the only chair, put his elbows on his knees, and leaned forward. "Grandma Draoi, I don't want you to worry about Maddie. I'm looking after her. You need to focus all your attention on getting better because she wants you to come home and be with her."

"Thanks, sonny."

His head jerked up so fast he heard a snap. Sharp green eyes peered at him with more than a hint of exhausted mischief. He opened his mouth to call out, but one frail hand settled on his forearm.

"Hold on, child, don't get in such an all-fired hurry. I need to tell you a few things."

"But Maddie will want to know— The doctor—"

"Yes, but first it's my turn. You're special, you know. No, don't interrupt me again. My time is limited. How have your emotions been?"

Stunned, Chase froze. "What?"

The mischief died away, leaving her very serious indeed. Her voice, barely a weak whisper, spoke faster. "Don't play dumb with me, boy. I know your emotions have been working overtime. At least, they better be, or I've really lost my touch."

"I don't understand." His pulse pounded. What had the old woman seen? Had she been watching Maddie and him all along?

She didn't waste breath sighing. "Of course you do. Listen and listen well. I was blessed with the same gift Maddie possesses, but when it passed to my daughter, my abilities changed. I successfully hid Maddie's presence from the dark ones until you and that Dougal kid arrived. Don't look so worried, child. It was inevitable. She had to be found."

Pain flitted across her face, but when he tried again to get help, she stopped him. "When I met you, I knew you were her protector, her defender. I could feel the power in you. I've been channeling her emotions to you to draw you closer. Now that I'm down, though, I fear the only way you'll *feel* her is when you physically touch. That's when your own abilities kick in. But you better not be doing that too much, do you hear?" Draoi drew in a deep, ragged, shaky breath. "Don't lift your eyebrow at me, sonny. I know you're a gray one—"

He didn't care if she knew of his alter ego or not. "Can you tell me why I'm changing? Please?"

"All I can say is there comes a point when love conquers all differences."

"But—"

She raised her hand. It only stayed up for a moment, then it sagged back onto the bed as if the last of her energy had seeped away. "Let me finish. I don't have the energy to explain everything to you. All I can say is protect Maddie, for she holds the key to life and death..." She stopped, gasping, and her fingers clenched.

Chase froze.

For a moment longer she glared at him, her eyes wide and staring. Then they clamped shut. Her next breath trailed off into a gurgle. Monitors blared and he jumped.

"Code blue, code blue!" rang over the ICU intercom. Dr. Gomez and several nurses and technicians flooded in and Chase was shoved aside. Heart pounding, he made himself as small as possible.

A wide-eyed Maddie appeared in the open doorway, complete horror etched on her face. He edged around the determined team and wrapped her in his arms. She buried her head against his chest. A doctor yelled, "Clear!"

Draoi Casey-Brennan's body thumped against the mattress. Maddie shuddered as they placed the paddles on her chest once more.

"Clear!"

Nurses and doctors stared at the machine. Seconds raced past. Maddie clutched his arm so tight he thought she squeezed bone.

"There it is. A regular rhythm."

Dr. Gomez checked the numbers on the machines and sent Chase a fierce glare. "What happened?"

He opened his mouth to say she'd spoken to him, but quickly changed his mind. Their discussion needed to remain his secret for now. "Nothing. One minute I was sitting there talking to her and the next the machines went crazy."

"Miss Clevenger, your grandmother is stable. You should head home and we'll call if there's any change."

"But—"

"She needs her rest and there's nothing you can do for her. I promise the nurse will call if there's anything new to report."

Maddie's shoulders slumped.

He should tell her what happened, he thought on the drive to his house. He wanted to. But he was afraid. How could he explain without telling her he was Alasdair? He just wasn't ready. And if he wasn't, she couldn't be.

At the house, Chase left Maddie in his mother's capable hands while he sought out his father. He found him in the workshop, reading yet another family journal.

"Dad?"

When Dad yanked off his glasses, he exposed his red-rimmed eyes. "Chase, I'm glad you're home."

"Me, too. I really need to talk to you."

"Same here, but you go first."

Chase gladly accepted the offer and Dad listened with rapt attention.

"It doesn't surprise me that the old lady knows."

"Why do you say that?"

"I wish she would have told you more. I've been reading the family's books all day and I am still no closer to the truth. I just don't understand it." He rubbed at a spot between his eyes. "All I know is that Cian and Arin weren't allowed to live in peace, because they trapped most but not all of the dark ones. Since Arin was the key to opening the door, the black gryphons threatened her, keeping her life in constant danger. Which meant Cian spent all his days protecting her with the help of others like himself."

"You mean there were more gray ones?"

"Yes. That's where we came from. From what I've read, there might have been an alliance between the gray gryphons and the village clans. The gray ones agreed to protect the key because of all the trouble their fallen brothers had caused, and in return the druids in the village gave them a gift."

Chase felt his eyes widen. "When love conquerors all!"

"What?" Dad shook his head, as if surfacing from deep

thoughts.

"Did Arin and Cian have children?"

"I think so."

"Now I get what Grandma Draoi said. It was kind of what you were reading before. When a gryphon finds his soul mate, he's able to transform at will. That was the gift given to them by the druids." He ran his hand through his hair. "What are we going to do? I don't think Maddie knows about her grandma being a druid and using her magic to pull us together. I want to tell her about all this, but if I do then I have to explain about me."

"You would also have to explain that she comes from Arin's line, which means she holds the same responsibilities. She holds the power to release one of the greatest terrors ever known. How would you tell her that she holds the key to life and death, not only for herself, but for the whole world?"

Chase could only stare.

25

Grandma Draoi's house seemed dark and foreboding, as if its soul lay unresponsive in the hospital and nothing remained for her inside. Chase tugged the passenger door open and peered inside. "Is something wrong?"

She faced him. "You tell me. Because I get the sense you're hiding something." They'd been silent all the way home and the truck cab had crackled with tiptoeing energy, afraid to put its foot down because something might explode between them.

He looked away and shuffled his feet. The non-answer and the evasive actions confirmed her suspicions.

Angered, she slid off the seat, pushed past him, and ran inside. In the foyer she dropped her backpack, rushed upstairs to her room, and slammed the door. How had her life gotten so complicated? In one week, everything had turned completely upside down.

She sat on the bench in front of her dresser mirror and pulled a brush roughly through her hair. Her reflection studied her in return. What was wrong with her? Why couldn't she have a normal life? Why was she surrounded by drama and constant uncertainty?

Because you're a dork, dork.

Thinking of those questions brought others. Like, what was Chase hiding from her?

Livid, she stalked downstairs, determined to get answers.

But the bottom floor was empty and Chase was nowhere to be seen. She stopped on the dilapidated porch and planted her hands on her hips, gnawing on her lip. She really should fix the broken slats before Grandma returned. Who knew what condition she would be in? She could put a foot through a hole and—

No. Not going there. Pushing those thoughts aside, Maddie trekked toward the river in search of Chase. She'd find him and she'd...

She didn't know what. And it didn't matter, because he wasn't there, either.

At the water's edge, the rotting dock floated, someone's canoe tied up alongside. The oar stood propped against it. No life jacket, no sign of the owner. But her father used to take her canoeing, and Grandma Draoi. It wasn't as if she didn't know how. And she really needed to get away, away from worries, stress, even Chase. Besides, it probably belonged to Mr. Temple, Gray Beauty's owner.

Old memories assailed her and before she realized it she had grabbed the oar, inspected the craft for seaworthiness, and stepped inside. One push against the dock and she was headed downriver.

Silence floated with her. Only the rippling of the current, the sloshing water dripping from her paddle, the occasional squirrel rustling the leaves, and her. Maddie closed her eyes, let the current take her, and let her body sway with the canoe's gentle ministrations.

It felt like no time at all passed. But when she opened her eyes, she didn't recognize the shoreline. The sun lowered in the sky and a cold icicle of fear shivered within her. No one knew her whereabouts.

Paddling hard, Maddie switched directions to head home, but the current was against her. No matter how fast she worked, the canoe never seemed to make progress along the bank. The sun set and the river noises became more pronounced. The mosquitoes feasted on her skin, but she kept paddling instead of slapping them away.

Counting strokes, she tried to be positive. *...forty-eight, forty-nine...* Finally she passed the rough-scarred section of the riverbank she'd been using as a guide. *...sixty-three, sixty-four...*

Something moved. Not the river, not her paddle. She'd only

spotted it from the corner of her eye. It had been huge. And it slid into the water behind her.

Her mind kept counting without her. ...*seventy-five, seventy-six*... But fear shot through her sluggish limbs. She trembled. What had caused her to believe boating alone in the evening was a good idea?

The river seemed to hold its breath. ...*eighty, eighty-one*...

The boat heaved beneath her. Maddie fought for balance. Something glided past her, barely visible in the dark. Something big, with pebbled skin. She heard it breathing. A single liquid eye peered at her, shivering with interior motion as it reflected the dark. Then it was gone.

A gator. One of the alligators that lived in the far crook of the river. Had she floated so far before waking up? Her heart hammered against her ribs. Her throat constricted. "Help!" A croak. *Good job, dork.* Louder, she yelled, "Help!"

In the old barn, Chase found lumber, a box of nails, a saw, a mitre box, and a hammer. He thought about telling Maddie what he was up to, but changed his mind. Hopefully if she walked outside, he would have time to warn her before she fell through a hole in the porch. But her moodiness had frustrated him. He needed to fix something. If he couldn't work on their relationship, the porch would do.

He sawed, beat, and banged for well over an hour, according to his cell phone. The sun lowered and he flicked on the porch light. Concern mounted when Maddie failed to come and check on the noise.

Circling the mess, he entered the house and took the stairs two at a time. Her bedroom door stood open. One glance inside told him she wasn't there. He ran back downstairs and searched every room. Not there, either. Stopping in the foyer, he massaged his temples. Where could she have gone?

Before he could answer himself, pain seized his stomach. Movement rippled down his spine, like fingers dancing on a keyboard, only beneath the skin, not on top of it. He doubled over. Sweat dripped down his face. He stumbled back to his room, stripping as he went. He fell to the rag rug and curled into a tight ball. There, the unfolding in his back, fur insulating his body, claws tangling in the rug, sharpening vision...

...and hearing. Someone yelled for help. *Maddie...*

He opened the window and climbed onto the roof, claws gripping the shingles. The ground seemed a long way down. He swallowed. He'd never tried to take off from a height. It would be like plunging into a pool, hopefully. Chase stepped from the roof. His wings flared out on their own and swooped down, thrusting him into the sky, and his heart soared with him. What was there not to like?

He soared over the treetops. There, on the river, some distance away. Maddie floundered in a canoe. The forceful current pushed her farther from home. She strained her muscles, fighting the water, paddling and staring at the bank.

Moonlight reflected off a long snout, glistening eyes, sharp teeth in a cavernous mouth. One of the alligators he'd seen when they'd first arrived in Coal Creek. Rage filled him. Chase howled and dove.

Dougal lounged on his chaise, devising his next move with Maddie. Chase had gotten to her. She no longer paid attention to his stares or flirting. He'd overplayed his hand with Stephanie and now it was too late.

Nor did he believe Serena's strategy would work. They could only threaten Chase so many ways. They could cut off his fingers, which held great appeal. They could crush his knee-caps, which made him even happier, but still, all that meant nothing if Maddie didn't care enough to open the door.

"She is in danger again," Serena said, covering a yawn.

"What?"

She rolled onto her side. "The girl. She is becoming more trouble than she is worth. What woman paddles a canoe into alligator-infested waters?" She sighed, flipped onto her back, and waved a careless hand. "I believe you should go and help her."

Dougal didn't wait. He raced to the end of the long tunnel, whispered the incantation, morphed into Doran, and jumped. He soared above the trees, scanning the landscape as he flew toward the river. Maddie. He longed to see her and flew faster. She'd filled his every waking thought since that day at the hospital.

After school, he'd wanted to whisk her away and reveal his

true identity. What would she think if she knew? His blood sang at the thought. Would she rush into his arms and demand his affection? Or would his black form and soul repulse her? He'd hold her and never let Chase near her again.

In his experience, women were attracted to his good looks and charm. His mysterious nature only made their interest even more intense. That was until they truly knew him. Then came the fear.

But Maddie was different. At the hospital, when he had cradled her in his arms, she hadn't seemed repulsed. Part of him whispered that was only because she didn't know him. Would her opinion change with the truth? She'd called him a friend, which still baffled him.

Just thinking of holding her reminded him of her scent. Her auburn hair smelled of flowers baking in the sunshine. It had taken all his strength to keep his fingers from running through her long tresses to see if they were silken, like he remembered. He wanted to pull her close and inhale her very aura.

Soft, feminine, her body against his. An innocent embrace. He'd hold her.

The wind changed and a new scent filled his nostrils. He breathed deeply of his enemy's essence. He would be ready.

Chase swooped low, wrapped his arms around her middle, and lifted her from the canoe. The alligator's mouth opened and clapped onto the canoe's side. It tipped, crunched, fell apart, and the pieces swirled away downstream.

Scratch one canoe.

Maddie screamed and trembled in his grasp. "Alasdair?"

He kept his focus ahead on the landscape. "Are you well?"

"I am now." She released a long, shaky breath and buried her head against his neck.

Fighting a smile, he drifted upstream toward the riverbank, well away from the alligators' haunt. No need to climb for altitude. He'd land and they'd talk, alone and cocooned in darkness, and maybe he'd hold her again until dawn.

A black shadowy form appeared, almost invisible in the night. It flew at them and rammed into his side. Pain exploded in his ribcage. They cartwheeled, his wings flailing. He lost his grip and Maddie tumbled toward the dangerous river, another scream falling with her.

His wings worked, pumping for altitude. No clue what hit them. He dove after her but more pain exploded in his head. White bursts of light shimmered behind his eyes. He plummeted. Without thinking about it, his wings extended into a glide, softening his landing.

He knelt on the cold ground and tried to breathe. The stars in his head were fading, but he still could see nothing in the night. Ears perked, he listened. The calls of crickets echoed against the water. No splashing noises, moans, or any other sign of Maddie. Wobbly, he staggered up and held his head. What had hit him? No, that didn't matter. Where was she?

"Sorry about that, youngster."

He looked up. A looming figure stood near the tree line, darker than the shadows around it. "Who are you?"

"Oh, I guess I should introduce myself. I'm Gregory, the Vigilant Watcher."

Right. Like he cared. "Where's Maddie?"

"Maddie? Oh, the girl. Don't worry about her. She'll soon be dead."

Horror seized him. He cried "No!" and ran toward the river, stumbling over fallen limbs and through scraggly bushes.

"Hey, boy, come back here. I'm on your side." Heavy footsteps followed him.

He whirled. "If you're on my side, then don't just stand there. Help me find her!"

Dark eyes blinked. A bronze glow began in their depths. "Why?"

He punched the dark form in the face, sending him staggering. "Do you know what you've done?"

"Of course! I've saved all humanity! With her dead, the line ends, the tower remains closed, and our evil brothers will stay locked in prison forever!"

Chase opened his mouth to scream with rage, but a noise like a wounded animal cried near the shore.

PART IV

B E G I N N I N G S

26

Her hands grasped at the air. Maddie screamed. The river roared below, and she braced her head and prepared for impact. Time slowed as she anticipated her demise. She expected terror, but instead, mathematical equations of speed and force from last year's geometry and physics classes flashed through her mind. Would hitting the water kill her? Or would it plunge her so far beneath the surface that she drowned?

Realizing no one was coming to her rescue this time, she closed her eyes and prayed. Sprinkles of water hit her face. The tips of her hair skimmed the water's surface as she was clutched around the middle and jerked upward. Wings pumped, the backwash spraying more droplets across her. She screamed again.

Her rescuer held her close. She couldn't see his face. But the fur beneath her clutching hands was dark and the odor invading her sinuses foul. Could this be the beast that attacked them? Now terror overwhelmed her. Screaming again, she squirmed and kicked.

"Please stop fighting me or I might drop you," came a gruff voice.

She knew that voice. "Doran?" She stilled.

"Yes."

She didn't know whether to fight him or hold on. Wind rushed around her head and filled her ears until she couldn't hear. She closed her eyes and tried to think through her next move. She could attempt to get loose, but she would plummet to her death. She could call for Alasdair, but if he was hurt could he help her?

She bit her lip and snuggled her hand against the black gryphon's chest. Beneath his soft fur, his heartbeat increased. The feel of him was vaguely familiar. His odor, the heat of his touch, his grip, all reminded her of someone. Who... when... The pain, when it hit her, was unbearable. She stiffened in his arms and he shook her slightly, bouncing them up and down on the air current.

"Are you well?" he asked.

"It was you," she whispered. The arms around her clutched more tightly. "You were there. You were the one who rescued me from the fire." Maddie waited, breathing in his strong musk. It was the same. No answer. He was strangely quiet and she burst out, "You left them! Why didn't you help them? Why did you only rescue me?"

She beat his chest with her fists. He twisted under the onslaught, then she raised her aim and he grunted with her first pounding blow to his face. The flight's angle changed, his weight shifting back and his wings pounding, then they settled on the ground. She jumped away from him and screamed, "Why didn't you let me die, too?"

For the briefest of moments, his eyes seemed to express pity. Then just as suddenly they changed and took on a horrifying bronze glow. His fangs bared and a snarl rumbled in his chest. "Get behind me."

Fear gripped her and she nearly ran. But no, he'd shifted his gaze and now looked past her shoulder. Maddie ducked around him, beneath the shelter of his rippling wings. He'd saved her twice; was he going to do so a third time? Peering around his side, she saw another dark form emerge from the woods.

The figure stopped, still within the gloom of the overhanging trees. "Doran, Doran, I knew it was you. You really need to find a way to mask that odor of yours."

Doran's wings rustled. "Gregory, is it? Nice to meet you. Well, not really."

"I have to ask. How come every time I try to kill this girl, you always show up and save her?"

Maddie froze, shocked at the casual cold-bloodedness. *Kill this girl... kill her.*

With a hesitant hand, she stroked the black wingtips flexing before her. They stilled. "Just my lot in life, I guess."

Gregory snickered and strode fully into the moonlight. "More like you're doing Serena's grunt work."

Doran tensed.

"Oh, don't get your fur in a wad." Gregory waved a careless hand, heavy with flashing claws. "I'm sure you want the tower opened for your own reasons, as well. It doesn't really matter why. All that matters is that it will never be allowed to happen."

Maddie stared at the newest beast, her heart pounding. How many of these creatures were there? How come they all seemed to want to either protect her or kill her? And what was this tower they kept talking about? Could it be the one from her dreams? But how? She had lots of questions but as they whirled around inside her head, she realized only one mattered at the moment. "Where is Alasdair?"

"Who?" asked Gregory, cocking a bushy brow.

She stepped from behind Doran's protection. She was going to give this Gregory a piece of her mind. But before she could get very far, Doran jerked her to his side.

"Don't go near him."

Gregory laughed raucously. "Yeah, don't go near me. I just want to kill you. No, stay with the beast that wants to use you, *then* kill you."

She looked up at Doran's black face. "What's he talking about?" She took a step back as she remembered the race through the woods with Doran on her tail. Had that been a dream or reality? She palmed her head. What was happening? She didn't know who to trust.

Gregory held out his hand. "If you come with me, I promise to make your death painless."

Doran grabbed her arm and squeezed until she thought it would break. She gasped.

Another gruff voice spoke from behind them. "Maddie, are you okay?"

She shifted her gaze. A third gryphon, this one pale yet somehow glowing in the moonlight. "Alasdair?"

With one smooth shove, Doran pushed her into Alasdair's arms. "Get her out of here."

"But—"

Doran glanced back. His eyes glowed like flames within bronze lanterns. "Don't argue with me. Get her out of here. Now!"

Alasdair hoisted her into his arms and took flight, wings pumping. She couldn't see the fight that erupted below but sounds like thunder vibrated her body as they flew away.

27

Dougal stroked the cold metal bars absently. While he'd attended school, Serena had purchased a zoo-quality cage and installed it in the cave. Chains securing Gregory's hands and feet were fastened to the cage floor, which in turn was bolted into the rock. The craftsmanship was impeccable, and Dougal found himself mesmerized by what it promised: a prison as unbreakable as the tower itself.

With one hand twisted between the bars, Serena doctored Gregory's wounds. "You know, you will heal faster when your brothers are freed," she said casually as she blotted at a raw area.

Since Dougal had tethered the battered Gregory within the pen, Serena had chattered away about how much better things would be once the tower was opened. Her words poured like a flood, as if Gregory's presence changed everything. But Dougal knew it didn't and he hid his skepticism. If half of what she said was true, then all the world's ills would vanish when the black gryphons were freed. He knew this could not be the case, but he went along with her plan—for one reason only. There was someone in the tower he yearned to meet.

"She's lying!" yelled Gregory. Dougal's heart jumped in his chest, but he didn't look directly at either of them.

Serena hissed and bared her claws, scratching a line along Gregory's already tender flesh.

Dougal swallowed his curiosity. "That's no way to treat our guest."

She hurled the ointment on the cage floor and slithered away. Crocodile tears coursed along her cheeks as she settled on her dresser stool. She threw a hairbrush at him, then a comb, and then everything she could get ahold of. "Don't believe me, do you?" *Clang* went the hand mirror against the cage's closest bar, then *rattle* and *smash* as it fell. "Believe an enemy over me!" A tube of hand lotion whirled between the bars, thudded against something soft, and Gregory yelped. "Both of you better sleep with your eyes open."

Her tail beat the uneven stones, whipping from side to side as she slithered from the main room. In his human form, Dougal stared at Gregory. For an old-timer, he had put up quite a fight. Cuts ran the length of his arms from the beating Dougal had given him, and the bruises were visible through his blood-matted fur.

Not his business, not his job. Dougal sprawled on the chaise and covered his eyes with his arm. Neither Serena nor Gregory could be believed. For just as he knew Serena's goal was to free the dark gryphons' leader from the tower and so regain her beauty, he also knew Gregory's goal was to keep the tower sealed forever.

And that was why Gregory had sought to kill Maddie. Again, and again, and again...

And that *was* Dougal's business. "Were there others?" He pushed himself back up and stared at Gregory.

"Other what?"

"Others like Maddie?"

Gregory shrugged. "There aren't any now."

Dougal thought about it. "What of Draoi Casey-Brennan, her daughter, and Maddie's mother? Did not all of them have the same power?"

"Aye, yes, Draoi. In direct line of the village witch! How could she be so lucky as to be in the line of Arin and a druid? The vixen hid herself, her daughter, and her granddaughter through trickery, at least until the great-granddaughter arrived. Then it was too much. *Madelyn.* The perfect name, don't you think?" Dougal didn't get his meaning, but he kept listening. "With her birth, Draoi again had to choose. If her grandson-in-law hadn't believed she was an eccentric old fool, then perhaps he would be still alive. But alas, I had to kill them to get to the girl."

"She's seventeen. Did it take you that long to track her down?" Dougal crossed his arms over his chest. A shudder raced through his body as he remembered the smell of charred flesh when he'd rescued Maddie from the burning house. Gregory had done that. The... the *beast*.

Gregory narrowed his eyes and squared his shoulders, as if insulted. "Maybe it did, maybe it didn't. The point is, she would've been dead and unable to free the dark ones if you had left her in the burning house!"

Exactly. Dougal grimaced. "I couldn't."

"Why not? Is it because of Serena?" Gregory huffed. "I hope you know she's lying. Nothing will improve if the leader returns. He will pillage, plunder, and decimate every village in Ireland. Then he will move outward until all that's left of the world is darkness. If any humans survive, they'll be his slaves and nothing more."

Finally Dougal looked at him fully. "Why do you care what happens to the humans?"

Gregory shifted nervously and glanced at the prison floor.

Dougal took a gamble. "You love one."

Something in the cage shimmered, like frustrated magic. Gregory folded his wings against his back and squeezed his eyes tight. It was as if he tried to change, but couldn't. It seemed cruel. Not that Dougal cared, he reminded himself.

With a sad tone, Gregory said, "I did love, once. But it was a long time ago."

"Was it Arin?"

Gregory shook his head. "No, it wasn't Arin."

Like a lightbulb being turned on, the answer came to him. "It was Mairin, Arin's sister."

"Aye, my beloved." The words sounded like a breathy sigh.

Anger rushed in behind the understanding. "You're the one who caused Cahal's imprisonment!" *All Gregory's fault. All of it.*

"I guess you could say that."

"If you'd left her alone or returned her when Arin asked, then Cian would never have imprisoned our brothers!"

"Aye, I know. Mairin begged for release, but I could not let her go. So beautiful, so..." Gregory swallowed. "I tried to make her understand my love for her. I explained how, if she loved me in return, I would morph into a handsome man, like none she'd ever seen! Yet she told me I was revolting. Can you imagine? All the females in our tribe vied for my attention. They sought my affections. I was known as Ailin Colin, handsome and virile. To have my child was considered the highest honor, but she thought I was revolting! I would've gladly exchanged my beast form to claim Mairin as my own, but without her..."

The words trailed off, and his shoulders drooped as he hunched over his gryphon feet. "She begged me to retrieve her sister. Arin was blind and alone. I agreed, but only if she would remain with me. She said yes and I flew away. I found Arin and Cian in the field in each other's arms. He had changed into a man! A man! How could that have happened so soon? The battle, it had just ended. He had betrayed Arin's people, yet she had already fallen into his arms!"

Gregory's voice rose to a crescendo. He jumped to his feet and leapt as far as the chains reached, grasping the bars and shaking them, rattling the cage and vibrating the cave walls. Then he deflated, fell onto the floor, and slowly crossed his legs beneath him. "Why should Cian be given happiness? Why was he allowed to change? Why did he have love when I did not? I returned to my lair without Arin. That was when I found her. Mairin had taken her own life rather than be with me."

He laughed hysterically. "Cahal didn't know I led the gryphons against the village. While Arin and Cian searched for her sister, I killed every Casey, every Clevenger, and anyone else that stood in my way. Cahal took the blame, of course, and afterward he vowed to kill me."

Dougal shook himself, shook off the lingering anger and horror. After listening to Gregory, he felt like he needed a shower. Maybe two. "Ah, so it's not your love of humans but your fear of Cahal that convinced you to hunt down Arin's line."

Gregory muttered. "I care nothing for the filthy humans. I have spent my time hiding in caves to just survive. If I thought Cahal would be of a forgiving nature, I would have freed him ages ago."

"Have you seen any more of our kind?"

"What kind would that be? I am purely dark. Black in color and in heart. That Alasdair character, her defender, as it were, is purely of the gray nature. He holds the pure heart of Cian and no doubt descends from the village clans." He scoffed. "But you, you are a nothing. You are merely the spawn of the dark that crossed over to mate."

Dougal ached to break Gregory's neck and clenched his hands until his claws extended and pierced his palms. "You know nothing of my history."

"I know more than you think." Gregory leaned his back against the bars and tucked his knees to his chest. "Otherwise, how would you change so easily without a true love?"

He turned his back on Gregory and left. Gregory laughed hysterically, the sound echoing within the tunnel, but he walked on without glancing back.

Alasdair dropped her in front of her grandma's home, at the edge of the wood, not far from where he'd left her once before. He set her on her feet and she grabbed his biceps to steady herself. Everything felt shaky after their desperate escape and the night loomed too closely. "Thank you."

He nodded.

"You always seem to be around just when I need you." Her eyes involuntarily ran the length of his body. A dark spot stained the fur on his right side, visible in the bright moonlight. Her hand went to the area and crusted blood flecked off. "You're hurt!"

"I'm fine."

"No, you're not! You need to come inside and let me look at it."

"No." He eased back, away from her.

"Alasdair, please, I need to make sure you're okay."

He removed her hand, turned his back, and started walking away. "I'm fine."

Maddie swallowed. He seemed so strong, so sturdy, whether he faced her or turned away, whether he flew or walked. "Did I hurt your feelings?"

He rounded on her, anger oozing from every pore. "My wound has healed. Only the old blood remains. I'm fine. Don't you need to check on your grandmother?"

"No, she's in the hospital. But you know, what I do need to do is check on Chase. We had a tiny spat and I probably owe him an apology."

Alasdair remained silent. For a moment longer he stared at

her, burning bronze behind his eyes. Then he pumped his wings once and flew away. Maddie reached out for him. *"Alasdair."*

Well, that wasn't going to help. Maddie let her hand fall back to her side and watched his diminishing form as long as she could make out his dark speck against the moon. He always saved her. And then he always left as fast as he could.

Dejected, she exited the woods, slipped across the yard, and plopped down on the porch steps. Her fingers were caked with mud. All of her was dirty, after an ill-advised canoe ride, a rescue, an attack, another rescue, and so on. Boy, how she would love to just talk with Alasdair, but he was always in such a hurry.

On the porch beside her, wood, nails, a saw, and a hammer littered the area. Apparently Chase had been thinking along the same lines as her... the porch needed repair. Only instead of just thinking about it, he'd actually done something.

She sighed deeply. Where was Chase? Just as she was about to search for him, he opened the front door.

He'd left Maddie in the grove and flown to the open second-story window. Now that the immediate danger was over, it was simple enough to change back into his human form. He dressed quickly and headed downstairs, ready to accept the forthcoming apology, since he knew in advance it was coming.

In the spill from the porch light, Maddie rested on the steps. She looked terrible. Her hair was wet and clinging to her head. Twigs stuck from her clothes, mud stained half of her, and her hair stuck out at odd angles. Scratches and goose bumps dotted her exposed arms.

"Maddie? Is that you?" He walked onto the porch, trying to keep his anger in check.

"Yeah, it's me."

"You look terrible. Where have you been? I've been looking everywhere for you."

"I went for a canoe ride."

"Were you inside the canoe?" Did the tone sound teasing? Or was he giving it away that he knew exactly what had happened to her? Would biting his lip help him keep his secret? He doubted it.

"What?" Confusion drew her brows together.

He shrugged, as cool as he could manage. "Well, you look like you were pulled along behind the canoe."

"Ha ha, very funny."

She shivered and he almost broke and told her everything. Instead he swallowed. "Maddie, come inside and change into dry clothes."

She rose and faced him, her body within inches of his. "I believe I owe you an apology."

Chase cocked his eyebrow. Although he'd known it was coming, hearing it from her lips still surprised him and kicked his heart into overdrive.

"I shouldn't have been so adamant that you share everything with me. I know if you could tell me, then you would."

His hand shot forward and plucked a twig from her hair, flicking it away. He stared into her doe-shaped eyes, the jade color darkening. They both held many secrets. Unwittingly she had shared most of hers.

Her innocence attracted him, and he leaned forward and sealed their lips in a kiss. Her hands moved between them and rested against his chest. He tangled his fingers in her hair, drawing her closer. She trembled, and he wrapped her in an embrace, sharing his warmth. When at last they pulled apart, they were both breathing heavily and some of her mud had shifted to him.

"I think you need a hot shower," he said gruffly. *And I need a cold one.*

"Why?" she whispered.

"You're shivering."

"Perhaps I'm not shivering because I'm cold."

The implication made his stomach knot, and he laughed to cover his feelings. He twirled a strand of her wet hair around his finger. "Why don't you clean up? I'll do the same here, then we can enjoy a movie and some popcorn or something. It's too early and I don't feel like going to bed yet."

"Okay," she said, not moving.

In a bold move, she wrapped her arms around his neck and drew his lips back down to hers. When she pulled back, a ruddy color darkened her cheeks. She extracted herself from his hold and ran inside.

Chase stared at her retreating form. His blood pumped so

loudly in his ears, he couldn't hear. They needed to have a serious talk. His attraction continued to grow. In his beast form, he was her protector and defender. In his human form, he wanted to be her mate and life partner. He knew they were young, but what would she say if he proposed? He pulled a small black box from his pocket and stared at it.

He didn't open it, but replaced it in his pocket. He picked up the mess on the porch. Ways to propose raced through his mind, ranging from simple to extremely romantic. His hand stilled and he noticed a scratch along his forearm. Until she knew the truth, he couldn't ask her. It wouldn't be right. But learning the truth could change everything.

28

Hot water cascaded over Maddie's mud-tracked flesh. She laid her head against the shower wall and watched the rinse water swirl down the drain, slowly running clear. Finally she washed her hair and scrubbed down.

What was she going to do? The whole thing was a disaster. Flying beasts trying to kill her, flying beasts trying to protect her—and all she wanted was to have a regular boyfriend and do teenage stuff.

Fully rinsed and clean, she stepped from the shower, dried, and dressed. In her room she combed her hair, allowing the damp tendrils to surround her face. Purple bruises wound around her wrists and cuts ran the length of her arms. She grabbed a sweater from her closet, donned it, and tugged down the sleeves. Now at least the mirror reflected a normal girl. She exhaled loudly. Why couldn't her life be simpler?

Plastering a smile on her face, she bounded downstairs. The aroma of popcorn filled the air.

Chase sprawled on the living room couch, his feet propped on the coffee table. A glass of iced tea rested in one hand, a handful of popcorn in the other. Several DVDs littered the table. He looked ridiculously comfortable, as if nothing had ever happened to her and the world was just peachy.

Fighting the urge to slam him with a handy pillow, Maddie sat beside him and tucked her feet beneath her. She shuffled through the movies. An old Western lay on top. "This is a good movie, but I'm not in the mood for horses and romance and riding off into the sunset."

Second was a dancing movie. "Love it, but I don't think I can do the musical scene tonight." It felt far too cheerful for her current mood.

Third was a romance. She set it aside because she didn't think he would like it, although she had to give him points for even setting it out for her consideration. But the fourth and last one was the best. "This is it."

"Really?" he asked, cocking a brow.

"Yep. This is definitely the one." She wished she could explain her choice, but it would lead to too many questions. Bruce Wayne was secretive, protective of his woman, handsome, rich, and reminded her of Alasdair.

Maybe Alasdair wasn't all those things. In fact, he favored a cat more than a bat—a big cat, like a pale panther. And she wasn't sure about his wealth. But he was secretive and protective. Part of her found him handsome, but not in the same way she viewed Chase. Chase was like Bruce Wayne, Alasdair like Batman. If only they were one and the same.

Besides, she got the impression Chase had put that movie on the table hoping she'd choose it. Who was she to disappoint him?

Chase inserted the disk and the movie rolled onto the screen. Maddie snuggled against his side, sharing the popcorn.

"Why do you think your grandma owns this movie?" he asked between bites.

"Hmm, maybe because Christian Bale is hot?"

"You think so, huh?"

"I didn't say that, but now that you mention it..."

He rammed his finger into her ribs and tickled her until she almost lost bladder control. Gasping for air, she called, "Uncle! Uncle!" To no avail; she fell to the floor and writhed, and still he tormented her.

"Nope. I can't stop until you take it back."

She opened her hands and shoved against his chest. "You're right! What was I thinking? I don't care for dark good looks."

Still he tickled her. "Not good enough. You're still saying he's good looking."

She enjoyed the attention so instead of pleading for mercy, she repaid in kind. She reached upward and dug her fingers into his side. Chase dropped to the floor, rolled, and begged for mercy. It felt great, and she chased him across the throw rug. Suddenly just before they rolled into the television screen where the movie played unseen, his laughter stopped, and no amount of tickling brought it back.

She straightened and placed her hands on her hips. "You're not ticklish, are you?"

He shook his head. "Not so much, no."

Jerk. She punched him in the arm.

"*Ouch.* What was that for?"

"For making me believe I'd won!"

Maddie placed her hand on the floor and pushed, but he grabbed her and drew her to his side. "Don't you realize you've won much more than a tickling contest?"

She hid her face behind a veil of hair, but he forced her to look at him. "Maddie, you've won my heart."

Maddie didn't have to reciprocate, but after his admission he expected some kind of response. Couldn't she find something to say? But the moment dragged, becoming increasingly brittle as he waited. *No, she couldn't*, and it felt as if his heart stopped beating.

She shoved off the floor and reset the movie back to the beginning before settling on the couch and pretending to watch it. He rose, too, intending to join her, but it suddenly felt like too much to handle, and instead he strolled outside to the porch and sat on the swing. He lost track of how long he sat there. The moon lowered toward the mountains and he yawned.

A beam of light appeared in the doorway. "Chase?"

"I'm over here."

Maddie shone the flashlight in the direction of his voice, but kept it low, so it didn't blind him. She hesitated, then crossed the porch to the swing. Once settled beside him, she blurted out, "Don't love me."

A deep snort left his throat. "Too late."

"Chase, you must understand—"

"Oh, I understand. I understand it perfectly. You love someone else."

227

"No! That's not it."

"You were awfully close to Dougal at the hospital."

"Chase!"

"What am I supposed to think? I've practically thrown my-self at you." The intensity of his voice increased. *Cool. Keep it cool.* "You must think I'm an idiot."

She cringed. A single tear escaped the corner of her eye. She wrung her hands. Angrily she shouted, "You can't love me! You can't!"

"Why not?"

"Because everyone who loves me dies, okay? And if any-thing happened to you then I— I don't think I could live with myself."

He glared at her. It seemed like the stupidest thing he'd ev-er heard. "So your solution is to push me away?"

Her chin firmed. "If it keeps you alive, then yes."

"It won't work. Besides, it's too late."

She shook her head hard.

"Why fight it? You know as well as I do that our destinies are intertwined."

"No..." she groaned.

"Yes."

"But—"

"No buts. We'll be together and nothing will stop us."

"But you don't understand—"

He swiped a hand between them, as if wiping away her doubts. "Then help me understand."

Her frustration mounted. "I can't!"

"You can share anything with me."

"No, I can't. I— I made a promise."

And suddenly he froze inside. Was the secret about Alasdair? If she revealed what she knew, could he keep a straight face? Would he give his own secret away? Instead of testing himself, he said, "Okay."

She looked stunned by his reply. "'Okay?' I reveal that I have a secret and all you say is 'okay'?"

Well, he was stunned, too. "I can't have you breaking prom-ises. One day you'll tell me." Chase almost repeated what she had said to him earlier.

"Yeah." She still stared at him, her lips gently parted. "Sure."

Her lips… no, enough of that. "Are you tired?"

She blinked, startled in a new way. "Yes."

"Why don't I take you upstairs?"

Pink invaded her cheeks. "I think I can make it on my own."

"I'm sure you can," and he hoisted her into his arms, "but I want to take you."

The tension melted from her shoulders. She snuggled against his chest, the embrace reminding him of earlier. When he looked at her, he saw the same perfect girl he'd always seen.

He ducked backward through the front door, carefully maneuvering her legs through, and took the stairs one slow step at a time. Then Chase stopped outside her door and lowered her to the floor, allowing her body to glide along his own. Every nerve ending screamed. Afraid to touch her more, he backed away and blew her a kiss. "I'll see you in the morning."

Her eyes softened and she touched her lips. Perhaps Alasdair needed to pay Maddie a little visit. His alter ego seemed to have better luck.

29

Sunlight streamed through the windows. Maddie rolled onto her side and groaned. Every muscle in her body ached from last evening's long adventure. If she'd known getting into a canoe for a little jaunt downriver would have cost her, and Alasdair, and Doran, so much effort... well, next time she'd stay home. But at least she'd learned it was Gregory who wanted to kill her, although she didn't know what to think about Doran, and besides, he stank... and she was going to be late.

She climbed from bed and attempted to lift her arm to run her hand through her tangled hair, but the pain was too intense and she dropped it back to her side. With short, stilted steps she headed for the bathroom, but stopped short in the doorway.

Chase stood before the mirror, his arm above his head as he removed a square white bandage from his side. A thin red line graced the length of his muscular torso.

She blurted, "How did that happen?"

Chase turned, his eyes widening. He looked like a kid caught dipping a hand in the cookie jar. "I— I, well, I— hurt myself yesterday."

"How?"

He pursed his lips. "Working on the porch?"

It sounded more like a question than a statement. Before she could ask further, he pulled his shirt over his head and tugged it down.

"I guess you need the bathroom, right?" He spoke fast, as if afraid she'd interrupt. "Yeah, of course you do. You better hurry or we'll be late for school. I'll meet you in the kitchen."

She gawked as he fled. She needed air after that encounter, but drawing in a deep breath caused pain to radiate along her upper chest and down her arms. Spots danced before her eyes and she leaned against the door facing to keep from hitting the floor. Too much exercise paddling the canoe. Too much fear when she'd fallen toward the river, when Doran carried her, when Gregory'd appeared. When she'd argued with Chase and tried to get him to leave. Just. Too. Much.

The dizziness passed. She clenched her teeth, brushed out her tangled hair, showered, and dressed. A glance at the clock showed she'd taken too long. Grabbing her backpack, she ran for the stairs. Midway down her feet tangled and she pitched forward. She shrieked, imagining her bones cracking when she crashed into the hard floor looming ever closer. Waiting for the crash, she wrapped her arms over her head.

A pair of hands snatched her around the waist and jerked her to a stop.

Maddie's first thought was that Alasdair had rescued her. But as she lifted her eyes, she realized she nestled against Chase's chest, against his gray sweater.

"Are you okay?"

Maddie waited until her breathing calmed. "Yes."

He righted her and eyed her curiously. "Are you really okay?"

Her ego was bruised, but she nodded. "We should go."

Both backpacks clutched in one hand, he headed for the truck and she trailed along behind, grabbing a granola bar for breakfast in passing. His biceps bulged against the sweater's seams. He'd been built when they'd met, but now he appeared even larger, broader of shoulder, stronger. He'd caught her without staggering. When had he had time to bulk up?

Questions compounded on one another. There were so many things she needed to ask, wanted to know. But how could she when she'd promised not to mention Alasdair? Not mentioning Alasdair probably meant she shouldn't mention Doran, either, or even that fiend Gregory. Why did it seem like she had to hide everything from Chase?

They drove to school in silence. He snuck a glance at Maddie, and caught her gazing out the window and absently playing with the door handle. He bit his lip and focused on driving.

The wound on his side had healed considerably. Amazingly, more like, as if he'd been injured a week ago. Maddie's touch when they'd tried to watch the movie, when they'd tickled each other, when they'd sat on the porch swing, their thighs pressing together—it seemed to have sped up the healing process.

He shifted and pain dinged his side. His secret had almost been revealed. But what did it really matter? She already knew Alasdair existed, so what would be the harm in telling her he was Alasdair?

They parked in the school lot, not too late. Maddie jumped from the vehicle and rushed for the door before he had the key switched off. He watched her closely as the engine died away. At the double doors she shot a glance over her shoulder, caught him staring, and offered a shy smile.

Privately he worried as he followed her inside. Maddie's preoccupation increased her clumsiness. Her trip down the stairs that morning replayed in his mind and he shuddered. What if he hadn't been close by? What if there came a time when he couldn't rescue her?

Dark circles rimmed her eyes; bruises from yesterday's adventure were highlighted by the school's fluorescent lighting, stark green and black against her beautiful skin. In homeroom, her eyelids drooped and her elbow shifted. She jumped, steadying herself, and grimaced. Later, she failed to eat lunch, instead laying her head on the table and napping.

And across the lunch room, Dougal stared.

Chase pushed his tray away. What should he do? If he told her the truth, would it put her mind at ease or would it only make her more preoccupied? Would it heap more on her tired shoulders or let her relax?

Lunch ended. When history class rolled round, Maddie seemed a bit more alert. Chase breathed a sigh of relief.

The history teacher, Mr. Stanley, sat atop his desk and drummed his fingers on the sides. "Today we're going to discuss names and their meanings. Let's start with you, Felicity.

Do you know the meaning of your name?"

"Nope," she said, smacking at a large wad of gum.

Mr. Stanley drummed again, leaned forward, and opened his hand, palm up. Felicity spit out the glob and shot him a goofy grin. He deposited it in the trashcan and retrieved a cleansing wipe from his desk. Wiping his hands and ignoring the class's verbal disgust, he said, "Your name comes from the English. It means happy or happiness."

"Cool."

He rolled his eyes. "Yes, of course, cool." He shifted target and pointed. "Now, Marley, your name is also from the English vernacular and it means pleasant wood."

Light laughter filled the room and Mr. Stanley cleared his throat. Everyone hushed.

"Stephanie, your name is from the Greek."

Preening, Stephanie faced the class. "You hear that, guys? I'm Greek. I wear long togas and golden leaves on my head."

Comments were made under students' breath—Chase privately agreed with them but refused to listen too closely—and Mr. Stanley shook his head in agitation. "Your name means..." he paused and grimaced, "...crown."

"I always knew I was a queen," said Stephanie, primping her hair.

Working his way around the room, Mr. Stanley revealed each student's name, its meaning, and where it hailed from. When he reached the last row, Dougal leaned back and crossed his legs at the ankles.

"Dougal Lachlan. A rich Irish name. Dougal means black stranger and Lachlan means lord of the lochs."

Mr. Stanley arched a brow as if he expected a comeback. When none was given, he adjusted his wire-rimmed glasses, straightened his bow tie, and moved on. "Well, then, I guess you youngsters don't find that interesting. What about this one? Chase, your three names are English, French, and Irish. I guess you couldn't have one origin."

He snickered, but the meaning was lost on Chase, and he lifted his eyebrows.

Mr. Stanley straightened his face and cleared his throat. "Anyway, your first name is Alexander, which means defender of mankind. Chase means huntsman, and Donovan means dark chieftain. A dark hunting chieftain that defends mankind.

You're a paradox, aren't you?"

Stephanie and her crew snickered and Mr. Stanley finally relaxed; hey, someone listened. Emboldened, he clapped his hands and drummed again. "And last but not least, Maddie. Your name is also Irish in origin. Madelyn means high tower and Clevenger means keeper of the keys. I guess that would mean you are the key keeper for a high tower." The class erupted in laughter.

Someone whispered, "We knew she was the keeper for something, but we would never have guessed keys since she doesn't even have a car!"

Dougal straightened and stared at Maddie. Chase's heart hammered. He bit his tongue to keep from jumping, grabbing her hand, and running from the room.

30

The school day dragged and Chase couldn't wait to leave. Dougal's staring intensified by the hour and Chase wished he could cloak Maddie in a shield to protect her. The constant barrage of attention from such an untrustworthy source twisted his gut and he worried he might morph into a gryphon during school. Oh, would that start the week off right.

Gym ended and he rushed Maddie to the truck. Awkward silence reigned while he drove her to his home. He couldn't stop mulling over the history teacher's lesson, the meanings of everyone's names, and wondering if they held significance. He should discuss it with Maddie. What did she think about it? He needed to know if it had made her see things that she'd missed before—like Alasdair.

He gnawed on his lip, ready to burst as they traversed the sidewalk and approached the front door. Before they made it inside, Colton rushed out and grabbed her hand. "Maddie, I want to show you something."

"Okay," she answered, flashing Chase a helpless look.

He grimaced. His younger brothers adored Maddie. The attention she paid them when she visited only exacerbated the situation. Colton running off with her and keeping her to himself was neither new or surprising. But he needed to talk with her!

The frustration was... well, frustrating.

Chase trailed behind them into the kitchen and leaned against the door facing while Colton wowed Maddie with his fossil collection, spread out on the table in Mom's way. The boy's giddiness was infectious and Chase found himself grinning along with them. But he still needed to talk with her—so instead, he backed out of the kitchen. If he couldn't talk to Maddie about what he'd learned, then maybe he could discuss it with his father.

He knocked on the workshop door. "Dad, are you in there?"

"Yes."

Chase opened the door and slid inside—and stopped short, blinking. The workshop had always been a well-kept and organized space. But now the floor was covered with old books, newspaper clippings, photo albums, and more. Where had it all come from?

In the center of the only clear place remaining, Dad pulled off his reading glasses and rubbed the bridge of his nose. He sat cross-legged on the floor and didn't look comfortable at all. "How goes it?"

"Is there a place to sit down in here?"

"You could try the floor."

"I think I'll stand."

"What's up?"

"No 'How was your day?' Just 'What's up?'"

"I assumed there's a reason you came to visit and continued to stay while I'm covered in this mess."

"Yeah, well, I can't deny you're right." He tiptoed between stacks, sending a pile of loose clippings slithering across the floor when he closed the door, then sighed and leaned back against an empty space of wall. "My history teacher gave an interesting lesson today."

Dad flipped over a page in the book stacked atop the pile in front of him, but suddenly stopped. "Okay, you've piqued my curiosity. What was the lesson about?"

"Names and what they mean."

Dad tilted his head. "And?"

"And my name means defender of mankind, a huntsman, and a dark chieftain."

"I already knew that. Go on."

"Dougal is a dark stranger who is lord of lochs."

"From your description of him, this doesn't come as a surprise. Continue."

"And Maddie, well, she's the key keeper for a high tower."

The book his father held slipped through his fingers and landed on the cluttered floor with a thump. "Just like in the dream," he whispered. "This confirms what we thought. She must be from Arin's line and she's the only one who can open the tower. Our family has been destined to protect her. No wonder you keep changing when she needs help."

"What's in the tower again?"

"According to the ancient texts, the dark ones are in the tower."

"And we're sure they're Doran's family?"

"Based on what you've told me, I think so. Somehow he escaped imprisonment and he wants Maddie to open the door and release the prisoners."

"But why?"

"I don't really know. Maybe to rule the world? Maybe to destroy the world? Or perhaps just to have his family back?"

Chase grimaced. "I wonder what Doran stands for."

Dad leaned across the floor, picked up a book from another stack, and flipped through a few pages. "Doran, of Irish origin, means pilgrim, stranger, exile."

"Doesn't it bother you to hold your brother prisoner?" Gregory asked.

"You're not my brother," answered Dougal. School had been atrocious and his head ached dreadfully. All he wanted to do was lie back on the chaise until the pain or the world vanished, and he didn't much care which. Unfortunately, Gregory was in no mood to let that occur.

"Oh, but I must be. For we are all related."

"Serena, can't you make him shut up?"

Serena threw something. Whatever it was clattered against the rock face then rattled to the floor. Nothing breakable, then. "I'm afraid not. If I could, I would've done so much earlier." Even her voice seemed agitated.

"Why should I be quiet? Free me and I'll kill the girl, and you and I can rule."

"What good would that do? There could always be another. Cian and Arin were quite prolific, I understand."

Gregory scoffed. "Have you not heard? They're all gone. She's the last one. With her vanquished, the tower will never be opened."

Silence fell over the cave. Not even the usual draft whispered. Dougal opened his eyes and glanced around. The tension radiating from Serena was palpable.

"He doesn't know anything," she said.

Out of Gregory's sight, Dougal wrung his hands. So there was something Serena hadn't known. Could it be true that Maddie was the last key holder? The last *eochair*? The pain behind his eyes pounded harder.

As if to hide her concern, Serena's voice turned soft. "We don't want to rule. We only want to reap the rewards of being on the winning side. For that to happen, the girl need only serve us with one small favor."

Gregory laughed outright. "What makes you think she'll do anything for you?"

"With the right motivation, she'll be more than willing. Trust me."

The dark gryphon's eyeroll spoke more than his words. "Doran, or Dougal, whatever you call yourself, why do you listen to this crazy woman? She's brought you nothing but grief, I can tell. She's only trying to fulfill her own desires, don't you see that?" He threw out his hands. "What possible hold could she have over you?"

Without responding, Serena stretched on the lounge and covered her face. Dougal watched her chest rise and fall with her breathing. She had no hold over him. He wanted the door open so he could have a relationship with his father, what he should have had as a young child. It was owed to him and he planned to have it. Whether he would sacrifice Maddie to get that relationship was becoming the difficult question.

Being around her had awakened a need in him. He could remain human if he could find his true love. What if Maddie was the one he sought? What if she could make him human all the time without Serena's spells? Was the paternal relationship he'd sought for years worth risking his ability to be human?

That was the million dollar question.

Maddie oohed and ahhed over Colton's fossil collection

while Carissa wound her way around them, setting the table. The boy was quite animated when he described something he enjoyed, but he didn't notice when Maddie grabbed the silverware from Carissa and slid it into position beside the plates. He was too busy pointing out something fascinating on his largest fossil.

Chase had disappeared. Carissa finally slid the last fossil from the tabletop to a nearby counter, then called everyone to dinner, and the family—including Chase and his father—gathered around, pulling out chairs and then tucking themselves behind their plates. Following grace, Maddie dove in elbow to elbow with everyone else, filling her plate. Chase smiled and sent her a thumbs up. Heat rushed to her cheeks and she let her hair cover her face.

When dinner was finished, Carissa refused her help with the clean-up. Instead Maddie curled her feet beneath her on the living room couch and listened to Craig strum his new guitar. She'd never had any little brothers, nor any little sisters, for that matter. Funny, how much she liked them.

"Are you ready to go?" Chase stood in the doorway, holding an overnight bag with fresh clothes.

"Ah, don't take her yet! I was just going to show her my newest song."

Chase collapsed beside her and snuck his arm across her shoulders. She snuggled into his side, enjoying the smell of his cologne while Craig warbled from one imaginative note to the next. When he finished his song, they clapped and whistled their approval.

"Thanks," said Craig, a flush covering his cheeks.

"Now we really have to go." Chase helped her stand. The electrical pulse that shot through her hand had a lower voltage than usual and she eyed Chase to see if he'd even felt it. His blue eyes burned brightly into hers and she gulped. He had.

Shouldering her backpack, she said, "I'm ready."

Carissa and Alex stood at the front door and waved as the truck backed from the driveway and headed toward the hospital. Once there, Chase waited in the lobby and worked on homework while she visited with her now lucid grandmother. Irritated by her forced stay, she tried to convince Maddie to take her home right then but the doctor had other plans.

On the drive home, Chase asked, "It's a good sign that your

grandma is finally awake, right?"

"Most definitely. Dr. Gomez seems to think she'll be able to come home in another day or so." Maddie refused to dance on the truck's bench seat, but it was a close-run thing.

"What do they think happened?"

But that question sobered her instantly. "They don't know. He said he ran every test he could think of and everything came back negative." She shrugged, watching his profile, little more than an outline in the truck cab as the world leaned toward sunset. "So maybe it was a spider bite, or perhaps she was just overly tired."

"Hmm."

Maddie shifted her gaze to the road. A shadow passed overhead, like an airplane. She twisted her neck and body around, struggling to get a better look.

Behind the wheel, Chase shifted. "Did you see something?"

She shook her head and settled against her seat. How could she tell him about the flying beasts that she kept seeing, without him thinking she was crazy?

He let her get away with the non-answer and instead took a deep breath. "So what did you think of Mr. Stanley's lesson today?"

Now that was a topic she could enjoy discussing. "It was *interesting*. Oddly enough, most of the meanings fit the person. I mean, Felicity is definitely a happy girl, always wearing that goofy grin, the typical bubbly cheerleader. And Kassandra, seducer of men, need I say more! And Mary! Whew! She is clearly the bitterest girl I've ever met."

"What did you think about the description of Dougal?" His knuckles tightened on the steering wheel and she swallowed before answering.

"A dark lord of lochs? Oh, yeah, captured him perfectly. And you? Great dark chieftain, huntsman, and defender of mankind." She didn't mention herself. She didn't want to draw attention, because the teacher calling her the keeper of the tower keys wasn't her finest moment—not with that recurring nightmare.

He cleared his throat. "And what of you? The keeper of the high tower's keys?"

He would ask. She swooped hair behind her ear and tried to be nonchalant. "Yeah, what a ridiculous description. My name means I keep keys. Why couldn't I have been named Belle, which stands for beauty, or something like that? Instead I am a key holder. Perhaps I have a future career as a locksmith." She laughed. Did her humor sound real? She hoped so. "Yeah, that's it. Dougal is a Harley Davidson gang member, you're a ninja, and I'm a locksmith!"

Chase snickered. "Oh, Maddie, you're too hard on yourself. Perhaps your name holds a deeper meaning that you're unaware of yet."

They stopped in front of the house—how had they gotten there so fast? When had she quit watching the road?—and Maddie scooted to the middle of the bench seat. She stared into his eyes. "How do you do it?"

"Do what?"

"Always say the right thing? The thing that will make me feel better, I mean. Do you want to make out?"

Chase spit and sputtered, and she used her hand to cover her mouth and stifle a giggle.

"What did you say?" he asked.

"Hmm, I'm not sure. I think I said you always say the right things and make me feel better."

"No, after that."

"Oh, I asked if you wanted to make out."

Her wide grin outweighed her seriousness. He nodded sagely, then leaned over and gave her a swift peck on the cheek before jumping from the truck. She leaned out the window and yelled, "Is that it?"

"Yup."

She grabbed her things and rushed after him. But he froze in the doorway, blocking her view, and she had no choice but to stop short behind him.

"Maddie, stay put." And now there was no laughter in his tone at all.

"Why? What's wrong?"

She peered around him and gasped.

Would he ever really be able to protect her from the evils that surrounded her?

Ugly words of hatred, and one word he didn't recognize, *eochair,* covered the living room walls. Someone had broken in—while her grandma was in the hospital, no less!—and sprayed graffiti everywhere. Not even very well; drips coursed down the walls from the straggling, malformed letters, as if the so-called artist hadn't known how to taper off the spray. At least he hadn't painted the floor, the drapes, or the furniture.

She peered around him again. "Who would do such a thing?"

He stared at her trembling frame and ran his hand through his hair. "We should call the police."

"No."

"Why not?"

"My grandma doesn't have the best reputation. They already think she's a little odd. You should've seen the woman at the hospital when I told her who they'd admitted. She gave me this knowing look like my grandma was a frequent visitor but really belonged in a loony bin."

Maddie sucked in a ragged breath. "I think it's probably best if we just keep this to ourselves." She huffed a sigh and eased farther into the room. Timidly, she stroked the dried red paint. Pointing at the last word, she asked, "What does it mean?"

"I don't know. We can look it up... later." He paused. "If you don't want to call the police, then we need to straighten this up before tomorrow. Can you imagine how your grandma would react if she came home to this?"

She whispered, "I can. Because it's probably how I'm reacting right now."

They straightened the room, then tackled the walls, scrubbing with sponges.

"This isn't working," said Chase, leaning back and studying their lack of progress.

"You noticed?"

"We've no choice. We have to paint."

Maddie stared at the floor.

Clearly he'd said the wrong thing that time. Chase tilted her chin upward. "What's wrong? It's not like these old walls didn't need a coat of paint anyway."

"It's not that. It's just, well, I don't have money to buy paint and Grandma doesn't give me access to her account."

Ignoring their sweaty clothing, damp from their scrubbing efforts, he encircled her waist with his arms, turned her around, and dragged her back against his chest. "Don't worry. I have some money left over from a summer job. We'll stop and get the paint tomorrow after school."

"Chase, that's very generous, but—"

"Don't argue. I want to do it."

She turned in his embrace and snaked her hands around his neck. "Perhaps I can repay you for your kindness with something other than money."

Oh, he liked the sound of that! He raised a brow. "What did you have in mind? Maybe washing my socks? Or babysitting my little brothers? Or cleaning my room? Or..."

She placed her finger across his lips. "I was thinking more along the lines of a few well-placed kisses."

"Hmm... that's not a bad idea."

The phone trilled—right then, *right then!*—and he groaned. Maddie smiled and wiggled free. But while she listened, occasionally murmuring some form of agreement, varied emotions flitted across her face. Finally she hung up, passed him, and plopped onto the couch. "That was Dr. Gomez."

"And?"

"And he said Grandma Draoi is as healthy as a horse, and her friend will bring her home tomorrow while I'm at school."

A million questions raced through his mind. Why couldn't the doctors find anything wrong with a woman who had been at death's door only a day before? And what of Draoi's unexpected release? The doctor had just told Maddie a few hours ago that it would be a couple more days before she could come home, and now a friend was bringing her tomorrow?

Skipping the complicated questions, he asked a simpler one. "What friend is bringing her home?"

"I don't know. I assume it's the same lady who takes her shopping and drives us to church most Sundays."

Huh. "Do you think we should stay out of school and pick her up ourselves?"

"The doctor insisted my grandma didn't want me to miss school."

"Okay." He sat next to her and twirled a strand of her hair around his finger. A thought struck him and he spoke it aloud. "So this is our last night alone."

31

At Chase's statement, all thought of painting over the vandalized walls fled from her mind. He was right. This would be their last night alone, at least for a while.

"I'm not saying let's ignore the damage," Chase said. "But for now, let's put it aside. Let's do something to make tonight special." Delicately he rubbed his hands along her arms.

Maddie shivered beneath his touch. How had she lived so long without it? "Yes. What do you have in mind?" Her heartbeat echoed loudly in her ears. Their last night already. It didn't seem right.

He snapped his fingers. "I've got it. There's only one problem; I need to drive to town." She groaned loudly and he laughed. "I promise I won't be gone long."

"What should I be doing while you're gone?"

"Hmm, why don't you take a hot bubble bath, dress in your fanciest dress, sweep up your hair, and wait on me?"

Anticipation heated her cheeks. "Okay."

Maddie almost jumped up and down like a bunny as Chase raced out the door, only stopping once to blow her a kiss. *A bunny?* She groaned again. Had she actually thought that?

Upstairs, she flung her closet door open and glanced at her gown choices. Grandma's attic had rejuvenated her wardrobe and she had two gowns from that source that she hadn't worn yet. So which should it be, the pale peach or the emerald green? Which should she wear? The peach hit right above her ankles; the emerald stopped above the knees in multiple layers of tulle and glitter.

The full-length mirror hanging to her left reflected her bright jade eyes, making her decision for her. She laid the emerald gown on the bed. Next she shuffled through the closet's bottom for the matching shoes, and giggled again at how little fashions had changed through the decades; her mother's old shoes fit her just fine and looked like the latest fad. When everything was picked, she grabbed underthings and raced to the bathroom.

She tapped her toes as the hot water ran into the tub, making a cascade of foamy bubbles. Chase had the best ideas.

Out of sorts, Dougal had left the lair. The constant aggravation of Gregory and Serena's pitchy whining had irritated his headache to a new level, and all he wanted was to feel the clean, cool wind in his face. Soaring through the night sky, finally finding release, he'd decided to check in on Maddie. By then she should have arrived at the farmhouse and found his handiwork.

Now, hanging outside the window and peering through, he watched with envious eyes. This was not what was supposed to happen. He had vandalized the walls to get her attention. If she had called the police, or took time to figure out the Irish word for key, *eochair*, then she would have run out of the house, away from her defender and the druid's protective spells, and been exposed. He could've taken her. He would've swooped in and rescued her, flying far away from everything and keeping her all to himself. But instead she was planning a private tête-à-tête with Chase!

His blood ran hot as Chase ran from the house and climbed into the truck. The boy was whistling! Whistling! How could that be? Dougal had desecrated Maddie's domicile, her sanctuary. Yet her defender acted as if nothing had occurred. It was outrageous.

And he'd been suitably outraged, until Maddie started running her bathwater. Then Dougal allowed himself to forget Chase as he peered through Maddie's window. He had never seen a more beautiful, rarer gem than her. A long, slender leg arose from the bubbles, glistening with foam, and she ran a razor along her heart-shaped calf. She hummed to herself, as relaxed and as comfortable as he'd ever seen her, even counting the time before her parents' passing.

She removed herself from the tub, wrapped a towel around her hair and another around her middle. After toweling, her hair fell to her waist in damp ringlets and she used the blow dryer, her head held sideways and her locks hanging free. He couldn't take his eyes off her as she entered her room and shrugged into the knee-length, old-fashioned, gorgeous green gown. He leaned forward, ready at any moment to burst into the house and whisk her away, if he could force himself past the druid's protections. In time he would convince her they were right for each other. If she wasn't the real one he sought, then perhaps she could be.

Dougal held himself poised with every muscle tense. But a motor revved and he shifted his focus. In the driveway out front, Chase's truck shuddered to a halt. The engine died. The annoying boy had returned, hasty footsteps crunching across the front lawn, and Dougal ground his teeth, claws digging into the tree branch.

The front door slammed and Maddie quickly drew herself to attention. Dougal could sense her increased pulse, see her flashing, excited eyes. It burned in his soul. She tilted her head to the side, as if she'd heard the steps across the entry, and rushed to the head of the stairs, Dougal flying from branch to branch, looking in window after window, to follow her path. But before she reached the bottom step, Chase yelled, "Can you go back upstairs for just a few minutes?"

She pouted as she turned on her heel and stomped upstairs, into her room, and flung herself across the bed. She pulled out a sketchbook and Dougal wished he could fly closer and study the pictures. But he dared not. If she'd glanced outside at any time while coming downstairs... but she hadn't. She'd been totally engrossed in that despicable boy.

No matter how much he desperately wanted to know what Chase was doing, he couldn't take his eyes off Maddie long enough to check. She swung her legs back and forth like a little girl, flipping through the pages of her book and sucking on her lip. All Dougal could do was stare at that lip, those legs, that hair. She was so beautiful.

Chase finally called, and she jumped up and ran down the stairs. Soon she was in Draoi's living room, twirling around in graceful circles, her gown's skirts flaring and rippling. Chase had lit the entire room with candles. The shiny green silk of her gown clung to her upper body as she moved into Chase's arms for an embrace.

Serena had goaded him into wooing Maddie in the beginning, but to what end? So he could be frustrated, no doubt. He would never have her, just like he never had Marissa, and Gregory would never have Mairin.

Dougal shuddered as the cold wind whipped around him, stinging his flesh even through his fur. He was in an agony of yearning and desire. Maddie's scent wafted through his nostrils, causing him added misery.

His body ached from the tussle with Gregory, his head hurt from the confusing thoughts of Maddie, and nothing could ever cure his aching heart. Nothing seemed to be going as he'd hoped. Gregory, the Ancient One, was an excellent warrior, but Cahal would surely kill him as soon as he was released. One couldn't imprison a gryphon leader and not expect retribution.

Dougal left those thoughts behind and concentrated on Maddie. What was Chase doing now?

Maddie gasped, the spectacle in front of her taking her completely by surprise. The electric lights were out and candles lit the entire room. "Unchained Melody" came through the stereo speakers, Bobby Hatfield's smoky countertenor turning the opening into pure soul.

And there... a silhouette walking toward her, backlit by tiny flickering flames. He wore a suit, she saw when he came closer, and carried one white rose. She took it from him, smelling its sweet scent. He reached down and clasped her other hand in his, lifting and kissing it. "May I have this dance?"

She could only nod as he enfolded her in an embrace. They glided around the room, holding one another tightly, the dethorned white rose between their clasped hands. Light from the fireplace flickered along the walls. The song changed to "When a Man Loves a Woman" and they continued to dance. The electric shock that happened when they touched ran rampant along her nerve endings.

Chase stepped in closer and leaned down, kissing her gently. When the song finished, he took her by the hand and led her to the table, set with candles and a single slice of chocolate-covered cheesecake with two forks. He helped her into her chair and scooted it closer to the table before taking his own seat.

"Maddie?"

"Yes?"

"I love you."

Her eyes flooded with tears. "Chase…"

"You don't have to reciprocate. It's okay if you think it's too soon. I just refuse to go another day without telling you how I feel."

She drew a ragged breath, feeling the surrender in every inch of her bones. "Chase, let me speak."

He nodded.

"I love you, too."

His face split in a huge grin. "I'm glad to hear it. I must say I was starting to get a little worried."

She stood up, walked around to where he sat, and settled on his lap. She leaned forward until their foreheads touched.

He said, "I have something to give you."

"Chase! You've already made this day more special then I could've imagined. What more could you possibly give me?"

He opened his hand. Nestled in his palm was a small black velvet box. Her mouth opened and she covered it with her palm. "Chase," Maddie whispered, breathlessly.

He removed her from his lap and swung her into his chair. Down on one knee, he opened the box. The ring caught the light and reflected it around the room in a thousand tiny rainbows. "Please hear me out. I love you. I want to spend the rest of my life with you. Will you promise to be mine?"

Before reality could interfere, she heard her own voice say, "Yes!"

Chase held her around the middle and slung her in a circle, her feet flying off the ground. The world spun around her. She shrieked with joy—how many times, in the preceding weeks, had she screamed with terror?—and held on for dear life. He set her down and grabbed her hands, supporting her when she wobbled. "Sorry. I'm not asking for full-blown marriage, because my parents would have a fit if I didn't finish school."

"Of course we have to finish school."

"So I'm just asking for a promise. A promise that we'll get through this and see what we have for each other on the other side. But I'm sure eventually we'll be making marriage plans. In fact, it might even be this summer. We could attend the community college. I could get a job." He must have noticed her frown. "What's wrong?"

Fears and doubts nagged at her mind. She deserved happiness like everyone else, right? Maybe it was all moving too fast. A promise to continue their relationship was one thing, but agreeing to marriage while they were in the middle of a crisis was another. What if he just liked her because she was a damsel in distress? What if they had nothing in common? What about the issue with Doran and Alasdair? There were secrets between them. What if they couldn't overcome those secrets? "Chase, there's so much about me you don't know."

"Before you go down that road, I've got one more thing to show you."

"Chase!" she said, exasperated.

His grin never wavered. "Just bear with me."

He took her to the newly repaired front porch and sat her on the swing, disappearing back inside. Through the curtained window, she could see candles winking out. When he returned, she started to stand but he held his hand up, palm out, for her to wait, and draped a shawl over her shoulders before withdrawing around the side of the house. When he returned, she couldn't have been more shocked. In his hands were a pair of leather reins, and trailing sweetly behind him was Gray Beauty.

32

Chase crooked his finger. In a trance, Maddie eased toward the horse, running a hand down her neck and marveling at her soft coat. The leather bridle gleamed in the moonlight as if freshly cleaned, and when Grey Beauty turned her head and whuffled, the skirts of the green gown billowed against her knees.

He mounted the mare bareback, then reached down a hand and helped her slide up in front of him.

"Chase? Where did you get this horse?"

"I asked Mr. Temple if I could borrow her."

"Okay." She gnawed on her lip. "Where are we going?"

"You'll see."

She glanced up at the moon, full and round overhead. "Do we really have time for a midnight ride?" Although it wasn't all that late.

"Trust me when I say this one is too important to miss."

Cool wind whipped past and teased tendrils of her hair as Grey Beauty walked along the forest's edge. Maddie shivered and snuggled back against his chest. "Are you cold?" he whispered in her ear.

"Yes," she answered, drawing the shawl tighter.

He slowed the horse, removed his jacket, and slid it around her shoulders. His warm breath stroked her cheek. "You look beautiful."

Heat flushed her face, warmer than his jacket. "Thank you." Tucking a stray strand of hair behind her ear, she said, "You don't look too shabby yourself. Where did you get that sway tux, anyway?"

"It was just hanging around in my closet for such an occasion."

"Chase!"

"I'm kidding. It was from my junior prom."

Which explained why it fit him so tightly. "Oh." Jealousy swelled in her breast. "Who did you go with?"

He shrugged. "Just some girl."

Maddie frowned but decided to drop the subject, not liking the way it made her feel.

He tugged one rein and Grey Beauty turned into the forest, winding her way between the massive tree trunks. It was warmer there, and she let her body relax into the mare's rhythmic strides until her eyes closed. A girl could dream on a midnight ride, oh, yes, she could.

And then Grey Beauty stopped.

"We're here," he said.

Startled, she looked around. They'd left the tree line and a rocky slope rose directly in their path, a deeper black hole buried among its center. The place seemed eerily familiar. "Where are we?"

"You don't remember?" A frown creased his brow.

For some reason she didn't understand, her heart began pounding. Not with love or excitement this time, but with something darker. She shivered again. "What do you mean? Why would I remember?"

He slid from the horse's back, gripped her waist, and pulled her down beside him. Carefully supporting her, he led her toward the dark blotch in the rock wall's center and suddenly she realized they were inside a cave. The noise of trickling water flooded her memory and she wailed, backing away.

"Maddie, are you all right?" He gripped her arm in support.

She wobbled, her unfamiliar formal shoes catching on the rough ground. "It can't be. It just can't be."

He slid an arm around her waist, holding her up. "Calm down. It's okay."

"Are you joking?" Her voice soared several octaves. "How could this be okay?"

He froze, as if she'd slapped him. "So, you *do* know who I am?"

"No, you're wrong." She backed away, her heart thudding ever harder. "I don't have a clue *who* you are."

He reached for her, but she scooted away.

"Please let me explain," he pleaded.

"If it was you, then why didn't you tell me? I don't understand. This whole time I thought *I* was lying to *you!*"

Chase drew in a ragged breath and ran his hand through his hair. In an agonized voice, he said, "I don't have an excuse. All I can say is my dad didn't want me to say anything until he figured out why we were changing."

His father knew? Does he think telling me I'm the last to know will help his case? Wait a minute—what had he just said? "We?"

"Yeah. My father changed the first time you two met."

Memories flashed rapidly through her mind, bringing a numb sort of clarity. "That's why he was late to dinner."

"Yeah."

"That was also why, when I touched his hand, it felt so weird. Just like the tingling sensations when we touch."

He shrugged. "Probably."

"So, he didn't want me to know?" She crossed her arms over her chest. "What changed to make you tell me now?"

"Because I thought you should know."

A new thought hit her, and she groaned. "If you're Alasdair, then Dougal must be Doran."

"What?" He appeared genuinely shocked.

And that seemed very strange to her. She figured it out so easily, and he'd known longer. Why hadn't he figured it out, too? "You mean you didn't know?"

"No, I didn't know. I wonder what that makes Gregory?"

"Gregory?" The memory roiled her stomach. "You mean the one that wanted to kill me until Doran, or Dougal, or whoever he is, told you to take me away?"

"This is getting more and more complicated." He ran his hand through his hair, and she found herself staring at his strong hand. Why hadn't she caught on to that action before? It was a tell. Alasdair and Chase both mussed up their hair in the same way. She should have noticed.

She gnawed on her lip and sat on the rock shelf, heedless

of the gown's delicate fabric. Why was all this happening, and now of all times? Her life had been so normal, plain, almost boring. There had never been anything special about it and now she had two gryphons seeking her attention. One had even asked her to marry him. But why?

"Do you hate me?" Chase's voice was so low, she almost missed it.

"No." She shook her head and swallowed. It was the simple truth, and she had no doubt it showed in her expression. It was the one thing she didn't have to wonder about.

He enveloped her in his arms. "We will get through this."

She nodded. She was so confused. She didn't know what to do or even think. She didn't hate Chase; that was impossible. Just to have something to say, she said, "Yeah, once we figure out what 'this' is."

He laughed quietly. "We should head back."

"Yeah, the morning is going to come real early." For the second night in a row, she wouldn't get enough sleep. She didn't care. Being with Chase made it all worthwhile.

"After I drop you off tomorrow, I'm going to feel completely lost."

"Me, too," she whispered, unable to fight the feelings she had for him. Even if she was upset that he'd kept his other self hidden, she found she couldn't hold anything against him.

They swung astride Grey Beauty and set out for home.

Dougal hovered above the horse at a safe distance. It wouldn't do for them to notice the odd shadows that danced overhead, nor for the mare to sense his presence and become frightened.

He'd followed them from Draoi's front porch to the forest's edge and then beyond. His frown had deepened when they'd dismounted and entered the damp cave. He'd edged closer, perking his ears and concentrating. His heart had slammed against his ribs—Alasdair was Chase. Then to discover that his father had changed, as well. And still the plot thickened!

He'd hung back and waited. This was the time for Maddie to become angry and stalk away from her protector. He had planned to snatch her away. He would take her to the lair for Serena—no, never mind that. He would take her far away, somewhere they could live in peace, where they'd never be found. He would tell her the truth and perhaps, maybe, just maybe, she would fall in love with him. He could be different; he knew he could. For Maddie, he could be anything. He could change.

But she didn't stalk out and leave Chase to wallow in self-pity.

Instead Maddie allowed Chase to touch her, to hold her and soothe her fears. How could she? How could she blow off his betrayal as if it were nothing? Perhaps she hid her true feelings. Perhaps anger bubbled beneath the surface, waiting to escape like an erupting volcano. She couldn't be so forgiving, could she? Could anyone?

Backing away from the cave mouth, Dougal found a spot in the trees and paced along a narrow limb. The clack of his claws irritated him and he wanted to morph to his human self, but feared discovery. But if he didn't chill, they'd hear his claws clacking.

He tapped a pointed claw to his forehead. If Maddie had forgiven Chase his indiscretion, perhaps, just perhaps, she would forgive him, as well. Yes, that was the answer. He would just tell her the truth as he had planned and she would forgive him. Then they could live happily ever after. Even if he had to hide her from Serena and Gregory forever, it would be no trouble.

Maddie left the cave, Chase supporting her arm, quieter than when they'd entered. Dougal needed to think of a way to get her away from Chase long enough to convince her he was the better choice.

Because of course he was. He had to be.

The trip home was awkward. Maddie held her silence, a troubled line between her brows, and he hesitated to bring anything up. What more could he say?

She held herself aloof, causing worry to gnaw at his gut. Would their relationship change because of what he'd revealed? He didn't see how it could possibly stay the same. But he'd had to tell her, before she fell in love with him forever, before they took the marriage thing too far. She had to know the truth about him first.

He tugged on the reins and Grey Beauty halted, slacking one hip. Maddie slid down and fled inside in a swirl of crushed silk before he could move.

The door slammed shut. He sighed and slid down, too. "Come on, girl, let's get you rubbed down."

He'd promised Mr. Temple he'd take care of Gray Beauty and that was what he intended to do. Earlier that day he'd prepared Draoi's barn, and he led the mare into the empty, bedded stall and unbuckled the bridle. Maddie had just vanished inside with his jacket, so he unbuttoned his cuffs, grabbed the body brush from the grooming bucket, and leaned into his strokes.

"I guess you could say this evening didn't go exactly as I'd planned." The horse didn't respond, just tugged a mouthful of hay from the hanging net, and he continued. "I thought she might be a little angry at me. Maybe we'd talk about it, or something. But I couldn't just say, 'Hey, you want to promise yourself to me?' and then turn around and lie to her." He sighed and ran his hand through his hair, remembering the way she'd stared at him when he'd done that in the cave. She must have just caught on to the action.

Brush replaced in the bucket, he checked her hoofs, patted her one final time, and secured the stall door behind her. Mr. Temple would pick Gray Beauty and her gear up in the morning and take her home. Missing his jacket in the cooling night air, he sauntered slowly toward the house. Lights backlit the curtains, giving the house an eerie glow.

As if someone lived there who'd be at home with a flying monster. Right.

Chase didn't stop in the dark, wax-scented living room, but proceeded upstairs. Maddie was just leaving the bathroom as he hit the landing. She shuffled her feet as he approached, but didn't run away. Instead, quickly, she pecked his cheek. She seemed fragile and it would be easy to frighten her; he was afraid to move. She turned on her heel and entered her room, the door clicking shut behind her. Already the closeness they had shared seemed to have melted away.

He studied the door. Maybe she just needed time to process what he'd told her. It couldn't be easy, knowing your boyfriend sometimes turned into a gray beast with wings.

He entered his own room and found she'd laid his jacket over the back of a chair. The thoughtfulness clenched his teeth and he paced. Tensed up from telling her and waiting for disaster to strike, there was no way he could sleep. Comfortingly, soft snores emitted from Maddie's room, and he breathed more easily knowing *she* slept.

Moonlight filtered through the bedroom window and pooled across the table. Silver keys sparkled. Might as well work, if he couldn't sleep. Keys and wallet gathered, he secured the house and climbed into the truck.

Ten minutes later he entered the hardware store, already emptied and half of the lights put out. When the bell dinged above the door, the owner turned and frowned at him. Apparently a last minute customer wasn't what he wanted.

Chase rushed to buy what he needed. With everything stacked in the bed of the truck, he drove back to Draoi's. He entered the silent house, walked upstairs, cracked Maddie's door, and peeked inside. She lay curled on her side, peacefully sleeping.

Time was limited. Downstairs he dragged a white paper suit over his clothes and mentally categorized what needed doing.

By night's end the room would look completely different.

33

The alarm blared. Maddie rolled onto her side, slapped the snooze button, and closed her eyes for nine more blissful minutes. When it blared the second time, she groaned and struggled her way to a sitting position. She stretched like a Cheshire cat, climbed from bed, grabbed her things, and headed to the bathroom.

Finally dressed and ready and with only minutes to spare, she grabbed her backpack and ran for it. But a whistle left her lips when she'd bounded downstairs. She dropped her chin and her fingers relaxed, sliding her backpack to the floor.

"You shouldn't throw your things," said Chase's tired voice. "I just cleaned there."

She glanced around and found him in the kitchen doorway. "Chase," she paused to take in a breath, "when did you have time to do this?" She pointed to the freshly painted walls. The room glowed a pale gold shade, new and inviting. She loved it.

"Last night."

"When did you sleep?"

He shrugged. "Sleep is overrated."

She hugged him and kissed his cheek, more grateful than words alone could say. Grandma Draoi would love it, too. She just knew it. "Chase, you didn't have to."

He clasped her upper arms and ran his hands along her goose-pimpled flesh. "I know, but your grandma didn't need to come home to that mess." He released his grip and Maddie shuddered from the loss of warmth. Turning away, he said, "Grab your books and let's get on down the road."

She complied and they left for school. The day was uncomfortable. Chase acted standoffish, like he wasn't sure about them any more. And Maddie didn't know how to rectify the situation. Instead of focusing on her failed relationship, she studied Dougal. Their discovery of last night had her searching for clues to his alter ego.

School ended as if she'd dreamed the day and Chase drove Maddie directly home, rather than stopping by his house for dinner. She found herself missing his little brothers already.

Neither of them mentioned his revealed secret. Maddie wished everything could go back to normal, or that she'd find and live some version of that word. Why couldn't he just be a regular hot guy and her a regular plain girl? Why couldn't they have the normal problems that came from being a teenager, like acne, bad hair, and what to wear? Granted, she really liked his wings...

Scenery flashed by the speeding vehicle. How was it possible the entire outside world was still the same when her world was falling apart?

Chase turned onto the driveway and braked at the far end. The truck shuddered to a halt, arousing her from her thoughts. A strange sedan waited in the driveway. Chase helped Maddie out of the truck and they walked toward the house.

"Have you ever seen that car before?" he asked in a hoarse whisper.

"No." She shook her head. "Nor have I ever seen it in the church parking lot."

"Who do you think it is?"

"I'm not sure."

A middle-aged woman, her arms laden with boxes, pushed roughly through the front door. "I'll just throw these away, Mrs. Casey-Brennan," she yelled over her shoulder. Facing them, she narrowed her eyes. "Hello. Can I help you?"

"I'm Maddie Clevenger." Maddie extended her hand.

The woman dropped the boxes at the trunk of the foreign-made car, dusted her hands on her pant legs, leaned back, and cocked one brow. "I'm sorry. Is that name supposed to mean something to me?"

Surprised by the woman's rudeness, Maddie said, "I'm Draoi Casey-Brennan's great-granddaughter."

"Oh, yes." The lady paused and eyed Maddie curiously. Finished with her blatant perusal, she added, "She has spoken of you."

Maddie waited for more but the woman clamped her heavily painted lips. She loaded the boxes in her trunk, climbed behind the wheel of her car, and sped down the road.

"How rude!" said Maddie.

"Agreed." The vehicle disappeared from sight, and Maddie and Chase entered the house. "Your grandma is asking for you. Are you going to be okay?"

"Yeah."

"Then I guess I'll go. I'll pick you up in the morning."

Already. Her heart felt as if it wanted to stop beating. "Will you call?"

He wrapped his arms around her waist and snuggled his nose against her neck. "Just try and stop me."

She planted a kiss on his cheek, glad for at least a small semblance of normality. "You better go. I'll be fine and if I'm not, I'll call."

"Promise?"

"Promise." She couldn't stop a small smile.

Maddie waited in the front yard until the dust settled. She dragged her feet as she drew closer to the porch. She was glad her grandma was home and yearned to speak with her; she needed to convince herself that Grandma Draoi was all right, but a tense ache filled her heart at being separated from Chase. Even if part of her was still aggravated with him over concealing the truth of his identity.

Holding the doorknob in her hand, she glanced at the golden band around her finger and then down the driveway. Tail lights faded as he joined the main highway. Sighing, she opened the door and entered. She froze and glanced around as bagpipe music flowed through the house.

"Grandma?"

"In here, dear."

In the living room, Grandma held a broom like a partner and danced. A smile creased her lined face.

"Grandma, are you okay?"

"Never better."

Well, she sounded good. "Can I get you anything?" Maddie eyed Grandma with curiosity and clutched her hands behind her back.

"Nope, I'm peachy." Grandma Draoi and the broom whirled together around the room. Neither one bent very well, though.

"Are you sure you're my grandma?"

She laughed, a strong and delightful sound. "Of course I'm your grandma. And I'm so happy to be alive."

Relieved, Maddie hugged her. "I'm glad you're alive, as well. Please don't scare me like that again."

"I'll do my best."

"I'm glad you're home."

"So am I. Did Chase bring you home from school?"

"Yeah. He's been staying with me since you've been in the hospital."

"Did he paint?" She and the broom whirled in a perfect circle.

She hesitated.

"Answer me, child."

"Yes."

"Was there a reason he painted my walls?"

"Yes." Maddie gnawed the inside of her cheek and tried to avoid saying more.

Grandma Draoi, despite her exertions, didn't seem breathless. "Well?"

She gulped. "Someone broke in and spray painted the wall."

The broom clattered to the floor and Grandma Draoi grabbed Maddie's upper arms in a vise-like grip. "What did the words say?"

Surprised, she stuttered. "Th-there were the obvious bad words a-and one word I'd never seen before."

"What was it?" Grandma's grip relaxed.

Maddie stepped back and massaged her arms, trying to make sense of everything. Surely she'd understand more if Chase was still there with her. "The word was *eochair*." She pronounced it phonetically. "Do you know what it means?"

"Yes." Grandma slid onto the couch and studied her worn hands. Her former partner lay unnoticed on the floor.

Maddie waited. When Grandma didn't say more, she asked, "Are you going to tell me what it means?"

"We'll discuss it later." She patted the seat beside her. "Tell me, how was school today?"

"Fine." But Maddie didn't want to discuss school. "How do you feel?"

"Fine. Great. Fabulous! Never better."

She sounded it. But strangely, Maddie didn't find that comforting. "Did the doctor give you any information on what happened to you?"

"No."

Figured. "Oh."

Grandma Draoi slapped her palms onto her upper thighs and bounced to her feet, as if the strange conversation had never happened. "Why don't you do your homework? After you finish, we'll eat supper and I'll tell you a story."

A story... Maddie's heart leapt. Like she wanted to do homework. Anxious about Grandma's health, and now convinced something was going on, she wanted to spend every available moment downstairs observing. But Maddie shook herself, agreed, and went to her room. Books spread on the desk in front of her, she struggled to focus. All she could think about was talking to Grandma later.

Sometimes homework passed the time. Sometimes it didn't. That afternoon, it didn't. Chase called, but even he couldn't do the trick. She was so distracted they didn't talk long.

Suppertime finally arrived, but still Grandma spoke of nothing but frivolities, as if she'd never been in a hospital in her life, as if their lives had never been interrupted. Maddie's patience wore thin. Tired of waiting, she said, "Grandma, when are you going to tell me what you know?"

Grandma Draoi chuckled. "Impatient, are we?"

"Yes!"

"I thought I would tell you a bedtime story."

"Fine, then I'm ready for bed."

Grandma grinned. "Okay, you prepare and I'll meet you upstairs."

Even though the sun had barely set and she still had enough energy to run laps around the forest, Maddie rushed upstairs and pulled on her pajamas. She skipped to the bed like a little girl and jumped in, her heart pounding. She'd learn something, and if the price included humoring Grandma's strange whims, then it was a cheap price indeed.

Soon Grandma ambled in, pulled the desk's chair close, and sat down. "What were we going to do?"

"Grandma!" *Not funny.*

Grandma giggled. "I'm just joking, child. Where should I begin? First of all, close your eyes."

"But—"

"Don't argue with your elders. Close your eyes."

"Yes, ma'am."

"Good. Now, let me see. How to start? Ah, yes. Long ago in a small town far away, there lived a beautiful young auburn-haired girl."

Maddie cracked open one eyelid and peered curiously up through her lashes. Grandma leaned back in the chair and a dreamy expression covered her face.

"The young girl lived in a village that was terrorized by a brutal army. One day, the beautiful young girl's sister disappeared. The young girl looked for her sister but couldn't find her. While hunting, she ran into a warrior and in desperation, she enlisted his help."

A warrior... The word echoed in Maddie's head as if shouted in a cave. *...warrior...* Her eye closed on its own.

"In exchange for his help, he made the young girl give him a promise. Actually, he asked for two things. One was her love. The other was even more important—she was to be a key."

"A key?" Maddie's body grew heavy as sleep threatened to overcome her. Wait, what had happened to all her energy, her impatience? If she hadn't known better, she'd have accused Grandma Draoi of casting a spell on her. *A spell... magic...*

The room darkened and her eyelids grew heavier.

"Yes," Grandma said, her voice measured and dream-laden, "a key. The warrior magically created an ivory tower and he planned to lure the brutal army inside. Once they were trapped, he would sneak out and she would lock the door. Special words were to be spoken which would seal the door, hopefully forever. Because once sealed, the door could only be opened by the girl's touch or by the touch of her descendants."

The last sentence was muttered in a breathy whisper and Maddie wasn't sure she'd heard it correctly. Before she could ask, Grandma Draoi's voice faded away and Maddie fell into a deep sleep.

34

Dougal tapped his fingers on the steering wheel. How could he get Maddie away from Chase? He'd tried the jealousy route using Stephanie, but it never seemed to work. If anything, it seemed to be sending Maddie closer to him.

Cool air struck his face and a hint of lavender drifted toward him. He abhorred the scent. Why was he still picking Stephanie up and carting her to school?

And then there was her voice.

"Hey, babe, why don't we go to the movies this afternoon? I hear that…"

He winced.

She droned on and on, but all he heard was *blah, blah, blah.* Yup, getting away from her was a must. He had one nagging woman at home in the cave; he didn't need one at school, as well.

Stephanie was still talking when he braked the SUV to a halt outside the school. She jumped out, still talking, and he released a pent-up breath. To get rid of her, he would have to do something dramatic, really dramatic. A simple *we're through* would never be enough. Perhaps he should kiss Maddie. A smile twitched his lips. That would do more than just get rid of Stephanie.

He ran his hands through his hair, thinking about Maddie's kiss.

"Are you coming?" Stephanie peered through the driver's side window.

He jumped. He hadn't even heard her approach. Maybe he should just open the door and knock her to the other side of the parking lot. That would do the trick.

Instead, he carefully stepped from the vehicle without touching her.

"If you don't want to see the movie, then we can go to the diner. I'm good either way."

They entered the school and he headed for his locker. Of course she followed him. His puppy dog was never far behind.

Marley rounded the corner. A smile tilted her lips and she waved in their direction. Hope lifted his spirits. He might have just found his saving grace. Dougal waved her over. Eyebrows arching, Marley pointed to herself. He nodded. She dipped her head and let her hair swoop over her eye. She was the perfect candidate. Now he just needed to wait for the right time.

The halls filled with teen chatter. He hated it.

He laid his arm across Stephanie's shoulders. Since their romantic evening, Chase and Maddie had been growing close, too close. He needed a drastic action so she would know he was still interested in other people, in her. Serena might not approve, but why did he care? Let her torture Gregory and leave the key to him.

As he should have done all along. He should have never listened to Serena's whining.

He arched his head back and sniffed. Ah, *there,* her scent; the key was close. He narrowed his eyes, feeling her mental touch. She watched him. Perfect.

He slid his arm free and shoved his hands in his pockets, secretly watching Marley's progress. She didn't count, either— only the key mattered now—but as a tool, she'd do.

Stephanie bumped his side. "Hey, what gives?" Her eyelid twitched.

He almost laughed at her worry, but instead clasped her hands and stared into her eyes. The dull, lifeless eyes of a normal person. Disgusting. "Stephanie, it's over."

"What?" She blinked.

With an exaggerated motion, he shrugged. "You're just not as popular as I thought. And your clothes!" He tsked and roved his eyes over her. "Totally last week. I can't date a girl who wears ugly clothes." Marley's approach brought her close enough. He grabbed her and pulled her into an embrace, stroked a strand of hair behind her ear, and smiled. She gaped like a dying fish. "Now you, you are gorgeous."

Stephanie cried out and ran from the hallway.

Had Maddie seen? He could almost feel her heartbeat increase. Oh, yeah, she had seen.

He put his hand on Marley's back and guided her to class. It was going to be an interesting day.

Maddie fell back against the lockers as a crying blond blur sped past. She lifted her head and stared back down the corridor, but Dougal had already turned and was heading the other way. Why had he done that? What was the point of pushing Stephanie away? But in all honesty... Maddie quirked her lips upward. Did she care? Stephanie had finally gotten what was coming to her. It aroused a twinge of guilt, but she quickly pushed it aside as Chase appeared and planted a kiss on her cheek.

"Why is everyone standing around and staring?" he whispered.

Should she explain what had happened? Yeah. Yeah, she should. "I think Dougal just broke up with Stephanie."

"Ah." He narrowed his eyes.

Was he worried? She turned into his arms. The teachers would pull them apart soon, but for now she would enjoy his touch.

His warm breath caressed her cheek. "Do you want to go for another hike on Saturday?"

She nodded. Of course she did. Judging by her own behavior, at least a part of her had totally and utterly forgiven him for keeping secrets, and she drifted through the rest of the school day with a goofy grin on her face that spoke of nothing but happiness.

The week had passed so slowly. Grandma Draoi hadn't spoken again of the story she'd told and Maddie hadn't asked. She'd slept so hard, so dreamlessly, that night that— well, when she'd awakened, she wasn't certain she'd heard the story properly at all. Nor did she want to think about it too deeply. With all her emotions about Chase in an uproar, she didn't have the energy for some unnamed girl from "far away" who had sealed a tower door, if she'd even heard that part right.

That afternoon, Chase dropped her off in her driveway and Maddie watched the truck's retreating tail lights until nothing but a speck remained, the way she watched Alasdair vanish in the sky after rescuing her. As usual when she found herself without Chase, the evening passed slowly. She finished her homework, watched a movie with Grandma Draoi, and climbed into bed. The sooner Saturday morning arrived, the sooner she could be with Chase. She planned to let him know she'd been wrong, that she knew he'd been protecting her with his secret and that she hadn't been ready to know the truth.

Her protector. Her *secret* protector. Every girl in the world should be so lucky. Well, except for one.

Early the next morning, Maddie waited anxiously for the honking of Chase's horn. She had already checked on Grandma Draoi. All the emergency numbers were programmed into the phone and Chase's parents had promised to call and check on her grandma at regular intervals.

What could possibly go wrong?

A knock interrupted her thoughts. She opened the door and Chase entered. "Are you ready?"

"Yep. Just let me tell Grandma goodbye and grab my jacket."

Chase paced and prayed Maddie would hurry. He... he wanted Maddie all to himself, without his parents, her grandma, or anyone from the school peering sideways at them. Was it too much to ask for them to be alone together, just for a while?

Maddie bounded back into the room. Her enthusiasm was infectious and he found himself grinning.

"You're happy today."

"Of course. Grandma's home and feeling better every day, and it's Saturday, which means I'm spending the entire day with someone very special to me."

Warmth invaded his heart. "Who is it? I want to know," he said in a jesting tone.

"Why, it's this really handsome, romantic, and considerate guy I met at school."

He groaned dramatically. "What will I do? How will I ever be able to compete?"

"I don't know. It's going to be hard. I think I forgot to mention how charming he can be and oh, he's also very humble."

Chase covered his mouth, but the laughter spilled through. Maybe being interrupted by Mom wouldn't be the end of the world. "I guess since I can't compete with your special friend, I'll just have to exhibit qualities he hasn't thought of yet."

She tilted her head and her eyes half closed. "Like what?"

"Like chivalry," he said, opening the back door for her and holding out his hand so she could walk through first.

She walked through but didn't look impressed. "What else?"

"Perhaps a display of strength." He picked her up, carried her across the little lawn, and deposited her in the truck before skipping around the hood and climbing behind the wheel. It wasn't the first time he'd carried her, but for some reason she seemed so light, as if she'd lost weight. But she hadn't, certainly not that much.

Still not impressed, she looked at him sideways. "And?"

He started the engine and shifted gear. "Laughter?"

Her lips twitched, but she controlled it. "I don't get your meaning."

He'd only driven a few feet, but that couldn't pass without challenge. The truck shuddered to a halt and he shifted back to park, then scooted closer to Maddie. Carefully he stuck his index finger straight up in the air, studied it, then casually jabbed it into her ribs.

She shrieked, squirmed, and tried to wriggle away. "Chase, I get it. I get it!"

"Good." Back behind the wheel, he shifted again and headed toward the main road.

Maddie folded her hands in her lap and stared at them. "Did you see the letter Stephanie wrote in the school paper?"

He didn't mind that she changed the subject. Lighthearted banter was just what the doctor ordered. "No, I haven't read it yet."

"She thinks they shouldn't vote for prom queen this year. In her humble opinion, and I quote, 'It would be a waste of time.'"

He snorted a laugh. "So she thinks she'll win no matter what. She wrote that before Dougal dumped her, right?"

267

"That's what it sounded like to me." But her smile was contented.

After thoroughly discussing prom, they moved on to other, less fascinating subjects until they arrived at the park. Chase helped Maddie from the truck and locked his doors. For some reason, they'd both forgotten their walking sticks. Chase humphed. Maybe they'd been too busy getting away to think straight.

"Are we ready?" he asked.

"Yep, we're ready."

They followed the lake trail, heavy with the scents of pine and damp earth, and memories of a night not so long ago flooded his mind.

Maddie drew in a deep breath. "This brings back memories, some good..."

"Some not so good," he finished for her.

In the daylight, the woods were not nearly as intimidating. They covered the trail in half the time, stopping to look out over the lake or just to enjoy an unusual tree or plant. The air was autumn crisp without being cold, and the sunlight glittered from the still water, turning it to liquid metal.

But in the heavy ground near the shoreline, Maddie narrowed her eyes and squatted. She touched her fingers to the gooey edges of what appeared to be an animal's pawprint. "What do you think it is?"

He hadn't even seen the print until she'd pointed it out. Chase glared around the sky and peered at the shadows beneath the tree line. "I'm afraid I might know."

She stood and rubbed her hands clean on her pants. "Do you think Dougal or Gregory has been out here? Surely this footprint couldn't have lasted all week?"

They'd had rain at some point, hadn't they? "I don't know." Chase bent and inspected the print more thoroughly.

The size and shape resembled the pawprint of a lion, only much larger and longer. The muddy impression seemed fairly fresh and it squished beneath his fingertips.

"What do you think?" she asked.

"I think we should keep moving."

"I second that. Oh, I forgot to tell you about this great story my grandma told me. Are you interested?"

Something like a warning stirred in his blood. But he kept

his voice casual. "Sure."

She led the way down the trail and spoke over her shoulder. "It was a love story. This warrior helped this girl search for her missing sister and in return he asked for her love and her help. She gave both."

So far he liked it.

She paused, waiting for him to catch up, and side by side they circled the lake. "He had some kind of dispute with his army unit and he needed to do something about them, or something. So he erected a huge, magical tower and asked her to seal the door once everyone was in and he was safely out. Then she and her ancestors would forever have the power to open the door merely by touching it. Why are you looking at me like that?"

It felt as if his blood turned to ice in his veins. "I'm stunned."

Her smile faded away. "Okay, why?"

"This whole time the answer was right in front of me." And now the last piece of the puzzle folded into place.

"Chase, what are you talking about?"

With one hand, he smacked his forehead. "It was so obvious."

"Chase? Seriously, what are you talking about?"

He grasped her by the shoulders. Her eyes, wide and frightened, stared back into his. At some deep, subconscious level, she knew, too.

"The story, Maddie. It's about Cian and Arin."

"Who?"

"It doesn't matter right now. What does matter is that, just like Dad thought, you're Arin's descendant. You're the key to opening the prison!" The words tumbled from him and everything became clear. The Donovan family had dedicated their lives as protectors of the key, while Arin's family *was* the key.

Beneath his hands, she shivered. "What are you talking about? I'm confused."

"I should have known as soon as I heard the meaning of your name. The word spray-painted on your wall, *eochair*, means key."

"Grandma didn't tell me."

He shook her gently. "That's why Doran wants you. *You* can free his family."

35

A slow, loud clapping echoed behind them. They whirled together. A dark figure loomed in the shadows of the trees. A stray shaft of sunlight pierced the pine boughs and flashed a rim of white fire along the upper edges of the figure's charcoal wings, arched above and behind its head like a dark heart.

"You finally figured it out. I was starting to wonder about your level of intelligence."

"Dougal?" Maddie asked. What was he doing there? That couldn't be good. And the black heart of his wings... she shivered.

The figure stepped from the shadows, and the sunlight revealed the dark gryphon himself. He spread his hands out to the sides as if presenting himself. Sharp claws gleamed. "In the flesh, or the fur, if you prefer."

"How did you find us?" Maddie asked, her palms sweating. She didn't know what Dougal-Doran was up to, and she didn't want to know. They had to get away.

He tapped one claw to his forehead. "Duh! Let's see. I can fly." He scoffed and shook his head. "Sometimes I wonder about Arin's children and their brains. Surely you've got it all figured out by now."

"No," she whispered breathlessly.

Beside her, Chase said nothing. But she could feel his presence like a scorching heat. When she reached out a hand, his fingers—human still—closed around hers. Good. He'd change into gryphon form and they'd escape.

"Well, then, let me say that your grandma is quite the little witch. She has been hiding you and your mother, and before that your grandmother, for years. But hiding two people presented a challenge, and somehow Gregory discovered your whereabouts." The fur covering his face let little emotion show through. But somehow she got the impression he wasn't nearly as pleased or victorious as he tried to sound.

She shook her head, shook off the thought, and tried to concentrate. "Gregory? What does he want from me?"

The big shoulders shrugged, the dark wings above and behind echoing the movement. "Oh, that's very simple. Like he said before, he just wants to kill you."

"Great. Why?"

"He was the gryphon who stole Arin's sister, starting the war and that little family feud you were talking about. He fears Cahal's release, so he has been killing Arin's offspring to ensure Cahal never returns. Simple, really. It's self-preservation."

"That's why he started the fire, to kill me? Then you saved me because you *do* want Cahal to be freed?"

"Yes, dear, you're correct."

"Why would you want Cahal to be freed? Right now, you're the only one of your kind." She tried to emphasize with her tone that he was special, unique.

But he didn't take her bait. "Not quite."

"Well, very close. So why do you want Cahal freed?"

She squeezed her fingers. But Chase didn't speak and she was running out of things to say to stall Dougal. What was wrong with Chase? Why wasn't he changing into Alasdair and flying them out of there?

Dougal laughed loudly and a figure left the forest shadows, slithering across the clearing like a snake and stopping beside him. Maddie gasped at its hideous form.

The snake-woman shook back her hair. Strangely, it was well-combed, styled in a fashionable up-do, with blond curls that danced on her shoulders. But the rest of her... "That's right. You're looking at a monster. My name's Serena, but I'm not myself. In truth," she laid one grotesque hand on her chest, "I am a beautiful woman." Enraged determination set her face in hard lines. "That is why Cahal must be freed."

Maddie let go of Chase's hand—*why wasn't he changing?*—crossed her arms over her chest, and attempted to put on a brave front. "That doesn't explain why Dougal is helping you."

Dougal guffawed. "She does have a point."

"Shut up, Doran," said Serena.

Maddie hoped it didn't hurt Chase's feelings but if he wasn't going to fly them out of danger, then she had to win Dougal to their side. She swallowed her fear. "I know Dougal has feelings for me, so I can't imagine why he would help *you*."

Chase fisted his hands.

Serena slapped her scaly tail against Dougal's dark-furred legs. "Answer the girl. Tell her what I hold over you." Dougal whispered the answer and Serena said, "Speak up, Doran, they can't hear you."

Doran shouted his answer and it echoed from the trees. "Serena has no hold over me. We were raised in the same village, nothing more. Are you happy?" He glared at Serena.

"No, I'm not." She gave him a little push. "Go on, tell your little love kitten why you're freeing your brothers."

Love kitten? Maddie felt like she'd been slimed.

He shrugged, "It's very simple—power."

"What?" Maddie said, shocked.

Serena slithered around him in a circle, running a long nail along Dougal's forearm. A thin red line appeared through the dark fur, then was instantly gone. "Honestly, darling, how can you be attracted to one so dumb? Please explain this to her, so we can get out of here. My head is beginning to hurt."

Dougal sighed. "Anything to stop your headache, dear," he said sarcastically. "Alasdair's line is of the grays, which are sworn protectors. But I'm different. After my father kidnapped my mother, he morphed to a human with the help of magic. My birth didn't occur until after the great imprisonment." He shifted out of Serena's circle and flexed his wings, forcing her away.

"Imagine my surprise to find out I was the only one! A freak! Everyone I knew grew up and died, but I stayed suspended in time as a young man, with no one like me. That's when Serena found me and explained that I wasn't the only one and that I didn't have to be alone. Now I want to free my father and the fallen gryphons, and take my rightful place as ruler of the world."

Beside her, Chase shifted. "Why do you think Alasdair exists?"

And suddenly Maddie realized why Chase hadn't changed: outnumbered as he was, talk was a better weapon than fists and claws. She forced a stoic expression, hoping to protect his secret.

Serena threw out her deformed hands. "Well, isn't it obvious? Alasdair is of the same race as Cian, the race of the grays, the defenders of mankind. After Cahal and his black warriors were imprisoned, Cian made a pact between the grays and the humans. The grays would spend their lives protecting the descendents of Arin and in turn her descendants would keep the tower locked. Alasdair has come into existence because Maddie is of the line of Arin and she has been threatened."

"How come his whole family hasn't changed?" His voice sounded strained and she wished she could squeeze his hand and offer reassurance. She should never have let his hand go.

"Because in order for a gray to change, he must feel the urge to protect. It's even stronger if the one in need of protection is his true love." Serena lifted her head to the sky, peering around. "By the way, where is your protector? Shouldn't he be here?"

She planted her hands on her hips. "Why? I'm not in danger, remember? You can't get me to open the tower if I'm dead." Hopefully her words would distract them from Chase's increasing tension. He felt like a time bomb beside her, awaiting the right moment to explode.

"Serena, she does have a point." Dougal grinned, but still... for someone who thought he was about to win a great victory, he seemed almost as strained as Chase.

Serena hissed. "She may not be in danger from death, but she is greatly mistaken if she thinks she is safe."

As if at a signal, Dougal whirled, stalked back to the forest's edge, and shoved bushes aside. Black fur, stained and matted—Gregory, bound with chains. Maddie started back, then froze. The black gryphon was even more hideous in daylight. His overly long black snout sniffed at the air. Long, thick, hairy arms were crushed to his sides. He stretched his wings behind him, fighting against the confining links. His eyes bulged as he stared at Chase. A chuckle rent the air.

He knows! Maddie shivered. She prayed he wouldn't say anything. After all, they shared a common goal. Neither one of them wanted the tower opened.

"What is he laughing about?" Serena frowned.

"Who knows?" Dougal-Doran shrugged. "He's obviously crazy."

"No, I think he has another motivation." Serena whipped her head up and again stared around the sky, her eyes bulging out.

A soft wind blew from off the lake, the first for hours. Maddie's hair teased her cheeks. Chase muttered something under his breath, shifting beside her. Dougal lifted his nose and sniffed.

Serena glared at Chase. Her eyes widened. "You!"

Chase's body convulsed, whirling, stretching, bulging. Fur sprouted, claws, teeth. He barely had time to morph before Dougal jumped on him and pinned him to the ground.

Serena droned on and on. Chase ground his teeth, taxing his energy to remain human. He was pretty sure he could outfly Doran, but Serena was unknown and her snake-like tail stretched longer than he liked. Who knew what she could do with it? Could she grab him out of the sky and dash them together on the rocks? Of course she'd make certain he landed on bottom; she wanted the *eochair* for her own use. And if he died...

Maddie would be alone.

Then Gregory snuffled the breeze. Chase swallowed. Gregory's changing expression caused his stomach to clench. Was the black gryphon going to give him away? *Maddie...*

But then Dougal lifted his snout and Chase knew it was over. He let go and the change coursed through his body. Now Dougal pinned him to the ground. The hundred-year-old black gryphon bared his claws and thrust them at Chase's neck. Defensively he raised his hands and instead Dougal swiped his side. Blood sprayed and Chase cried out.

Maddie screamed and ran to help, fists clenched. But Serena's tail whipped out and wrapped around her, yanking her back. He wanted to tell her to stop fighting, that he'd be fine. His wounds had all healed in the past. Surely these would heal, as well.

Without releasing his hold, Dougal heaved Chase from the

ground. Chase grabbed blindly over his shoulder, but he couldn't even get a handful of wing feathers before the lakeshore whirled around him. Thrown about like a rag doll, he realized his folly. Instead of romancing Maddie, he should've been learning more of the necessary skills to defend her. Instead he'd left it all to his instincts. But surely the black gryphons had the same instincts, and after a hundred years of life, Dougal knew in his bones how to fight.

Suddenly the ground was there. Chase's wings tried to extend—they knew what to do, even when he didn't—but Dougal twisted his hold. Chase crunched face-first into the rocky shore.

"How pitiful." Dougal grabbed his wing and leaned on it. Pain wracked up Chase's back into his chest. "If the gray gryphons can defend no better than this, it's no wonder Gregory was able to annihilate all the *eochairs*."

Once more Chase tried to wrestle free. Once more Dougal smashed his face into the ground and leaned on his wing. Through the blood dripping into his eye, Chase watched as Maddie wept silently.

Serena jerked her hair. Speaking to Dougal, she said, "Are you ready?"

"Yes." Dougal's voice didn't even sound winded. Humiliating.

Serena spoke unintelligible words. Chase's head swam and lights swirled around him. He closed his eyes and when he opened them, he lay face-down atop purple heather. So the snake-woman could work magic, too. His heart sank within him. It was hard to convince himself they weren't doomed.

"Where are we?" Maddie's eyes were wide with fear.

"In Ireland, my dear."

Slowly Chase lifted his head. The heather extended in all directions, to a distant stand of dark trees on the left, and on the right...

A pale tower shimmered into focus.

Maddie squirmed and struggled against her captor. "I won't do it!"

"Madelyn, dear, you can only open the door if you do so willingly. And we both know you want to open the door." Dougal's voice made the words sound like dripping poisoned honey.

"That's where you're mistaken." She fought harder, her hair falling over her eyes. "There's no way you'll ever get me to open the door."

Serena's tail snaked farther up Maddie's struggling body. Dougal scoffed and gave Maddie an evil smile. With the distraction, Chase's— no, *Alasdair's* strength and hope increased. He lunged, but Dougal was too quick. Again Alasdair found himself eating purple heather. He screamed in agony as Dougal sank his claws into Alasdair's side and ripped off a chunk of the repairing flesh.

Alasdair collapsed, lights flashing before his eyes, and he struggled to stay conscious. Dougal held the chunk of flesh for Maddie's inspection. She turned an unsightly shade of green.

"Do you see this? This is only the beginning. If you wish for him to live, then you will open the door."

As quickly as that, all his hope died. "No," Chase moaned in a ragged whisper.

No more.

Maddie cast a final glance at Alasdair—her own beloved Chase, now beaten and bloody—and stepped forward as Serena's tail fell away. The entire scenario reminded her of her dream; only this time it wasn't a dream. It was most definitely real. The grass with the purple flowers was indeed a field of heather in Ireland. The tower that once shimmered in her dreams now loomed, solid and forbidding. And she'd hear Chase's agonized scream in her soul for the rest of her life.

As she strode forward, the heather tickled her legs through her jeans. If she closed her eyes, she could almost imagine herself home in bed, sleeping and dreaming the nightmare that never ended.

She glanced back over her shoulder.

Gregory lay bound, chains wrapped around his wings and body. Dougal-Doran stood over Gregory with fangs and claws bared, daring him to break free and try to escape. Alasdair, her loving Chase, curled on the ground with Serena's tail now writhing around him, his side sliced open, the ground blackened with his blood. The beast part of his body tried to heal the wound; she could see it starting to close, but then Serena squeezed him with her tail and fresh blood spurted. He choked out another hoarse scream, weaker now.

"Go on, lassss," hissed Serena. Triumph twisted her face into even more of a mockery. "Touch the tower."

Maddie drew in a ragged breath and walked on. With luck, she'd die before she reached the gleaming white tower.

As she approached it shone, beautiful and pristine, the white reflecting the sun like polished ivory. Even in her terror, she thought it amazing and beautiful. However, the closer she drew, the more the tower changed. No longer white and inviting, it slowly changed to gray, drab stone. Forbidding, she thought, and her breath hitched in her throat. As she neared, wails and moans drifted from between the bars that appeared like magic on the outside walls.

"Let us out! Let us out!" It seemed thousands of voices screamed.

Maddie's heartbeat raced and she backed up. *If they got free...*

She blinked and the scenery around her changed. No longer did she stand mesmerized by the forbidding prison tower amidst the heather. Instead it seemed she crouched behind a huge, moss-covered tree trunk. A massive dark flying beast, more demon than gryphon, laughed and dragged a screaming woman from her hiding place behind another tree. A man leapt out beside her, awkwardly swinging a cudgel. But the dark gryphon whipped out one claw. Blood sprayed, the farmer gurgled and collapsed, and the gryphon yanked the woman into his arms and flew away, wings pumping. Her screams trailed behind them. Maddie turned, spied another dark beast hovering behind her, fur matted with blood...

But she blinked again and it was all gone. She stared at the tower, watching the spurting blood in her memory. No. *No.*

Behind her, Serena hissed, loud enough to be heard across the field's expanse. "Go on, lasssss, or lover boy here is a goner."

"Don't do it, Maddie!" Chase howled, but fought to choke out words even through his pain. "The whole world is at stake! Those *things* destroyed Arin's village and if you let them out, there's no telling what havoc they might cause!"

"Shut up!" yelled Serena, squeezing Chase until he let out a yell of pain.

Maddie didn't know what to do. Serena would kill Chase if she didn't open the tower door, but the escaping dark gryphons could destroy the whole world, bit by bit, if she did. She had no doubt she'd seen a memory from Arin's village, perhaps floating loose in the rampant magic of Ireland.

She looked at Dougal. He turned away, and a thread of hope twined around her thoughts. She needed to see his face. Surely there was some good in him. How many times had he saved her? Had he saved her only so he could have the prisoners released? A part of her said there was more to it. Hadn't he seemed torn earlier, not really happy that they'd won?

"Dougal, would you look at me?" Maddie called. The wind surrounding the tower sucked away the words and she yelled the question a second time.

She expected him to ignore her. Instead he faced her but didn't speak.

Surprised, she swallowed. "Won't you help me?"

He studied the ground. Serena laughed maniacally. "Are you kidding? He has wanted to use your kind for a full century!"

So much for Dougal. She aimed her next words at Serena. "What's in this for you?" She couldn't help but ask. Dougal had said it was power and surely freeing his family, as well. So what did Serena want? Maddie needed the truth. But more so, she needed to stall. Surely someone would come to her rescue. Someone had always come to her rescue. But how much time did she have? The wails and moans of the prisoners grew louder. Had they sensed her approach? Could they smell her? Her heart pounded harder.

"What's in it for me?" Serena paused, then shrugged. "Well, I'll tell you. Once I was a beautiful young girl, but I fell in love with the leader of the Ancient Ones. He promised me long life and eternal beauty if I would stay with him forever. And I promised him I would." For a moment her smile was tender, like a young girl in love for the first time. It didn't last long. "Then Cian and Arin locked him in prison! Without his presence, his magic, I turned into this horrible snake creature. I have been this way for over one hundred years and it stops now!" She contracted her tail and squeezed until Chase screamed. "Here's your last chance. Open the door or he dies."

Maddie glanced once more at Dougal. Tears raced along her cheeks. "I called you *friend*," she whispered, as she touched the door and entered the tower.

PART V
C H O I C E S

36

The door melted from in front of her. Maddie stepped through the opening; it felt like walking through mist. Solid walls of looming gray stone surrounded her. She couldn't see the bars or hear the prisoners' wails. She couldn't hear anything, not even the popping flames of a torch, and felt more alone than she had since her parents died.

"Well, this is a sticky pickle you've got yourself into." She wrung her hands and considered her next move. Fact was, she didn't know what to do next.

Light flowed from a narrow tunnel ahead. Behind her was nothing but wall, the mist-like opening and the solid wooden door both gone. She gulped and followed the tunnel. Stark stone towered over her, around her, cold and dry. The light was steady, not flickering, as if it were magic, not flame.

At the tunnel's end, she entered a hollow room. Maddie lowered her chin and gnawed her lip, too terrified to breathe. What was she supposed to do now? She'd touched the door as Serena had demanded. Surely that wasn't all of it. She couldn't just be expected to walk around this room for eternity.

She swallowed. Could she?

She turned in a circle, stopped at the halfway point, and stared. The tunnel had vanished, just like the door and mist-like opening. Where they'd been stood a platform. A lone chair resided in the middle of the raised dais, statues on each step.

Otherwise the room was empty. Steady light kept the soaring room bright, although it didn't seem to have a source. It just was.

She studied the chair without approaching it. Was she supposed to sit in it? Was that how she released the prisoners? Or had she already released them?

What had happened outside the tower when she'd entered? Did Serena continue to squeeze the life from Chase? Did Gregory fear for his own existence? Did Dougal feel remorse over allowing her to go inside?

What was she going to do?

She backed up, leaned against the wall, and slid to the floor. Cradling her head in her hands, she tried to make sense out of what she saw and what had happened.

"Why put a seat in the room if it wasn't meant to be sat on?"

Shoring up her resolve and sucking in a deep breath, she stood on wobbly legs and strode forward. Questions kept bobbing to her mind's surface. If she sat in the chair, would the whole world perish? What would happen to her? What would happen if she didn't?

That was the only question she thought she knew the answer to—Chase would die.

Three steps led up to the wooden seat. Three times bigger than any chair she had ever seen, it had massive armrests and a width made for three giants. Not a chair; a throne.

On the ends of each step poised gray stone statues. On the first step was a statue of a lion and another of an eagle. The rest of the stairs held statues of gryphons in various stages. One looked like a man with the lower half of a lion. Another was a man's legs with the upper half of an eagle. On and on it went, gryphon and man in interchangeable forms.

Maddie placed her foot on the first step and a red light glowed behind and above her. She stepped on the second step and the light glowed yellow. *Would green be next?*

She would have laughed at the craziness of the notion if she hadn't been so terrified of taking that last step. But she had to find out. She drew in a ragged breath and lifted her foot one more time. As her foot descended, a green glow bathed the room. Warning bells and alarms went off with a sound like an air raid siren. She covered her ears and fell into the chair.

37

Dougal squinted across the field of heather, watching. Maddie entered the tower and it took on a translucent look, letting him track her progress through the changing interior. Serena's face held a smile of delight. Gregory wailed and thrashed against his padlocked chains. Chase remained in beast form, lying on the ground in frozen despair. No one paid him any attention. Dougal remained still, pretending to guard the captives but instead reviewing his betrayal.

Earlier, in the forest, he could've revealed Chase's secret identity. No telling what had held him back. Perhaps he hadn't wanted to hurt Maddie—as if he hadn't when he'd ripped a chunk of flesh from her irritating defender's side. Perhaps he'd thought if Chase could get away, then Chase would leave Maddie to her fate and save himself, giving Dougal an opportunity to play hero and rescue her again. But in the end it hadn't mattered. Chase had changed to Alasdair and Dougal had been forced to crush him. He couldn't let Serena know his loyalties wavered.

In the end, Serena had been right. Injured, either form of Chase had been enough leverage to make Maddie open the tower. His heart hammered against his ribs, jealousy eating at him. What would it feel like to know someone loved you so much she would sacrifice the whole world for your life? That was the bad part about being a beast; you never wanted to share. Madelyn *should* have loved him, just as Arin's daughter should have loved him. Cian and his heirs had taken love from him for the last time. Maddie would just have to perish, as Serena had suggested.

Dougal watched Maddie from outside, sensing her fear. Through the tower's magical walls, she looked ethereal, like a beautiful ghost. She was so small against the towering fortress, so hesitant. The urge to be by her side was overwhelming. If he moved, Gregory would have a greater chance of getting free, as the watcher in his chains could easily twist his wings and let the padlocked links slide away. No, Gregory was no longer his problem.

His heart pumped faster, his sight swam before him, and his blood churned. Dougal took a step toward the tower. If he let her sit in that chair, she would be stolen from him forever. His last chance at love would be lost. Had he rescued her from the fire just so she could be a pawn in Serena's games? Had he saved her from Gregory's hand only so he could watch her die? He'd survived without his family for this long; why not continue? Which love was more important, the one that would set him free or the one from a father he'd never known—and who'd never known him?

Before he could overthink it and change his mind, Dougal leaned forward and pumped his wings, shooting straight up into the air. He swooped low, lining up with the shimmering opening. Surely now that she had walked through the magical door, it would be open to all.

Serena wailed. "Doran!"

But it was too late. Dougal folded his wings and shot through the misty door feet first. Pain ripped through him, as if he'd forced a path through solid stone or wood. He screamed. His wings convulsed and he landed on the other side in a heap. The pain radiated through him, pounding like a sledgehammer in his head, wings, and torso.

There—through the translucent walls, straight ahead, Maddie hesitated in front of the massive throne on its dais. The yellow glow surrounding her changed to green as her foot moved to the top stair.

He dragged himself up by his arms, not having the strength to stand. "Maddie, wait!" he yelled, but it was no use. "No!"

Covering her ears, she sat upon the chair and disappeared.

Chase winced and looked away. Dougal lay bruised and battered on the floor of the tower with his arm outstretched; for a moment it had looked as if he'd survived smashing through the misty doorway, but then he'd yelled something and collapsed, and hadn't moved since.

Serena laughed wildly, somewhere between hysteria and victory, relaxing her tail's grip. Her bulging eyes focused on the tower and didn't shift. Distracted; good. Chase tried to will a change to his human form, but it was useless. With the wound in his side, even though it was trying to heal, he was too weak.

Then the earth rumbled and the ground beneath them shook. The top of the tower opened and black shapes poured out, swirling in the sky. It looked like a black tornado heading for them. Cold fear solidified in his middle. Desperate, Chase glanced around again. While they'd been distracted, Gregory had escaped from his bonds and wisely had vanished. The empty chain sprawled on broken stalks, gray against purple and green. Serena ignored him, her eyes lifted to the sky as she slithered forward, her great snake's tail weaving behind her.

Chase lay on the ground as motionless as possible, still in his beastly form. Without Serena's constant squeezing, his body would heal. If Maddie touched him, would the healing have been quicker? The tingle when they touched could have been Maddie's innate *eochair* power seeping into him. That would explain why Serena had separated them.

Focusing forward, he groaned. He could no longer see inside the tower. The transparent effect had begun to dissipate after Maddie sat in the chair and disappeared. She had indeed been the key to the lock; now the door was opened, and the key was stuck inside.

A large black shape floated down from the sky toward a waiting Serena. "Cahal!" she exclaimed excitedly.

Chase closed his eyes and pretended not to exist. If he didn't move, maybe they wouldn't notice him.

The black gryphon backwinged and then settled with one final stroke. Chase swallowed. It was the biggest gryphon he'd ever seen, making his father and Gregory seem small, dwarfing Dougal and him. As if nearsighted, the gryphon peered at the snake-woman. "Aye, it is I. And who are you?"

Serena threw out her arms as if inviting the big black gryphon home. "Cahal, how can you say such a thing? It is I, Serena."

Insulting laughter escaped his eagle's beak. "You're joking, of course. Serena is a beautiful young lass."

Her tail whipped from side to side. Chase buried his head in the heather as her tail cracked like a whip over his head.

"It is I, I tell you. I was transformed when you were imprisoned."

"Oh, that is a shame." Cahal turned his back to her and lifted his hands. The flying black gryphons, turning barrel rolls and looping in the air like freed children, began swarming toward their leader.

Chase tried not to hyperventilate. There had to be thousands of them.

Serena narrowed her eyes. "Cahal, I freed you!"

"Thank you," he said, without facing her.

Impulsively, she grabbed his arm and yanked him around. One claw flashed out and sliced through her neck. *All the way* through—her head sailed through the air and her body crumpled to the heather, crushing more stalks.

"Hideous beast," murmured Cahal.

Chase hid his face and wished he could stick his head in the ground like an ostrich and hide. Swallowing back bile, he waited for Cahal to say something to him, but the black gryphons' leader ignored him.

Thousands of dark winged forms amassed in front of Cahal, too many for Chase to distinguish individuals in the throng. He shuddered and eased himself forward, sliding on his belly through the crushed heather like a soldier in no man's land. *Had to get away.*

Or die.

Cahal held out his arms in greeting. "My brothers!" The black gryphons cheered and he raised his hands, quietening them. "This day we have been freed!" Again the cheers rose, this time to overwhelming volume. And this time Cahal allowed the noise to escalate to a fever pitch before he shushed them.

"You!" One gryphon held up his hand. "Yes, you and your troop. Fly around and check the area. Set up a perimeter we can defend. And you, establish base camp." Cahal directed his men like a military leader. Assignments were barked out and black gryphons flew.

How long would he be ignored? Was it safe to try and reach the tower? He had to rescue Maddie. Might not hurt if he could save himself, as well. Pulling himself along by his weakened arms, Chase was halfway to the tower when a gryphon's gravelly voice yelled, "Sir, there's a gray gryphon headed toward the tower. Should we stop him?"

"I thought he was dead." Cahal's voice rose to a shout. "Yes, you fool! The last gray-haired gryphon imprisoned us for one hundred years!"

His fear vanished, leaving Chase calculating possibilities. He had one chance. He pretended to be more hurt than he was, rising on his legs and shifting as if drunk or about to collapse. Black gryphons closed in on him from all sides. He allowed them to get a bit closer, then he spun on his heel and shot into the sky, breaking free from their encircling wall. Because they were so close, when they tried to follow they ran into each other, wings tangling and voices shouting, and half of them collapsed back to earth.

Pulling his body in and creating a narrow shape, Chase raced for the tower's door, no longer misty and magical but once again iron-braced wood. It loomed ahead. Too late to change direction; too late to find another plan. He braced his shoulder on the uninjured side and aimed for the door. The black gryphons yelled behind him, voices rising in anticipated victory. Ignoring them, Chase concentrated on Maddie. He had to rescue her, protect her. He hit the door with his shoulder. Pain smashed through him and radiated to his injured side and neck. The wood splintered and gave way.

He'd made it. He was on the other side, and a few cautious flaps of his wings settled him on the stone-flagged floor.

Outside, the black gryphons massed around the door but none of them were willing to walk through. Their victorious yells rose into howls of rage. Well, if he'd been imprisoned for one hundred years, he might not willingly walk back into the tower, either. Turning his back, Chase jogged along the long narrow tunnel, entering the chamber.

No sign of Maddie. Even the magical green glow was gone. Still in Doran's beast form, Dougal sat on the lowest step, the one with the red glow, holding his head in his hands.

Fear twisted in Chase's gut. He collapsed beside Dougal

and tried to decide what to do next.

Maddie blinked. The tower room vanished and something else took its place. But no light penetrated and whatever surrounded her remained hidden. All she heard was her own ragged breathing; the scent of heather was gone. She slid off the chair, held her hands before her, and shuffled forward. Striking her knees against stone wouldn't be fun, but the anticipated pain never came. Was there anything around her? It felt as if she'd walked a long way.

Suddenly a beacon of light blazed out. Maddie squeezed her eyes closed against the brightness, paused to calm her pounding heart, then edged closer. The light appeared to come from a figure of some kind, like a torch held overhead.

"Who are you?" Maddie asked, fighting a consuming fear.

"I am Cian Conn." The light moved aside, out of her eyes, and she gasped. He was breathtaking. Shaped completely like a man, with no hint of his former gryphon self, he shone gauzily like a rare opal. His eyes glowed amber; one hand, held over his head, blazed with light. When he spoke it was like listening to a legion, with scores of voices underlying his own.

The shock didn't dissipate and Maddie wished for something to hold onto. With bravery she didn't feel, she asked, "Are you the one who helped Arin?"

"Aye, I am."

Sadness pervaded the room like a mist and Maddie shivered. But instead of elaborating, he fell silent. Glancing around, she gnawed her lip. A circular room soared overhead and all around, completely enclosed, with no windows and no doors. However she'd arrived, she could see no way out.

The silence bothered her. She cleared her throat. "What happened to you?"

He shrugged. "That depends." It seemed as if fewer of his vocal legions spoke with him now, more of the underlying echoes falling away with each syllable. Strong and reassuring, his own baritone voice wove a tranquil spell around her drained body, and the light from his hand softened, too.

"What?"

"When do you mean?"

"I— I guess I mean, how did you get here, in the tower."

He looked away, as if into the distance. "We are not in the tower."

"I don't understand."

"Of course not."

Again she gnawed on her lip. If she wasn't in the tower, where were they? Had she died when she sat in the chair? Had she given her life to protect Chase? Strangely, the possibility didn't bother her. If he remained safe and alive, then the trade was worth it.

With a sigh, Cian settled on the ground, stretching out his legs. The light seeped from his hand into the wall behind him, softening further and giving the stone a gentle glow, and the last of his legion of voices died away with his first words. "Long ago I was a gray gryphon. One day, I decided I wanted to be a great warrior." His sarcasm made her wince. "My clan was always on the defensive, letting the battle come to us. We always protected others. We never attacked. I decided I wanted more. I wanted to make a name for myself. I wanted glory and honor. So I joined the other side. Only unlike most of my kin who had fallen away, my color never changed. I remained gray." He frowned. "And I don't know why. But because of it, I was never completely trusted. I was ostracized by the black clan as well as by my gray brothers and every village in Ireland, until I met Arin. She gave me a new family. A new hope."

"Where is Arin now?"

"Alas, she has gone to the other side." He lowered his gaze.

"I don't understand."

"Arin died, my dear."

Sadness welled in Maddie's heart. "When?"

"A long time ago." He stared off again, as if looking into the past.

"Have you been here since then?"

"Yes."

"So when she died you just slipped into this place and started glowing?"

He laughed under his breath and rubbed a spot between his eyes. "Not exactly. When she passed, my will to live diminished and I allowed myself to perish. When I awoke, I was here."

"Where is here?"

"Here is here."

"Oh." She paused. "Where am I?"

"You are here."

"Why?" There seemed little point in asking about *here*. Cian obviously wasn't inclined to share the details, if he even knew them.

"Because you opened the tower door."

Maddie shifted in place, ignoring a vague sense of guilt. "Yes. I did."

He shook his head and wrung his hands. His voice hinted of desperation. "Why would you do such a thing? The door has remained closed for over a hundred years. No daughter of Arin has ever opened it."

"I had to," she said, a single tear escaping and rolling down her cheek.

"Why?"

"I had to open the door to save Chase."

"Who is Chase?"

"It's a little hard to explain. He's a boy, but he's also a gray gryphon. L-like you."

Cian nodded approvingly. "Ah, a brother. A defender. So the pact worked; it held. I always wondered." He paused. "You did not open the door *for* him, but to *protect* him?"

"Yes."

"Who bid you open the door?"

"Dougal— I mean Doran. And Serena."

"Ah, Doran." Cian grimaced. "Cahal's son."

"Cahal's son!"

"Aye. He was born after the black gryphons were imprisoned, and orphaned before he was a man grown. Arin and I tried to help him settle in the village since he was alone, but because he was the only black gryphon remaining, he always thought he was different. I tried to convince him otherwise. When he asked for my daughter's hand in marriage, I agreed. Perhaps a little too reluctantly." He paused. "You see, he was no different than my own children, but he refused to be accepted. He believed the color of his fur also determined the color of his heart."

Compassion for Dougal consumed her. He'd been bitter, dissatisfied, and alone for his whole life. Her life had only been bad for a handful of months, and that had seemed disastrous enough. How would it feel to think you were all alone for over a hundred years?

She had to get out of there. She would tell Dougal he wasn't alone, she was his friend, and she'd convince Chase to befriend him, too. "So what happens now? I sat on that chair back there and then I arrived here. How do I go back to Chase?"

"I am afraid you cannot."

"What? B-but—"

A hint of the legions returned, strengthening his voice. "The tower must be filled, either with its prisoners or with the key." It sounded like a prophecy.

Maddie dropped to the floor, bruising her knees. It was made of some reflective material, something like glass, and felt like it, too. She caught sight of herself and groaned aloud. Heather stems and twigs stuck out at odd angles from her hair. Her clothes were ratty and ripped. Her face and hands were covered in dirt. What a way to meet one of your ancestors!

"So what happens now? Will Chase survive?"

"My child, do you not understand what you have done? Because you opened the tower, no one will survive. Cahal will wreak havoc upon the entire world."

Tears flowed freely down her cheeks. By rescuing Chase, she'd not only destroyed him, but doomed everyone! Grandma Draoi, the Donovan family, the little brothers who'd treated her like a sister...

No way could her day get any worse.

38

"Where is she?" asked Chase. He winced. His voice sounded so defeated.

Dougal shifted in place. "I don't know."

"What do you mean, you don't know?"

"I don't know, okay? She disappeared before I could get her attention."

Chase stretched. No pain; his side had fully healed, yet he remained in his gryphon form. He grabbed Dougal by the scruff of the neck and twisted. Dougal yelped and tried to wriggle free, but Chase twisted harder. "You're going to get her back! She did this for you. Now your accomplice is lying dead back there and those black flying friends of yours are plotting to take over the world!"

"I know," Dougal whispered, staring at Chase's chest.

"Then what are you going to do about it?"

"I don't know."

Furious, Chase shook him. "Dougal, why did you want them freed in the first place? I can't believe you sacrificed Maddie for power."

Dougal quit fighting and his face twisted. "Cahal is my father."

Not what he'd expected to hear. Chase released him and fell back against the stairs.

Dougal rubbed his neck. "My mother was one of the women

he kidnapped from the Irish villages. She was physically taken against her will and I was the by-product. She loved me dearly all her life and told me daily I didn't have to be like him, but the other villagers didn't see it that way. With a druid's help I stayed in my human form, but sometimes the beast would arise and I would do something atrocious. Cian claimed he tried to help me. But he imprisoned my father and was the reason for my problem, so why should I listen to him?"

He sighed, rubbing his furry palms together. "Then I met Serena. She'd been a druid who secretly lived in the next village over. She fell in love with my father while she was his captive. Stockholm syndrome, I believe it's called today. Anyway, she fell in love with him and offered her soul to remain young and live with him forever. When he was taken from her and imprisoned, she turned into a hideous beast. That's when she sought me out and convinced me that if we opened the tower, we would both be free."

Un-be-*liev*-able. "So for more than a hundred years you sought the key for this door? You could've done all kinds of things. Made money, started a company, met the woman of your dreams and started a family, but this is what you chose to do?"

Dougal's laugh sounded hollow. "Seems like a waste, huh?"

"Yeah, it does." Too furious to sit any longer, Chase pushed himself to his feet and stalked around the room. "How did you know how to open the door?"

"Serena knew all that." Dougal shrugged, his feathers rustling. "Hey, she was the one who knew all the old legends. She told me we needed a daughter from the line of Arin and she knew the girl had to open the door willingly."

Punching the stone wall would hurt, and Chase kept reminding himself of that fact. "She was probably the one who knew how to rescue Maddie, too."

"Yeah, probably." Dougal studied his clasped hands.

Chase threw out his hands. "So what do we do now?"

"A better question would be, are we trapped?" Awkwardly, Dougal rose and walked back along the narrow tunnel, his black wings drooping. Chase trailed behind, seething.

In the entry, the translucent mist still filled the doorway but the wooden door lay splintered across the floor. Chase swallowed, remembering the smashing pain that had telescoped along his back and shoulder. He'd forced his way through that?

"Hard to get in, was it?"

"Let's just say I didn't have time to think of a way to do it gracefully."

Carefully Dougal touched the doorframe. Sparks flew and he yelped, retracting his hand and cradling it to his chest. "I think it's electrified."

"Just great." Chase paced the tunnel. "How are we going to get out of here?" He snapped his fingers. "I have an idea. Why don't you just do that cool rewind thing you did in class?"

Dougal frowned, his snout twitching.

"Don't play dumb. Remember when we were in chemistry and you had Stephanie sit down in slow-mo? The room got all fuzzy and..."

"Yeah, I remember." Dougal shook his head. "But that took a ton of energy. I'm not sure I have enough left to make it happen and even if I did, I don't know if it would work."

"Great." Chase stretched his wings and paced with frustration.

"What are you two doing?"

Chase jumped. Not Dougal's voice. He twisted, peering past his pinfeathers. A small, shadowy form stood on the far side of the electrified doorway.

Whoever it was planted fists on hips. "We can't rescue Maddie unless you get out here and help Gregory round up the black gryphons."

Only one person sounded that imperious without also sounding arrogant. "Mrs. Casey-Brennan?" Chase squinted into the sunlight.

"Draoi, remember? I'm named for the druids of old. And if Serena knew how to get a daughter of Arin in, you better believe I know how to get one out."

"How did you get here?" Dougal sounded just as puzzled as Chase felt.

It was difficult to make out more than her outline, peering out into the glare. But it looked as if she huffed. "Well, I thought about taking a plane, but that seemed a tad pricey. I'm an old woman on a budget."

Dougal looked at Chase. Chase shook his head.

She threw out her hands. No need to guess about that motion. "I wished a spell, like Serena did. How do you think I got here?"

Chase felt heat rush to his cheeks. "We're stuck."

"Not for long."

She closed her eyes, lifted her hands, scrunched up her face, and whispered unintelligible words before yelling, "Hurry!"

Startled, Chase jumped again. But his wings swooped down without waiting for him to think about it, throwing him into flight. He flew through, Dougal almost close enough behind him to tangle their wings, and she collapsed. Chase landed next to her, cradling her head in his crooked arm.

She pushed him away. In a strained voice, she said, "Now, boys, go round them up."

"How?" demanded Dougal. "It won't be easy to trick them back into the tower. When Chase flew in, they weren't willing to enter even to catch him."

"Never mind all that." Chase helped her up. "Are you okay, Draoi?"

"I'm fine." She trembled in his supporting arm and her face was pale and waxy. "I haven't had this much fun since I was a young girl." She breathed deep but couldn't stop trembling. "Here's the plan. I've spoken with Gregory and he's willing to help us corral them again. He'll pretend to be on the black gryphons' side, which should be easy enough, since he looks like one of them. With an illusion, I'll conceal the tower's true form and cause it to look different. Then you two turn into humans and stand on the battlements, pretending to guard it.

"The idea is, we'll make it look like a great fortress they can use for a military base. And as soon as they're inside, I'll release the concealment and the black gryphons will be trapped. Once they're inside, Maddie will be released." She swallowed. "At least, I think that'll work."

Again Dougal looked at Chase. And again Chase shook his head. "Are the black gryphons really so dumb they'll fly into a fortress and not know it's the same place they just left?"

Dougal shrugged. "I'm not sure. I wouldn't think so. But maybe Gregory will bring them a different way. Maybe fly them around in circles. So maybe, maybe not."

"It will work." Draoi straightened, stepping away from Chase's supporting arm even though she still trembled. "It has to." One more deep breath, and some color returned to her face.

"Now go. Stand on the battlements and look fierce." She turned and stumbled across the heather to the distant line of dark trees.

Dougal started to call after her, but stopped himself and grimaced. "How are we supposed to get out when the tower closes again?"

Good question. "I'm sure Draoi has a plan."

"I hope you're right."

The tiny druid vanished into the trees. Chase waited, wishing he could give her some of his returning strength. But within seconds, a ripple of something invisible swept across the heather. The tower seemed to twist, growing taller, stretching into a curtain wall, and morphing into a medieval castle. A moment after that, two thick branches appeared on the ground in front of them; seconds later, they faded, shifted, and changed into two iron-headed spears.

Once again Dougal looked at Chase. Once again Chase shook his head. Together they took off and flew to the battlements, spears in hand, and took up positions as if they were lookouts.

Dougal sucked in a deep breath. "I'm sorry I was blinded by selfish desires."

Still too angry to reply, Chase grounded his spear. The hardwood handle grated on the stone beneath his feet. It sounded, looked, and felt real.

"Do you think Maddie will forgive me?"

"I don't know."

"You do realize I care for her?"

"Yes." Chase squirmed.

Spear held across his body, Dougal paced across the raised walkway behind the crenellations. "You know, if not for her, I wouldn't be helping you. I would let you all die. She's the only human who's ever been nice to me."

Sounds like blustering. "What about Stephanie? She seemed pretty friendly with you." Chase fought sarcasm. He had to work with Dougal and couldn't afford to alienate him.

But Dougal's glance aside was cool. "Stephanie was only out for herself. She thought I looked good and she liked my car. If I hadn't been popular or mysterious, she would never have hung out with me." His grimace faded. "On the other hand, I acted strange with Maddie, and yet she told Draoi I was her friend."

That sounded like Maddie, and warmth drove out the jealousy in Chase's heart. "When did she do that?"

"When she visited Draoi in the ICU."

Wait a moment. "How did you know?"

"I was listening."

"You mean eavesdropping."

"Yeah, I guess I was. I must tell Draoi sorry for that, as well as for other things. If not for Serena, she would never have been in the hospital in the first place." Dougal stared out at the empty Irish sky, turning on his heel. The butt of his spear clanked against the merlon and he pulled it closer to his chest. The iron spearhead gleamed in the light, utterly real. "I'm still not sure what Serena did to her. She said something about an herb, but I wasn't close enough to tell."

Chase held back his retort and focused all his energy on remaining human rather than attacking and killing Dougal. Then he stiffened. His fingers tightened around the spear. A crowd of black creatures flew their way. "I don't believe it."

"What?" Dougal turned and froze beside him.

"Gregory must really want the black gryphons locked back in the tower." Chase released a breath. "Look alive, here they come."

They screamed and shouted, using the tower's hollowness to make their voices echo and multiply. But just as the black gryphons came close enough for Chase to see individuals, half of them split off. His stomach knotted. "This is not good, not good. What are we going to do?"

But Dougal appeared dazed. What was he staring at? Chase traced Dougal's focus to the tower's base. At the head of a small horde of black gryphons, Cahal gazed upward and cocked a brow.

Dougal whispered, "He knows."

Wings buffeted the air. Eyes wide, teeth bared, Gregory barreled past and roared through the open sally port. Moments later, a squadron of furious black gryphons followed him. The pounding of their wings deafened Chase. They looked like a never-ending black tide, pushing and shoving in pursuit of their mortal enemy, fighting each other to be first through the port. At that speed it was hard to get a good look at them, but he glimpsed ragged feathers, clawless hands, malformed arms and legs.

As the others rushed inside, Cahal stayed outside. Hundreds of black gryphons circled behind him, never landing, strong wings pumping. And Chase understood. Cahal kept the strong and able-bodied with him, and sent the weaker ones chasing after Gregory, right back into captivity.

Dougal was right. Cahal knew.

Something clattered against the stone. A spear rolled on the stone walkway, unregarded, and behind it Dougal transformed. He flew over the fake easement and soared down to the gate. Sunlight flashed off his wings, highlighting each dark feather as he backwinged and landed before Cahal. Cahal didn't shout. He just stared at Dougal.

Leaning between two crenellations and peering down, Chase stifled a curse. There went his last hope. Draoi was busy concealing the tower. Gregory was trapped inside with his victims. Dougal had apparently forgotten the plan—which left him. What could he do?

"Father?" Dougal said, reaching out his hand.

"Father, you say?" Cahal scoffed. "Are you Serena's son? For you do not belong to me."

Dougal froze. His hand stayed frozen in place, reaching across the distance between them. "Yes, I do. You're my father. Don't you remember Caitir? You took her from her family. When she came home, she had me."

Cahal rolled his eyes, as if at a fool. "Of course I don't remember! How can you expect me to remember every child I sired with those village wenches?"

Somewhere in the fake tower below Chase's feet, a man screamed. It sounded like Gregory's voice, and suddenly Chase realized that Draoi hadn't let the traitorous black gryphon fly back out of the prison. He was trapped in the tower along with half of the company he'd helped trick one hundred years before. She'd taken her vengeance upon the man who'd murdered her granddaughter.

Not good. Not good at all, and Chase huffed a breath and transformed, feeling the crawling sensation along his spine as his gryphon self burst free. All he could do was work a con of his own. Wings spread, he flew over the purple fields of heather. The free gryphons swirled in a type of circular formation. Heart in his teeth, he joined their ranks, hoping to survive the trickery.

A punch struck his cheek and he reared his head back. *Oh, great start, just great.*

A black gryphon hovered in front of him, eyes wide with disbelief. "What are you doing here?"

Chase spit blood. "I'm here to prove that I'm better than you."

Several black gryphons laughed. One said, "Is that so? And just how do you plan to do that?"

The one who hit him flexed his claws. A scar ran across his cheek, an old wound that had healed wrong, and it made him look especially ugly when his teeth bared. "There are many of us and only one of you. We could kill you in an instant."

True, that. His heart hammered against his chest. Swallowing back his fear, he cocked a brow, "You have to catch me first."

His wings flared, pumped, and Chase punched the ugly gryphon in passing. With all the speed he could find, he roared from the circle, yelling as loud as he could, and raced toward the fake fortress. Voices rose behind him as the black gryphons followed.

Can't make it too simple. Instead of flying straight into the tower, Chase banked, circled around boulders, and skimmed over the heather in nap-of-the-earth flight. Suddenly he flashed over what was left of Serena. Already flies gathered upon her dead flesh, and his pumping wings threw them everywhere. Fighting the urge to retch, he banked again, passing over and circling around Dougal as he confronted Cahal. Their argument raged as if he'd never been there. He didn't stop. If only he could have signaled Draoi and asked for help.

The assault caught him unaware. A strong punch landed from above. He was knocked in the side, throwing him off balance and sending him plummeting to the ground. His wing smacked on impact and he grunted.

"Better than us, are you?" The ugly gryphon stalked around him. Chase's punch had landed on his other cheek but had already healed, giving him a matching set of scars.

Another gryphon kicked him in the ribs; another spit at him.

He ducked and rolled, then used his arms and pulled himself toward the tower, as he'd done earlier when trying to escape Cahal. If they thought he sought the fake fortress as ref-

299

uge, maybe they would bar his way.

They did, gathering in a pack ahead of him, between him and the tower. Chase leapt to his feet then bounded into flight. His wings tilted, turning him away as the black gryphons scrambled to follow, then his wings folded along his back, diving him beneath them and back toward the open sally port.

Hope flared in Chase's heart. Maybe they would enter before him. He yelled with all his might, "I'm coming, darling, just hold open the door!"

The black gryphons howled with laughter. A pack of them split off and raced through the sally port, folding their wings as they vanished inside. Another fist flew at Chase. He dodged, dodged again. "No!" he shouted. "No!"

More of them split off and ducked inside the tower, then more. Chase wove through the boulders, screaming as if in a rage and trying to force a path through the remaining black gryphons, but they kept massing between him and the port. As they tired, they retreated inside. None came out; Draoi was keeping up her end of the plan.

Finally only the ugly scarred gryphon lingered and Chase had had enough. As they circled around each other, he grabbed Ugly's wing and heaved. A hard pump with his wings, another heave, and Ugly, startled and yelling, sailed through the sally port. Electricity crackled, blue lightning rippling across the fake fortress, then it vanished and the pale tower remained, glowing in the sunlight.

The wails rent the air. Chase did a fist pump. He flew to Dougal and landed behind him, panting for breath.

Cahal's furry face had twisted and specks of spittle sprayed as he yelled. But Chase could feel Dougal's rage. It burned like a fire, billowing in almost visible waves around them. And Chase pitied him. All that time Dougal had dreamed of fitting in. He'd thought if only he could rescue his father, he would have a family. But all his hopes were being dashed.

"You don't even remember her! I've spent my entire life trying to save you and you don't even remember my mother!"

Cahal straightened. He glared past Dougal at Chase, as if finally realizing what had happened. "It would be easier to feel gratitude if you hadn't kept me distracted while your friends again entrapped all my brothers. But there it is. Now, how would you like to help me rule the world?"

Dougal stretched to his full height, spread his wings as far as they would go, and yelled, "Chase, tell her I love her."

He took flight, swooped straight toward his awed father, grabbed him, and hauled him bodily through the open tower door. Once inside the tower, Dougal was trapped. He had sacrificed himself to save them all.

Inside the circular room, the ground shook. Even kneeling on the glass floor, Maddie had to crouch or fall over. "What's happening?"

"I don't know." Cian spread his arms for balance. A hint of his legions returned, deepening his voice. "But I wonder…"

Maddie blinked. She could see the glass through her hand. Her eyes widened in horror. "I'm fading! Am I dying?"

Cian smiled. "No, my dear. The prisoners have been reinstated and you are going home."

The last word faded into a many-voiced echo. The enclosing room vanished. Suddenly a sweet-scented breeze blew across her face. Sunshine blazed around her. Startled, she wobbled and landed on her bottom with a hard plop—in a field of heather.

Dazed, she looked around. Grandma Draoi sat on the ground nearby, holding someone to her bosom. Maddie scrambled to her feet. Drawing closer, she gasped. It was a black gryphon. No—it was Gregory, and she didn't have to look twice to see that he was dying. He'd been battered, great chunks of flesh torn from him. Golden fluid like blood poured from his wounds.

"Grandma, what are you doing?"

"Oh, my dear." Grandma Draoi wept, tears coursing down her wrinkled face as she rocked the black gryphon like a child. "Gregory tried to escape the tower once the door was closed and this is what happened to him." She sobbed. "I should never have locked him in there. It's my fault, all my fault."

Maddie looked around at the carnage and wreckage. Large trees had been uprooted; small animals lay dead. It looked like a tornado had swept the area. Then she saw him. He was in human form, standing on two feet not far from the tower entrance, and completely whole. The door behind him was again iron-bound wood and impenetrable.

With a glad cry, Maddie ran to his side. He opened his arms to her and she ran into them. He hugged her.

"Chase!"

"Yeah, it's me. Are you okay?"

"Yes, I'm okay. Are *you* okay?"

"Oh, yeah."

She pulled back, her hands around his neck, and asked, "Where's Dougal? I need to tell him—" But the expression on his face stopped her.

He didn't want to say, she could tell. He glanced toward the tower then back at her.

Her breath caught in her throat. "He didn't?"

"He did. Cahal realized we were trying to trick him. But we tricked him again. Then Dougal rushed him and pushed him in."

"Why didn't he come out?" Maddie peered over his shoulder. The tower door loomed beyond, like an ugly mouth. She shuddered.

"He couldn't. Didn't you see what happened to Gregory?"

Hot tears slipped onto her cheeks and she swiped them away. Pulling away from Chase, she ran to the tower and lifted her hand.

"No! Maddie, stop. You mustn't open the tower."

Maddie froze. Two stories up, one of the barred windows framed Dougal. He waved his arms and shook his head frantically.

She cupped her mouth and yelled back, "But Dougal, I have to save you. I'll open it and you can rush out."

She could see him. He was alone in a small room, debris piled against the barred door as if to wedge it shut. Wailing echoed around him as his brothers screamed in woe. "It will never work."

"But—"

"Madelyn, you have your whole life ahead of you. Marry Chase and be happy. But remember this—I will always love you."

Chase came up behind her and wrapped his arms around her. She fell against him and he pulled her away. As they left, she heard a whisper on the wind. *"You opened my eyes and took the darkness from my heart."*

Dougal's fur changed to gray as he and his family disappeared behind the ivory stone walls.

E P I L O G U E

Months passed and school ended. Chase and Maddie graduated from Coal Creek High School with plans to attend the local community college in the fall. Their associates degrees would transfer to the state college if they wanted to continue their educations, and in the meantime they could stay close to their families.

Draoi spent the morning helping with preparations. The wedding was to be held at their church at two o'clock that afternoon and everyone was late. The cake had yet to arrive, the bridesmaids were still at the hairdresser's, and the groom's tuxedo didn't fit. If it could go wrong, it had. But it was still going to be a gorgeous wedding; she could feel it in her old bones.

During yesterday's wedding rehearsal, both Maddie and Chase had had the same thought at the same time. They'd stopped in the middle of the aisle and stared at each other while the music had slowly died around them.

"Protectors can only have sons." Chase's eyes had been wide as baseballs.

Maddie had laughed. "And *eochairs* can only have daughters."

After a breathless moment, Chase had joined in. "Oh, man, this is going to be fun!"

Rising from the last flower arrangement, Draoi drew in a deep breath. Once Maddie had a child, whatever it turned out to be, it would be in immediate danger. No more gryphons had been spotted since that ill-fated day, but Draoi knew better than to take anything for granted. It seemed impossible to believe that all of the black gryphons had flown back into the tower, that none of them had snuck away and remained at large. She thinned her lips. She hadn't protected her daughter, granddaughter, and great-granddaughter to let her guard down now.

The wedding hour approached. Chase stood at the altar with the minister. He looked handsome in his rented tuxedo. His father walked a blushing Maddie down the aisle, then stood with his son as best man. As Maddie and Chase said their vows, a feeling came over Draoi. She looked at the back of the church but saw nothing. But someone was there, watching; she could feel it.

When she returned her gaze to the couple, they were being introduced as husband and wife. And then she knew. From somewhere unseen, Cian and Arin smiled upon them, together again. Light filtered through the stained glass windows and Draoi felt the power of darkness lift from her family. Dougal had found redemption and Maddie and Chase had found love. What more could a grandma ask for?

"He has delivered us from the power of darkness and conveyed us into the kingdom of the Son of His love, in whom we have redemption through His blood, the forgiveness of sins."—Colossians 1:13-14

The End

ABOUT THE AUTHOR

Felicia Rogers, born and raised in the southern part of the United States, is a Christian wife and mother. She is just your average, ordinary woman, with a side interest—writing.

For eleven years, every waking moment of her life was consumed with changing diapers, wiping noses, and kissing scrapes. But now that her children are growing up and she enjoys a modicum of freedom, in addition to taking care of hearth and home, she writes! She enjoys adding a flavor of realism and humor to her all-too-real romance stories. For what is love without a little laughter!

Also by Felicia Rogers

Contemporary single titles:

The Painted Lady
The Holiday Truce
The Perfect Rose
Love Octagon
All I Have
A Month in Cologne

Wounded Soldiers series:

Diamond Mine
Pearl Valley
Emerald Street

Historical romance:

The Ruse
The Rescue

The Renaissance Heart series:

There Your Heart Will Be Also
By God's Grace
Labor of Love
Beyond a Doubt
Letters in the Grove

Southern Hearts series:

Millicent
Amelia
Cora

writing as F.A. Rogers
The Board series:

Maralie
Reuben
Vanessa
Simon
Darla
Daniel
Irving
Levi
Francesca
Benjamin
James

don't miss the next book!

Mara's Secret

1

Awareness swam slowly to the top of Dougal's thoughts. Voices... voices he didn't know.

"Can I keep 'im, Ma?"

Weird voices. Or at least, weird people.

"Maude, don't be silly. You don't have any idea where he's been."

A new voice, a male one, cleared his throat and interrupted. "T'aint it obvious where he's been? Look at all those scars. He's been in the war and from the looks of him, he must've taken a good beating."

War. That didn't sound good. Dougal risked slitting his eyes open. The old man who'd carried him sat at a plain wooden table, scratching his head and staring at Dougal. "I wish he was wearing more of his uniform. If he was wearing more blue, I'd put him back out in the field."

"Pshaw. You'll do no such thing," said Ma. The woman speaking bustled around out of Dougal's sight. A pan clanked down on a stove; at least there was one sound he recognized.

Pa shook his head. "Maybe he's a deserter. I'm surprised the feller ain't been shot. You heard about them two boys who were on their way home. Poor fellers were let out of the army, done injured and discharged. They got plenty close and the neighbors thought they'd deserted, so they shot 'em." He paused. "Maybe he didn't leave his company, maybe he was in a battle and they thought he was dead, and they left 'im behind. Could be that's why they didn't shoot 'im."

"Should we turn him in?" Another male voice, but younger.

Pa scratched his head. "Naw, Junior. Your ma's right. We should let the poor soul rest. Since we don't know where he came from or why he was about these parts, we should give him a chance to explain himself."

The voices continued, but they didn't seem to pose any immediate danger and exhaustion won. Dougal drifted back into a deep sleep.

Later, when he again awoke, his chest felt tight and heat tortured him. Pain throbbed in his forehead. A glance showed that someone had draped heavy covers over him. He grabbed the quilts' edge, flung them aside, swung his legs up and around, and settled his feet to the floor. The smooth-worn planks felt like a freezer's interior and he shuddered.

Sunlight filtered into the empty room through scrubbed-clean windows. The family from before—Ma, Pa, Junior, and covetous Maude—weren't around. The cabin was simple—thick logs planed smooth and grouted with mud, notched together at the ends. Dried pelts hung from the rafters. Metal cooking utensils hung from nails beside a stone fireplace. In the middle of the room stood a plain wooden table and six chairs. The construction details were different, but overall, the cabin reminded him forcefully of the primitive home where he'd grown up.

No people, weird or otherwise, darkened the interior. Good; he could think. Dougal grabbed his pounding head. Bits and pieces of the earlier conversation drifted back to him. They thought he was a soldier in a war with blue and gray, a soldier who had abandoned his unit or been left for dead. Did that mean he was in the United States during the Civil War?

No, that would be some bizarre form of time travel and that couldn't be right. How could that even be possible? His pulse pounded, matching his head, and he swallowed his fear.

"Get ahold of yourself, Dougal." His voice sounded thin and raspy, not reassuring at all. "Maybe you're in one of those reenactment battles or something." Right. "Sure, that's what it is." Oh, yeah, right.

Another shiver rippled through him, and he looked around for a pair of shoes, socks, anything to cover his poor cold feet. No clothing, but the shiver segued into a tingle that raced along his spine, as if someone had touched him with an electrical current. Dougal lifted his head.

She stood silhouetted in the open doorway, twisting her white, almost translucent gown between her slender fingers. Long black hair hung unfettered to her waist. Her eyes were the color of blue steel, her beauty like that of a statue in a world-famous museum. He couldn't look away, didn't want to, didn't want to ever look away from her again. The tingle up his spine deepened until he felt he'd shake apart.

As he stared, her breath burst in and out and her color melted away, leaving her ashen. He lifted his hand toward her, wanting to comfort her fear, but his throat had dried and all that came out was a croak.

Nope, that wasn't going to help.

She glared at his hand, her eyes widening. A moan escaped her. She turned on her heel and vanished.

A ghost. He'd been visited by a ghost, while trapped in a Civil War reenactment. Dougal collapsed back onto the bed and yanked the quilts back over him. Something—okay, *nothing* was right, but he couldn't put his finger on it...

Even outside, in the clear pine-scented air, Mara's chest heaved as she struggled to breathe. The stranger had *looked* at her. He'd even lifted his hand, as if he wanted to *touch* her! Just the thought made her tremble. She didn't like strangers. Strangers did bad things to people. Strangers tricked you into doing things you didn't want to do, like holding your tongue.

Still rattled, Mara settled on the tree swing, her favorite spot for thinking, and laid her head against the rope. She looked across the pond and eyed the cabin where the stranger lurked. Yesterday morning, when Pa and Maude had brought him home, the only clothes covering his body had been a pair of tattered breeches. The sight of his exposed chest had caused heat to flush her cheeks, and finally Ma had shooed her from the room. She'd climbed into the loft and peered over the edge, watching while Ma had treated the wounds carved upon the stranger's body and he'd groaned and moaned as if dying.

Pa said the stranger had received a beating and he was lucky to be alive. She didn't know if she agreed, but why else would the young man have been left in the field?

She glanced around the farmyard. The cow chewed her cud under a shade tree but otherwise Mara was alone. She bit her lip. Would it be safe to hum? Or maybe sing quietly to herself? Technically it wasn't talking if no one was listening, and the sweet sound of Sunday hymns took her mind off her troubles. Soon Ma would call her in for dinner and she'd have to blink, and play dumb, and help in her mute way.

Mara squeezed the swing's rope until frayed fibers cut into the tender flesh of her palms. If only she had stayed away from the creek.

When Dougal awoke again, the family sat around the table praying over a meal. He remained silent and peeked through his lashes. He needed more info so he could figure out what to do next. If he could only remember more—but there seemed to be a hole in his memory. Darkness, then light, then… something.

Middle-aged mother and father and three grown children raised their heads with a rousing "Amen!" Ma lifted a ladle and spooned steaming liquid into each raised bowl. The smell of rich broth tantalized him and his stomach growled. Loudly.

Maude swiveled around. She cocked a brow before pushing back her chair and ambling toward him. Blond hair pulled back in a severe bun highlighted her defined cheekbones and hazel eyes. Her small, round frame reached his side and she leaned over. A smile tugged at the corners of her rosy lips as her gaze followed the length of the bed.

No, not the bed. His body.

Great. The strange one. Not the silent, pretty one, staring at the table and shredding a roll with nervous fingers. Not even Ma, with her safe, wrinkled face and stern, measuring eyes. No, of course not. He had to attract attention from Maude.

"I think he's awake, Pa." The grin reached her eyes and Dougal gulped.

Pa didn't even glance up. "Good. Get him some food."

She patted his hand. "Are you hungry?"

Dougal nodded, and the girl shuffled back to the table and retrieved her bowl. When she returned, she dragged over her chair, settled her curved body with a wriggle, and began to spoon broth into his mouth.

It tasted as good as it smelled, all savory warmth and goodness. He twitched his lips upward in a practiced smile. A flush stole over Maude's face, and she blinked shyly and looked away. He hadn't had a chance to study his appearance since his arrival, but thankfully his good looks appeared intact. At least he still had the ability to make a young woman blush.

She fed him another warm spoonful. Maybe he'd get a chance to enjoy the meal, after all. At the thought, he smiled again—a real smile this time, surprisingly, not one of his practiced concoctions designed to get a reaction from a girl. Strange, how good a simple smile could feel.

Maude leaped from her chair. The bowl flew through the air, spreading his meal across the floorboards, and clattered to a halt upside down. Dougal sighed. It had been good while it lasted. He'd have to turn down his wattage.

"Maude, what are you thinkin', child!" Ma's voice sounded irritated.

Maude ran to the table, clutched her parents around their shoulders, and screamed with delight. "Ma! He smiled at me! Can you believe it? He is one mighty fine specimen. Should we send for the preacher?"

What twilight zone had he been dumped into? With two fingers, Dougal pinched himself. This had to be a nightmare, right? If not, he might soon be standing in front of a clapboard church with shotguns cocked on either side while he waited for his fate to be sealed!

The other girl, the quiet one, reminded him of the girl from his dream. Was she real? She'd held her peace, but at Maude's declaration, her steel blue eyes widened as if horrified.

Pa's spoon paused halfway up. "Now, Maude, you stop with such silly talk. You're upsetting Mara."

Mara...

As if Dougal had spoken the name aloud, the quiet girl glanced in his direction. His breath caught. It *was* her, the one who'd fled so fast she'd seemed to vanish, like a ghost. She was real and even more beautiful than he'd remembered.

The black hair that had hung freely was now braided and draped atop her shoulder. Her translucent gown had been changed for a yellow one, which highlighted her tanned skin.

Again he couldn't stop staring at her. He gave her the same smile, the one that sent Maude leaping for joy, but Mara trembled, shaking so violently her chair bounced. What was wrong? His looks had never caused that kind of response. Unless...

Ma cocked a brow. "Mara, what in heaven's name is wrong with you?"

Mara didn't reply. She shoved back from the table and bolted for the door, sending her chair reeling backward and crashing against the floor.

As if nothing had happened, Maude resumed her seat, plopped her elbow on the table, cradled her chin in her hand, and whined in a nasally wistful tone. "I ain't never gonna get married. Every time someone looks at me, you say no. It ain't fair."

"Now, Maude, we've done been over this. You are spoken for. You can't just go off and try for another beau. It ain't fittin'." Pa eyeshot a glance in Dougal's direction.

Maude's fingers plucked at a loose string on her dress. She looked up and her heated gaze fell on Dougal. *Great, just great.* He shifted on the bed. She smiled. "But he's so purdy."

Pa rolled his eyes. "It don't matter. If he's a deserter, they might want him back once he's well."

Oh, yeah, he needed to get out of this madhouse. He had no intention of marrying Maude or anyone else. Nor did he have any intention of being taken by an army he'd never joined in the first place. How he'd gotten there and why—those were his current concerns. Little else deserved his attention. Well, maybe Mara...

Ma frowned and patted Maude's hand. "We ain't arguing about that. What we're sayin'—"

"What do you mean?" interrupted Pa.

"Mean by what?" asked Ma.

"By what you just said?"

"I don't understand your question."

"Are you tryin' to say you find this here feller attractive?"

Ma leaned over the table and stared into Pa's eyes. "You don't need to worry, dear. I haven't seen an attractive man in the last twenty-five years."

Dougal restrained his laughter as the old man attempted to use his fingers to count. Perhaps he was trying to decide whether he should be offended or not.

Thanks for reading! Dingbat Publishing strives to bring you quality entertainment that doesn't take itself too seriously. I mean honestly, with a name like that, our books have to be good or we're going to be laughed at. Or maybe both.

If you enjoyed this book, the best thing you can do is buy a million more copies and give them to all your friends... erm, leave a review on the readers' website of your preference. All authors love feedback and we take reviews from readers like you seriously.

Oh, and c'mon over to our website:
www.DingbatPublishing.ninja

Who knows what other books you'll find there?

Cheers,
Gunnar Grey,
publisher, author, and Chief Dingbat

δ
Dingbat Publishing

www.ingramcontent.com/pod-product-compliance
Lightning Source LLC
Chambersburg PA
CBHW070631260626
47161CB00007B/2660